Advance praise for Tom Mendicino and
The Boys from Eighth and Carpenter

"*The Boys from Eighth and Carpenter* is a heartfelt story of two loving brothers as well as a compelling crime drama all set in the changing city of Philadelphia. Tom Mendicino is a supremely gifted writer with an eye for the most telling of details, and I loved this novel!"

—Lisa Scottoline, *New York Times* bestselling author

"At the heart of this capacious and suspenseful novel is the bond between two very different brothers, but its larger context is the Italian-American family: its values, loyalties and responsibilities. Tom Mendicino writes with honesty and compassion, and the reader can't help but root for his endearing characters."

—Christopher Castellani, author of *All This Talk of Love*

Books by Tom Mendicino

PROBATION

THE BOYS FROM EIGHTH AND CARPENTER

E-Novellas

KC, AT BAT

TRAVELIN' MAN

LONESOME TOWN

Published by Kensington Publishing Corporation

The Boys from Eighth *and* Carpenter

TOM MENDICINO

KENSINGTON BOOKS
www.kensingtonbooks.com

To the extent that the image or images on the cover of this book depict a person or persons, such person or persons are merely models, and are not intended to portray any character or characters featured in the book.

KENSINGTON BOOKS are published by

Kensington Publishing Corp.
119 West 40th Street
New York, NY 10018

All Kensington titles, imprints, and distributed lines are available at special quantity discounts for bulk purchases for sales promotion, premiums, fund-raising, educational, or institutional use.

Special book excerpts or customized printings can also be created to fit specific needs. For details, write or phone the office of the Kensington Sales Manager: Kensington Publishing Corp., 119 West 40th Street, New York, NY 10018. Attn. Sales Department. Phone: 1-800-221-2647.

eISBN-13: 978-1-61773-795-4
eISBN-10: 1-61773-795-X
First Kensington Electronic Edition: September 2015

ISBN-13: 978-1-61773-794-7
ISBN-10: 1-61773-794-1
First Kensington Trade Paperback Printing: September 2015

10 9 8 7 6 5 4 3 2 1

Printed in the United States of America

For my sister, Pamela, who did everything I couldn't

There were two brothers called Both and Either; perceiving Either was a good, understanding, busy fellow, and Both a silly fellow good for little, King Philip said, "Either is both, and Both is neither."

—Sayings of Kings and Commanders, attributed to Plutarch

. . . and remember, a boy who won't be good
might just as well be made of wood.

—The Blue Fairy

Prologue

giuramento di sangue

April 14, 2008

Promise me you'll always take care of each other. Frankie, you make sure you tell your brother I asked you both to do that when he's old enough to understand.

Frankie (morning through the late afternoon)

He's going to the Hair Show just as he'd planned. Frankie Gagliano, proprietor of Gagliano Cuts and Color, Family Owned Since 1928, always goes to the Hair Show. People would notice his absence. But now that he's sitting in the parking lot, he's wavering, questioning the wisdom of his decision and lacking the stamina to engage in the usual banter about how quickly time seems to fly and that it's hard to believe it's been a year since the last trade show. And, of course, he no sooner picks up his badge than he finds himself face-to-face with Beppe Lopato, his nemesis back at South Philadelphia Beauty Academy, who's wearing a pair of snug, crotch-grabbing jeans and looking like he subsists on steroids and nutritional supplements. Beppe strikes a pose, giving Frankie a dramatic once-over. Frankie feels the perspiration dripping from his armpits, fearing guilt is written all over his face. Even a Neanderthal like Beppe Lopato can see it.

"I hope the other guy looks worse."

The swelling has subsided and the bruises are beginning to fade from purple and green to yellow. The cut on Frankie's lip hasn't completely healed. He'd considered covering the damage with makeup, a little foundation, something subtle, of course. But in the end he decided to show himself to the world and resort to the tale of an errant taxi running a red light if anyone asks.

"It's very butch. I like it!"

Frankie doubts his sincerity. Beppe, one of those unfortunate Sicilians who resemble the missing link in a Time-Life series on the history of man, has always been envious of Frankie's blue eyes and fine features. He'd mocked Frankie in beauty school, calling him Fabian, after the baby-faced erstwhile teen idol from South Philadelphia.

"Are you doing Paul Mitchell? I'm headed over to the booth. Walk with me, Frankie, and let's catch up," he says, obviously curious about who's been using Frankie as a punching bag.

An internationally renowned expert on color application is lecturing in ten minutes and Beppe wants to get a good seat. Frankie begs off, saying he's signed up for the extensions demonstration at the Matrix exhibit. They part ways, air-kissing, swearing to have lunch or cocktails soon, a promise made and broken every year. Frankie wanders the two acres of concrete floor, from Healing HairCare to Naturceuticals to Satin Smooth Full Body Waxing. His mind is distracted. Nothing registers. He needs to sit for a few minutes, and the "Be a Color Artist, Not a Color Chartist" presentation is as good a place as any.

It's still 1983 here at the Valley Forge Convention Center Hair Expo and Trade Show and Michael Jackson has never gone out of fashion. Over the years, Frankie's seen thousands of stylists choreograph their presentations to "Beat It" and "Rock with You." The kid onstage is shimmying and shaking to "Wanna Be Startin' Something," brandishing a pair of shears and a can of hair spray like he's headed for a high noon showdown. The boy wasn't even born when *Thriller* topped the charts and wouldn't recognize the King of Pop in a picture taken when he still had his own nose. It's exhausting watching him multitask up there, demonstrating a revolutionary new color system while auditioning for *Dancing with the Stars.* Frankie's seen enough and trudges back onto the exhibit floor.

He's restless, living on caffeine. He's barely slept since he flushed the Ambien down the toilet, a terrible mistake. Those pills were his opportunity to take the easy way out. It was a rash decision he deeply regrets, forcing him to choose one of the more grisly, and likely more painful, alternatives, any of which is still less terrifying than the possibility of being confined behind bars for the rest of his life, spending the next two or three decades as a caged animal.

An army of bitter and burnt-out old stylists flocks to him, sensing fresh prey. They harangue him with brochures and order forms and discount coupons for the products they're hawking. He'd had the good sense to hide the color-coded ID badge identifying him as a PROPRIETOR in his pocket, but they're still circling him like vultures descending on fresh carrion, their instincts sensing he's a salon owner with a shop to stock and inventory to replenish.

"Francis Rocco Gagliano. You get more gorgeous every year. And that black eye is *sooo* sexy!"

He's staring into a blank slate of chemically induced preternatural youthfulness. He loves her cut, though, a no-nonsense *Klute*-era Jane Fonda shag that looks shockingly hip and contemporary.

"It's me, Estelle Prince!"

"Oh my God. What's the matter with me?" he apologizes, though she's been remodeled beyond recognition. "You look incredible."

She assumes he means it as a compliment. Parts of her face, the moving ones, seem to be made of putty. She seems perpetually startled, a talking wax doll who's been zapped by a stun gun. She babbles on, much ado about nothing, and he shakes his head in agreement though his mind is elsewhere and he doesn't hear a word she says. He knows now it was a mistake coming here. They'll all agree in hindsight he was acting strange at the Hair Show. Most people will say they didn't know he had it in him. A few will claim the news came as no surprise. *He wouldn't look me in the eye, now that I think about it. It's a damn shame, but what can you expect if you get mixed up with those kind of people?* But he foolishly agrees to join Estelle for a glass of wine after the "Beyond Basic Foiling" presentation. They embrace, promising to meet in forty-five minutes. He waits until she disappears into the crowd and turns toward the exit, attempting a quick getaway, and nearly collides with the young woman who steps in front of him, blocking his way.

"You cannot say no. I'm going to make you an offer you can't refuse."

She's the very model of scientific efficiency, dressed in a crisp white lab coat, cradling a clipboard in the crook of her elbow. She's wearing *I-mean-business* eyeglasses, the tortoise frames suggesting the serious dignity of a wise owl; her hair is pulled back in a ponytail with a few tendrils liberated to flatter the strong cheekbones of her lovely face.

"You get a fifty-dollar honorarium and a sample selection of our top-of-the-line hair product. And you'll leave the show today a new man with a brand-new look. Satisfaction guaranteed."

He's about to politely decline her generous offer when she introduces him to the stylist, licensed as both a barber *and* a cosmetologist, an expert, she assures him, in both professions. Vince is his name, and his Clubman Classic aftershave, crisp, antiseptic, is vintage 1967, the year Frankie's papa put his seven-year-old son to work sweeping clippings from the barbershop floor and emptying ashtrays heaped with smoldering cigarette butts. His younger brother, Michael, had resented being conscripted into Papa's labor force as soon as he was tall enough to push a broom, but Frankie never minded. He would linger in the shop after his chores were done, too young yet to understand why he was drawn to the longshoremen and refinery workers who sat flipping through ancient issues of *Sports Illustrated* and *Car and Driver,* crossing and uncrossing their legs with casual grace as they waited their turn in the barber chair. Their loud, deep voices rumbled as they argued about sports and politics. They called him Little Pitcher, a reminder that certain language wasn't meant to be overheard by Big Ears, and teased him about his long eyelashes and wavy hair, saying it was a shame Frankie hadn't been born a girl, all those good looks going to waste on a boy. Forty years later, he's still aroused by the memory of their unfiltered Pall Malls, the Chock Full o'Nuts on their breath, and the Brylcreem they used to landscape their hair.

"You game, my friend?" Vince asks. "Feeling brave today?"

He's neither short nor tall; broad through the shoulders and barrel-chested. He's thick around the waist, not quite potbellied, certainly not sloppy but carrying a few extra pounds; his loose Hawaiian shirt, a relatively sedate design of bright green palm leaves on a navy background, is a generous fit. His forearms are sturdy, built for heavier labor than barbering, and dusted with a fine spray of sun-bleached hair. The visible tattoos are Navy port-of-call vintage, clearly not the handiwork of a punk-rock skin-art boutique. He's wearing Levi's 505s, full cut, and Sketchers, probably with inserts for extra support. He's a man who's clearly comfortable in his own skin. His blunt, still-handsome face is branded with a raised, flaming-red scar from his right earlobe to the corner of his mouth, a warning he's a man with a past: mysterious, dark, dangerous, the survivor of a bar fight or a prison term in the Big House or a tour of duty in the first Gulf War.

For all his foreboding appearance, Vince is a friendly enough guy, approachable. He tells Frankie he has fifteen years experience cutting hair and owns a small shop in Johnstown, Pennsylvania, where he makes a good living doing volume in ten-dollar haircuts. He recently moved in with a "special lady" he met in his motorcycle club and he's paying to put her through beauty school. He suggests a much shorter cut for Frankie, to give him a more masculine look. He'll try a fade on his neck and up the sides, something that won't need any upkeep or grooming. He'd like to bring a little color back, nothing terribly dramatic. He suggests they try a Number Two solution for a natural-looking blend.

"Get ready to rock and roll!" Vince says as he leads Frankie to the chair.

His gruff but soothing voice preaches the gospel of men's styling as a life raft in tough economic times to a rapt audience gathered for the demonstration on his willing guinea pig. *Do the math: more potential bookings per week, none longer than twenty minutes and most of them in and out in ten, more visits per year, every two weeks for most men, none less frequent than monthly. Pay close attention now,* he cautions, demonstrating the most effective way to use a number-one guard on his clippers while eulogizing the dying art of scissors-over-comb. He promises his skeptical audience the product he's about to demonstrate will break the final barrier of a guy's reluctance to color his hair. *It's a simple shampoo, leave it in five minutes, a quick wash, and they're out the door. The construction workers and long-distance haulers who come into my shop wouldn't be caught dead under the dryer.*

Frankie surrenders to the strong hands massaging his scalp. Vince lowers the chair to rinse his hair with warm water and briskly dries it with a barber towel.

"So there you have it. A fresh new look in nineteen minutes."

The audience approves of the results, nodding and throwing a thumbs-up.

"So, whaddya think?" Vince asks, spinning the styling chair so Frankie can face himself in the mirror.

He's showing more skin than he expected, especially in the close-cropped area above his ears. He likes the cut; it's a clean look, almost military. And the color is soft and natural, even to his critical professional eye.

"Thank you, brother. Don't forget to pick up your free sample bag," Vince says as he shakes Frankie's hand and quickly dismisses him, turning to introduce himself to his next challenge, a faux-skateboarder/bike messenger with spiky extensions who's about to be transformed into G.I. Joe. Frankie tosses the bag into the nearest trash can as he walks to the exit. He won't be needing conditioners or gels to maintain his "brand-new look." He hadn't bothered to collect his fifty-dollar honorarium. There's nothing to buy and no use for money where he's going.

An overdose would have been calm and peaceful, but his internist won't refill the Ambien and the Ativan. She suspects he's abusing since she called in a month's worth just last week. Swallowing a bottle of an over-the-counter drug wouldn't be lethal and he would end up in the ER, having his stomach pumped. He doesn't own a gun and his hands would shake too badly to attempt slitting his wrists. Drowning would be painless, but those few moments before he loses consciousness would feel like an eternity, enough time to regret what he's powerless to reverse as his lungs fill with water. Same problem with jumping off a building. He doesn't want his life passing before his eyes as he falls twenty stories. Hanging is too risky. If his neck doesn't snap, he'll strangle to death, clutching at the rope and gasping for breath.

He's considered all the alternatives and the swiftest, most efficient way to do this is to step into the path of an approaching train. He'll leave the car in the wasteland of cargo terminals and storage units surrounding the airport and walk to the railroad tracks with his iPod set at maximum volume, Stevie's magical voice singing "Rhiannon" and "Gold Dust Woman," the last sounds he wants to hear as he leaves this earth. In a few hours he'll know whether there's a heaven waiting to welcome him or a hell to which he'll be condemned for taking his own life or if it's all just a black nothing. He's collected all of the official documents Michael will need to put his affairs in order—his will, the deed to the building, the insurance policies, the numbers of his various bank accounts. They'll find his wallet with all his ID on the driver's seat of the abandoned car. This morning he locked the doors of the home he's lived in his entire life for the very last time. He didn't leave a note. His reason will be obvious. Not immediately, but soon enough.

"Frankie! Frankie! Did you forget our date?"

Estelle Prince, laden with shopping bags full of brochures and samples, is chasing him, teetering on her skyscraper stiletto heels.

"Should we take one car or two?" she wheezes.

It's likely the most exercise she's had in years and left her short of breath. Thankfully, she doesn't object when he suggests they drive separately. He considers losing her in traffic, but fortifying his resolve with a liberal dosage of alcohol isn't a bad idea. Estelle insists the local outpost of a national chain of "authentic Italian bistros" has a decent wine list. A lone salesman is nursing a bottle of beer at the bar and two well-heeled blue-haired old ladies are lingering in a booth. The hostess seats the latest arrivals, offering menus, which Estelle refuses, saying they're just having a drink.

"We have a nice selection of wines by the glass," the young lady offers.

"We need more than a glass. You don't have anywhere you have to be, do you, Frankie? Let's share a bottle. Red or white?"

Frankie shrugs and says he'll be happy with whatever Estelle chooses.

"Chardonnay," she predictably instructs the server. "The one from the Central Coast. Not one of those ridiculously expensive bottles from Sonoma."

"Bring us the Cakebread Cellars. My treat, Estelle."

His last glass of wine should be a good one.

Estelle's not about to argue with his generosity. Frankie waves away the cork and tells the server to pour. He's sure it's fine.

"What are we celebrating?" Estelle asks, proposing a toast.

"Nothing. Nothing at all."

"We have to celebrate something! Let's toast your new look

then. Oh, sweetie, the color takes ten years off your age. I hope you're ready for all the young men who are going to be running after you!"

She's far too self-absorbed to question Frankie's insistence on quickly changing the topic to her favorite subject—herself. All he's called upon to do is occasionally nod his head in agreement to encourage her to keep the one-sided conversation going. He settles back and lets his mind wander, allowing her to vent about her philandering soon-to-be-ex-husband and the crushing legal fees she's paying her attorneys to punish him in the divorce settlement.

"We'll have another bottle," he tells the server as she approaches the table.

"Are you planning to get me drunk so you can take advantage of me?" Estelle teases.

He laughs mirthlessly and swallows a mouthful of wine. When the time comes to settle the bill, he'll be as ready as he'll ever be. He remembers a line in a song about finding courage in the bottle, but doesn't recall who sang it. Estelle says she's getting light-headed and places her hand over her glass when he offers a refill. *More for me,* he thinks. The alcohol doesn't exactly transform fear into courage like the song promised, but it's loosening his grip on any remaining doubts about stepping on to the railroad tracks. He needs to finish the job before the effects of the wine wear off and cowardice and misgivings weaken his resolve.

"Are you sure you're okay to drive?" Estelle asks as they walk to their cars.

He brushes off her concerns. He's not stumbling or slurring his words, but he's clearly under the influence, which, of course, is exactly where he needs to be.

"Don't worry. I'll stop for a coffee at the Wawa before I get on the expressway. I promise."

It's a few minutes past five, according to the digital clock on his dashboard. The evening rush hour is building to full force and traffic is at a near standstill. At least he doesn't have to worry about drifting between lanes at sixty-five miles an hour. He squints and peers over the steering wheel, not trusting his ability to accurately gauge the distance between his front bumper and the brake lights of the car ahead. He's confused by the jumble of directional signs overhead. South to West Chester. The Pennsylvania Turnpike to Harrisburg and points west. East to Center City Philadelphia and the Philadelphia International Airport. That's the direction he needs to travel. Distracted and anxious, he nearly misses the access road to the interstate and makes a sharp right. In his confusion, he's misread the road signs and doesn't realize he's trying to enter the expressway on the one-way exit ramp until he hears the siren and sees the flashing blue dome light in his rearview mirror.

MICHAEL (EVENING AND INTO THE NIGHT)

"You know, I could just put you out in Norristown and let them press charges, if that's what you want."

News travels fast and bad news flies at the speed of sound. The Upper Merion Township police had contacted the young on-call prosecutor of the Office of the District Attorney for Montgomery County, who then called her supervisor for guidance after Frankie had disclosed his brother, Michael, was Chief Deputy District Attorney in the neighboring county. After a brief phone conversation between Michael and his peer, the officer in charge told his partner to tear up the report he'd begun to write and released Frankie from custody. Michael made arrangements to pick up Frankie's car in the morning. He'd assumed Frankie was too embarrassed to face Michael's wife and son (a nine-year-old asks a *lot* of questions) when he'd refused the offer to spend the night in their guest room in Wayne. He'd pleaded to be dropped at the nearest station so he could take a train back to the city. He'd only agreed under protest to allow Michael to drive him home and has been sullen and hostile the entire ride.

"So I take it you're not talking to me. Fine. I won't ask again what happened to your face. Last month you tripped. Now you tell me your taxi ran a red light. If you ask me, I'd say someone's put the *maliocch'* on you."

Michael's sarcasm fails to get a rise out of his brother.

"Jesus, how long have we been sitting here? At this rate I won't get home until midnight."

He's staring at a seemingly endless ribbon of red taillights on the road ahead, waiting for the traffic update on news radio. The headlines of the day are the same as yesterday's and the day before that. Natural disasters. Military skirmishes in distant lands with unpronounceable names. Domestic tragedies. Children killed in crossfire between street gangs. Hillary. Obama. The Dow Jones. The five-day weather forecast for the Delaware Valley.

Somewhere in that mash-up between the important and the inconsequential, all stories read in a comforting monotone, he's startled to hear a sound bite of his own voice. Was it only this morning he'd spoken to the press on behalf of the District Attorney, announcing the decision *". . . to not seek a retrial of the first-degree murder charge of Tommy Corcoran, whose capital conviction on that count was recently overturned by a federal court. Corcoran continues to serve a life sentence without parole on the remaining charges. Now on to traffic and transit. Eastbound traffic is experiencing forty- to fifty-minute delays from 202 to the Vine Street underpass due to an overturned tractor trailer."*

What began as a trying day is ending on a bad note. Michael's unhappy about being forced to suffer this endurance test on the expressway. It would have been perfectly reasonable, not to mention convenient, for Frankie to stay the night in Wayne. There's only one explanation for Frankie's anxiety about rushing back to the city. He's worried that goddamn little Mexican illegal is pouting in front of the television, feeling neglected and abandoned. It astounds Michael that his brother trusts the kid with the key to his house and thinks nothing about leaving him there alone.

"We could sit here for hours," Michael grumbles. "Call him and tell him you'll be back as soon as you can."

"He isn't there."

"Where is he?"

"He's gone."

"I hope you told him not to come back. That little shit. I knew this was going to happen. How long did he smack you around before you gave him what he wanted? How much money did he squeeze out of you before saying *adiós?*"

He immediately regrets his angry, aggressive tone. He'd intended to give Frankie time to recover from the shock of being arrested before resuming the interrogation about this fresh set of bruises and split lip. He feels as if he's kicking a wounded puppy.

"It doesn't matter. He's gone. He's gone and he won't be coming back," Frankie says wearily.

"He'll be back when he needs a quick cash infusion or a roof over his head. And when he shows up again, I'll call the authorities myself. I mean it, Frankie," Michael swears as traffic begins to move, a crawl to be sure for the next mile or two, then slowly gathering steam as they pass the accident site.

Michael and his wife need to start throwing age-appropriate gentlemen with steady incomes at Frankie until one finally sticks. Looking back, he should have appreciated the fifteen years of relative peace and quiet when Frankie was involved with that pompous alcoholic high school teacher. He should have been less critical, more welcoming, of the harmless old fool. Sometimes he thinks Frankie believes he's never really accepted his lifestyle. But Michael stopped resenting his brother's sexuality years ago, though he still isn't going to be marching in any parades to celebrate it. It's Frankie's poor choices and naïveté that make Michael uncomfortable. He wouldn't take the odds against Frankie running into his own Tommy Corcoran someday and ending up like the ill-fated Carmine Torino. His worst fear is that this Mariano is just a test drive for a more lethal liaison yet to come.

"I don't know how you do this every day," he complains, growing more frustrated by the minute.

He's circling the block where he and Frankie grew up, searching for that elusive place to park within walking distance of Eighth and Carpenter and the house where they lived as boys. Years of suburban living have dulled his parallel-parking skills, but he manages to squeeze the car into a tight space, much to the horn-blaring frustration of the driver trying to pass him on the narrow street. He hasn't eaten yet, having gotten the call from his colleague in the

Montgomery County office before dinner, and insists they stop for a slice. Standing at the register, his stomach rumbles and he orders an entire pie, large, half sausage, for him, half mushroom, for his brother.

"What are you doing?" Frankie frets as the girl at the cash register counts out Michael's change.

"I thought we'd go back to the house and share it. Do you have any cold beer? I'd settle for a Bud Light. For me. You've had enough booze for one day."

"You don't need to come back with me. I just want to go to bed," Frankie insists. "It's been a terrible day and I want it to be over."

He seems a bit too despondent to Michael for the circumstances. He's assured Frankie no DUI charges will be filed. No report will be made. The arrest never happened. There won't be any points on his license or need to attend a mandatory alcohol-counseling class. No one will ever mention it again. He wonders if Frankie's on some medication that's causing him to act strange. He realizes he has to piss too badly to wait until they're back at his brother's house.

Frankie's gone when he emerges from the men's room. Something feels out of kilter, ominous even, and he wonders if it's safe for Frankie to be alone. He grows antsy during the interminable wait before the counter girl announces his order is ready. He opens the box and practically swallows two slices whole as he walks back to the house. He tries slipping his house key into the locked door of the private entrance in the alley on Carpenter Street, but the blade resists sliding into the keyhole. The shop key doesn't open the Eighth Street entrance, Frankie must have changed the locks after the kid took off and forgotten he hasn't given Michael the new keys. He sets the pizza box on the sidewalk and dials his brother's number on his cell, but Frankie doesn't answer. So he stands in the middle of Eighth Street and shouts his name. The lights are burning on the upper floors so he knows Frankie's in there.

He's surprised some neighbor trying to sleep isn't shouting profanities through a bedroom window. A strange, cold fist grips his heart. He tries calling Frankie's cell one last time, then calmly, purposefully, walks around the side of the building and kicks in the back door. He runs up the stairs, taking two and three steps at time, until he reaches the bathroom off the master bedroom on the highest floor, where he finds his brother slumped on the commode, cradling his head in his hands. The ceramic lid of the toilet tank is lying on the floor, near the tub. Frankie looks so pitiful and helpless sitting there, needing comfort and reassurance, and all Michael has offered is an unpleasant harangue and criticism.

Frankie barely resists as Michael walks him to his bed. He doesn't protest when his younger brother unbuttons his shirt, unzips his pants, and takes off his shoes. He's lying in bed, his eyes wide-open, when Michael turns off the light and urges him to try to sleep. He calls his wife with the good news that the parasite is gone. The bad news, though, is Frankie's acting odd and Michael doesn't want to leave him alone overnight. *Something doesn't feel right. I think he colored his hair. No, I didn't ask him about it. He cut it too. It's shorter than he usually wears it. He doesn't look like himself and he sure as hell isn't acting like himself.* He asks if his son is disappointed. Michael had promised him a trip to the mall after dinner to buy a new pair of sneakers. The Nikes Danny's been wearing have fallen out of style. *Tell him we'll go tomorrow night. I love you, too. Talk to you in the morning.* He hopes there's beer in the fridge and he'll finish off that pizza if some street dog hasn't run off with it. But first he needs to secure the back door. The tools and nails are in the basement, likely untouched since the last time he did a minor repair.

Everything down here is just as he remembers. The damp moisture of the earthen floor. The metal storage shelves, odd pieces of furniture and broken lamps, the wide, deep freezer chest, an ancient Frigidaire model, antediluvian, but still serviceable. His eyes are slow to adjust to the harsh light of the bare ceiling bulb and he slips in a puddle underfoot, noticing an odd smell, fetid but not overpowering, the distinct scent of meat beginning to rot. There are two trash bags on the floor, not full but securely tied. He opens one and finds chicken breasts and cuts of beef soaking in water and blood. The freezer must be broken, despite its gently purring motor.

"What the fuck are you doing down there, Mikey?" Frankie shouts from the top of the stairs, his voice shrill and twisted in his throat as he races down the steps, sweating and gasping for breath.

"You need to replace this goddamn freezer."

"There's nothing wrong with the freezer," Frankie insists, grabbing the trash bag from his brother's hand. "Go upstairs and I'll clean up this mess."

"Let's put this shit back before it stinks up the entire fucking house," Michael says, opening the lid before Frankie can stop him. A blast of arctic air slaps his face and he blinks and jumps back, confused, staring at Frankie in disbelief, not trusting his eyes, needing a moment to gather his wits before confirming that, yes, Frankie's little Mexican is lying in the freezer, shrouded in frost, his twisted and contorted remains a snug and cozy fit.

Book One

parenti serpenti

1920–2007

PAPA AND HIS WIVES, 1920–2001

"Please, Boo. Please!"

"Tonight. Just for one night. You're getting too old for this," Frankie said, finally relenting and lifting the covers so Michael could slip into his bed. Michael's thoughts were racing too quickly for his older brother to keep pace. He'd been spinning in circles since the service and funeral lunch for the stepmother he'd become deeply attached to. He should have been exhausted, but he was too agitated for sleep and began peppering Frankie with questions.

"Do you think Papa hates us?"

He was never Dad, certainly not Daddy. A father who allowed his brats to call him Pa or Pop wasn't worthy of his children's respect. He was Papa, as the man who had sired him had been. His children's few words of Italian were awkward, barely recognizable to a man who had never heard, let alone spoken, English until he was almost nine years old. His boys understood enough of the dialect of Calabria to get the gist of his outbursts whenever he relapsed into the language of his childhood, but always responded in their own native tongue. Michael, always the more willful and bolder of his two sons, would grow up to be a resentful teenager who referred to his father in the hated American vernacular as his *old man,* drawing empty threats of banishment with no possibility of ever returning. Michael was defiant, unbowed. He complained that none of his friends had to live in a dark apartment above a barbershop, with holy pictures on the walls and plaster saints on every table. Michael would live with Sal Pinto if Papa didn't want him around. And once he was gone he would never come back.

Michael's grandfather would have thrown his son into the streets if he'd ever dared to challenge his unquestioned authority. This country had made Papa weak, a man who allowed his children to run wild and treat him with contempt. His naturalization papers, granted after his service in the war, had made him a citizen, but Luigi Rocco Gagliano only finally, truly, became an American the day Michael turned his back on him and walked away, suffering no consequences for calling his father an embarrassment, a stupid old wop with an accent, who should go back to Italy if he hated the *medigan'* so much.

"Was Papa always so mean?"

"You're a lucky boy, Luigi. You're going to live in America."

Even at the age of eight, he knew his mother was frightened and wary of leaving the only home they'd ever known. She'd been a white widow for so many years, left behind when her husband crossed the ocean, that she'd begun to think of herself as a maiden. She was only a girl when she married her husband, a man who'd come back to Calabria to take a bride after emigrating at seventeen. He'd returned to his life in America less than a month after the birth of his son. His letters were short, to the point, hardly filled with the romantic declarations a young girl yearned to read. But the money he earned put meat on the table and paid to repair the roof when the rain leaked through the seams. She received frequent gifts of bolts of expensive cloth and small luxury items like lavender sachets and combs and hair clips made of ivory and tortoiseshell. Luigi was likely the first boy in Italy, certainly Calabria, to own a bright red Liberty Coaster wagon, elevating his status among his cousins, who vied for the privilege of pulling him through the streets of the town.

Then, finally, instructions arrived with the name and address of a man who had booked their passage on the *Konig Albert* departing from Naples. His mother tried consoling Luigi as they sat in the cavernous terminal waiting to board the ship.

"We'll come back soon to see Nonno and Nonna," she promised, assuming the separation from his doting grandparents was the cause of his despair.

A man wearing a uniform and a whistle around his neck was calling names from the front of the room.

". . . Gagliano, Santamaria; Gagliano, Luigi Rocco . . ."

He pulled away when his mother tried to take his hand. He wasn't a baby. He could walk by himself. He knew she needed the reassurance of his touch and wanted to punish her, refusing to forgive her for promising the wagon to his cousin Aldo when they left for America.

Nonno had tried to console him, promising him that, in America, he would have two or three wagons and live in a palace like the Savoy kings. His father was a rich man now, a person of stature and influence, a citizen of the United States with money to grease the palms of the right people in America and Italy to spare his son from a life under the boot heel of Il Diavolo, Nonno's name for the godless Il Duce. But the old man's words failed to comfort and, late in the evening of his last night in the village, Luigi climbed a steep hill, dragging the wagon behind him. He'd stood at the edge of the cliff, tears running down his cheeks as he threw his beloved Liberty Coaster from the rocky precipice and watched it disappear into the leafy ceiling of the trees far below.

"Why doesn't Papa ever talk about when he was a kid?"

The stranger who met Luigi and his mother at the port when they arrived in America was a terrible disappointment to a boy expecting to be greeted by a hero. Salvatore Rocco Gagliano was barely taller than his wife and looked much older than the man in the wedding photo his mother kept on a table beside her bed. The first meeting was awkward, formal, without kisses or an embrace. They boarded a train in a town called Newark and traveled to a city named Philadelphia, arriving after midnight at an enormous building with a barbershop at the street level. S. GAGLIANO, BARBER, EST. 1928, was painted on the window glass. Luigi awoke early his first morning in America, eager to claim the Liberty Coaster wagons his *nonno* had promised awaited him. His mother fed him a simple breakfast of bread and cheese, telling him to eat quickly as he was needed downstairs.

"Do as he says, Luigi. He's your father."

The barber had decided his son was old enough to be put to work and ordered him to wash the shop windows with water and vinegar. Perfection was expected. Being an eight-year-old boy was no excuse for streaks on the plate glass. His efforts were rewarded with a blow that knocked him to the sidewalk. He knew his life had changed, his position in the world diminished, when his mother rebuffed his tearful attempts to seek consolation and sympathy, deferring to her husband in the discipline of his son.

"Who's going to be Papa's wife in heaven?"

Luigi returned to Italy to take up arms against his own blood, fighting in the Battle of Anzio. He returned with an honorable discharge and enrolled in barber school. He assumed his place beside his father in the shop, renamed S. Gagliano & Son, Since 1928, their chairs only a few feet apart. Ten hours a day, six days a week, he suffered endless criticism about squandering his money and his time drinking alcohol with his worthless friend Sal Pinto. What had his father done to be cursed with a *minchione* who chose to keep company with cheap sluts, *donnaccias,* unsuitable to be a wife and mother?

The deal was brokered before Luigi met the woman who would become his first wife. The Gaglianos had known the Avilla family for generations. Pasquale Avilla's two daughters, the loveliest girls in the neighborhood, fair-skinned and blue-eyed, had survived near fatal infections of streptococcus, developing rheumatic fevers that had kept Teresa, the oldest, bedridden for seven months, and her sister, Sofia, ten years younger, for nearly a year. Doctor and hospital bills had left the family deeply in debt, making the offer of money for the hand of Avilla's eldest daughter impossible to reject.

"She is a very pious girl," Luigi's father advised him on his wedding day in 1949. "Don't tear her apart the first night with that big, fat cock you're so proud of."

She'd bled for two days after their wedding night. But she seemed to take to the act quickly, even enthusiastically, until he struck her, calling her a *puttana,* when she made the mistake of touching his prick. Their first child was born within a year, a girl named Paulina Rosa, as useless to Luigi as her mother would become after two miscarriages and years of marriage without giving him a son.

Desperate, she risked damnation of her immortal soul by consulting the local shaman, seeking talismans to protect her from the evil eye that had cursed her womb. The baby was a boy, carried to term, perfectly formed, eight and half pounds. He was delivered stillborn, never drawing a single breath. Luigi would have dragged his wife from her bed and beat her if the priest and Sal Pinto hadn't been there to restrain him. He accused her of being a witch and a whore. God had taken his son to punish him for marrying a woman who practiced the black art of forbidden sorcery. He said she was cursed for bargaining with the devil. He refused to sleep in her bed again, barely exchanging words with her until she died, literally, from a broken heart, its valves corrupted by childhood disease.

Luigi waited the obligatory year of mourning, then, in 1959, married Sofia, as lovely as her sister and with the same quiet, resigned disposition. Eleven months later, she delivered the long-awaited heir and, after five years, provided Luigi with another son. The second pregnancy had been difficult to consummate and the delivery of a ten-pound baby was fraught with risks. She never fully recovered from the caesarean, and congestive heart failure made Luigi a widower a second time when his youngest son was three years old.

"Who will be my mother in heaven?"

Sal Pinto's wife had a friend named Eileen Costello who had been on the New York stage; her husband had died, leaving her no money. Dire circumstances had forced her to take a job giving dancing lessons at Palumbo's. No one could conceive of Luigi choosing a *medigan',* Irish no less, a woman unafraid to speak her mind, to be his wife and mother to his boys. She'd had a mysterious past, actresses being women of questionable reputation, and had already put one husband into the ground. The women of the neighborhood, loyal to the memories of the sainted Avilla sisters, gossiped that she'd put a spell on Luigi, blinding him to the plain and unremarkable face she painted with makeup. Their husbands, though, lusting after *figa,* envied the carnal pleasures to be had between her long legs.

Miss Eileen, as Papa insisted his sons call her, restored calm and a sense of order to the house at Eighth and Carpenter. Luigi's new wife had an uncanny gift for calming gathering storms and had mastered the art of gentle but firm persuasion, prompting her husband to take pause and reconsider before raising his hand to his children. Papa still believed in corporal punishment, but physical abuse was far less frequent and always less severe. Still, his older son clearly resented her presence, though he was always polite and respectful. She refused to allow her husband to pressure the boy into accepting her. She lavishly praised his mother's beauty and gentle nature, which she said was obvious even by her pictures, trying, without success, to relieve Frankie's aching heart.

Michael, though, adored her, embracing her from the outset. No other woman had ever gently cleaned and bandaged his frequent cuts and bruises or praised his smallest achievement and fussed and clucked over his appearance. Miss Eileen provided a lap where he could rest his head while they sat on the sofa, laughing at the antics of Lucy and Jethro Bodine. His own mother existed only as an image in the framed photograph beside their bed, a benign specter whose presence hovered over their lives like a guardian angel or Mary, the Blessed Mother. Miss Eileen was flesh and blood. She smelled of Estee Lauder Private Collection, Virginia Slims, and cinnamon sticky buns. She loved him fiercely, as if he were her own child, and he sought comfort in her arms whenever he was tired or sick.

"Lou, bring the car around," she'd insisted one cold, rainy night. "His fever is a hundred and five."

Michael, always large for his age, was almost too heavy to carry two flights of stairs to the sidewalk where her husband was waiting. She held him in her lap and stroked his head, calming and reassuring him. Her clothes were damp with his sweat when they arrived at the emergency room. The nurse had to pry Michael from her neck to lay him in bed. Frankie and his father, banished to a hallway, could hear his terrified voice behind a pulled curtain, calling for his stepmother, as they sat, useless, unneeded, out of the way.

"Mama! Don't go! Mama!"

"I'm here, baby," she assured him as she held his hand. "I'm right here. I'm not going anywhere."

"Is Papa going to get married again?"

No one expected Luigi to take another wife. Eileen Costello's death seemed to have broken him. His sons would hear him sitting alone in the darkened living room, having one-sided conversations with her about the events of the day. His hair had turned white; his face was gaunt and haunted, his back more stooped. His quick temper returned, unrestrained by any calming influence, and he began swinging his belt again out of anger and frustration at the slightest provocation.

His sons said nothing when he brought a woman home one Sunday evening and announced the banns of marriage would be published in the next week's parish bulletin. Frannie Merlino, recently widowed, was a constant complainer, happy only when Luigi conceded to her demands he spend money on a Mediterranean color television console and a pale blue Ford Fairlane with the title in her name. Knowing he'd spoiled *that dance hall girl* (an insult she never dared utter in his presence) with annual vacations, she insisted her husband take her on expensive trips, cruises in the Caribbean and a fifth-anniversary excursion to Europe. Luigi even agreed to spend one week each July sweltering in a vacation trailer in Virginia left to her by her first husband. She tried to win Michael's affection, but he would never grow attached to another of his father's wives after losing Miss Eileen. She was cold and arrogant toward Frankie, treating him as something vile and disgusting, stalking him like a starving cat, waiting for any opportunity to expose him as a disgusting degenerate who should be cast from their home. She was a patient woman, knowing the day would come when she would hold the evidence in her hand.

Papa was waiting for Frankie as he let himself in the back door.

He assumed his father was angry because it was long past midnight. Frankie and his friend Jack Centafore had gone to see Barbra Streisand in *A Star Is Born,* both agreeing once wasn't enough, and had stayed to watch it from beginning to end a second time. But when he saw Frannie Merlino standing behind her husband, clutching the torn pages from a magazine in her hand, he knew he was being confronted with something far more serious than breaking his curfew.

"I found this under your mattress," she hissed, gleeful in her triumph. "Do you think we don't know what you're doing with this in your bedroom?" she said, tearing a photograph of a bare-chested Robby Benson into shreds as if it were the vilest pornography.

Papa seethed with rage, his face flush with blood. He held his clenched fists at his side, having been warned by the priest of the consequences if he ever left marks on his sons again. Michael, awakened by the shouting, wearing only his underwear, stood on the staircase, ready to attack if his father dared to raise a hand against his brother.

"*Finocchio.* Queer. Thank God your mother is dead or this would kill her."

Frannie Merlino, too self-absorbed to gauge her husband's fleeting moods and shifting loyalties, gloated over her victory, seizing an opportunity to continue the humiliation.

"At least you can be grateful one of your boys is growing up to be a man and not an embarrassing faggot."

Papa's voice was even, but cold and chilling. Frannie Merlino's face blanched at her husband's reproach.

"This is my house. You live under my roof. If you cannot respect my children, pack your suitcase and leave."

As fate would have it, Luigi's most miserable marriage was the longest, lasting fifteen years until she made him a widower a fourth time. Obsessed with clean teeth and fresh breath, Frannie Merlino Gagliano had been too engrossed in searching her pocketbook for a Chiclet to see the Number 57 bus jump the curb. Neither father nor sons mourned her passing and rarely spoke her name after the day she was buried.

"How many wives is Papa allowed to have?"

* * *

Helen Constanza, Luigi's last wife, was happiest working in the kitchen, standing at the stove from morning until night. She treated his sons with deference, insisting on feeding them whenever they walked through the door, regardless of the hour of the day or night. Michael, then a hardworking assistant prosecutor residing less than a mile away in an apartment he shared with the young nurse he intended to marry, returned infrequently and then only to see his brother, a grown man, who, though a successful stylist, still lived under his father's roof. It was the great mystery of the family at Eighth and Carpenter that Michael, who had only occasionally suffered from the barber's temper and moods, despised the man, while Frankie, the brother their father had treated so harshly, had remained the loyal son.

Both boys were genuinely fond of Helen Constanza, Frankie in particular. Frankie invited her to nights at the Forrest Theater and dinners with his friends, the ugly priest and the fat schoolteacher. Luigi began to become confused and forgetful, sometimes referring to his wife as Eileen and insisting she wear the green dress he admired so much. He would scoff, becoming angry when she reminded him that Eileen Costello had passed many years ago and would accuse her of thinking him an idiot. Of course he knew who was dead and who was living flesh and blood. Helen's daughter in California insisted on moving her out west after she suffered a mild stroke, fearing that Papa, then in the obvious early stages of Alzheimer's, was unable to care for her. Luigi refused to consider a request from Helen's children that he agree to an annulment and they remained married until a fatal aneurysm did them part. He'd raged at his son the lawyer, calling him useless, when Michael wouldn't sue the Constanza family for cremating their mother, whose remains Luigi insisted were his legal property as the widower, and scattering her ashes at a marina in San Diego.

"Will Papa be nicer in heaven?"

All but his most loyal customers gradually began drifting away. Even Sal Pinto feared his shaking hands and dreaded his lapses into irrational rants about the Polish Pope being a plant by the

Kremlin. Frankie reluctantly conceded when Michael insisted their father surrender his license. But he was adamant he would never condemn him to a nursing facility where Michael argued he could be cared for and protected from himself. Frankie kept him at home as long as he could, up until the day Michael received a phone call from a colleague in the Philly DA's office, saying he was having a hard time persuading an irate family from pursuing a private complaint against their father.

"I know I told you about it," Frankie insisted when his brother confronted him. "You must have forgotten it, Mikey."

"No," Michael assured him. "I'm goddamn certain I would remember hearing my father had been arrested in a school zone, sitting in a parked car with his limp pecker in his hand."

"Not arrested," Frankie corrected him. "He was picked up," meaning he'd been rescued and escorted safely home by the Ottaviano boy on the force, who was kind enough to wrap an Eagles commemorative fleece blanket around Luigi to cover his nakedness.

"Paul Ottaviano," Frankie explained. "The one who looked like Elvis. He had an older brother, Bobby. Their parents had that luncheonette at Fifteenth and Dickinson. *You're a very lucky man, Papa,* I told him. *You'd be sitting in the lockup if some stranger had picked you up, some Irish cop or a* moulinyan. They would have treated him like a pervert, a *vecchio schifoso,* and charged him with indecent exposure."

"Did Paul Ottaviano accuse him of that?"

"He just said he found him with his sausage in his hand and his pants and boxers on the passenger seat, neatly folded, with his shoes and socks on the floor. He didn't accuse Papa of anything. He said Papa must be confused. I thanked him and told him how much I appreciated him looking out for the old man. After he left, I asked Papa why he was driving around South Philly bare-assed. He stood there with his big fat schlong hanging to his thigh and told me I was crazy. He said I was his curse, unholy, and that only an ungrateful *finocchio* would make up such hateful lies about his own father."

Luigi lost his ability to speak even the most basic English after being admitted to a dementia unit. Frankie was secretly relieved of the responsibility of caring for him, no longer torn between the demands of his father and those of Charlie Haldermann, his schoolteacher "friend." He dedicated three evenings a week and Sunday afternoons to sitting with Luigi. Michael, at his brother's insistence, came to the nursing home on his father's birthday and Christmas and an occasional weekend when he couldn't bear Frankie's nagging any longer. His sons were puzzled by their father's frequent crying jags. Frankie could make out a few of his words, but they amounted to nonsense, something about a red wagon. Michael shrugged, not terribly interested, and said whatever memories tortured him would forever remain a mystery. Maybe they'd been fooling themselves and Papa had known all along about the secret they and Miss Eileen had conspired to keep from him that long ago Christmas Day. Luigi faded slowly, his limbs withering with atrophy, refusing even small bites of food. He died two days short of his eighty-first birthday. His funeral Mass was ten a.m. on Tuesday, the eleventh of September, 2001.

Only his sons and the pallbearers accompanied the body to the cemetery. The other mourners had raced directly to the Speakeasy, where the staff brought television sets into the private dining room Frankie had reserved for the funeral lunch. Luigi was an afterthought at his own wake, the guests too preoccupied by the unimaginable images of horror ninety miles to the north to mourn him. The booze flowed and everyone lingered long after the meal, eyes riveted to the screen.

It felt like an eternity before Frankie was able to collapse on the sofa with a vodka tonic, his first drink of the day. He remembered Helen Constanza had had a son who worked at the Trade Center and offered a quick prayer he wasn't among the many lying in the rubble. He reached for the remote, having seen enough death and tragedy for one day. He heard Jack Centafore's heavy footsteps on the back staircase, returning with Indian takeout despite Frankie's protest he had no appetite. The vodka went to his head quickly and he decided he shouldn't have a second, knowing his embarrassing tendency to get sad and sentimental when under the influence. But he didn't argue when Jack poured him a refill, even stronger than the first, and turned on the television.

"Can I ask you something?" Frankie ventured, emboldened by the liquor.

Jack nodded his head without looking away from Peter Jennings reporting live from the smoking rubble.

"Were the terrorists good men?" he asked.

Jack stared at him as if he were crazy.

"What do you think? I can't believe you would even ask."

"Do you think they're burning in hell?"

"That's a better fate than they deserve."

"Was my father a good man?"

Jack carefully chewed his food, cogitating, trying to compose a diplomatic answer.

"That's not for us to judge, Frankie. The only opinion that counts is God's," he said, contradicting his own knee-jerk condemnation of the men who had brought down the tallest buildings in New York.

"What would you say if I told you I didn't believe in heaven or hell? That when you die, you die, and there's nothing more to it."

This time Jack was quick to respond.

"I'd say you're exhausted, you're grieving your father's death, and you're starting to get a little tipsy."

It was pointless to argue and Jack was right. He was a little drunk.

"You know what I've never understood?" Jack asked, finally posing a question that had perplexed him for years. "Why did your brother hate your father so much? If anyone had a reason to despise the old man it was you."

"It's my fault. I'm to blame. Even when he was a little boy he thought he had to protect me. He would cling to Papa's leg, crying when Papa would hit me with the strop, begging him to stop. He threw a can of tomatoes at Papa's head for slapping my face when he was only seven years old. God only knows what Papa would have done if Miss Eileen hadn't been there. Mikey hated Papa because of me."

Frankie, 1966

She was the most amazing creature in his world. Each day after school he sat at the kitchen table, waiting patiently to hear the clacking sound of her shoes and the static feedback on her transistor radio as she climbed the wooden staircase. She called him her shadow when Papa and his mother were in earshot and, affectionately, her little shit-bag when they weren't. It was his special nickname, a secret, one of many shared between them. Frankie was his half sister's sounding board, her confidante, an enlisted ally in her war against their father.

The baby still slept in Papa and Mama's bedroom and Frankie's bed was in a small space, not much larger than a walk-in closet, behind the kitchen. Polly's room, on the third floor, across from her father's, the one Frankie would later share with his younger brother, had a window facing Carpenter Street and, at night, the streetlight cast a warm glow through the pink sheer curtains. He would stand at the door, waiting to be invited into this magical refuge in the otherwise dark and dour house. Polly would sigh and call him a pest, barely tolerated. It was part of the game. The difference in their ages meant they could never be real friends. But a six-year-old boy was a perfect acolyte for a sixteen-soon-to-be-seventeen-year-old adolescent needing constant, adoring reassurance of her attractiveness and desirability and an audience for her rants about the strict rules enforced by Papa and the harsh penalties imposed whenever they were transgressed.

Frankie would sit cross-legged on her bed, rapt, listening to her stories of life at her all-girls high school under the strict supervision of the "crows," the black-bonneted Sisters of Charity. To an impressionable little boy, it was a place as mysterious and enchanted as Oz, populated by wicked nuns wielding yardsticks rather than broomsticks and an ever-shifting cast of best friends, enemies, and rivals. There were brash girls with fierce tempers and girls too timid to speak. Some were loyal girls who had your back and others were treacherous sluts who would stab you in the chest. Worst of all were the smug little brats, hated by all, who curried favor with the crows in black, informing on who was smoking in the bathroom and who rolled up the waists of their skirts, exposing the white skin of their thighs, when they loitered outside the entrance to the boys' high school two blocks away.

Frankie's favorite of her stories were her tales of those boys, especially the ones about the efforts, not entirely unwelcome, of Bobby Ottaviano, whose beauty rivaled that of Rodney Harrington on *Peyton Place,* to persuade her to "go all the way." She told Frankie he would understand what she was talking about when he was older, but he already knew how it felt to be in love with Bobby Ottaviano. But, even at six, he sensed he could never share his secret with anyone, not even Polly, that there was something wrong and shameful about his feelings for his half-sister's boyfriend. Boys were only supposed to fall in love with girls, not other boys.

Frankie hated whenever Papa and Polly fought, which seemed to be almost every night. His mother tried to comfort and counsel her niece and stepdaughter, only to be cruelly rebuffed with tearful recriminations. *You're not my mother. I hate you. I wish you were the one who died.* Even Polly knew she'd gone too far when she called Frankie's mother a mean and ugly cunt. She begged her stepmother not to tell her father, fearing the certain brutal consequences of her filthy mouth and disrespect. Frankie watched his mother take Polly into her arms, assuring her it was their little secret. She stroked her sister's daughter's hair, a simple, kind gesture that unleashed the girl's inconsolable grief over being abandoned by a mother who had loved her and rejected by a father who treated her like an unwanted reminder of a former life.

Polly was heartbroken, swearing she would never get over it, when Bobby Ottaviano told her they were breaking up after she finally relented, believing his promises of an engagement ring, and let him put "it" in her. She was certain he would change his mind if she were prettier, like her mother and aunt, not a drab brown hen whose only good feature was her piercing blue eyes. She enlisted Frankie as her accomplice one Sunday afternoon when Papa and Frankie's mother drove to New Jersey to visit an ancient dying Avilla aunt who had never seen the baby. They made a mess of Papa's shop, slopping peroxide on the floor as they stripped the mousy color from her hair, transforming her into a bleached blonde who could pass as Nancy Sinatra's twin. Polly was in a celebratory mood, shocking her little brother by pulling a pack of Salems from her purse and puffing away as if she had been smoking for years. Frankie followed her to her bedroom and watched with rapt attention as she frosted her lips and made up her eyes.

Papa was enraged to return home to find his daughter looking like a cheap *puttana.* Frankie's mother had to plead with her husband to persuade him not to strap the girl to his barber chair and shear her head down to a clean scalp. Polly wept bitterly, conceding defeat, accepting the compromise punishment of being forced to restore her beautiful blond hair to an approximation of its natural color with a bottle of Nice 'N Easy from the Sun-Ray Drugstore. That night, Frankie sat on the floor beside her locked door, forbidden by Papa to enter to comfort her, whispering in a voice loud enough for only her to hear. She looked beautiful, he assured her, prettier than Nancy Sinatra, prettier even than Connie Stevens. She'd be a movie star someday, he promised, just like she dreamed, and Papa would regret being so mean and hang her pictures on the walls of his barbershop for everyone to see.

Frankie and Michael, April 1968

Michael didn't struggle as Frankie slowly marched him down the long, brightly lit corridor. He was big for his age, sometimes mistaken for a child of five, and had inherited a stubborn, sometimes ornery, personality from his father. At home he could be loud and boisterous, running from room to room, jumping on the furniture until the heavy thumping on the ceiling summoned an angry Papa from the barbershop below. But the hallways of Methodist Hospital were unfamiliar surroundings, patrolled by intimidating women in starched white uniforms with funny hats pinned to their hair, and he shrank behind his brother's back as a fierce-looking nurse approached them.

"Are you boys lost?" she asked as they stood by the elevator, placing her hand over the call button before Frankie could reach it.

"No, ma'am," Frankie assured her, afraid to admit he might have gotten confused and taken a wrong turn, forgetting Papa's careful directions.

"Where is your mother?"

"In her room," he answered.

"Is she a patient here?"

"Yes."

"Does your father know where you are?" she asked.

"He told me to take my brother to the cafeteria."

"How old are you boys?" she asked, skeptical that a child as young as Frankie would be charged with supervising a toddler, especially with all the terrible things on the evening news the past few days.

"My brother is gonna be three and I'm eight."

"All right, go on then. But don't let go of his hand now, you promise?" she said, sending them on their way against her better judgment, her voice softer and kinder.

"I won't," he said as the elevator door closed behind them.

The cafeteria was filled with empty tables. An old colored man sat alone in a far corner of the room, drinking coffee and listening to a transistor radio. Frankie put his arm around Michael's shoulder as the cashier took their money, holding him tightly to keep him from wandering off.

"You boys sit where I can see you," she said as she handed Frankie his change. "You come tell me if that nigger says anything to you."

Michael ate a few bites of his hot dog and drank a carton of chocolate milk. Frankie felt safer knowing a grown-up was keeping an eye on them. Sal Pinto was supposed to be watching them, but he'd gone home to check on his wife and daughters, worried the riots were spreading to the streets of South Philadelphia. Everyone was talking about what they would do if the *moulinyan* tried to burn down their houses. Sal Pinto said he had a shotgun and Papa swore he would crack open the skull of anyone who tried to break down his doors.

No curious nurses stopped them as they made their way back to their mother's floor. An old woman sitting in the visitors' room looked up from her rosary beads as they opened the door. The thermostat in the boiler room hadn't been adjusted for the warmer temperatures of spring and the radiators banged and hissed, pumping heat into the stuffy, windowless space. Papa had dressed his sons in heavy wool sweaters and Michael was cranky and agitated, tugging at the scratchy collar rubbing against his neck. The woman put her rosary in her pocketbook and picked among the butts in the overflowing ashtray, finally choosing a suitable one to smoke.

"He should be in bed," she snapped.

"He's just hot," Frankie said as he yanked his brother's sweater over his head. He pulled a frayed copy of *Go, Dog. Go!* and a Hershey bar from his book bag, hoping to pacify Michael until their father returned. Maybe Sal Pinto would come soon to take them home. Sal Pinto, unlike Papa, didn't care that it was a school night and that *Bewitched* didn't start until after bedtime. Michael was squirming in his seat, his face bright red. Frankie looked up from the book and saw his father in the doorway, seething as his youngest son smeared melted chocolate across his white dress shirt. Papa's aim was sure, the slap crisp and sharp, hard to enough to break the skin of Frankie's upper lip.

"What did I tell you? You were supposed to watch him," Papa said, never raising his voice.

Frankie's eyes swelled with tears and his lower lip trembled. The old woman cackled at his misfortune, covering her stained teeth with her hand.

"Stop it, before I give you something to cry about," Papa snapped as he grabbed Frankie by the chin to inspect the damage. "It's just a little bit of blood. Take your brother to the bathroom and clean him up, then wash your face and comb your hair. Hurry up, now. Your mother's waiting."

"Yes, Papa."

"Stand by the bed and hold her hand. Don't complain. Do you understand me?"

"Yes, Papa."

"Go on, now. Don't make me come looking for you," his father said as he turned and walked away, still looking fresh and pressed, his clothes unwrinkled, his hair neatly parted, forever and always the impeccably groomed barber.

Frankie washed Michael's face, doing his best to make him presentable, then took him by the hand and slowly walked him from the bathroom to their mother's room. A plaster statue of Our Lady of Lourdes was on the table by the bed, a burning red votive candle at her feet. A wilted Easter lily and a vase of carnations sat on the windowsill. Voices were whispering in Italian behind the drawn white curtain separating the patients in the semi-private room. Michael clung to his brother's arm, turning away from the thin and brittle woman propped up against a bank of pillows, a sheet pulled up to her chest.

"Come here, closer, so I can see you," she said, speaking with difficulty as she struggled for breath.

"Go ahead, Mikey," Frankie said, encouraging him.

"I don't want to, Boo! I don't want to!" Michael insisted, burying his face in Frankie's chest. Boo had been Michael's first word and the name he'd christened his older brother. Papa called it childish gibberish, baby talk, but Mama said it was a harmless endearment he'd soon grow out of.

"I'm right beside you," he promised, urging his brother to go to the bedside.

She was wearing a pretty pink cotton dressing gown with a white lace collar buttoned at the neck. She'd put on red lipstick and a touch of makeup to brighten her face and Papa had washed and brushed her hair.

"Go to your mother," Papa pleaded as he tried to pry Michael from his brother.

Michael started to howl, refusing to leave Frankie's side.

"He's scared, Mama," Frankie said, finding his tongue, almost as frightened as his little brother by the long plastic tube dangling from her nose. "Let's go say good night, Mikey. Me and you," he said quietly, gently easing Michael toward the bed. Frankie picked up his mother's hand and held it, heeding his father's warning.

"Such handsome boys! The girls are going to fall in love with you!" she gushed, pausing between words to catch her breath.

Frankie was blue-eyed and fair, like his mother. Michael was dark, his features less chiseled and perfect than his brother's, with brown eyes that seemed to sink into his face, giving him a gravitas unusual for a boy of his age. They shared a dignified Roman nose worthy of a marble bust, marking them as true Gaglianos.

She sank back into her pillows and closed her eyes, gasping for breath through her open mouth. But her grip on her oldest son's hand was firm, unwilling to release him. Frankie stood perfectly still, not daring to move. His mind began to wander, his thoughts drifting to Samantha Stephens and Endora and Gladys Kravitz, the nosy neighbor across the street. He couldn't see the face of his wristwatch, a Timex his godfather Mr. Ferri had given him the morning of his First Communion. He made a bold move, twisting his forearm to check the time, knowing that nothing, not even the slightest movement, escaped Papa's eyes. Eight o'clock was fast approaching, when, just like magic, summoned by Samantha's twitching nose, Sal Pinto arrived to take them home.

"Frankie," his mother whispered as he gave her a good-night kiss.

"Yes, Mama?"

"Promise me you'll always take care of each other. Frankie, you make sure you tell your brother I asked you both to do that when he's old enough to understand."

"Yes, Mama."

"Remember to say your prayers."

"I will," he promised, growing anxious again. They would have to hurry if they were going to make it home on time.

"You send them straight to bed, Sal," Papa insisted. "Don't let that one tell you he can stay up all night watching television."

Sal drove through the traffic lights, not bothering to stop. The streets and sidewalks were deserted. Everyone was barricaded behind locked doors, waiting for angry mobs to invade their neighborhood. They arrived home to find shattered pieces of a broken Coke bottle on the sidewalk at the barbershop door, evidence, according to Sal, of an attempted break-in. He quickly led the boys upstairs and told them to sit quietly on the couch. He picked up the receiver of the kitchen phone to call his wife, clearly shaken by the booming crack of an engine backfiring on the street below.

"All right, all right," he said, trying to calm the frantic woman on the line. "You and the girls stay upstairs. Don't come down. I'll come home and make sure the back door is locked," he reassured her.

"Yo, Frankie," he shouted. "I gotta run back to the house for a few minutes. Don't you move off that couch until I get back."

Frankie nodded and sat quietly, waiting until he heard the barbershop door slam shut before running to turn on the television. Samantha was just beginning her sidesaddle broomstick flight across the starlit sky as he settled back on the sofa. Only Huckleberry Hound or Woody Woodpecker, not suburban witches, could hold Michael's attention and he quickly drifted off, his head in his brother's lap, contentedly sucking his thumb.

Michael was cranky and tired in the morning. Still groggy with sleep, he needed his older brother's steady hand on his shoulder to march him to the bathroom. He protested when Frankie pulled down his pajama bottoms and lifted his butt onto the toilet seat. He wasn't a baby anymore and wanted to stand and aim for the bowl like Frankie had taught him. Frankie promised he could pee like a grown-up next time, but this morning there wasn't time to waste wiping up the floor if Michael missed his mark as he most often did.

"Stand still, Mikey," Frankie pleaded as he washed and dried his brother's hands.

Michael kicked his legs when Frankie sat him on the edge of the bed, thinking they were playing a game. He curled his toes, resisting his brother's efforts to slide his feet, broad and long for a child, into his slippers. He ran to the kitchen and crawled onto a chair at the table.

"No!" he insisted when Frankie offered him a bowl of Raisin Bran.

Michael knew what he wanted and wasn't shy about demanding it. He picked out the desiccated pastel marshmallow Lucky Charms from the bowl and left the cereal swimming in the milk.

The clock on the wall said seven thirty, meaning Frankie would have to dress quickly and run three blocks to Saint Catherine of Siena Elementary. Sal Pinto wandered in barefoot, having slept on the living room sofa, and lit his first cigarette of the day. He seemed uncomfortable, avoiding looking Frankie in the eyes when he told him he wouldn't be going to school today. "Your father will be here soon," he mumbled as he searched for an ashtray and, finding none, flicked his ash into the kitchen sink. Frankie knew then, without needing to be told, his mother was never coming home.

Polly argued with Papa that Michael was too young to attend the open-casket viewing and, for the first time Frankie could remember, Papa conceded to one of his children. But he'd insisted both sons attend the funeral Mass and the graveside rites. Michael was restless, banging his Buster Browns on the wooden pew, not understanding that his mother was in the sealed box before the altar. Polly stood close to Papa at the cemetery, keeping vigil as they lowered the casket in the grave, but he shrugged off her arm, not wanting to be touched, when she tried to comfort him.

That night, lying in his bed, unable to sleep, Frankie cringed at the loud, harsh voices shouting downstairs. His father and sister were fighting, Polly insisting *I'm not leaving without him.* He was only three, she argued, still a baby, too young to live in a house without a mother. Papa replied that no son of his was going to be raised by a whore. A shotgun wedding to the man who'd gotten her pregnant last year hadn't redeemed her in her father's eyes. They argued back and forth, accusing each other of terrible things, of being unfit to be a parent. Frankie rolled on his back and stared at the ceiling, praying his half sister would have her way, trying to imagine a life without Papa. Polly was his friend. He was her shadow, her little shit-bag. She wouldn't whip him with a leather belt or take a barber's strop to the back of his legs. She wouldn't lock him in a dark, cold basement and force him to sleep on the floor. For a few moments, Frankie could hope for a chance to live without constant fear of a backhand to his face. But Polly's next words cut him deeply, more painful than any physical punishment Papa was capable of giving.

"You'll still have his brother. You won't be alone. He can cook and clean for you. You can treat him like your little wife."

It wasn't her horrible words and sneering voice, mocking him as more girl than boy, that wounded him. She was trying to steal the one thing in the world that belonged to him, the only thing he loved. She would leave him alone, without a mother or a brother, to live with a father who rarely spoke to him and then only to criticize and threaten him. The voices below grew louder as they shouted over each other, waking Michael, who ran to Frankie's bed. He burrowed under the covers, clinging to his brother, his arms, strong as a little bull's, around Frankie's neck, nearly choking him.

"I want Mama," he cried, his voice muffled by Frankie's chest.

"Mama went to live with the angels."

"Where?"

"Angels live in heaven."

"What's heaven? When is she coming home?"

"She has to stay with the angels. They'd be sad if she left them alone."

"Doesn't she like us?"

"She loves us, especially you. You're her special boy."

"Are you going to go live with the angels, too, Boo?"

"No. I'm going to stay with you, Mikey."

"Okay," Michael said, easily comforted as only a child soon to be three could be. He fell asleep quickly, feeling safe in Frankie's arms. Frankie would be bruised in the morning from Michael kicking his legs while he slept. Mama had said Michael would be as tall as a giant when he grew up, big and strong, but Frankie would always be older, someone his young brother would look up to. Papa and Polly could fight all night. He didn't care who won the argument downstairs. He'd made a promise to his mother and no one would ever take Michael away from him.

FRANKIE, CHRISTMAS 1969

The morning of Christmas Eve was unseasonably warm, but Miss Eileen insisted on wrapping a wool scarf around Michael's neck and stuffing his chubby hands into a pair of mittens.

"It's pneumonia weather, Frankie. Don't argue with me today. Just bundle up so we can be on our way."

Frankie was nine and a half and too old to believe her dumb stories about disobedient boys who had caught their death from running around outdoors in the month of December with bare heads and their coats unbuttoned.

"Tell me their names!" he demanded.

"Oh, you wouldn't know them. They all lived in Holmesburg when I was a girl and they died long before you were born. Mikey, if I let go of your hand you have to promise not to run out into the street."

Frankie tried to act blasé, as if he couldn't care less, but his heart began fluttering as soon as the Broad Street Woolworth's was in sight.

"You're going to have to help me carry everything back. I only have two arms and need eyes in the back of my head to watch your brother."

Last-minute shoppers swarmed the aisles of the five-and-dime. Several women from the parish stopped Miss Eileen, trying to engage her in gossip, but she smiled and wished them a Merry Christmas, *I guess I should say Buon Natale,* and, pleading a million things left to do, shepherded her stepsons toward the boxes of ornaments.

"You have to help me pick out what to buy, Frankie. Which of these do you like the best?"

They were all beautiful to his awestruck eyes. He chose silver and red and green and gold shiny glass globes that would reflect the light of the colored tree lamps.

"You don't know how lucky we are these days. When I was your age, the whole string would go dark when one bulb burned out."

She told them each to pick out one "special" ornament. Michael, of course, wanted a crudely molded Santa. Frankie chose a delicate glass snowflake. The only disappointment was settling for a star to top the tree because the angels were out of stock.

"Next year," Miss Eileen promised. "We'll come the day after Thanksgiving and buy the biggest one in the store."

Sal Pinto was steadying a fragrant pine by the big window on Eighth Street when they arrived home. The greatest miracle of all had occurred. Papa had relented, giving in to his new wife's pleas that it wouldn't be Christmas without a tree. The immigrant from Calabria believed only the idiot *medigan'* dragged a dead tree into their house. Every year there was a story in the paper about some crazy family that had been burned to a crisp after an electrical short caused the cursed fire hazard to burst into flames. In Papa's household, the Birth of the Savior had always been observed by displaying the elaborate wood-and-terra-cotta *presepe* his mother had had shipped from Naples and by hanging a wreath on the barbershop door. The flame-haired woman had accomplished the impossible, though she couldn't persuade her husband to actually walk to the corner to buy the tree and haul it up the stairs. Sal Pinto offered to string the lights, saying it was a man's job, and teased Miss Eileen about showing him a few of the tricks she'd used to force the old goat to live in the twentieth century. She warned him about being fresh and told him to behave himself since *that one,* she said, nodding at Frankie, *doesn't miss a trick.*

She put Frankie in charge of decorating the tree and loaded a stack of holiday LPs—Perry Como and Bing Crosby, Nat "King" Cole and *The Little Drummer Boy*—on the hi-fi turntable. She announced that decorating was thirsty work and made cocoa, which Michael spilt on the floor, setting off a frantic rush to mop up the mess before Papa climbed the stairs after his last trim of the day.

"Isn't it beautiful, Lou?" she asked. "Frankie did it all by himself. All I did was hang the ornaments on the branches that were too high for him to reach."

Papa was ungracious in defeat.

"No smoking in this room until that thing is out on the street where it belongs."

Papa and his bride squabbled when she pulled a casserole of macaroni and cheese from the oven to take to Sal Pinto's Christmas Eve dinner.

"For God's sake, Lou, they're little boys. You can't expect them to eat that stuff. I can hardly look at it myself."

The smelly fish were the only bad part of Christmas. Miss Eileen slapped Sal Pinto's hand at the dinner table, much to the pleasure of his beleaguered wife, for tormenting her stepson by dangling a greasy dead smelt inches from Frankie's face.

"She's spoiling you, Francis," Papa said as they walked to Saint Catherine's, where Frankie was serving at Midnight Mass. Miss Eileen had taken Michael home with strict instructions from Papa to give him a spoonful of Benadryl if he was too excited about the visit from Saint Nicholas to sleep.

On Christmas morning, Miss Eileen chased Michael with an Instamatic, taking pictures as he tore through the wrapping paper, barely taking time to look at one toy before moving on to the next. Frankie made a major haul of board games and model planes (he had no interest in aircraft, but loved the meticulous task of assembling the pieces) and an army of plastic Roman centurions. Miss Eileen raved about the drugstore perfume he'd selected when Papa warned he wouldn't be able to sit for a week if he didn't buy *his mother* a present.

"How did you know Jean Naté is my favorite?" she gushed. "Mikey, that's an outdoor toy! Not something to play with in the house!" she chided as Michael raced from room to room with his brand-new Little Red Wagon Radio Flyer.

"Lou, you look like you're going to meet the Queen of England!" she laughed when Papa came downstairs from dressing.

The part in his hair was meticulous and his mustache freshly trimmed. He was wearing a three-piece suit and he'd spit-shined his black leather shoes. He was holding a fedora, perfectly blocked, in his hand.

"Would you please put on an overcoat?" she pleaded, clucking over the risk he was willing to take with his health. "You're as bad as the boys."

As president of the parish Holy Name Society, it was Papa's solemn duty to dispatch the members of the confraternity to deliver generous cash gifts, raised by the Society's monthly 50/50 raffles and weekly bingo games, to the widows and homebound invalids of the neighborhood. Most of the men would stumble home drunk to their Christmas feasts since it would be an insult to refuse to raise a toast with their grateful beneficiaries. Not Papa, of course. Frankie had never seen him get loud and silly like Sal Pinto and Pete Delvecchia after a few shots.

"You'll be home by three," Miss Eileen reminded him. "Remember. You promised."

Papa had wanted to make his wife happy and reluctantly agreed to load the trunk of the Oldsmobile sedan with gifts and travel to the Holmesburg section of the city, no less foreign a destination than if Miss Eileen had suggested Marrakesh, to have Christmas dinner with her brother's family. Frankie had heard his father speaking Italian with Sal Pinto on Christmas Eve (Sal Pinto, born in Philadelphia to immigrant parents, couldn't sustain an entire conversation in the old tongue and frequently lapsed into English, his first language), expressing his disgust at the prospect of being served dry turkey and slimy yams by dry spitting on the floor.

"Don't let him get overheated," he said, nodding at Michael, who was clambering to be set loose outdoors to take the Radio Flyer on a test run. "I bought that bastard Imperiale a new car with the doctor's bills I've paid him this year."

The temperature had plunged overnight, falling more than forty degrees, well below the freezing point. Miss Eileen stood at the barbershop door, soliciting Frankie's promise to walk slowly while pulling his brother in the wagon.

"You boys be careful. That's black ice on the sidewalk. You don't want to spend Christmas in the emergency room."

Michael grew restless after two laps around the block and tried to climb out of the moving wagon. The Radio Flyer tipped, spilling him on the concrete. The thick cushion of his mittens protected the meaty flesh of his palms when he used his hands to break his fall. He escaped without cuts or bruises, but the shock of finding himself facedown on the sidewalk was reason enough for him to begin to wail.

"Come on, Mikey. Stop crying. You're not hurt," Frankie reassured him as he lifted Michael to his feet.

Neither of them saw the Radio Flyer drift down the sidewalk or knew that it had jumped the curb and rolled into the street until they heard the metallic crunch of it being crushed beneath the wheels of a baby-blue Cadillac. The driver jumped from the car and did a quick 360 around the vehicle, searching for damage.

"You fucking kids are goddamn lucky that thing didn't scratch my car or I'd break both of your scrawny necks," he panted, even the slightest exertion being a strain on his corpulent body.

He was the *capo di tutti capi,* a man who commanded such respect that Papa's boisterous and argumentative customers fell silent, greeting him with deference born of fear, when he arrived at the shop for his weekly trim, *take a little off the top and clean up the neck.* A woman with heavy jowls and a short neck opened the car window, exhaling a thick cloud of cigarette smoke. She wore a ring on every finger and the white skunk strip in her kinky, long hair reminded Frankie of Cruella de Vil.

"For Christ's sake, Angelo, it's Christmas. Stop torturing those poor boys."

The *boss of bosses,* chastised by his wife for being a Scrooge, gave Frankie a crisp ten-dollar bill and a lecture about the dangers of playing in the street. Michael, wary and frightened, as if the mangled wagon were a dangerous beast poised to attack, ran indoors, seeking the comfort of Miss Eileen's arms and soothing words.

"Don't worry, sweetheart. Tomorrow we'll take the subway to Wanamaker's and buy a new wagon. We won't say anything when your father gets home. It'll be our secret. Just the three of us. He'll never know. Now come on, both of you. Stop frowning. Show me what handsome boys you are when you smile."

Papa was pleasantly surprised to learn Miss Eileen's brother had married an Italian girl whose holiday lasagna was light as air and whose *pizzelles* were crisp and fragrant with anisette. His *medigan'* in-law had developed a taste for Sambuca and insisted he and Papa share multiple toasts. It was almost midnight before Papa carried a sleeping Michael to the car.

"No, honey. Sit up front with your father," Miss Eileen told Frankie. "I'll ride in the back with your brother."

"Don't slam that door and wake him up, Francis. And put those cookies away before you get crumbs all over the seat," Papa warned.

He heard Michael stir and Miss Eileen quietly singing a carol to lull him back to sleep. Frankie hated her more at that moment than at any time since the day Papa brought her into their house. He and his brother had only each other after their mother died. Michael belonged to this stranger now and Frankie belonged to no one. He bit his lip, drawing blood, determined that no one see him cry.

"It's late, Francis," Papa said when they arrived at Eighth and Carpenter. His youngest son was dead weight in his arms. "Don't make me come back down these stairs to chase you to bed."

"Yes, Papa."

He waited until he heard the tip-tap, click-clack of Miss Eileen's heels on the creaking floorboards overhead. He acted quickly, snatching the glass snowflake from the tree, and wrapped it in his scarf. In the morning, he hid it in the deep pocket of his toggle coat and smashed it on the sidewalk on his way to church to serve at morning Mass.

Frankie and Michael, 1970–1973

The promise of a few hours away from the critical eye of Papa, no one snapping at him or threatening him with the open palm of his hand, sustained Frankie throughout the week. He was still too young to be trusted alone at home with Mikey when Papa and Miss Eileen went dancing at Palumbo's on Saturday night. It was Father Parisi who made the suggestion. *It's not a problem at all. It's an early night for me anyway, just putting the finishing touches on my sermon, a glass of wine and bed. It'll be fun. Don't worry about feeding them. The housekeeper always makes a pot of gravy. We'll watch a little television. They'll keep me out of trouble.* He winked at Frankie as if they had a secret conspiracy to stay up all night drinking Pepsi and playing Parcheesi. *Why don't the boys just stay overnight? Frankie can serve at eight o'clock Mass.*

Father Parisi had picture books of Bible stories and, as Mikey grew into a precocious young reader, serious tomes from the rectory library like *Lives of the Saints* and *The Greatest Story Ever Told* to keep him occupied while Frankie listened to the priest rehearse his sermon. (Useful training, Frankie later realized, since there was no course in beauty school to teach aspiring stylists how to look fascinated and engaged when they're bored to distraction, their minds a million miles away from the client droning away in the chair.) Frankie would bring his favorite records, and the priest never complained the volume was too loud or, like Papa, called the Jackson 5 *moulinyan* who belonged in jail. Frankie, so quiet at mealtimes at home, talked a blue streak at the dinner table, and Father Parisi pretended to be fascinated by the latest plot twists on *General Hospital* and *All My Children*. The priest never chastised the brothers when they argued, which was often, Mikey seizing any opportunity to grab his share of attention. There was always chocolate cake for dessert and Michael always asked for a second slice.

After supper, they watched Archie Bunker and Mary and Rhoda and, if Father Parisi was in a particularly good mood, Frankie could stay up for Carol Burnett. The priest would listen to the boys' prayers, then tuck them into his double bed. If Frankie and Mikey were too wound up to sleep, Father would come knocking on the door and threaten ever so gently that one of them was going to have to take his blanket and pillow and move to the floor unless they settled down and behaved. And sometime in the middle of the night, awakened by a police siren or a loud drunk voice on the street, Frankie would sit up in bed and take comfort in finding Father Parisi, fully dressed, snoring in the armchair at the foot of the bed, where he'd dozed off watching over them as they slept.

He woke them early in the morning. The priest insisted they take a bath before dressing for church, both brothers in the tub together so Mikey couldn't dawdle. He would knock on the bathroom door, hurrying them along, opening the door just wide enough to hand Frankie fresh towels.

"Make sure his feet are dry, Frankie. I don't want your father saying I let him catch cold."

The two of them would quickly dress in Father's bedroom. Frankie was charged with making sure his younger brother didn't miss any buttons and that his shoelaces were tied. Father would always inquire if they were decent before entering the room.

"Let's hurry now, you two. We can't be late for Mass," he said, holding his Polaroid Land Camera in hand.

He was only interested in formal portraits, his subjects wearing white shirts and ties, never candid shots. The poses never varied: Frankie and Mikey standing side by side in the rectory living room, facing forward.

"Look into the camera, boys; be serious, no giggling or smiling."

Frankie loved watching the images of the solemn, sad-eyed brothers emerge from the stinky film.

"Why do you take so many pictures of us?" Frankie asked, knowing they didn't look any different from week to week.

"Because you're such handsome boys," the priest explained, "and I'm so proud of you I want to show all my friends."

MICHAEL, 1972

The blazing sun was pushing the temperature above ninety as high noon approached. Better than rain, Father Parisi reminded the groaners who had already begun complaining before the step-off. He whistled, corralling the morning's First Communicants to their honored position behind the brass band at the head of the annual Procession of Saints through the streets of the outdoor market. Michael hovered at the back of the group, intending to sneak off in search of a bathroom, but the priest called his name and ordered him to take his place at the front of the line.

Most of the boys had stripped off their neckties and freed their shirttails from the waistbands of their pants. Some of them had been allowed to change into Keds for the long march on the broiling asphalt. Mothers had collected the stifling veils of their daughters and any pretense of sacred solemnity had melted with the punishing heat. But such disrespect was unthinkable for any son of Luigi Rocco Gagliano, the strict enforcer of ritual and formality. Michael's starched dress shirt was damp with sweat and perspiration was dripping from his armpits. His First Communion gift from Papa, the Saint Rocco medal worn by his father and brother and generations of Gagliano men, felt like a chain around his neck. His collar was buttoned at his throat and his white silk tie knotted beneath his chin. His hands were folded in prayer, a model of sincere devotion. The old women admiring his piety would have been shocked by the sweet-faced boy's thoughts of taking murderous revenge against his tyrannical father.

The brass band struck its first chords, off-key and shrill, and the procession of plaster idols, liberated one day each year from the dark, shadowed niches of the parish, began its slow, stately shuffle through the adoring crowd. Women and a few men, mostly elderly, many needing assistance, approached with crumpled bills in their fists, seeking the favor of the passing saints. The Blessed Mother. Saint Joseph. Saints Francis of Assisi with his bleeding stigmata and Anthony of Padua, the Holy Infant clinging to his neck. Shy and virginal Saint Lucy, her eyeballs offered to her Savior on a silver platter, and Saint Agatha, her breasts sacrificed for her commitment to purity. Mary Magdalene de Pazzi and Nicholas of Tolentino and Philip Neri, all venerated by Italians for reasons long forgotten. Papa and Miss Eileen brought up the rear, pushing the trolley cart bearing Saint Rocco, the family's patron saint, the protector from plagues, his faithful dog at heel and his exposed leg revealing pustules of rot and disease. Papa's loyal comrades, Sal Pinto and Pete Delvecchia, marched at his side, accepting tributes—fives and tens and twenties—to pin to the ribbons draped over Saint Rocco's shoulders.

Father Parisi, dressed in full vestments, conceding nothing to the heat, walked behind the saints, sprinkling holy water from his aspergillum to bless the sweating faithful. His trusted aide, the Sacred Heart Boy, an honor awarded Francis Rocco Gagliano three years in a row, marched lockstep at his side, cradling the silver bucket from which the priest refilled his holy wand. The final benediction and hymns from the makeshift stage on Washington Avenue seemed interminable to Michael. The hot and cranky members of the First Communion class jostled and pushed, vying to stand in the stingy corner of shade under the tarpaulin. Michael, though, stood still, his face baking in the sun, knowing Papa was watching from the crowd and feeling his eyes bearing down on him. Father Parisi introduced the May Queen, an almond-eyed ten-year-old beauty, to a round of applause. The Sacred Heart Boy was greeted with a loud ovation, the neighborhood's own little Fabian, with a face kissed by God and perfect manners demanded by his father.

After the ceremony, Luigi rolled Saint Rocco up the aisle of the church and safely restored him to the altar in his prominent side chapel behind the baptistery. They could hear the rowdy sounds of the festival on the streets as Luigi gathered his family at the altar rail to lead them in a rosary. The church was hot and stuffy and Michael began to fidget, praying for Papa to go faster, trying to ignore the pressure swelling in his bladder as his father slowly plodded through the Five Glorious Mysteries. He bit down on his tongue, setting his jaw, concentrating his energy on controlling the powerful urge to urinate. He grabbed his crotch and squeezed, sinking into despair as a stream of warm piss flowed down his leg, a puddle forming on the marble beneath his feet.

Papa's first instinct, as always, was to strike. But sensing the disapproving gaze of Saint Rocco upon him, he tore a strip of bunting from the trolley cart and thrust it into his son's hands, pushing him to the floor. Michael fought back tears, making a mess as he took wide, careless swipes. Frankie knelt beside him, Miss Eileen, too, offering assistance, both of them ignoring Papa's angry insistence that Michael clean it up himself.

"Either help us or leave us alone, Lou," his stepmother said in a calm and measured voice. After they finished, she lit a vigil candle and whispered in Michael's ear that his patron saint would grant him one wish on the day of his First Communion. *Please, Saint Rocco,* he prayed with all his might. *Make Papa wet his pants so everyone will laugh at him.*

FRANKIE AND MICHAEL, 1973

No one could remember S. Gagliano and Son, Since 1928, ever closing for business except for the funerals of the proprietor's parents and first two wives. Someone in the family must have died, they all agreed. Why hadn't Luigi hung the traditional black wreath on the shop door? The news that he and his third wife were lounging on deck chairs on a cruise ship in the Mediterranean spread through the neighborhood like wildfire. The women of their parish whispered that the painted *medigan'* had some kind of unholy power over him. They'd never known Luigi to leave the city limits or allow his boys to stray far from his critical eye. Sal Pinto had seen his closest friend's sons safely aboard a westbound train traveling across the state. Polly's husband, smelling of beer and cigarettes, met his young, not entirely welcome, houseguests at the station and loaded their suitcases in the trunk of his car.

"She's in a bad mood," he warned as he dropped them at the front door before returning to the bar. "Don't piss her off if you know what's good for you," he said, laughing as he drove away.

They found their half sister in the kitchen, her hands submerged in dishwater, a burning cigarette in her mouth. Embraces and kisses would have felt awkward.

"This isn't a hotel," she reminded them as she stacked the

dishes. She looked tired and worn, much older than a girl of twenty-three. Her mustache needed bleaching and the dark roots of her hair were showing. "Learn the rules and we'll get along fine," she warned as she counted the bills in an envelope, making sure Papa hadn't shorted her on the negotiated price to provide room and board to his sons for a month. The money was generous and she desperately needed it. Her husband earned good wages as a steelworker, but the mortgage installments and the monthly car payments were high. Most of his paycheck went to supporting their young son and the three stepchildren she inherited when she was knocked up at seventeen under the Atlantic City boardwalk by the handsome thirty-six-year-old widower of an unlucky soul who'd died in a car crash. Whatever remained ended up in the cash register at the neighborhood bar.

After a few days, Frankie and Michael adjusted to the rhythms of a different household. The chores and responsibilities assigned by their sister were far fewer than the many duties imposed at home by their demanding father. They were expected to pick up after themselves, to weed the vegetable garden, and water the grass. They were conscripted to slap a coat of paint on the front porch. But most days they were left on their own, unsupervised, free to come and go as they pleased as long as they didn't interrupt Polly during the afternoon hours she devoted to her "stories," *The Guiding Light* and *One Life to Live.*

Michael fell in with a group of local boys, who, impressed by his strength and speed, recruited him for pickup games of kickball and baseball that lasted the entire afternoon. Frankie was charged with looking after his young half nephew Sonny, who quickly grew attached to him. He spent his free time on a chaise longue in the backyard, flipping through the pages of *Tiger Beat* and *16*. Polly's stepdaughters, Laurie and Marybeth, had an extensive record collection and an encyclopedic knowledge of the bubblegum scandals of the teen fan magazines. They had lasagna and meatballs, *pasta e fagioli* and fresh tomatoes, for dinner, not the greasy corned beef and cabbage and heavy stews Miss Eileen put on the table, and Polly's cakes didn't come from a box. There was French toast and bacon for breakfast and always a cold pitcher of Kool-Aid in the refrigerator. Polly's husband was a happy drunk, with change in his pocket to share with any kid willing to rub his shoulders or scratch his back.

Frankie and Michael might have even enjoyed their rural exile if it hadn't been for Carl, Polly's stepson. A tall and hulking Slav, with a broad face and blond brush-cut hair, fully formed at fourteen (a mere nine years younger than his stepmother) with the body of a man, he was loud and rowdy with an unrestrained mean streak. The neighborhood boys excluded him from their games despite his strength, calling him doofus and retard, fearing the fierce tantrums that erupted whenever he didn't get his way. Too many of them had been left bruised and bleeding in the dirt when they dared to challenge him. Their parents had complained to Polly to no avail, their protests rebutted by her sharp rebuke that she had no sympathy for sissies unable to defend themselves.

Carl's greatest pleasure was making Frankie cry, pushing his face into his crotch and laughing, saying he knew Frankie wanted to blow him. His double bed slept two comfortably, but not three. Michael was given a sleeping bag and air mattress on the floor below the creaking coils of the box springs. He hid his face in the pillow and put his fingers in his ears, not wanting to hear the harsh commands Carl whispered to his brother.

"Just do what I tell you to do if you know what's good for you. Put your hand on it. Now put it in your mouth."

At the breakfast table in the morning, Laurie and Marybeth ignored their brother's insults as they teased Frankie about his devotion to the blond Brady daughters. The girls loudly scorned his choice of the hangdog Jan as the prettiest over the saucy Marcia or the pig-tailed Cindy.

"Well, she's my favorite and I am not changing my mind!" he insisted.

"Well, she's my favorite and I am not changing my mind!"

Carl's affected high-pitched voice with its ripe, fruity tones was clearly intended to mimic and mock his stepmother's less masculine half brother.

"You shut up, Carl," Laurie insisted.

"You shut up," he snarled.

Polly ignored the rising tension, her back toward the table as she flipped pancakes on the griddle. Frankie flinched as Carl flicked his index finger against his cheek.

"Well, she's my favorite and I am not changing my mind!"

He pinched and twisted Frankie's ear, making him cringe in his seat.

"Leave him alone," Michael said quietly.

"Shut up, you little snot. Frankie likes it, don't you, Frankie?"

"No," Frankie whimpered. "Please stop."

Michael jumped up from his chair and charged, stabbing the tines of his fork into Carl's fleshy arm. The boy screamed and fell to his knees, a stream of blood dripping from his elbow onto the linoleum floor. Michael braced himself as Polly turned from the stove, standing defiantly to accept his punishment. But, surprisingly, his half sister went for her stepson, yanking the dangling fork from his bicep, then slapping him hard across the face, twice, until he curled up in a ball of the floor, wailing for her to stop.

"Get up and go wash off that blood and bring me the iodine and a cotton ball. The rest of you finish your breakfast and stay out of my way the rest of the day."

She turned toward Frankie, the boy who had adored her only a few short years ago, and spoke with a barely concealed disgust.

"Shame on you, Frankie, for making your little brother do your fighting for you."

FRANKIE, 1974

He'd turned fourteen that day, old enough for a grown-up celebration, something more than cake and ice cream and party games. Papa gave his sons fresh haircuts for the occasion and insisted they polish their dress shoes. Frankie looked sharp in his dark blue suit and Michael wore a sweater and tie. Miss Eileen looked like a movie star in a stiff green dress that rustled as she walked. A fierce-looking giant with a shaved head and a gold tooth greeted them at the door and led them to a table in the front of the room, next to the dance floor, near the orchestra. Papa ordered the veal and Miss Eileen couldn't decide between the lamb chop and the stuffed flounder, finally settling on the scampi. Frankie and Michael both had spaghetti and meatballs and glasses of ginger ale with bright red cocktail cherries.

After the birthday toast, Papa gave his oldest son a twenty-dollar bill and Miss Eileen presented him with a tie clip studded with a diamond chip, which she insisted he wear immediately. Michael gave him the original cast recording of *West Side Story,* chosen and paid for by Miss Eileen, who'd assured her younger stepson it would be his brother's favorite present. The bald man carried a cake with a single dazzling sparkler to the table as the waiters sang a rousing "Happy Birthday" and urged Frankie to make a wish. He closed his eyes and prayed for Miss Eileen to drop dead at the table, which, of course, she didn't, the only disappointment on an otherwise perfect birthday. Then the lights went dim and the room grew so quiet he could hear the snapping of cigarette lighters as the audience fired up their Winstons and Camels. The bandleader lifted his baton and led the orchestra through the opening bars of "There's No Business Like Show Business" as the bald man stepped up to the microphone and asked the ladies and gentlemen to clap their hands and welcome the greatest star on Broadway, the legendary Miss Ethel Merman!

The audience went wild as she stormed out from the wings, smiling and waving. Planting one hand firmly on her hip, she cocked her head and asked when the hell Philly got so shy, challenging everyone to shout themselves hoarse to let her know how glad they were to see her. Frankie was mesmerized, barely believing that this larger-than-life creature he knew from the Mike Douglas and Merv Griffin shows was close enough to reach out and touch, not that he would ever dare! Her glorious voice tore through the room, rattling the chandeliers as she sang all of her famous songs. She joked and bantered, ribbing the men and teasing the women, and suddenly, unexpectedly, Frankie was staring into a microphone, his heart in his throat, his pulse racing, terrified, unnerved by her simplest questions—*what's your name? where do you live? how old are you?*

"I guess the cat's got our young friend's tongue tonight. Look at those lashes," she said, tousling his hair and admiring his bright blue eyes. "Watch out, ladies. This one is going to be a real heartbreaker."

He was too excited for bed when the magical evening ended and begged to be allowed to stay up to listen to the album his little brother had given him for his birthday. He kept the volume on the hi-fi console turned low so he wouldn't disturb Papa and Miss Eileen sleeping one floor above. He played the entire record twice, from beginning to end, dancing around the living room in his pajamas, miming the lyrics to "America" and "I Feel Pretty," oblivious to his stepmother standing in the doorway, smiling as she watched him perform.

"I love this song! Please don't stop!" she pleaded, but he was too embarrassed to continue, mortified at being discovered acting like such a sissy, fearful she'd tell his father, who barely tolerated his oldest son's interest in actresses and singers.

"Come on then, come over here and sit beside me," she insisted as she settled on the sofa, lighting a cigarette and blowing the smoke across the room. "Did you have a good time tonight? Your father tried to argue with me, saying you and your brother were too young to go to a nightclub, but I wouldn't take no for an answer. I wanted you to have a birthday you'd remember the rest of your life."

If she'd been anyone else, an aunt or a neighbor, the mother of one of his schoolboy friends, Miss Eileen, glamorous and elegant, would have been irresistible to a starstruck boy like her stepson. He would have sat at her feet, a willing captive, enthralled by her tales of eating clams with Frank Sinatra in Atlantic City, drinking daiquiris with Sammy Davis, Jr., at the Latin Casino, borrowing lipstick from Natalie Wood in a powder room in Miami Beach. She'd left her home in the Holmesburg section of the city at sixteen and found her way to New York, where she'd danced in the chorus of Broadway musicals, *The Pajama Game* and *L'il Abner.* She claimed her first husband had died under mysterious circumstances, hinting of gangster connections and Mafia hits, but Papa scoffed at the story, saying he was nothing but a lowlife drunk who broke his neck in a fall down the stairs. A youngish widow, she'd supported herself giving dance lessons at Palumbo's where she'd met Papa. Frankie would have worshiped her, hung on her every word, lit her cigarettes, and brought her Pepsi-Colas, if only she hadn't married his father. She was an intruder, the woman who'd encouraged his little brother, unable to remember the mother who had died before his third birthday, to call her Mama.

"Yes, ma'am," he answered, surrendering to the arm she draped around his shoulder, pulling him in for a hug.

She looked different without her makeup, pale and drawn, with black circles under her eyes. Her skin appeared dry, almost chapped, translucent, the bright blue blood vessels shimmering just below the surface. She took a drag off her cigarette before stubbing it in the ashtray, coughing as she sucked the smoke deep into her chest.

"Wasn't the show tonight wonderful?" she asked, sounding wistful, as if she missed her long ago days on the stage.

"Yes, ma'am," he repeated, not resisting the kiss she planted on his forehead. The tobacco and talcum powder couldn't completely mask the unpleasant sour milk-smell of her breath.

"Don't stay up too late, Frankie. Your father wants to go to eight o'clock Mass in the morning," she said as she rose, a bit unsteady on her feet, and said good night. After she'd gone, he stared at the bloody tissue on the coffee table, the one she'd used to cover her mouth when she coughed. She would be bedridden by midsummer and dead before Thanksgiving. Frankie wore the tie clip she'd given him on his birthday to her funeral, then put it in his sock drawer and never took it out again.

MICHAEL, 1974

Michael was tired and irritable. He missed the routine of his everyday life, spending his days at school, his evenings at the kitchen table doing his homework before *Happy Days,* then reading in bed until he fell asleep, rousing adventures like *Kidnapped* and *The Hobbit* that swept him away to more exciting worlds. Papa had insisted on a three-night viewing for his third wife, grousing that the younger generation had no respect for the dead, hardly waiting until they were cold before putting them in the ground, out of sight and out of mind. Michael had overheard Sal Pinto telling his wife that Luigi couldn't bear the thought of letting her go. Tomorrow would be a long day: the funeral Mass, the long trip to the cemetery, the catered lunch in a banquet room at Palumbo's.

"Mikey, Papa is looking for you. He wants you in the viewing room. You better hurry up. Father Parisi is going to start the rosary."

His half sister Polly had found him sitting alone, hiding in a dark, quiet corner in a back room of the funeral home. He resented her bossing him around, trying to take charge while Papa was preoccupied.

"I have to go back to the house to help Mrs. Pontarelli and Mrs. Delvecchia put out the food." The women of the neighborhood had prepared an elaborate feast of hams and turkeys, trays of ziti and pots of meatballs and sauce, cakes and pies and mountains of cookies, to feed the visitors who came back to the house after viewing hours to eat and drink and smoke, staying long after Michael and Frankie had been sent to their beds. "Don't make him come get you if you want to be able to sit tomorrow," she warned.

As soon as Polly left, he ran up a wide, carpeted staircase, certain no one would follow. He reached the landing and slowly made his way down the hall to find somewhere to hide, the prospect of getting caught by Papa being far scarier than meeting a flesh-eating zombie in search of fresh blood. At least he could fight back against a zombie, killing it by bashing in its brain. He saw light from an open door and heard music, not the funereal organ dirges piped through the speakers on the floor below. The radio was tuned to "Fridays with Frank," the same station Papa and Miss Eileen listened to during dinner. Mr. Casano was sitting at his desk, his glasses pushed up on his head, singing along to "That's Life" as he worked.

"You like Mr. Sinatra, young man?" he asked, smiling as he looked up and found Michael standing in the doorway.

"He's okay, I guess."

"I suppose you like the more modern music, don't you? Who's your favorite singer?"

"I don't know. I don't have one," Michael mumbled, stricken by an attack of awkward shyness.

"You don't like music? That's a shame." Mr. Casano clucked. "Music is one of the great joys of life."

"I like Fleetwood Mac," Michael insisted, citing Frankie's favorite group, not wanting to disappoint Mr. Casano.

"Well, I don't know who that is, but I'm sure he's very good," Mr. Casano agreed, reaching into his desk drawer for a Snickers bar to hand to Michael as he waved him to a chair. "I need to go back downstairs, but you can stay up here while you finish your candy bar. You can change the radio station, if you like."

Mr. Casano had rescued him from being forced to do the awful thing against his will. He sat in the chair, swinging his legs, eating slowly to make the candy bar last. He found a station that played the Top 40, "Bennie and the Jets," "You're Sixteen," humming along as he chewed. He thought he was safe, that he'd never be found, only to see Frankie standing in the doorway.

"Papa says you have to come downstairs now."

He knew better than to argue. He'd run out of options.

"It's not so terrible, Mikey. I'll do it first. It only takes a second."

He swallowed the last bite of Snickers and followed his brother into the viewing room, where they knelt beside their father on the floor while Father Parisi droned through the Five Sorrowful Mysteries. After the prayer, they took their place beside the casket, thanking the visitors again for coming, nodding their heads as their friends and neighbors shook their hands and embraced them, assuring them *she looks so peaceful, at least she isn't suffering now, Casano did a beautiful job.* And then, after the last condolence had been shared and the three of them were alone, father and sons approached the stiff, cold woman lying in the open casket. The strange lady in a bright orange wig, with ruby-red lips and robin's-egg-blue eyelids, looked nothing like the sweet and gentle stepmother who had sung "Mr. Sandman" when she put Michael to bed. He'd heard the old black-clad crones from the parish whispering among themselves, scandalized by the plunging neckline of the emerald-green burial dress chosen by Papa because his wife looked like Angie Dickinson in *Ocean's 11* whenever she had worn it.

Frankie, as commanded, bent down and kissed Miss Eileen on the lips. He whispered in his brother's ear, offering encouragement, telling him there was no reason to be scared. Miss Eileen couldn't hurt him.

"Why do I have to do it, Boo?"

At times, when Michael was exhausted or frightened, he would regress and become a needy little boy again, using the name he'd stopped calling his brother after starting school.

"You don't have to kiss her on the mouth, Mikey. Just do it quick and it will be over."

Michael felt Frankie drape his arm around his shoulders to steady and reassure him. With his brother standing beside him, he found the courage to lean over and barely touch his lips to his stepmother's cold, smooth forehead.

Frankie, 1974

Bless me, Father, for I have sinned. It has been two weeks since my last confession.

"Is that all you have to confess, young man?"

"Yes."

Frankie's voice was wobbly, strained and high-pitched. Father Parisi would know he wasn't telling the truth. It's another sin, lying to the priest in confession.

"Are you sure?"

"Yes, Father."

He'd already run through the litany of pardonable transgressions. Lying to his father six times. Being mean to his little brother twice. Cheating at Monopoly.

"Remember, there's nothing Jesus hasn't heard before. Nothing He won't forgive."

Father Parisi was wrong. Jesus would never forgive Frankie for praying for Miss Eileen to die.

"Your penance is two Our Fathers and three Hail Marys. I know you're a good boy, Frankie. Don't ever be afraid to come talk to me if you're ever worried you've done something wrong."

But Frankie had known as long as he could remember there are some things that couldn't be shared and to trust no one with his secrets. He knelt in the front pew before the altar, head bowed, back straight, hands folded in prayer, promising to never wish anyone dead again, the picture of saintliness to the approving old women of the parish waiting to make their confession.

FRANKIE, 1975

They'd been inseparable as boys, their lives intertwined since their first day at Saint Catherine of Siena Elementary School. Jack, left sallow by chronic anemia, had shyly approached and asked if he could join Frankie at the lunch table. The girl sitting with Frankie picked up her tray and walked away, claiming the unwelcome intruder smelled funny, which he did. Jack had an odd scent that lingered after he left a room, reminiscent of mothballs and dirty clothes and, strangely enough, licorice. He was a weird-looking kid, with pointy ears and a mouthful of sharp, crooked teeth. His nose was runny and he breathed though his mouth, whistling as he inhaled. He'd been a change-of-life baby, his only brother almost twenty years older, and was a lonely child, left on his own, his parents preoccupied with running their corner market. Miss Eileen had set a place for him at the dinner table most evenings and he spent many nights sleeping on a makeshift bed on the floor in Frankie and Michael's room. Papa never objected to his presence since Jack was quick to offer to help Frankie with the chores in the shop, sweeping the cuttings from the floor, stacking the magazines, emptying ashtrays, always soliciting favorable comparisons to Papa's lazy and ungrateful eldest son.

Their friendship deepened as they grew older and became even more isolated and estranged from the cliques that absorbed their classmates, each dependent on the other for companionship. Frankie thought of Jack as a second brother. He never suspected Jack had different, stronger feelings until a blistering August afternoon in 1975. They lay side by side, working on their Hollywood tans, only a beach towel protecting them from the scorching concrete of the deck of the Montrose Street municipal pool. Frankie's transistor radio was tuned to WFIL and the hottest hits of the summer. "Jive Talkin'." "That's the Way (I Like It)." "The Hustle." Frankie was roused from his stupor when the lifeguard blew on his shrill whistle, checking to be sure Michael wasn't drowning in the deep end of the pool. He squinted into the sun, half asleep. Jack was lying on his side, propped up on an elbow, staring at him. Frankie felt exposed and awkward. He closed his eyes and faced the sun, acting as if he hadn't noticed the bulge in Jack's trunks, and reached for a towel to hide the obvious one in his own. Later that afternoon, the first of many times, they locked themselves in Jack's bedroom in the apartment above his parents' store. One day, when Jack's mother was upstairs recovering from the flu, Jack suggested they go to Frankie's house, but Frannie Merlino kept knocking on the bedroom door, asking what they were up to and why they were so quiet, insisting they let Michael join them.

It became a routine and began to feel like a dreaded chore to Frankie. Jack was always the instigator. Frankie was the passive one, lying on his back as Jack unbuckled his belt and slipped his hand into his underpants. Frankie was a reluctant participant, needing to be begged and cajoled, agreeing only to spare Jack the humiliation of rejection. He would close his eyes while Jack was blowing him, pretending it was Paul Ottaviano or Joey Criniti, the handsome boys he fantasized about whenever he stuck his finger up his ass when he lay in bed at night, unable to sleep. But he never let Jack kiss him again after the first time they had done it. He always turned his face and clenched his jaw, repulsed by the vivid memory of Jack's sharp teeth and the unpleasant taste of his mouth.

Frankie and Michael, 1976

Things were different after the night the old priest showed up, unannounced and uninvited, and insisted on speaking to Papa. Frankie and Michael were sent to their bedroom and told to shut the door. They heard loud, angry male voices downstairs, but couldn't distinguish the words. Frannie Merlino's pleas, though, were clear and distinct, begging her husband not to argue with a man of God.

"I showed Father Parisi the back of my legs," Frankie confided. Michael could smell his brother's terror, fearing Papa's wrath for daring to reveal family secrets to an outsider. His punishment would be swift and severe.

Frankie ran to his closet and began stuffing as many clothes as he could in his St. Philip Neri High School gym bag. He dropped to his knees and hugged his little brother.

"I'll come back for you as soon as I can, Mikey. I promise you."

Michael, confused and frightened, begged Frankie to take him with him. Frankie flinched when the bedroom door was flung open, expecting the sting of leather on his back. Papa was clearly enraged, too angry to even speak, but he didn't raise a hand or take a step toward his son. He spit out some phrase in Italian, then turned and walked away, slamming the door behind him.

Father Parisi's threat to report his most devout parishioner to Protective Services kept him from ever striking his sons again. But Papa was creative, finding ways to punish his children that were far crueler than any beating. The list of offenses was exhaustive. Disrespect. Unreliability. Failure to obey. But the worst transgressions imaginable to the man of many wives were the sins of the flesh, which included a pre-pubescent boy's healthy and normal curiosity about the human body.

Michael learned how to swear on the asphalt parking lot that served as a schoolyard. He took great delight in hearing the sound of his voice forming the forbidden words. He was still too young to understand the mechanics of *blow me* or to know exactly which bodily fluid *cream* referred to. He and his friends spent their entire lunch hour in the damp, smelly restroom, arguing about the physical differences between boys and girls. He'd begun noticing the sullen teenage girls in their high school uniforms, palming lit cigarettes as they sauntered along the sidewalk. They wore tight, clingy sweaters and their blouses were unbuttoned to expose the crucifixes dangling in their cleavage. Titties, he knew for sure what titties were, and titties were what he committed to paper, drawing stick girls with every shape and size breast imaginable. Round ones as big as basketballs. Long, skinny ones that drooped to their knees. Every girl had identical heart-shaped lips and wavy, long hair and fried-egg eyes. Only their titties were different.

"Disgusting. Filthy, disgusting boy," Papa spit as he tore the drawings into shreds, threatening to make Michael chew and swallow the pieces. The actual punishment was worse. Michael pleaded for mercy, promising to confess his impure thoughts on Saturday, to do whatever penance the priest required, as his father slammed the door in his face and turned his key in the lock.

It was just a basement, ordinary, no different from the cellars of every house on the block, with a dirt floor, exposed ceiling beams, and cinder-block walls that had never been whitewashed. A single hundred-watt bare bulb cast a circle of stark, bright light in the center of the room. An entire nocturnal world existed at the bottom of the stairs. Silverfish slithered across the floor and centipedes climbed the surfaces of the walls. In the summer, crickets chirped in their hiding places and, come winter, tiny field mice took refuge from the snow and ice, seeking warmth and food.

Michael spent hours in exile, without clocks or a watch to measure time. Soon enough he felt pangs of hunger and his mouth was dry with thirst. He cupped water from the faucet of the utility sink into his hands and tipped it into his mouth. It tasted putrid, like rust and chemicals. The floorboards above creaked as Papa readied the shop for his first customer in the morning. He heard the echo of his father's footsteps fading as he climbed the stairs to the kitchen, where his dinner and a glass of dago red awaited. Michael refused to cry. Only babies cried. He couldn't shout or scream. No one could hear him. Papa wouldn't return until morning. The dirt floor was cold and there was nothing to use as a sheet or a blanket. He sat crouched on the staircase until his back ached, cradling himself with his arms for warmth. He pissed in the sink when his bladder was full and tried to ignore the stabbing stomach cramps from the dirty water he had drunk. The pains grew sharper and he gripped his belly, gritting his teeth until his jaw ached. He fought the terrible urge as long as he could, until he couldn't control it any longer. He cursed his father for making him lay in his own shit and surrendered to tears.

Sometime before morning, while Papa and his wife slept, he heard the key slip into the lock and the dead bolt slide open. Frankie helped him out of his soiled pants and socks and shoes and handed him a towel to wrap around his waist, preserving his modesty as they climbed the stairs. He stood Michael in the shower and Michael didn't complain or resist when his brother put him to bed like he had when he was still young enough for bedtime stories. He turned his face to the wall, angry and humiliated, and muttered promises of revenge that Frankie pretended not to hear.

MICHAEL, 1976

"Where did you get that book?"

Father Parisi was horrified to discover Michael with his nose buried in such blasphemous atheist propaganda as *Lord of the Flies.*

"Do you know who the Lord of the Flies is? I didn't think so. The Lord of the Flies is Beelzebub! It's the devil, Michael!"

The old man threatened to report the local librarian who'd suggested this trash to an impressionable young reader who was quickly bored by the childish books on the middle school recommended summer reading list. God created man in his own image, the priest lectured. A creature born with a soul isn't a savage driven by murder and bloodlust.

"I won't tell your father about this if you hand that over so I can return it in the morning. And I want you to say an Act of Contrition. Now this was one of my favorites when I was boy," he said, pressing an ancient copy of *Ben-Hur* into Michael's hands.

Michael took Father Parisi's book to bed with him that night, reading the same three dull paragraphs over and over. He closed the cover and turned out the lights. In the morning he would cross Broad Street to a different branch of the Free Library and check out another copy of *Lord of the Flies.* He would be more careful this time, hiding the book even from Frankie, who believed every word from that creepy old priest's mouth. Back when Papa was married to Miss Eileen and he and Frankie were forced to sleep at the rectory every Saturday night, the priest always insisted "his handsome boys" pose for a photograph on Sunday morning. Michael never smiled for the camera, feeling awkward and not knowing why he felt naked while the priest snapped the picture. Frankie defended Father Parisi if Michael called him weird or complained about the frequent outings to amusement parks and state parks, insisting they should be grateful for his generosity.

He read the forbidden book in secret, shoving it between his mattress and box springs when he heard Frankie's footsteps approaching their bedroom. The dilemma of the story troubled him. What would he do if he were stuck on a desert island? Would he follow the rules he'd been taught when there was no one to impose them or would he paint his face and run wild, turning into a scary savage? He liked some of the other books on the advanced reading list, *Dracula, The Red Pony,* and especially *The Outsiders.* Others he couldn't finish, like *Wuthering Heights.* But Ralph and Jack haunted him the rest of the summer, never far from his mind. Was he the brave young hero rescued by the naval officer on the beach or was he the villain, standing abashed, wearing a tattered black hat and a pair of broken specs around his waist? He'd just turned eleven and was still naïve and impressionable, too young to comprehend that he, like all men, was both, and that life would eventually reveal the best and worst in him.

FRANKIE, 1977

Mr. Montesserri was known to be generous to his young assistants, a succession of pretty, effeminate St. Philip Neri High School boys he hired to help the overworked staff at Montesserri's Creative Floral Designs. He took a special interest in fair-haired boys with blue eyes. Frankie always seemed to be assigned to jobs old Mr. Montesserri was personally supervising. That night had been a particularly stressful engagement. The wedding of the goddaughter of the fearsome *capo* Philip "Chicken Man" Testa to the son and heir of New Jersey's largest cement contractor had required bouquets and boutonnieres for a bridal party of twenty-two and centerpieces for tables to seat the guest list of five hundred. Afterward, Mr. Montesserri insisted on a "special celebration" for select members of the team. Carlo Cesa, Michael Stupak, Johnny Caprogimo, handsome young Patrick Ryan, blessed with long eyelashes and thumbprint dimples, and Frankie. Frankie was both excited and terrified by the idea of actually entering a gay bar. He didn't need to worry that Papa would be standing at the door when he returned in the middle of the night since he and Frannie Merlino had gone to Providence, Rhode Island, to attend a Merlino family christening. And Michael wasn't home because Papa had sent him to Sal

Pinto's overnight, insisting his irresponsible twelve-year-old son would burn down the house if left on his own.

"Welcome to the Sisterhood," Patrick whispered in Frankie's ear as they swept past the doorman at Equus, greeted like arriving royalty, without even a cursory glance at the ID of the sweet-faced seventeen-year-old.

The Sisterhood formed a protective half-circle around Frankie as he sat at the bar, their sharp elbows discouraging any besotted drunken queen from approaching their young charge. Frankie sipped the sweet rum and Coke through a swizzle stick, shyly averting his eyes from the lascivious stares of the supplicants who approached Mr. Montesserri. The florist had changed from his dark tailored dress suit into a mint-green jumpsuit unzipped to the navel and was holding court, looking regal as he accepted tributes. Frankie shrank behind Patrick Ryan's broad back as an aggressive older gentleman slipped through the human barricade, angling for an introduction.

"Wanna dance, Frankie?" Patrick asked.

Mr. Montesserri gave his blessing, trusting Patrick to protect Frankie from the pack of starving wolves eager to sink their teeth into such an alluring piece of fresh meat. Frankie's knees wobbled as Patrick picked up his hand and led him to the dance floor. They wandered into the crush of sweating bodies, dodging stamping feet and flailing arms, finally reaching a small pocket of space that felt almost like solitude. Patrick lifted his arms above his head and swayed to the music, encouraging Frankie to do the same.

San Francisco! SAN! FRAN! CIS! CO!

Frankie was shy and self-conscious, fearing that all these incredibly handsome men, more than he had ever seen in one place, were watching him. But no one seemed aware of him; they were all lost in their own private worlds, their faces transfixed by some kind of religious euphoria. The pounding bass lines rocking the floor beneath the soles of his feet charged him with energy. The music swallowed him up. He squinted into the piercing strobe lights, mesmerized by the spinning colors of the laser beams that swept across the room. Patrick wrapped his arms around Frankie's back and nuzzled his neck, shouting above the deafening din of the Village People.

"You are so fucking beautiful. You know that, don't you?" he asked as he led Frankie off the dance floor, pushing and prodding him through the crowd. He motioned for Frankie to follow him into a small bathroom behind the bar, kicked the door shut, and locked it.

"Here, do some of this," he said, showing Frankie how to snort a line of white powder through the tip of a swizzle stick. "Go ahead. Don't be a pussy."

Frankie inhaled and held his breath, just like Patrick told him. He felt like he was collapsing in on himself, but in a good way, as if he were a warm puddle slowly spreading across a glass floor. Patrick unbuckled Frankie's belt and pulled his pants and underwear to his ankles. Then he spit into his hand, promising Frankie it would only hurt when he put it in, then it would feel really good. The sharp pain in Frankie's ass surprised him, but subsided quickly, as Patrick urged him to relax. It was a strange feeling, a fullness, an urgent, not unpleasant, sensation, like having to go to the bathroom. Someone was pounding on the door, shouting, demanding to know what they were doing and why it was taking so long.

"Go the fuck away," Patrick shouted, grunting harshly, then collapsing onto the toilet. He closed his eyes, breathing deeply, leaving Frankie standing there, with Patrick's semen dripping down the back of his thighs.

"Are you okay?" Patrick finally asked as he thoughtfully wiped Frankie's tender butt with a wet paper towel.

"Yes," Frankie said, confused by surging waves of conflicting emotions, assuming this was how you were supposed to feel when you first fell in love.

"Don't tell Montesserri about this, okay?" Patrick asked, sounding younger than his twenty-one years.

"I won't."

"You're a good kid, Frankie." Patrick smiled as he slipped out of the cramped bathroom, closing the door behind him. "See you around."

Mr. Montesserri was sipping from a tall glass as Frankie approached him self-consciously, fearing it would be obvious to the old man and everyone else what Patrick had just done to him.

"Are you having fun, Frankie?"

"Sure."

"Go dance. Burn off some of that energy. It will be last call soon."

Emboldened by the cocaine, Frankie pushed his way through the tangle of sweaty, bare-chested men on the dance floor, drawn toward the spinning mirror ball in the center of the room. He tried resisting, then finally surrendered to their groping hands, melting into the music, disappearing, snakebitten by the voice of an angel chanting *oh, love to love you baby.*

MICHAEL, 1977

Papa and Frannie Merlino needed a little privacy after six days and five nights with two adolescent boys in a cramped and stuffy vacation trailer in a Virginia oyster village. Papa gave Frankie the keys to the Oldsmobile, warning him he'd written down the mileage on the odometer and knew the exact distance to the drive-in across the causeway. Michael, who'd already seen *Star Wars* twice in the city, was obsessed with the rebels of the Galactic Empire, but Frankie was bored by the adventures of the Jedi warriors after an hour. He told his little brother he was going for popcorn and Cokes and to lock the doors until he came back. When he didn't return by the time the credits rolled and the cars began snaking toward the exit, Michael, emboldened by the courage of young Luke Skywalker, went searching for him.

The young girl bagging trash at the concession stand mumbled that the counter was closed, the movie over. She laughed when Michael said he'd lost his brother, commiserating that her own had gone AWOL and left her with all the cleanup chores.

"Tell him I'm tired and want to go home if you see him," she called after him as she dragged the trash bags out to the cans. "He's got red hair so you'll know it's him."

He wandered toward a distant copse of pines, unnerved by the croaking tree frogs, and called Frankie's name softly. Deer flies nipped his bare legs, drawing blood, and he stepped into a sinkhole, his shoe sucked into the muck. He stumbled through the brush, tripping over a tangled knot of vines, and fell to his knees in a shallow pool of water.

On the far bank, two figures were draped in deep shadows, one crouched over the trunk of a fallen tree, the other naked from the waist down, the bright light of the full moon flashing across his bare white buttocks. At first he thought Frankie was in danger, that he was groaning in pain and needed a hero to rescue him. Then, frightened and confused, Michael turned and raced back to the car, running from the sound of his brother's voice begging the grunting red-haired boy to keep going, not to stop, telling him how good it felt.

"Sorry, I got lost," Frankie apologized when he finally returned, tossing Michael a box of Good & Plenty, insisting they stop at Dairy Queen for banana splits on the way home.

In the morning, they sat facing each other at the tiny table in the trailer, eating coffee cake out of an Entenmann's box. Frankie acted as if nothing out of the ordinary had happened the previous night. Michael was unusually quiet, tentative, unable to find the courage to speak.

"What's the matter, Mikey? Something's bothering you. I can always tell."

Just last month, he'd punched Phil DeStefano in the face and knocked Junior Curcio on his ass when they mocked Frankie and taunted Michael, saying he would grow up to be a fag like his brother, who let guys put their dicks in his mouth. *Everyone knows it, Mikey. It must be weird living with a queer.* He defended his brother from the ugly rumors, even though he worried they were true. Carl Shevchek *had* put his dick in Frankie's mouth, but only because Carl was as strong as he was stupid and had easily overpowered him. It didn't mean Frankie was a homo. Michael had asked Sal Pinto how you could tell if someone was a fag (a question he could never ask Papa). His godfather minced across the room, swinging his arm as if he were twirling a purse.

That's how you tell if someone is a leccacazzi*!*

Frankie didn't walk like that, but he did carry his schoolbooks like a girl, clutching them to his chest. Sometimes he would cross his leg at the knee and Papa would blow up, demanding he sit like a man with both feet flat on the floor.

"Frankie, do you know that guy?" he mumbled as he picked at the coffee cake.

"What guy?" Frankie asked, curious, offering Michael the last of the pastry.

"The red-haired guy at the drive-in."

"What red-haired guy at the drive-in?" he asked, crushing the empty box and tossing it in the trash.

"I don't know," Michael said. "Never mind."

"Papa said we can have the car tonight. Do you want to see *Star Wars* again?"

"Sure," he said, without any great enthusiasm, knowing Frankie secretly planned to slip away again tonight. Now that he knew the things people said about Frankie were true, everything felt different. Nothing was the same. He wanted Frankie to be the brother he had been before he changed, the one he'd run to with every bruise and cut, who taught him how to tie his shoes and pee like a man, who read him *Go, Dog. Go!* so many times he'd memorized the entire book, who let him crawl into his bed when he was afraid of the dark, who promised to never go away and leave him alone. He didn't want to believe Frankie *hadn't* changed and he'd always been a homo. And maybe those idiots DeStefano and Curcio were right and Michael was a homo, too, and just didn't know it yet.

FRANKIE AND MICHAEL, 1978

"Night Fever" was the theme of Frankie's senior prom. He was the chair of the decorating committee, of course. The "night" part, at least, was easy. He'd designed a billowy sky of bedsheets dyed a deep indigo. The janitor bitched about hanging four dozen foil stars from the gymnasium ceiling. Frankie painted the cutout of the smirking Man in the Moon (without, of course, the cocaine spoon) he'd seen in photographs of Diana Ross and Liza dancing at Studio 54. Mr. Montesserri had helped him find a real mirror ball and knew a designer willing to lend him revolving color wheels to illuminate the fantasy sky.

Everyone agreed Frankie had done a beautiful job. Even Jack Centafore, the only St. Philip Neri senior who couldn't find a girl to agree to be his prom date. Frankie had his choice of young women, being the best-looking boy in his class. Every girl without a steady boyfriend was willing to enter the gymnasium on his arm. She knew not to expect any romance beyond a chaste kiss good night and that he wouldn't beg for a blow job like the louts doing shots in the boys' room. But Frankie would look wonderful in the prom photos. Years later, she could prove to her skeptical daughters that she had indeed been taken to the prom by the most handsome young man in South Philadelphia, a boy who ought to have been a movie star.

Frankie slept late the morning of the prom, waking in a deep funk, dreading the dance. He had asked Cecilia Forte, a girl burdened by extra pounds and a homely face, who could have never dreamed of going to the prom if Frankie hadn't been kind-hearted, with a weakness for misfits. Cecilia was funny and smart and had won a scholarship to Smith College, where she was going to major in journalism and follow in the footsteps of her idol Barbara Walters. But he longed for what he could never have. Paul Ottaviano, who in a few hours would be crowned Prom King, would never sweep Frankie up in his arms and lead him around the dance floor to the lush chords of "More Than a Woman."

"Don't think I'm going to fix you anything at this late hour. If you want breakfast get out of bed with everyone else," Frannie Merlino snapped when he finally wandered into the kitchen.

He was resigned to the misery of life with Frannie Merlino. He'd learned to accept her as his punishment for the awful way he'd treated Miss Eileen, who had loved Frankie and Michael as if they were her own sons. He could have had a second mother for a few years at least if only he had allowed himself to love her back.

Michael was still hanging around the house, which was unusual for him on a beautiful spring morning. He spent as little time as possible under Papa's roof lately, but he'd been waiting hours for Frankie to get out of bed, needing his brother's opinion on an important decision he had made.

"Do you think it's okay? Is it good enough? Do you think I should take it back and buy her something else?"

Michael rarely confided in Frankie anymore and never asked his advice.

Frankie made a thoughtful appraisal and asked several pertinent questions before passing judgment.

"Are you sure she has a charm bracelet?"

Of course he would know. He knew everything about her. He'd been swooning over Barbie Giorgini since the beginning of the school year.

"Why a ballerina charm?"

"She wants to be a dancer."

"Is she any good?"

"She's excellent!"

"Have you ever seen her dance?"

"Not yet."

"Then how do you know she's excellent?"

Michael's cheeks flushed as if he were about to erupt in one of his frequent outbursts, and Frankie wisely decided not to tease him any further.

"She's going to love it," he declared. "What's the special occasion?"

"It's her birthday."

"Do you know if she really likes you as much as you like her?"

"We're going to go steady when we're fifteen. We already talked about it. That's how old she has to be before her father won't hit her for chasing boys."

Frankie knew his little brother well enough to understand there was some other question he needed answered, one he was too embarrassed to ask.

"What is it?"

"What if she asks me to dance at the CYO party?"

"Then dance with her."

"I don't know how."

"Come on," Frankie said, motioning for his brother to follow him into the living room. He shuffled through the record albums until he found something appropriate for a slow dance. Frankie was incredibly patient, never getting frustrated, dropping the needle on the record track over and over again. He had a million things to do before picking up his prom date, but everything would have to wait until Michael knew how to lead his partner, where to place his hands and how to move his feet, even if it took the entire afternoon.

MICHAEL AND FRANKIE, 1981

The last scheduled arrivals at Thirtieth Street Station had been posted on the board: an eastbound train from Harrisburg and a northbound one from Washington, D.C., on time and twenty minutes late, respectively. One final departure for Penn Station, New York, was boarding in ten minutes. The ticket counters had closed at ten and wouldn't reopen until five in the morning. The station shops were dark, their doors locked, and the only vendor still open for business was the newspaper kiosk selling early editions of the Sunday *Inquirer* and *New York Times.* A transit cop sauntered through the nearly deserted station, ominously tapping his nightstick against his leg as he cast a wary eye at the few remaining weary travelers checking their wristwatches, waiting for their boarding calls.

An older man had given Frankie a tip once after blowing him in the men's room: have a valid ticket in your pocket if you're confronted by one of the uniformed Amtrak Nazis and threatened with arrest for loitering. But the cops never bothered Frankie. He wore a backpack slung over one shoulder and sometimes carried one of Mikey's Penguin Classics, easily passing as a Penn or Drexel undergraduate heading home for the weekend. The only time an officer ever approached him was to warn him to be on the lookout for queers on the prowl late at night. *Stay out of the bathroom unless it's an emergency and, if you do have to go and you see someone suspicious, come looking for me.*

Frankie cruised the perimeters of the station, making eye contact with some men and avoiding it with others. He stopped to stare in the window of the bookshop, conscious of a tall fellow following him at a safe enough distance to not be too conspicuous. He studied the dust jackets of the best-sellers on display, waiting for the man to approach. Charged with nerves and sexual energy, he let his eyes drift upward and saw his admirer's face reflected in the shop-window glass.

He was much younger than Frankie had expected, not like the older trolls who usually stalked him. The man pulled a pack of Marlboros from his pocket and offered one to Frankie, who declined. He struck a match and lit the tip of his cigarette, then casually walked away, occasionally looking back to demonstrate his interest. He stopped to linger in front of the florist shop, staring boldly now that a mutual attraction had been firmly established. Frankie, brimming with confidence, walked toward him, ready to introduce himself, but the man crushed his cigarette beneath the sole of his shoe and turned his back before Frankie could speak. He crossed the station with purpose, taking long strides, and disappeared into the corridor leading to the men's room.

Frankie watched the clock on the arrivals and departures board, patiently waiting for a few minutes to pass before following him. He expected to find him at the urinal, stroking his cock, waiting for Frankie to sidle up beside him and unzip his pants, the first step in the ancient ritual of tearoom seduction. But the men's room appeared deserted. Frankie assumed his pursuer had lost interest, had a change of heart. He was about to leave when he saw the door of the last stall of the cavernous bathroom slowly open. The man, knowing Frankie would follow, stood with his back pressed to the wall, his jeans around his ankles. His swagger had disappeared. He seemed nervous, jittery, rushed, as if he were anxious to get it over with.

"Suck me," he insisted, grabbing Frankie by the shoulders and pushing him to his knees.

Frankie dropped his backpack and took the man's flaccid penis in his mouth. The man grew frustrated when he couldn't get hard. He grabbed Frankie by the hair and shoved his limp, but thick, cock down his throat until Frankie gagged.

"Get up. I'm done," he said, pulling his pants to his waist. "Give me twenty dollars, faggot," he said, tugging at his zipper.

"I don't have that much money," Frankie said, hoping the transit cop would come strolling into the bathroom to rescue him.

"Fuck! Fuck!" the man said, slamming his fist against the door of the stall.

"I have seventeen dollars. Here, you can have it," Frankie offered, pulling the bills from his wallet.

The man snatched the money from Frankie's hand and crumpled it into a ball, shoving it into his pocket without counting it.

"Fucking faggot," he spit, slapping Frankie's face twice, hard, with an open hand. Not satisfied that he'd sufficiently demonstrated his disgust, he clenched his fist and punched Frankie in the gut.

"I ought to kick your fucking pretty face in," the man threatened, punching Frankie again, this time in the ribs, then pushing him aside, leaving Frankie gasping for breath as he fled.

After years of begging for hand jobs and a chance to feel up her tits, Michael finally discovered the magic word to persuade Barbara Giorgini to "go all the way" on the linoleum floor of his father's barbershop.

Pre-engaged.

He'd expected that afterward Barbie would be quiet, contemplative, respectful of the solemn event that had taken place between them. Losing their virginity was a sacred rite of passage, binding them together the rest of their lives. No one else could ever be the other's first.

But she chattered incessantly as he walked her home. Should they share the news of their pre-engagement or keep it secret? Would their parents give their blessing or would they separate them, hoping time and distance would be fatal to young love? He was going to buy her a ring, wasn't he? Should she come with him to choose it or should he surprise, and possibly disappoint, her? She kissed him on her doorstep after planning a trip to Jewelers' Row Saturday afternoon. She didn't expect a diamond since they weren't actually engaged, not yet. A birthstone, innocent seeming, was an appropriate symbol of their commitment; they would call it an early birthday present if her parents asked. She had a fleeting moment of nostalgia for her maidenhead as they said good night and made Michael swear he loved her and always would. He answered her truthfully, *Of course, I do and I always will,* assuring her he could never love anyone else. Except, of course, for Valerie Bertinelli, who was only a fantasy and not an actual possibility, a secret crush he knew better than to admit.

What the hell did "pre-engaged" mean anyway? he wondered as he crossed Federal Street, slowly making his way home. It was only a promise to make a promise, two degrees away from the Sacrament of Marriage. Still, the idea would set Papa off like a bottle rocket. He'd accuse Michael of being a fool, of stepping into a mousetrap set by a conniving girl, his promising future (top of his class at the Academy, the prospect of a good college, becoming a doctor or lawyer) over before it had even begun. The elder Giorginis would condemn him as a scoundrel who'd tricked their daughter into surrendering her virtue, the first step on the long descent to becoming a slut. Maybe it was a mistake, maybe they shouldn't have done it, at least not tonight. He should have waited for a more romantic moment to make his move. She'd resent him one day for taking her virginity on a cold linoleum floor. Papa and his fourth wife were sailing the Caribbean on a seven-day cruise and Frankie rarely came home before midnight from his mysterious nighttime prowls. He could have taken her up to the bedroom he shared with his brother, allowed her the comfort of lying on a soft mattress as they made love the first time.

He didn't feel any different from how he had a few hours ago when he was still a virgin. There hadn't been any fireworks. It wasn't like the movies, soft focus with a string section as background music. He wasn't even sure they had done it right. He knew she hadn't liked it by the grimace on her face. His dick hurt from the effort it took to get it all the way in and he'd shot in the condom as soon as he penetrated her. He felt relieved that it was over, nothing more. He'd always stood quietly when his friends and teammates bragged about their escapades, which he knew were mostly exaggeration or outright lies. They argued and debated about who put out, which girls could be persuaded to give a blow job and which ones were prissy cockteasers who acted as if they were handling a poisonous anaconda if they agreed to jerk you off. They talked about the places they'd screwed and the acrobatic positions they'd tried. Michael shrugged off their persistent questions about how many times he and Barbie Giorgini had done it and if she did more than lie on her back as if she were dead. His friends assumed Michael was too deeply in love to share the details of what they imagined was an active, enthusiastic sex life. They'd never suspected the real explanation for his reticence was that his lack of experience left him nothing to talk about. At least now he could never be exposed as a virgin or accused of having no interest in girls.

Not that anyone ever questioned his masculinity or whispered he might be "a fairy nice boy" like his brother. He was All-Catholic, feared and respected on the field. He lettered in wrestling after football season. The entire neighborhood and his class at the Academy had witnessed the consequences of provoking him. They'd heard the stories of how he'd kicked more than a few asses of dumb shits who were stupid enough to call his brother a queer or faggot. (*Ignore them, Mikey, they're ignorant,* Frankie would say, proud and unfazed.) It was his duty to stand up for his flesh and blood, but he resented Frankie becoming a homo. Sometimes he understood how his brother's tormentors felt. More than once he'd caught one of the hateful epithets about to slip from his tongue when Frankie did something that angered or frustrated him.

If he had a normal brother, he could confide in him about his confusion over the events of the night. He could ask Frankie to explain why losing his virginity had left him anxious and depressed and Frankie would assure him he'd felt the same way his first time with a girl. But there was no way he could ever talk about sex or love with someone who did the disgusting, gross things Michael had seen in the collection of magazines he found when he stole the key to the locked suitcase Frankie kept under his bed. Men with pricks up their asses and cocks in their mouths, sometimes both at the same time. He hated that the brother he'd once loved more than anyone else in the world, and probably still did, even more than Barbie Giorgini, was a pervert.

He entered the house through the barbershop and gathered the soiled towels they had lain on to toss in the washing machine. The pipes of the old house creaked whenever water was running upstairs. Frankie must have come home while he was gone and was still awake upstairs, probably washing his face and brushing his teeth before bed.

"Are you sick?" he asked, surprised to find Frankie with his head in the toilet, vomiting into the bowl.

"I'm all right," Frankie answered. But his upper lip was bloody and his right eye was swollen shut. He tried pulling himself off the floor, but slid back onto his ass, groaning and clutching his chest. "Go to bed, Mikey. I'm all right."

"Your shirt's torn! What happened to you?"

"Nothing. I tripped on the steps coming up from the subway. That's all. Just help me stand up."

Frankie gasped as Michael lifted him and steadied him on his feet. Frankie ran his palm along his left rib cage, as if he were feeling for something. He took short, shallow breaths, wincing as he inhaled. Michael remembered an Academy teammate's painful breathing when he'd broken a rib during a preseason scrimmage. The fractured bone had punctured his lung, putting him out his entire senior season.

"We got to go to the hospital. Something might be broken. You might be bleeding."

Michael was visibly shaken by the thought of Frankie dying. He would rather have a homo for a brother than no brother at all.

"I'm all right, Mikey. Stop overreacting. It's just a bruise. I'm not going to die."

"You don't know that," Michael said, growing more anxious. "The same thing happened to Sean Matthews and his lung collapsed. We have to go to the hospital."

"Look, don't tell Papa about this when he gets home. Promise?"

"I won't," Michael said.

Michael understood why Frankie insisted Papa could never know about tonight. He hadn't fallen in the subway. Someone had punched and kicked him because he was a queer.

"Did they rob you, Frankie?" Michael asked.

"What?"

"Did they rob you? Take your money?"

"No, no," Frankie said, suppressing a bitter smile. "I gave him the money; he didn't have to steal it."

"Then why did he beat you up?"

Frankie walked to the refrigerator, opened a can of beer, and gently lowered himself onto the sofa.

"Hey, what do you think you're doing, big shot? You're sixteen years old," he said, chastising Michael for following his lead and casually popping the top of a can of Schaefer.

"I am sixteen going on seventeen," he sang, mocking his brother's love of show tunes in a futile attempt to lighten the mood. "We're celebrating. I got pre-engaged tonight, Frankie," he said, hoping the news might cheer his brother up.

"Jesus, Mikey, what the fuck do you think you're doing?" Frankie said, squirming in discomfort as he tried to find a comfortable position. "Papa is going to kill you."

"Fuck Papa," Michael said, full of bravado, though he dreaded his father's reaction if he ever learned of his and Barbie's plans. "Besides, I'm not gonna tell him. And neither are you."

"You know what that little girl is up to, don't you? She's not going to let you go easily. You be careful, Michael. You want to get out of here, don't you? That's what you always say."

Michael watched Frankie as he sipped his beer. He looked smaller, more vulnerable than usual, someone who needed to be protected. Strangers rarely recognized them as brothers despite the prominent nose they'd both inherited from their father. Michael was already taller than six foot and was still growing, fortunate to have been blessed with a recessive gene that had produced one towering uncle on his mother's side. He had wide shoulders and a narrow waist and legs as thick as tree trunks. His olive complexion tanned easily in the sun and the black pouches under his dark brown eyes never completely faded with eight hours of sleep. He looked like Pacino in the *Serpico* poster, at least to his admiring girlfriend, although, unlike the movie star, he kept his black, wiry hair—his heritage from Papa—cut short, close to the skull. Frankie was five-eight by a generous reading of the tape measure. He was their mother's boy, fine-boned and fair. His thick, wavy hair, once the color of straw, had darkened a bit with age and his pale blue eyes were set off by his long, curling lashes.

"Bring my car around to the front door, Mikey," Frankie said as if he had suddenly awakened from a trance.

"Huh?"

"I left my backpack at the train station. I have to get it back."

"Why were you at the train station?"

"It doesn't matter. Just help me. I think they lock the bathroom doors after midnight. We have to go now."

Frankie told him to wait in the car when they arrived at the station, that he'd be back in a minute, but Michael insisted on parking and going with him. He wasn't going to let Frankie be beaten twice in one night. The men's room hadn't been locked yet. An old man was mopping the floor and the place smelled of chlorine and soap.

"I left my backpack in here tonight. Did you find it in one of the stalls?" Frankie asked, sounding as casual as possible, hoping not to raise any suspicions.

The old man studied them for a long minute, his eyes filled with disgust.

"I ain't seen no backpack," he said, his voice defying any potential challenge.

"In the last stall. Down there. I'll go take a look."

"Them floors are clean, kid. Don't go fucking them up. There weren't no backpack in there," the man said, a simple statement clearly intended as a threat.

"Can I just look?"

"You callin' me a liar?"

"No. No," Frankie said, defeated and dejected.

As they walked toward the door, Michael clearly heard the janitor snicker and murmur the word *faggot* under his breath. He ran back, fists clenched, ready to punch the bastard, but stopped dead in his tracks at the sight of the fear in his old eyes. So instead he reached down and grabbed the man's bucket and smashed it against the wall, splashing filthy black water across the room.

"Fuck you, asshole. I ought to break your fucking neck for talking to my brother like that," Michael said, his voice steady and calm, as he emptied the contents of the trash can on the floor and plucked the backpack from the wet paper towels and empty coffee cups. "Open your fucking mouth again and I'll bust you up," he promised as he slowly and deliberately followed his brother into the station, his cocky jaunt daring the old man to raise his voice to call for help. He wasn't happy Frankie was a homo, but it was their own business—his and his brother's—and he would rearrange the face of anyone who hurt him again.

"You don't have to fight my battles and you can't solve every problem with your fists. You need to control that temper. You're gonna hurt someone one of these days. Stay out of trouble. You've got too much to lose now," Frankie lectured as they walked to the car.

Everyone told Michael he had a promising future. The world was his oyster. College recruiters were competing to get him to sign a letter of intent in the spring. He could go anywhere. His coaches, his adviser, his most trusted teachers, all believed he would make his decision based on academic rankings and his likelihood of making the squad. None of them would have suspected he had already made his choice and intended to accept the offer of the school the greatest distance from Eighth and Carpenter. He'd sworn to go away and never come back. But driving home from the station, he understood he could never leave Frankie behind, alone, with no one to watch over and protect him. He didn't remember his mother's face or how her voice had sounded, but he knew what she had asked his brother as she was dying.

Promise me you'll always take care of each other. Frankie, you make sure you tell your brother I asked you both to do that when he's old enough to understand.

FRANKIE AND MICHAEL, 1984

"He doesn't like me, Frankie. I told you he wasn't going to like me," Charlie Haldermann whined when Michael excused himself, saying he needed to use the men's room.

"Of course he likes you," Frankie insisted, trying to assure his new lover he was misinterpreting Michael's sullen demeanor. "He's shy around strangers. That's all."

"Shy? The kid looks like he could tear the phone book in half. What the hell does anyone who's built like a steamroller have to be shy about?"

It had been a bad idea. Frankie had been naïve to think Mikey would be happy, or at least relieved, that his older brother was finally ready to settle down. Ruddy and stocky, Charlie was more likely to die of a heart attack than AIDS. Michael finally could stop handing him feature articles he'd clipped from the newspaper about the brave struggles of the gaunt and doomed victims, stranded in a hellish medical purgatory between the dead and the living. He wouldn't feel the need to give Frankie the third degree at least once a week. *What are you doing? Who are you doing it with? Why can't you just stop? Not forever. At least until they find a cure. Wasn't watching Michael Montello waste away to nothing enough to con-*

vince you to take a vow of celibacy? Do you want to go blind, too? Don't you think you're being selfish putting yourself at risk? Don't you know the cunt would hound Papa to throw you out of the house if you got sick? Have you ever stopped to think how I would feel if you caught it and died? But it had been wishful thinking, foolish even, to think Michael would embrace Charlie with open arms. Michael would find a hidden character flaw in Jesus Christ himself if He took up a relationship with Frankie.

Frankie and Charlie had a minor, quiet squabble about ordering another bottle of wine while Michael was in the bathroom. They'd already gone through two, at twenty-five dollars apiece, or, more accurately, the Gagliano brothers drank two glasses each while Charlie sopped up the rest like a thirsty sponge.

"Well, he drove an hour to meet me and he's been acting like he can't wait to leave since the moment he got here," Charlie complained, pissy about facing an empty wineglass after losing the argument.

Michael had made Frankie beg before agreeing to the introduction. He'd insisted he was too burdened by academic and athletic responsibilities to spare the time to come home. He hadn't even seen Barbie in nearly a month. The Tigers had traveled to Cambridge and Hanover for away games the past two weeks, and he would be expected to devote time he couldn't spare to her if he showed his face in Philadelphia. But Frankie was persistent. Bucks County was close to Central Jersey. They could have a nice dinner in New Hope.

A steak house was neutral territory. Frankie was certain his brother was blowing them off when he failed to show more than thirty minutes after the reservation. But the threadbare tires of Michael's beat-up Gremlin were to blame as he'd had to stop and change a flat in Lambertville. Frankie worried about him traveling in that ancient junk bucket held together with duct tape and rubber bands and planned on leasing him a snappy new Civic CRX for Christmas. He'd quickly built a loyal clientele and had plenty of disposable income since Papa refused Frannie Merlino's nagging appeals that Frankie be made to contribute room and board, saying no child of his would ever be asked to pay to live under his roof.

"I'm going to the piano bar and request that Twinkle Fingers play 'Send in the Clowns.' Is there something your brother would like to hear?"

Frankie doubted the shellacked Liberace-wannabe knew "Thunder Road" or "Born in the U.S.A."

The waiter presented the bill when Michael returned. Michael frowned when he saw Frankie offer his credit card without dividing the check and collecting a share from this garrulous, eager-to-please Charlie.

"What's wrong, Mikey?"

"Where did you find this prize?"

"A friend of a friend introduced us during the intermission of a Gay Men's Chorus benefit for the AIDS Task Force."

"Didn't you say he looked like Kris Kristofferson? You must be going blind, Frankie. He doesn't look like a movie star to me."

"He's a little heavier than when we met, but he still has those beautiful eyes and a full head of hair."

"Is it true?"

Barbie's mother had heard from one of her friends whose sister was a client of Frankie that Frankie was giving his new friend a substantial down payment on a large residence with a view of the Delaware River.

"Is what true?" Frankie asked.

"Is it true you're buying him a house?"

"Jesus, how rumors fly. I'm lending him a little money and cosigning on the mortgage loan."

The school district where Charlie taught high school music, also serving as chorus director and the drama club faculty sponsor, kept him leashed to Bucks County by a residency requirement. Frankie thought Charlie was suggesting they live together when he asked to borrow the money. He was surprised when Charlie didn't seem enthusiastic about the idea of Frankie leaving Philadelphia, and he was hurt when the man who professed to love him actively discouraged him from making inquiries if any of the better local salons had an open chair. It had been a crazy idea anyway. Frankie was a city boy and didn't like the pitch black of suburban nights or the sounds of four-legged nocturnal visitors foraging in garbage pails. He would have felt responsible if Papa "accidentally" tumbled down the staircase and broke his neck while living alone at Eighth and Carpenter with Frannie Merlino. Michael said his brother's suspicions were preposterous, that Frannie Merlino was many evil things, but a killer wasn't among them. He'd laughed and said Frankie spent too much time watching old movies and scoffed at the idea that their stepmother was Barbara Stanwyck and had sweet-talked Papa into taking out a secret policy with a double indemnity clause. *Always the drama,* he'd sighed, dismissing Frankie's fears as the product of an overactive imagination.

"You'll never see that money again, Frankie. Don't sign those papers."

"Stop it, Mikey."

"And tell him to stop calling me that. No one but you can call me that."

"Promise me you'll try to like him."

"He's a hundred years old and he's fat and loud."

"He's fifteen years older than me, which would make him thirty-nine. He's hardly an old man. He's got a big heart. You'll see. Give him a chance. Salazzo gave me Saturday afternoon off so we can come to the game when you play Penn at Franklin Field. Charlie bought a Princeton sweatshirt he's dying to wear."

The desperation in Michael's eyes was startling.

"Don't bring him, Frankie. Please. Don't. Please."

"Why?"

"Just don't. Don't."

Michael pushed his chair from the table and looked at his wristwatch, announcing he had to leave.

"It's late. I've got two chapters of Latin to translate and I have drills at five thirty in the morning."

"Walk with me to the piano bar. Charlie will be hurt if you don't say good-bye."

"You say good-bye for me," Michael said, turning his back and walking toward the door.

Charlie was sitting at the piano, his voice dominating a loud sing-along, pausing only to sip his cocktail. He lifted his glass and beckoned Frankie to join him. Frankie resigned himself to a long evening. Charlie had settled in until last call. He'd be too drunk to get it up when they got into bed and he would fall asleep as soon as his head hit the pillow.

FRANKIE, 1985

Frankie wanted to surprise Charlie Haldermann and make this birthday the best he'd ever had. He'd stowed his overnight bag in the trunk, along with a bottle of Moët & Chandon (no cheap sparkling wines for his Charlie), a dozen roses, and a chocolate birthday cake from the bakery on Christian Street. He'd reserved the best room, one with a working fireplace and a four-poster bed, at the most expensive inn in New Hope. He couldn't wait to see the look on Charlie's face when he opened the gift box and found a TAG Heuer Carrera, the same model the salesman said Steve McQueen had worn.

It was going to be the perfect celebration, as special for Frankie as it was for the birthday boy. Frankie had never been in love before, not really, not with someone who loved him back. He'd been blessed to find his soul mate in the eye of the storm swirling around him. Half of the boys in his graduating class at South Philadelphia Beauty Academy were dead. A client's son who had seen Patrick Ryan in San Francisco said his face was spotted with purple lesions. Frankie had sat at Michael Montello's bedside three nights a week until he passed, reading aloud from Stephen King novels after CMV retinitis had left his dying friend blind. Frankie had confessed to Jack Centafore he often felt guilty being so happy in the midst of such terrible suffering. But Jack had promised him God surely wouldn't begrudge Frankie some small measure of contentment, seeming to encourage the relationship, though, in truth, he resented Charlie and rued the day the teacher had come into Frankie's life.

Frankie didn't recognize the van parked in Charlie's driveway. He rarely made it to Bucks County before eight on Saturday nights and hadn't told Charlie he was only working half a day today, not wanting to give him any reason to suspect he had something special up his sleeve and ruining the surprise. It probably belonged to a friend who had stopped by to wish Charlie a happy birthday, another teacher or a member of his Lutheran church choir. Frankie felt a slight twinge, knowing Charlie liked his cocktails and would certainly have insisted on making a toast in honor of the day. *Let's hope it's just one,* he thought as he slipped his key in the front door.

"Hello?" he called, more a question than a greeting as he stepped into the foyer.

He heard music playing in the living room, Madonna singing "Into the Groove," an odd choice for Charlie, whose taste ran to *My Fair Lady* and Bach chorales unless it was Sunday tea dance at the Raven or the Cartwheel. Frankie found an open bottle of wine and two empty glasses on the coffee table. A pair of Adidas and rumpled Levi's were on the floor. Charlie never wore sneakers or jeans. Frankie felt a stabbing pain in his gut and fought back tears as he climbed the staircase and opened the bedroom door, finding Charlie naked and on his back, his legs flailing in the air, urging a handsome young man to fuck his tight pussy and treat him like his dirty whore.

Frankie turned and fled, bolting down the stairs and out the door, with Charlie, wearing a flapping open robe, in pursuit. Charlie was surprisingly nimble for a fat man and managed to pull Frankie from behind the wheel of his car before he could close and lock the door. He pleaded for a chance to explain, and Frankie, despite his best intentions, sobbed into his faithless lover's chest.

"He's nobody, Frankie. Nobody," Charlie swore.

Frankie didn't want to know, and Charlie didn't confess, who the dark-haired stranger was, how he and Charlie had met, how many times they had done it. He didn't extract a promise it would never happen again, knowing Charlie would willingly say whatever he knew Frankie wanted to hear to buy forgiveness and some small measure of trust. It was enough that Charlie had sworn the man meant nothing to him, that he was nothing but trade (probably the truth), and that Frankie was the only man he could ever love (most likely a lie).

The sneakers and jeans were gone when they went back inside. Charlie poured Frankie a rum and Coke, then gathered the empty bottle and glasses and carried them to the kitchen. Frankie walked to the window. The van was gone. Charlie returned wearing his cords and flannel shirt and fleece-lined slippers, his hair neatly combed and parted.

"I know this is your favorite, Frankie," he said, changing the record. They settled on the sofa, Frankie yielding to Charlie's affectionate embrace and finding comfort in Stevie Nicks's plaintive voice. "Feeling better now?" Charlie asked.

Frankie, his face still wet from tears, breathing through a nose full of snot, nodded his head.

"Who's my honey bun?" Charlie asked in that coy voice he used when he wanted to sound endearing.

Frankie resisted the temptation to say he couldn't answer that question since he didn't know the stranger's name as they hadn't been introduced. It was over, done with, the subject put to rest, never to be raised again. Charlie loved his birthday surprises, all of them. It became a tradition, the two of them returning to the same room in the most expensive inn in New Hope every year until Charlie died.

He would never trust Charlie again after that notorious birthday. Charlie was supposed to be his safe harbor in the maelstrom of the epidemic and, instead, he had carelessly, recklessly, thoughtlessly, put Frankie at risk. Frankie thought about leaving him, but in the end, decided to stay with the devil he knew, at least until a cure was found and the threat was over. But he never let Charlie near him again without a condom. And after the dying stopped and the fear subsided, he could never quite find the right time to end the relationship. There was always some reason—a prepaid Caribbean cruise, Charlie's emergency gall bladder surgery with serious complications—to postpone the breakup. Frankie could always soldier through a few more months. When Papa began to fail, needing more and more of his attention, he was grateful he had a lover who made so few demands on his time and who was content filling his evenings and weekends with other distractions, sometimes not seeing Frankie for weeks at a time.

For fourteen years, until the last time he used his key to gather the clothes he kept in his dead lover's bedroom, Frankie felt his shoulders tense each time he turned the corner onto Charlie's street. Holding his breath, he braced himself, preparing for the worst, always expecting to discover a strange Ford Taurus or Jeep Wrangler parked in the driveway. He never caught Charlie red-handed again but would often stumble on the telltale signs of infidelity. A used rubber under the bed. First names and telephone numbers scribbled on scraps of paper. Nothing to get worked up about. It didn't mean anything. At least Frankie was still alive. He'd survived the epidemic. And, all things considered, being with Charlie, or with anyone for that matter, was better than being alone.

MICHAEL, 1987

The days turned cooler, the nights cold enough for down jackets, and the branches of the trees were stripped of any dead, brown leaves. The best and the brightest, used to constant affirmation of their gifts, were unsettled, on edge. Penn Law was brutal, unforgiving, without quizzes and midterms to allow anxious first-year students an opportunity to gauge their progress mastering the concepts of property and contracts and civil procedure. They had only one chance, a single test given at the end of the semester, to prove themselves worthy of their admission to one of the most selective schools in the country. Entire futures rested on the answers they would commit to the pages of their blue examination books.

The palpable nerves of his classmates were a balm to Michael, boosting his confidence. He thrived on competition, determined to succeed. He burrowed into a carrel in the Biddle library every night, drafting detailed outlines of the copious notes he'd taken since September. Frazzled, weary-looking One Ls lingered by his desk to make small talk, complaining and cracking nervous jokes. He knew they sought him because of his thick working-class Philly accent and his notoriety as the Godfather, a two-time All-Ivy center. He could read it in their faces. *Look at him. Listen to him.* It gave their fragile egos comfort, knowing there was a gorilla in their midst. *At least there's one person here I don't need to worry about as competition for selection to the Law Review.*

The weather had been raw, two days of cold, driving December rain, but the sky had cleared and the air was crisp as an apple when he emerged from the library the night before his torts exam. He zipped up the varsity jacket he'd earned at the Academy, worn as a badge of honor of his row house roots, and slung his backpack over his shoulder. Ordinarily, he would have waited for a southbound bus, but the night was a pleasant reprieve from the wet, humid weather so he decided to walk through the Penn campus and across the bridge spanning the Schuylkill River. His thoughts were consumed with the recitation of the essential elements of simple negligence and the concept of *res ipsa loquitur.* He was barely conscious of his surroundings, and at first didn't notice the woman ahead of him. The streetlights were dim and the massive walls of the football stadium loomed overhead.

He couldn't see her face, of course, but there was something familiar about her confident carriage. He was fairly certain it was Amy Morganthau. She'd spoken to him tonight in the library, briefly, pleasantly, told him her little brother, three years behind him at Princeton, had been impressed when he learned the Godfather was her law school classmate. Even her jeans and sweatshirt couldn't camouflage that she and Michael belonged to different species. Women like Amy, members of a privileged tribe whose rituals and language he didn't know, intimidated him like no hulking ogre on the defensive line ever could. He'd avoided them his entire four years at Princeton, preferring the comfortable familiarity of his high school sweetheart.

He lingered far enough behind to not be recognized should, for some reason, she turn and look behind her. He questioned the wisdom of her walking these streets alone at night. An ancient rusted Impala passed him, traveling over the speed limit, and he tensed, sensing trouble, when he saw the red brake lights and heard the squeal of rubber tires skidding on the asphalt surface as the car came to a sudden stop beside the lone woman. Two young men jumped from the car. One snatched her sack purse and book satchel. The other grabbed her by the waist and started dragging her to the car, intending to throw her into the backseat.

"Hey, motherfuckers!" Michael screamed, dropping his backpack and running toward the car. The taller of the two men drew a knife, clearly rattled when the weapon didn't deter Michael from attacking. Michael felt the blade pierce the flesh in the thickest part of his haunch, and, enraged, broke the boy's jaw with his first punch, knocking him on his back. He heard a car door slam, and the racing motor of the Impala driving away, the coward abandoning his friend to Michael's wrath. He gripped the boy's throat with one hand, not allowing him to beg for mercy, and struck him, each punch gathering force, fueled by years of rage at his father's cruelty, beating the kid's face to a bloody pulp. He would have killed him if Amy Morganthau hadn't jumped on his back, sobbing, trying to restrain him.

"Please, stop. Stop. Stop. I'm okay now," she pleaded.

The influence of the Morganthau family extended far beyond the Borough of Manhattan and criminal assault charges were never filed against Michael Rocco Gagliano. Amy tried to acknowledge her appreciation, but Michael rebuffed her offer to pay for the ER to stitch his knife wound, saying it wasn't her responsibility. He even refused to be her guest at an expensive steak house, saying he didn't think it right for him to accept a gift for simply doing what any decent man would do. She was used to getting her own way, she told him, and sooner or later she would find some way to repay him, even if it took years for the right opportunity to present itself.

MICHAEL, 1989

She was a write-on, not one of the elite who'd risen to their lofty position as Law Review associates on the basis of their grade point average. Michael Rocco Gagliano, the newly elected Note Editor, who would go on to graduate ranked fourth in his class, had taken an instant dislike to her as he undertook the extensive edits necessary to prepare her submission to the venerable publication. His own well-reasoned, impassioned argument in favor of allowing criminal defendants to waive their Sixth Amendment right to counsel during police interrogation had needed only minor revisions last year, and Michael had been deferential to the senior editor assigned to his project, willing to accept his suggestions. This chick was something else, confrontational from the outset, insisting on an extensive debate over even a minor change to a footnote. She'd clearly resented his lack of enthusiasm for her deadly dull (for him at least) topic, debtor abuse of the automatic stay provision of the bankruptcy code.

"It's Kit," she corrected him when he mistakenly called her Kathy.

"I go by Michael," he informed her when she referred to him as Mike.

It would be years before they learned they were known as Doozy and Mikey to their respective families, names more suitable for Mouseketeers. Michael did call her Princess Leia, not to her face of course and only to a select group of trusted intimates on the Law Review editorial board, and not because she shared a physical resemblance to Carrie Fisher. But Katherine Morris Scott did seem to have been spawned on another planet, *a long time ago in a galaxy far, far away*. She was nothing like the women he'd grown up among, creatures who took elaborate measures to emphasize their physical differences from men. Kit, lithe and muscular, her dirty-blond hair pulled back from her face, unadorned by any makeup other than an occasional touch of lipstick or any jewelry except for the small gold hoops in her pierced ears, would have seemed like an alien among the Catholic school girls of South Philadelphia. Most men would consider her attractive, he conceded, not a great beauty, but a handsome woman with good features that would age well.

"You must think I'm a complete bitch," she said, surprising him with a quick about-face as they sat at a small booth in a West Philadelphia deli favored by generations of Penn Law students for its generous portions of potato salad and matzo ball soup.

"Huh?" he grunted, grabbing a napkin to sop up the oil dripping from his hoagie onto the edited pages spread across the tabletop.

"Oh God, I just made you blush!" she laughed.

"Look, I just want to finish up here and . . ."

"You must really hate me," she said, interrupting him.

"No, I don't," he said, but knowing that he easily could, especially now that she was obviously changing tactics, trying to disarm him with insincere apologies and self-deprecating remarks. She'd clearly overestimated his ability to be charmed into submission by a seductress without a pair of big tits. He knew her type from his days at Princeton. A woman with a storied Philadelphia surname who believed he was nothing more than some big stupid jock, the beneficiary of an affirmative action program for athletic scholarship recipients from ethnic minority neighborhoods. Easy prey for patrician mockery.

"Are you going to eat that or let it go cold?" he asked as she played with her food.

"The soup is kind of greasy," she complained, claiming a complete loss of appetite. "Do you want to finish it?"

"It tastes okay to me," he said, having grown up believing that wasting food was the most grievous of sins.

"You're funny," she announced.

"How so?" he said, picking up the bowl to tip the last bit of soup into his mouth.

"You just are. My father would really like you. He's always wanted another Tastykake."

"What are you talking about?" he asked, bristling slightly, assuming that being referred to as a lunch box snack cake, a Butterscotch Krimpet or Chocolate Junior, was an emasculating insult. *You really are a bitch,* he decided. Thirty-two blocks from here, in the neighborhood where he'd been raised, they would call her a cunt.

"That's what he called his favorite clerk. Alan Jablonsky from Trenton. His father was a maintenance man at the state capitol. Alan was Harvard Law. He's at Sullivan and Cromwell now. Represented Dow Chemical in that big antitrust case last year. My father loved him. All hard work and no attitude, he said. You should apply."

"I'm not interested in writing someone else's opinions for two years. I'm going straight to the DA's Office after graduation."

"So? My father went to St. Paul's with her right-hand man. The city of Philadelphia will somehow survive for two more years while you clerk for my father. I know he's still interviewing," she persisted.

The Honorable Augustus Ballard Scott, appointed to the Third Circuit Court of Appeals during the first term of the Reagan Administration, was known as a law-and-order jurist, referred to affectionately as Gruff Gus by those who argued before him. A clerkship in his chambers wasn't considered a plum by Michael's peers on the editorial board, whose academic résumés had earned them consideration by liberal icons and Federalist Society heroes sitting in the most prestigious circuits. Still, it was an appellate clerkship and one of Judge Scott's own had gone on to a position in the chambers of the Supreme Court, clerking for Chief Justice Rehnquist, no less.

"What's in it for you? Does your old man pay you a finder's fee?" he asked, not trusting her intentions.

"You really are a complete and total asshole," she said, laughing, without malice so he knew she wasn't really offended.

"So I'm told. On a daily basis. At least once an hour."

"By who?"

"Well, you just did, for one."

"Anyone else?"

"You name them, they say it."

"Your girlfriend? You have one, I assume?"

"My fiancée," he said, not intending to sound resigned to his fate.

"What's her name?"

"Barbara," he answered, truthfully, though he'd rarely known anyone to refer to her by her formal name.

"Is she an undergraduate? You strike me as someone who needs to be adored by those worshipful coeds who study in the law library, hoping to make the acquaintance of a future partner at a Wall Street firm."

"She's a nurse. She works in the Emergency Department at St. Agnes."

"Oh," she said, sounding almost incredulous, as if he'd just revealed his fiancée was a circus performer. "How long have you been together?"

"A long time."

"What does she look like?"

"What difference does it make?" he asked, growing irritated by the game of twenty questions. "Why do you care what she looks like?"

He wanted to finish the edits, turn the goddamn thing in to the executive editor. It was getting late and he'd promised to pick up Barbie at the end of her shift, her nerves still unsettled by an off-hours rape on the Broad Street Subway line last month.

"I bet she looks like Diane Keaton."

"That's ridiculous," he scoffed, trying to visualize his Italian-Polish fiancé in an Annie Hall getup.

"Because you look like Pacino."

Michael had long been weary of the frequent comparisons to a pipsqueak who needed lifts to reach five-foot-six. Still, he couldn't deny the resemblance and, over time, had embraced the nickname, Godfather, given to him by his Princeton teammates.

"When are you getting married?" she asked.

"Soon," he said, the same answer he always gave the woman waiting to become his wife.

"I think my fiancé and I are breaking up," she announced.

"I'm sorry to hear that."

"He's sleeping with this little bitch in Boston. Some Brahmin whore he met at the Business School. He keeps denying it, but I know he's lying."

"Maybe he's not."

"I bet you don't sleep around on Barbara."

"No, I don't," he answered truthfully. He didn't. He hadn't. Not one time since they lost their virginity together on the cold linoleum floor of his father's barbershop. Not during his four years at Princeton. Not since they'd begun sharing a cheap apartment near the river in Grays Ferry when he entered Penn Law, ignoring the laments of her disapproving parents. Never. Ever. Ever.

"I knew it. I could tell," she said. "Don't be embarrassed that you're actually a good guy."

"I'm not embarrassed," he protested, sounding defensive.

"So, how about it?"

"How about what?"

"Meeting my father. I'm going out to the house tomorrow. You should come. You can bring Barbara."

"She works tomorrow. She gets premium pay for Sunday shifts."

"Then come by yourself. For drinks and dinner. I just know the Judge is going to love you."

"We'll see," he said, not ready to commit, but already considering which of his ties would make the best impression on Gruff Gus. After all, a clerkship would be a nice little résumé credential for a man with ambitions of one day being elected DA himself. He'd wear a rep. Red, white, and blue, of course. And a white shirt. Maybe after a few stiff drinks the old patriot would even confuse his olive-skinned guest for a real American rather than a yard worker who had wandered through the front door. "I'll meet you at the law library," he said. "What time do you want to pick me up?"

MICHAEL, 1992

"I can't fucking believe you are doing this! You've known my Tony your entire life. You made your First Communion together. Your father gave him his first haircut."

The distracted young ADA, looking down at the notes he'd scrawled on a legal pad for his opening statement, made his best effort to ignore Tony Valentino's haggard-looking mother as she stalked him in the courthouse hallway. The way she was carrying on you would have thought Michael was sending the scrawny little junkie to Graterford state prison for life instead of asking for a one-year sentence in the county jail.

"You little fucker. You think you're better than us now, don't you?" she said, insisting on a confrontation.

He'd known the day would come when he would have to choose between old loyalties and his sworn oath to uphold the law. He just hadn't expected it to arrive this soon. But this is the life he wanted. This is the work he'd fought to do. Penn Law grads, especially one who'd been an editor of the Law Review and had completed a two-year Third Circuit clerkship, rarely came seeking employment opportunities in the District Attorney's Office, and those few who did were expected to contribute their superior abilities to the more intellectually challenging arena of appellate work. But Michael had resisted his new employer's efforts to confine him to the tedium of brief writing and insisted he be assigned to the trials unit. They'd thrown him in with the other puppies to cut his baby teeth on preliminary hearings where they struggled to hold the attention of bored and distracted judges. Michael was a quick study, the first of the litter to draw blood with his bite. Four weeks after being sworn in as an assistant district attorney, he was assigned a bench trial in a simple assault second-degree misdemeanor charge.

"Come on, Mikey, cut me a break. We'll plead to a third-degree misdemeanor and enter court-mandated rehab. You'll be lucky to get even that after the bartender testifies Tony was only defending himself," Tony's lawyer whined. Michael knew him from the neighborhood—one of those shingle-hanging hacks who trolled the courthouse in their cheap, ill-fitting suits, handing their cards to potential clients who couldn't afford to pay a decent attorney to take their cases.

"That's not what she said in the police statement," Michael said, eager to get his first trial under his belt.

"What's the matter with you, Mikey? I been loyal to your family for years. I stuck with your old man until he retired, even after he almost clipped off a piece of my ear."

Even Michael's supervisor, the venerable Walter Rudenstein, was surprised by the vehemence with which his young protégé argued against agreeing to the lesser count and a lenient sentence of probation, rehab, and a thousand-dollar fine. *It was a fucking bar fight, Michael,* the jaded prosecutor chided. *You'd think this pathetic little junkie was Manson and John Wayne Gacy rolled into one. What are you gonna ask for when you're trying real criminals? That the poor bastards be drawn and quartered in the village square?* But in the end, Walter Rudenstein, impressed by Michael's tenacity, gave his blessing. Yeah, it was just a bar fight. A bar fight provoked by a defendant with three prior misdemeanor convictions and two failed stints in recovery programs. Tony Valentino was a bully and a coward, a fucking sadist who deserved the maximum punishment.

"Just be sure this isn't personal, Michael," Walter Rudenstein cautioned.

He assured his boss he had nothing against Tony Valentino personally. He'd known him all his life. They'd made their First Communion together.

The victim, a nervous lowlife reeking of Paco Rabanne, alcohol, and dirty underwear testified he hadn't given Tony Valentino the slightest provocation to smash his fist into his face three times, causing a hairline fracture below his right eye socket. The bartender corroborated the sorry old drunk's story. The judge sentenced Tony to nine months in county, eligible for release in six if he successfully demonstrated a commitment to recovery. Mrs. Valentino, an unlit Virginia Slim in one hand and a bejeweled cigarette case in the other, was waiting for Michael as he emerged from the courtroom. She spit in his face, twice.

"Once for you. Once for your faggot brother."

The cop who'd testified for Michael grabbed her by the elbow and twisted her arm.

"You stupid fucking cunt. That's a fucking felony, assaulting an officer of the court."

"Let her go. She's not worth the fucking trouble," Michael said as he calmly wiped the spit from his face and watched her slink away, no more threatening than an insect he could have crushed beneath his heel.

MICHAEL, 1997

"Would you mind keeping an eye on her for a few minutes? Just make sure she doesn't drown."

Scottie Lippincott, all of six years old, reminded him of the pigs-in-a-blanket being passed around by the catering staff—a pink, plump Vienna sausage wrapped in puffy orange pastry. He pulled off his shoes and socks and rolled up his pant legs, dangling his legs in the water, ready to dive to the rescue if the little girl defied the physics of her Navy Seal–approved flotation device and plunged to the bottom of the pool. He soon realized her mother's fears were completely unfounded. Poseidon, Lord of the Watery Underworld himself, couldn't have vanquished the feisty kid. Scottie was a turbo-charged dynamo, furiously slapping the surface of the water with her chubby arms, determined to propel herself the length of the pool.

"Here, you've earned this," Kit said as she sat down beside him and handed him a beer.

"I can see she has your personality," he commented.

"I wish. She's her father's daughter, through and through. I should have married someone like you, Michael. Then my child would be as solid and earnest as her very serious old man." She laughed. "I bet you'd make a wonderful father."

It made him feel good, having his old nemesis flirt with him. He knew he was blushing, as awkward at being the object of a female's attention as he had been at fourteen.

"Look at me, Mama! Look! Look!" Scottie shouted. She wasn't doing anything remarkable, nothing she hadn't been doing the entire afternoon, but several minutes had passed since she'd had her mother's undivided attention.

"I see you, Scottie. Stop splashing Mr. Gagliano."

"What makes you so sure I'd be a wonderful father?" he asked. "How do you know I wouldn't take a barber's strop to their little bums if they looked cross-eyed at me?"

She seemed startled that her little flirtation had taken an unexpected, ugly turn.

"That's ridiculous. People don't treat their children like that."

"My father did. Well, mostly to my brother. He'd hit me sometimes, but not like the beatings he gave my older brother."

"That's really terrible, Michael."

"That's my only role model. That's what I know about parenting. Not everyone was lucky enough to have a father like the Judge."

The Judge was wandering among his guests, tumbler of Maker's Mark in hand, a potentate in madras shorts and boat shoes, basking in the affection of the pillars of the legal community whose careers had been launched from his chambers. Each and every one of his former clerks knew to never schedule a conflicting obligation for the second Saturday of July, the date reserved for the annual reunion on the lovely lawns of Highbrook. Chicken and beef rolled off the grill all afternoon and drink glasses were never empty. The guest list grew more distinguished each summer as the alumni climbed the ranks of the profession. Michael spotted one incumbent congressman who was rumored to be running for the Senate in the next election cycle. A newly appointed federal district court judge, two members of the Commonwealth Court, several law school faculty members, and too many partners of prestigious law firms to count were milling about the lawn, impressing one another with their latest accomplishments. A current clerk, a ginger-haired ectomorph, was accepting congratulations on his recent hire by Justice Thomas. Michael was a sluggard by comparison despite his promotion to

Chief of the Major Crimes Unit in the Philly District Attorney's Office.

"Yes, I have to keep reminding myself how fortunate I am to be sprung from the loins of a saint," she said mockingly, a surprising undercurrent of bitterness in her tone. "Come on, Scottie. Time to get out of the water."

The child was defiant, her already red face blazing a deeper scarlet. Michael stood and lifted the bawling child from the pool. He whispered something in her ear that stopped the tantrum and made her giggle.

"Dodie's fixing you a hot dog," Kit promised to placate her. "This kid will do anything if you bribe her with food," she confided to Michael. "I asked her pediatrician if I need to put her on a diet. I'm worried about her weight."

"She looks fine to me," Michael said, having grown up in a neighborhood where a few extra pounds on a healthy six-year-old was called baby fat and mothers indulged chubby sons and daughters with soft pretzels and Water Ice.

"It's genetics. My former husband's waist has expanded to forty-two inches and I don't see it getting any smaller."

Michael drew in his breath, hoping she noticed the excellent shape he was in.

"Go on, Dodie's looking for you," she said as she freed her daughter from the restraints of her lifejacket. "Don't run. The wet grass is slippery and you're going to fall." She turned her attention back to Michael.

"Good God, Michael, you're soaking wet. You didn't need to fish her out of the pool."

He didn't shirk or back away as she fussed with the rumpled collar of his shirt.

"I'm not going to melt."

"You know, Michael, I'm surprised you've never married. What happened to the nurse?"

He reached for his shoes and socks and she handed him a towel to dry his feet.

"She wanted kids so she married the vice president of marketing for Tastykakes, which I'm sure you find terribly amusing."

"What do you have against kids?" she asked.

"Nothing. I love kids."

"Then what was the problem?"

"Nothing . . . I mean . . . it's too complicated to explain."

"It's not that complicated. You've got yourself twisted into knots for no reason. I've known you for quite a few years. Not well, but well enough to know you would never take a barber's strop to your son's behind. You and I should go to dinner. I bet you live on leftover takeout and warm beer," she suggested.

"Sure," he said, a vague commitment at best.

"How about Tuesday night? You choose the restaurant. My treat," she said, closing the deal, the matter settled, his fate sealed. He'd walked willingly into the trap, flattered that a Scott of Chester County considered him worthy of the hunt.

Michael, 1998

They were married in a civil ceremony. Judge Scott officiated. Kit's mother, Dodie, who Kit had threatened to banish from her life if she ever used the word *dago* in her soon-to-be-husband's presence again; her daughter, Scottie; and Frankie were the only witnesses. Dodie, a harmless, soft-spoken, and genuinely kind woman whose epithet had amused rather than offended Michael, expressed her sincere regrets that Michael's father wasn't present to see his son married. Michael thanked her, knowing Papa, confined to a dementia unit, would have boycotted the nuptials, protesting the absence of a priest and the existence of a living ex-husband. Papa always insisted the vows of matrimony were sacred, being an expert on the sacrament after having taken five wives. Marriage was a commitment *till death do us part* and the Church provided no exemptions, no get-out-of-jail card, for a woman who had unwisely chosen to bind herself to a philandering scoundrel.

After the ceremony, Frankie drove them to JFK, where they boarded a flight to Rome. Kit had been an art history major at Yale, with a special interest in Italian Baroque, and had spent an undergraduate year in the ancient capital. She playfully called her new husband Michelangelo the moment the plane landed, which embarrassed him but didn't faze the natives. Shopkeepers and waiters appreciated her fluency, complimenting her accent while feigning complete ignorance of the snippets of Calabrian dialect Michael had learned from his father.

He'd never been out of the country and she delighted in showing him her favorite galleries and palazzos and churches. He pretended to be interested in the gloomy oil paintings and excessively ornate interiors while his thoughts wandered to his next glass of *rosso* and bowl of *penne alla carbonara.* But he happily trailed his bride through miles of apses and naves as she tutored him on the Splendors of Rome, none of which made much of an impression until he found himself standing before an unassuming side chapel in a modest church, face-to-face with an image he recognized from an old postcard Frankie had tucked into the frame of their dresser mirror when they were boys.

A neighbor or a customer on a package tour of the Italian Peninsula had sent it to Papa. Frankie had rescued it from the trash and preserved it as a holy relic, an object worthy of veneration. Caravaggio's Madonna of the Pilgrims was a rather plain young woman, more weary than radiant, physically exhausted by the large child, years beyond infancy, in her arms. Lovely in her ordinariness, her mind seemed elsewhere as she gazed benignly at the adoring pilgrims, distracted by nagging thoughts of all the humble household tasks that needed to be finished before the day was over and she could fall into her bed. The Madonna in the postcard had the same kind eyes and comforting expression as the woman in the black-and-white photograph Frankie kept beside his bed, the mother that Michael never knew.

Kit was deeply moved by the tears running down his cheeks as he stared at the painting, his face illuminated by electric candlelight. Her new husband was revealing himself to be full of surprises. She would have never expected him to demonstrate such a profound appreciation of the Master of the Baroque. She whispered in Michael's ear, pointing out the powerful humanistic details like the dirty soles of the pilgrims' feet that made the painting so compelling.

"We had a postcard of this picture in our bedroom. Frankie told me she looked just like our mother and I would pray to her every night, asking her to come back."

He turned away from his new wife, embarrassed by the raw honesty of his confession. He knew she couldn't understand the painting's power as an icon. To her, it was something to be admired as a technical achievement, for the painter's mastery of shadow, his powerful use of darkness and light. He felt stupid, exposed.

"I was just a dumb kid. I'm sorry. I'm sure you already regret marrying such a sentimental idiot."

A light drizzle was falling as they walked back to their hotel, a romantic little hostel just off the Campo de' Fiori, lingering to watch the market vendors breaking down their stalls for the day and stopping to warm their hands and faces by the flames of the fires in the metal trash cans. Her body, pressed close to his, radiated with sexual tension. He kicked the door behind them as they entered their room. They fell on the bed and he penetrated her before they could undress, never before wanting any woman as much as he wanted her at that moment. When they finished, she confessed she'd been attracted to him since their days on the Law Review and her only regret about marrying him was it had taken so long to catch him.

Later that night, she took him to her favorite *trattoria* in Trastevere where the owner and his wife remembered her from years past and kept their tumblers filled with the fruity house red. She was full of questions, fascinated by his stories of his childhood. She was curious about Frankie, intrigued by the bond between brothers who couldn't be more different. She envied their relationship and confided she felt a silly twinge of jealousy. She had four siblings of her own, none of whom she'd ever been close to. The eldest, a sister, has been MIA, presumed dead, since running away from a New England boarding school with a local dealer at the age of sixteen. Of her two surviving brothers, Henry, the oldest, finally graduated from Temple after a spiraling academic career at successively less competitive schools and was now living on a small stipend teaching history and coaching lacrosse at a Quaker Friends school. Her younger brother had dropped out of Dartmouth and eked out a meager subsistence giving snorkeling lessons in Maui on the rare days he wasn't too hungover to crawl out of bed. A third had died of AIDS in the early years of the epidemic without ever coming out to his father.

She confided her own youthful miseries, shocking him with deep and unsuspected resentments of her parents. Her mother was weak, a coward, the doormat Kit swore she would never become, a woman who willfully turned her head, ignoring what was common knowledge to the rest of the world, including her own children once they grew old enough to understand. Her father was a selfish bastard who'd carried on a long, indiscreet affair with his wife's sister throughout Kit's childhood, a misalliance that ended only with his lover's painful death from pancreatic cancer. Her worst memory was a Christmas Eve when she was only eight and wandered upstairs during the family party and stumbled upon her drunken father and aunt groping each other in a darkened bedroom in Highbrook, her mother's sister's hand deep inside his zipper.

"They say a woman always marries a man like her father. I made that mistake once already." She snorted bitterly. "You're not like my father, are you, Michael? Stop. Wait. Don't answer. I know you're nothing like him."

Michael's pledge of fidelity came out sounding more indignant than comforting and reassuring. He couldn't, wouldn't confide in her that she had no reason to worry. His brother was the only living soul he trusted with the truth. She'd think him strange, unmanly, his status in her eyes diminished if she knew he could count the number of women he'd slept with on one hand without needing to use his thumb. He'd had a one-night stand with an ADA from New Orleans at a conference after Barbie had decamped with her Tastykake executive, and then entered a committed and exclusive long-distance relationship with an obstetrician in Manhattan who worked the same long hours as he did.

There was nothing wrong with him. His libido was as strong as—likely stronger than—any other man's and his cock was nothing to be ashamed of, not as large as his father's and brother's, but certainly more than adequate. It was simply that Michael was incapable of infidelity. A shrink would have a field day if he ever agreed to take to the couch. He could spend a lifetime in therapy and only scratch the surface of why a boy who had never had a mother would be too traumatized by the possibility of losing a wife to ever consider betraying her.

FRANKIE, 1999

At least Charlie Haldermann got to go quickly, if a few decades prematurely. He always said he wanted to die while seated fourth row center at the Shubert Theater on Forty-fourth Street in the heart of Manhattan's Theater District, during the first act of *South Pacific* as the glorious voice of Emile de Becque celebrated "Some Enchanted Evening." The Lord came damn close to granting Charlie his wish, striking him dead while he ran through his notes for the first rehearsal of the school's spring musical, a full orchestra production of *Guys and Dolls.*

Charlie's immortal soul may have been tap-dancing in the chorus on the Great White Way in the sky, but his earthly remains were put to rest in a churchyard in Lancaster County. The Haldermann sisters, a pair of overweight, overbearing, Pennsylvania Dutch garden slugs, swept in to claim the body, never asking if Charlie had left instructions on how he wanted to say farewell to this earthly life. The modest and humble Christian eulogized at the funeral was a complete stranger to the man who had slept with the deceased for fifteen years, one who Frankie learned for the first time during the service was four years older than the fifteen-year age difference Charlie had acknowledged between them. The Haldermann family had never wanted to know anything about their loving brother's life after he'd left for Penn State at eighteen, and Charlie had accommodated them, keeping them in blissful ignorance, insisting he was picky, just waiting for the right girl to come along. Frankie was banished to a seat twelve pews back from the altar at the service, treated like an unwelcome intruder. The good Mennonites shunned him at the church basement reception after the burial, the deceased already forgotten as they passed plates of cherry cake and paper cups of fruit punch and grumbled about the migrant workers infesting the county and the legislature's attempt to tax smokeless tobacco.

The afternoon forecast had called for a late winter storm, no accumulation, a mix of ice and sleet, dangerous enough to justify a traveler's advisory. The Haldermann sisters didn't urge their brother's "friend" to delay his departure or wish him a safe journey as he took his leave. Traffic on the turnpike was light, most commuters having left work early to avoid slippery highways and poor visibility. Frankie, ordinarily a cautious and timid driver, felt possessed. He pressed his foot to the floorboard, pushing his sedate Volvo sedan to the limits of endurance, and cranked up the volume of the disc player, tempted to smash his car into the flickering taillights of the tractor trailer ahead. He pounded the steering wheel as the lyrics of "Magic Man" and "Barracuda" throbbed through the speakers, cursing Charlie for dying.

They'd never shared a home. Even after Frankie had been relieved of the day-to-day responsibility of taking care of Papa, he wouldn't consider living more than five minutes from the nursing home where he and his brother had imprisoned their father. And Charlie was a spendthrift, bad with money, relying on Frankie to bail him out whenever he fell behind on the mortgage payments on his Washington's Crossing dream house. Frankie learned to tolerate his lover's frequent infidelities in adult bookstore arcades and his risky liaisons with strangers he'd met in AOL chat rooms. The three-martini happy hours and pack-and-a-half-a-day habit had certainly contributed to his early death.

Charlie, always full of surprises, had one left up his sleeve. Six weeks after the funeral, New York Life notified Francis Rocco Gagliano that he was the beneficiary of a generous life insurance policy paying seven hundred fifty thousand dollars on the event of the death of Charles Martin Haldermann. The unexpected windfall liberated Frankie from the yoke of the tyrannical daughter of the late Victor Salazzo, the proprietor of Salazzo's Corona di Seta, a garish temple of South Philadelphia grandeur, decorated with red-flocked wallpaper and plaster busts of Diana, Goddess of the Hunt. Frankie had apprenticed there during beauty school, learning under the stern eye of a master the art of weekly wash-and-sets and the care of nicotine-ravaged complexions. Papa had coerced him into accepting a permanent job after graduation, the Salazzo and Gagliano clans having been close back home in Calabria. He'd intended to stay for only a year, then swore he'd leave after five. By his tenth anniversary, he knew that the window of opportunity to be offered a chair at a Center City or Main Line salon had closed. He suspected the friends and colleagues he greeted at hair shows snickered behind his back; they pitied him, maybe even mocked him, for rotting in a backwater beauty shop, catering to working-class matrons who hadn't changed their hairstyles in decades. He'd lost confidence in his talent and abilities, accepting his fate, assuming he'd work at Corona forever, suffering Victor Salazzo's indignities and insults and, later, those of his bitter daughter when she inherited the shop.

The insurance proceeds allowed him to gut the top two stories of the house at Eighth and Carpenter, knocking down walls to create airy, sunlit open spaces showcased in the Urban Habitats column of the *Philadelphia Inquirer* Sunday Styles section. At the street level, he transformed Papa's old barbershop, shuttered for years, its ancient fixtures shrouded in dusty old sheets, into a sleek salon. Salazzo's daughter threatened legal action, accusing Frankie of soliciting her clients and slandering her business with whispers about unsanitary conditions in her shop. A strong letter from a scorch-the-earth litigator at his sister-in-law's firm promising extended expensive litigation that would undermine the fiscal stability of Salazzo's Corona di Seta put a quick end to that folly. At long last, Frankie was living the life he richly deserved. All he needed was someone to share it with.

MICHAEL AND FRANKIE, 1999

Frankie escalated from astonished to angry to panicked when Michael announced his son would be named Daniel Pugh Scott Gagliano, needing two acceptable surnames from his maternal grandparents to offset a last name ending in a vowel. Not that Kit was explicit about her concerns about their son's birthright to attend the Assembly Ball and claim membership in the venerable Philadelphia Club when they were considering possibilities, but Michael knew she was conscious of the attitudes and prejudices of the small, privileged world she had never entirely rejected despite her progressive politics and open-minded embrace of a wealthy bohemian lifestyle.

"Mikey, I think you're doing this just to get back at Papa. The poor old man doesn't even know who or where he is now!"

"No. I'm doing it because my wife wants it."

Michael denied it, but he was as uneasy about insulting Saint Rocco as his brother. But Kit's tolerance for religious superstitions had its limits and he was leery of pushing her any further. He'd won the one concession that mattered when she'd agreed that their son, who would be raised a Protestant, would be entrusted to the authority of the Jesuits when Danny was old enough to enroll at Matteo Ricci Preparatory Academy.

"Let me talk to her."

"I can hear *that* conversation, Frankie. *Please, Kit, you don't understand how important Saint Rocco is to our family. He's protected us from the evil eye for generations. Why tempt the fates?*"

Frankie would be willing to compromise. It had made little difference to Michael, who set foot in a Catholic Church once a year to make his confession on Good Friday and only then because some habits were too ingrained to shake, if his son was baptized an Episcopalian. But Frankie had been shocked by Michael's casual rejection of the religion in which they had been raised and, after consulting with his friend the priest, had upset his brother and his wife by politely and respectfully declining the honor of standing as godfather to his nephew in a *Protestant* ceremony. It was a decision he would now reconsider if a concession were necessary to steer the *maliocch'* from an innocent child.

"Just let me talk to her. She'll understand."

Which she didn't, but she surrendered, wary of creating a rift between her husband and his brother, and on the morning of his nephew's christening, Frankie stood in the baptistery of St. Peter's Episcopal Church and recited the words of the Book of Common Prayer, vouching before the Lord Jesus Christ in the name of Daniel Rocco Gagliano that his godson did, indeed, renounce Satan and all his works.

The ceremony was mercifully brief, followed by a gathering at Highbrook that threatened to go into the evening hours. The Judge was in unusually high spirits, both figuratively and literally, courtesy of Maker's Mark bourbon. Kit thought his frequent memory losses were the consequences of years of alcoholism, but Michael recognized the same early signs of dementia he'd seen with Papa. The assembled descendants of storied Philadelphia families engaged in the perfunctory oohs and aahs and good-natured (but purely polite) arguments about which parent young Danny, the mirror image of his father, most resembled, before drifting off to engage in more pressing conversations about recent scandals involving the inhabitants of their rarefied world.

Kit, ever vigilant for the sounds of activity on the baby monitor, was engaged in the kitchen and sent her husband upstairs to check on their infant child. Danny was red-faced, crying out for someone to change his soaked diaper. Michael, who had never held, let alone changed, a baby before his son was born, was amazed by how much poop such a tiny creature was able to produce.

"You're all nose and hose," he said as he sprinkled talc on his boy's tender skin. His son had inherited the noble Gagliano beak, and Michael took paternal pride in the impressive length of his penis. He picked up Danny and held the crown of his child's head close to his face. It was a smell like no other, sweet and gentle and fragrant. Michael had never felt more content, at peace, than he did when he was holding his son, breathing in his essence, and his wife would find him in the wee hours of the morning dozing in a chair, his baby cradled in his arms.

"He's so beautiful. Just like you when you were born."

He hadn't heard Frankie creep up behind him and the sound of his brother's voice brought unexpected tears to his eyes.

"Tell me I'm nothing like him, Boo," he whispered. "Please. Say that I'm nothing like Papa or I'll walk out that door and never see my boy again."

"You're nothing like him, Mikey. Nothing at all," he said, neither a lie nor the complete truth.

Michael had inherited his keen intelligence from his astute, if unschooled, father, a fact he only begrudgingly admitted. They both had quicksilver tempers and were prone to act before thinking. But Papa was an angry, bitter man. He was cold and cruel while his younger son had a tender heart, despite his best efforts to conceal it. Michael had tamed the wild beast that lived inside him, and Frankie, who knew him better than anyone, even his wife, assured him he would never lift his hand to strike his child.

"How do you know that, Boo? How can I be sure?"

"I just do, Mikey. Trust me. I just do."

FRANKIE, 2000

"Now aren't you glad that I insisted we do this?" Jack asked as they ended the third night of Frankie's fortieth birthday cruise with a nightcap after winning big in the casino.

With Jack traveling incognito, in civvies and no clerical collar, they were quickly adopted as "the boys" by middle-aged couples who wouldn't invite two obvious fairies to their dinner tables in their provincial hometowns. The husbands were amused by their wives' coy flirtation with Frankie, feigning indignation over their admiration of his dimpled chin and long eyelashes. Claiming two left feet and trick backs, they encouraged Frankie and Jack to partner their women on the dance floor, busting a gut as their graceless wives attempted cheesy lounge act favorites like the Electric Slide and the Macarena. Frankie and Jack were in constant demand, the most popular men on board, even recruited to judge the Annette Funicello look-alike contest after the movie night viewing of *How to Stuff a Wild Bikini.* Everyone competed for "the boys" to sit at their table, and the women prodded Frankie to indulge in two rich desserts every night.

All good things must come to an end. The days passed quickly and suddenly it was the last night on board: one final dinner with new friends, phone numbers and e-mail addresses exchanged, solemn promises made to stay in touch. The priest made the last toast of the evening, his oratorical gifts on full display, and the couples all dispersed to their cabins, leaving Frankie and Jack alone. The band, playing to a near empty room, took all their requests: "Rhiannon" and "Landslide" for Frankie, "Close to You" and "Goodbye to Love" for Jack. Usually so garrulous, they were strangely quiet, each lost in his own thoughts.

Frankie realized he hadn't thought of Charlie Haldermann even once during his week at sea. The hard truth was that the past year had been the most peaceful he'd had in over a decade, blessedly free of any stress and strife other than the predictable difficulties of dealing with a demented Papa. Charlie was dead and no longer needed to be rescued from creditors and hustlers and law enforcement agencies threatening to prosecute another DUI. Surely God would forgive Frankie for being grateful for having such a burden lifted from his shoulders. He'd envied the relationships of his friends. True, some of them went after each other like cats and dogs while he and Charlie never raised a voice against the other. And none of them were monogamous, either by agreement or deception, but they shared an intimacy Frankie and the schoolteacher had lacked.

The thoughts preoccupying his friend must have been much darker than his own, judging by the black clouds of anger that had settled upon his face. Jack tossed back four shots of Sambuca, then bellowed at the bartender to put the bottle on the table. He snapped at Frankie's suggestion they call it a night, drinking until he could barely lift his head, babbling almost incoherently. The only words Frankie could understand were ones he pretended he didn't hear. He led Jack back to their cabin, staggering under the dead weight of a stumbling drunk. Jack came to life as he kicked the cabin door behind him. He tore at Frankie's shirt, buttons flying across the room, and dropped to his knees, struggling with Frankie's belt buckle, finally burying his face in Frankie's crotch, crying tears of frustration. Frankie stood erect, immobilized by the arms wrapped tightly around his legs. Jack moaned, then pushed Frankie away, scrambling on his hands and knees to reach the toilet. Frankie gagged, sickened by the smell of anise-sweetened vomit on the cabin floor.

* * *

Jack was already awake when the rocking of the boat roused Frankie from a deep sleep. Frankie heard the soft rumblings of the priest's voice and rolled to his side, opening his eyes. Jack, dressed in a white T-shirt and his black dress cleric trousers, knelt beside his own bed. His back was toward Frankie, his Breviary in hand, the yellow soles of his bare feet and the black stole draped across his shoulders in plain view as he recited the solemn prayers of his Daily Office. Frankie closed his eyes, allowing Jack his privacy, and drifted back to sleep, comforted by the gentle murmur of the holy words.

God, come to my assistance; Lord, make haste to help me.

Jack was gone, his packed suitcase on his bed, when Frankie awoke. He quickly showered and threw his last dirty clothes in his bag and rushed upstairs to the breakfast room. He found Jack sitting alone at a table, staring into a bowl of cold cereal.

"Good morning! Did you sleep well?" he asked, his voice full of false cheer.

Looking into Jack's sad, bloodshot eyes, he knew it was useless to try to erase last night's sordid events with willful ignorance.

"Thank you," the priest whispered, his dry throat cracking as he spoke.

"For what?" Frankie asked, not understanding what he had done to earn Jack's gratitude.

"For being stronger than me. For not letting me break my vows."

Frankie felt his cheekbones blazing with shame. He was afraid to look Jack in the face, knowing the truth would be apparent in his eyes. It hadn't been noble thoughts that had caused him to refuse to yield to a tortured plea for a single kiss, but revulsion at the thought of having his ugly friend's tongue in his mouth.

MICHAEL, 2005

If anyone could pull off a surprise party for Michael's fortieth birthday, it was Katherine Morris Scott. Either she was deft and skillful—not one of the dozens of clever invitations with the black-and-white snapshot of Michael as a fifteen-year-old boy celebrating the 1980 World Championship found its way into his hands—or he was simply too oblivious to notice, having lately been entrenched in spearheading the Commonwealth's latest challenge to yet another of the seemingly endless appeals of the capital conviction of the killer of the tragic Carmine Torino. She'd called him at his office, where he was spending yet another Saturday afternoon, to ask him to pick up Danny at his grandparents'. Nothing seemed suspicious as he drove the long, winding entrance road to Highbrook, and his only thoughts were about how he was going to need to talk his son off the sugar ledge after twenty-four hours of unlimited access to candy and cupcakes. Later he learned the guests had been instructed to park at a neighboring estate and arrived at Highbrook by party bus. He nearly pissed his pants when three hundred of his friends and colleagues pounced as he walked through the front door, shouting *Surprise!* in his face.

Kit had thought of everything. She'd rented amusement rides for the kids and hired a member of the Charlotte Ingersoll School swim team to act as a lifeguard so that parents could enjoy their cocktails without needing to worry about their offspring drowning in the deep end of the pool. Michael never knew so many people genuinely liked him. Teammates from the Academy and Princeton. Colleagues from the Law Review. The once-young bucks who had cut their teeth with him in the Philly DA's Office. He was touched that his old mentor Walter Rudenstein, now the Dark Prince of the Defense Bar, had made the effort to attend. Steven Kettleman, District Attorney of the County of Delaware and Michael's boss, not only made an appearance, he lingered and mingled until after the cutting of the cake. Even Kit's childhood dance teacher, the imperious Miss Peterson, had deigned to hold court.

"Now please, will you forget about Carmine Torino for one day," Kit whispered in his ear as she refilled his glass with small-batch bourbon.

Carmine Torino had been a loner, harmless and shy, whose life had peaked at twenty-seven when he was promoted to manager of a Wawa convenience store. Slightly overweight, bald by twenty-eight, he lived alone in a third-floor walkup apartment and drove a six-year-old Hyundai. The poor bastard had left a seedy Ridley taproom one fateful night, giddy with excitement, probably pinching himself, thinking he was having a wild dream from which he would abruptly awake. He would never have had the nerve to invite a pair of hard-bodied, good-looking young men to come home for a nightcap. But his new friends wanted to keep the party going, hinting that things could get a little crazy after a few more Jack and Cokes and a hit or two of Tina.

The tenant of the apartment below had called the fire department at 5:16 in the morning. Carmine Torino's body was slightly charred, his killers being too impatient or too high on crystal to start a proper blaze. He was lying on a blood-soaked mattress, naked, bound and gagged with duct tape. The coroner concluded he'd been kicked or punched in the head multiple times. The lacerations to his neck, throat, and face were too numerous to count. One eye had been gouged and his fifth and sixth vertebrae had been severed. In the pathologist's expert opinion, the victim had aspirated on his own blood five to ten minutes before expiring.

Eyewitnesses had placed Billy Kucic and Tommy Corcoran at

the bar and seen them leave with the victim at last call. Corcoran's fingerprints had been found all over the duct tape, but the only prints on the hunting knife used to shred Carmine's throat matched those on record for Kucic, who'd just been released from prison after serving a sentence for assault. Kucic had somehow eluded custody. Unsuccessful leads had placed him in Canada, New Mexico, and an island in the Caribbean. In the Commonwealth, an accessory is guilty of murder in the first degree, punishable by death, if proven he had the same intent to kill as the actual perpetrator. Corcoran, fair and doe-eyed, a man who might even be called pretty, had taken the stand in his own defense, crying convincingly, swearing he didn't know his friend was going to kill the guy. They were just going to knock him around, steal his car and his wallet. He feigned revulsion at the events of the night and claimed to have fled the sickening scene of Kucic hacking at the victim's throat. At least one member of the jury might have believed that the baby-faced and soft-spoken altar boy on the stand was incapable of wanting to carve up another human being with a hunting blade.

Fortunately for the prosecution, Kucic and Corcoran were stupid fuckers who had made the mistake of seeking refuge at the nearby house of a friend, a biker named Thornton, who'd testified under oath and over objection that Tommy Corcoran, covered with the same blood as Kucic, was the more agitated of the two, insisting the victim himself was to blame. *I told him not to touch me. I told him I wasn't no fag. I told him. He should have listened to me.* His words were persuasive evidence of the intent necessary for the death penalty. Michael wasn't a religious man, but he'd prayed as he stood in the courtroom waiting for the foreman to deliver the verdict, haunted by a vision of Frankie bound and gagged, lying on a bed, his face mutilated beyond recognition.

"Where's my brother? Where's Frankie? It's my birthday, Kit. Why isn't he here?" he asked his wife, who calmly explained to her frantic husband that Frankie was in the kitchen assisting with the supervision of the catering staff.

Where else would he be? Michael realized. Better to stay occupied, making himself useful, than to stand awkwardly on the periphery of the conversations of strangers with whom he had nothing in common. Michael doubted any of them had ever known a stylist other than the one who cut their hair. Not a single person from his life at Eighth and Carpenter other than Frankie was present. Not even his godfather, Sal Pinto, who had first put a football in his hands, had been invited to cross the impregnable border between the life of the accomplished and respected family man who lived in a House with a Name, "Sleepy Peter's Quiet Nook," and the childhood of Michael Rocco Gagliano, son of the neighborhood barber.

It was for the best. He would have been on edge the entire party, waiting for Sal to malign the *moulinyan* or brag about how he'd Jewed down a car dealer. A polite invitation to that horse-faced priest who trailed his brother like a lovesick puppy should have been extended. But the list of names from his past that might have been included stopped there. He'd renounced his citizenship in the neighborhood when he moved away and a language barrier had arisen in the ensuing years, making it impossible to sustain a conversation with those who had known him as a boy.

Everyone wanted to offer a toast to the man of the hour, and no one, not Kit, not his brother, discouraged him from drinking his fill or nagged him to limit or at least slow down his alcohol intake. When the sun went down, he stripped off his shirt and cannonballed into the pool to the shrieking delight of a dozen waterlogged kids. A local Springsteen cover band played until midnight, and Michael, usually so reluctant to demonstrate his lack of rhythm, stomped barefoot on the makeshift dance floor. He hadn't needed convincing to step up to the microphone and take the lead vocal on "Born to Run."

It was nearly three in the morning when Kit surveyed the wreckage of a very successful party. Tomorrow would be soon enough to begin to clean up the mess. It had been a long day and every muscle in her body ached for the bed in her old room upstairs. But the birthday boy had gone missing and a little reconnaissance would be necessary to reel him in.

"Michael! Michael!" she called, her voice loud enough to carry without needing to shout. "Michael, the party's over! It's time for bed!"

Her brother-in-law responded, *This way, over here.* She found them propped against the trunk of an ancient oak, her husband sprawled on the ground, snoring, his head resting in his brother's lap.

"Go on to bed, Kit. He's dead to the world. I'll bring him inside when he stirs enough to wake him."

She nodded and walked away, self-conscious, feeling she had intruded on something intimate, private, a place where no one else was welcome, sealed by a locked door without a key.

FRANKIE, 2007

The revenues were healthy from the day Frankie opened the doors of Gagliano Cuts and Color, Family Owned Since 1928 and grew steadily each year. The stylish shop even attracted the new arrivals to the neighborhood, young urban bohemians with sizable incomes attracted to the ten-year tax abatements for purchasers of the expensive new town houses built by ambitious developers. He had an easy rapport with a breed of woman who pushed Maclaren strollers and carried yoga mats and eco-friendly Whole Foods shopping bags. But he'd learned early on to carefully schedule their appointments, separating them from his longtime regulars, though his dotty assistant Connie occasionally fucked up, leading to an inevitable and uncomfortable exchange of opinions on the politics of George W. Bush and the archdiocese's culpability in the pedophile scandal in the Catholic Church.

It all made for long, exhausting days, often twelve or thirteen hours, Tuesday morning through Saturday night. Success left Frankie little time to dwell on the fact that the likelihood of ever finding someone to share his life with was growing dimmer and dimmer. He'd tried dating, letting himself be fixed up with a succession of middle-aged florists and church organists and real estate agents who his matchmaking clients insisted were absolutely "perfect" for him.

He'd suffered through too many long dinners and meet-for-drinks-or-coffees with these promised soul mates, trying to feign interest in an unattractive stranger's tales of his prodigy nieces and nephews and pampered and adored cats. Worse yet was the occasional rejection by the rare possible suitor he found himself attracted to, like the handsome, barrel-chested, sandy-bearded delivery truck driver who sheepishly apologized he had only agreed to meet Frankie because he didn't want his sister to know he was only interested in black men with prominent scars and criminal records.

Solitude had its advantages. He had Jack for companionship and, though his brother was often distracted, occasionally irritable, Michael had drawn him into the heartbeat of the family he had made with his wife and son, the bond between motherless boys being impossible to sever.

And if physical desires were not yet completely extinguished, they, at least, were more infrequent, and easily satisfied by the services of the city's premier escort agency, all companions bonded and regularly tested for STDs. He'd grown quite attached to Stefan from Prague, a gangly six-foot-seven blond, who had even accompanied Frankie on a weekend jaunt to the Bahamas for the reasonable fee of fifteen hundred dollars. Frankie was far more devastated than he should have been, considering Stefan's exclusively mercenary interest in spending quality time together, when the agency explained Stefan had an unfortunate encounter with Homeland Security and would no longer be available for "modeling" sessions.

But after the occasional extra glass of Pinot (a rare indulgence for a man who strictly monitored his calories), nursing a mild buzz while he wept over tearjerkers like *The Notebook,* he would yearn for his own Ryan Gosling to enter his life. And then he would tumble into a blue funk. His capacity for self-pity surprised him. But he longed to know how it felt to be truly, deeply loved, and the clock was ticking, the window of opportunity closing. He wanted to feel something more than the convenience and apathy, the habit and familiarity, of his years with Charlie Haldermann. He wanted to hear the words *I love you* from someone who loved him like he had once loved Charlie before the drinking and debts and infidelities slowly but steadily drained the passion, and eventually even the affection, from his feelings.

The days felt endless and he would fall into bed early in the evening and sleep until morning, exhausted by the effort of simply going through the motions, smiling and exchanging pleasantries, concealing his despair. The most recent black mood had been the worst yet. An unrelenting pessimism had poisoned his thoughts, his situation seemingly hopeless, until the bitterly cold Valentine's Day night when a beautiful young Mexican, a boy whose smooth cheeks had never seen a razor, shyly approached his table in a low-rent *tacqueria* and handed him a folded napkin with his phone number scrawled in crooked letters.

Book Two

riti familiari

March 4, 2008–April 13, 2008

MARCH 4, 2008

When you think Tim McGraw . . .

Frankie can't get that damn song out of his head. His own divas were all legends before the dawn of the Reagan administration and the heyday of Alexis and Krystle. There's Barbra and Miss Ross, Aretha and Cher, and of course, Stevie, the woman who stole his soul the first time he heard "Rhiannon," casting a spell that's endured for decades. She *is* a witch, a benign one, of course, a sorceress, a wizard who conjures up mystical potions of pain, loss, and love. One minute she's a dervish, an apparition of swirling chiffon and lace. Blink your eyes and she's an urchin in ruffles and feathers and leather boots, veiled in a sweeping gossamer shawl. She's beauty and power and mystery. Her top hat from the 1977 *Rumours* tour, bought for six thousand dollars at a charity auction, is preserved in a glass shrine for all who enter his shop to admire and revere. No one will ever write a song as haunting as "Landslide" or one as powerful as "Dreams." No one will ever inspire him more.

But lately he's been making an effort to keep up with the times, or trying to at least. His iPod doesn't terrify him anymore and he's learned how to download tunes. He's been listening to Beyoncé and Rihanna and Shakira (all true divas need only a single name), though, if truth be told, he has a hard time telling one from the other since all of their songs sound alike, all beats, no melody. But he's fallen in love with this little girl Mariano worships, Taylor Swift, just eighteen or nineteen years old. He's been playing her music incessantly in the shop until his clients have begun teasing him about jilting Stevie for jailbait. He humors them, knowing they're not actually talking about the music, that they're gently mocking him for taking up with a nineteen-year-old boy. It's taken time, but they've begun to believe the sincerity of the young man's feelings for him, most of them at least.

He turns on the television while he waits for the coffee to brew. Hillary looks absolutely stunning in canary yellow. Whoever's dressing her these days deserves an award from *Women's Wear Daily*. His ring tone, "Gold Dust Woman," announces an incoming call. Michael. Again. He'd better answer this time before the cavalry arrives at the front door to rescue him from whatever crisis is fomenting in his brother's overactive imagination.

"Have you forgotten how to answer your telephone?"

"I just sent you a text, Mikey."

"I tried to reach you three times yesterday. Why the hell didn't you call me back?"

No excuse will satisfy his brother so the question just lingers in the silence, unanswered.

"Kit is expecting you to come out for the neighborhood festivities Sunday night. Act surprised when she brings out your birthday cake."

"Jack is taking me to the opera on Sunday."

"You're going to a matinee. Come out later. Bring the damn priest if you want."

"Please don't waste good money on a birthday cake, Mikey."

Frankie refuses to commit unless a formal invitation is extended to Mariano, a Rubicon Michael refuses to cross.

"We're expecting you. Don't disappoint my wife."

Michael pauses, then asks a question.

"Are you all right? Is everything okay down there?"

Michael has an almost preternatural way of sensing trouble. Frankie sometimes thinks his younger brother was born with a microchip in his brain cell that sounds a red alert at the slightest indication that things are off-kilter, out of alignment.

"What's wrong, Frankie?"

"Nothing's wrong."

"I can hear it in your voice."

"Nothing's wrong. Honestly."

It's the God's truth. Nothing's wrong, at least not anything serious. It's just a deep bruise. There's nothing to do but take ibuprofen for the pain and give the swelling time to subside. The next few days will be awkward, trying to navigate the salon with an ACE bandage wrapped around his hand. He can handle the wash-and-sets and the color jobs. He's rescheduled any cuts for later in the week when he'll be able to grip the scissors. It was his own fault, really. He should never have tried to reach for the door as Mariano slammed it in his face. His brother, as always, would jump to conclusions if Frankie told him about the accident. He would assume the worst, accuse Mariano of assault, threaten to notify Immigration and Citizenship Services of an undocumented alien residing at Eighth and Carpenter. It was nothing but a silly tantrum. Over and forgotten. Frankie admits Mariano can be high-strung at times. He's young, impatient, and wants his own way. A nineteen-year-old boy needs breathing space to grow.

And certainly the good things in their relationship far outweigh the bad. Frankie had thought his best days were behind him, that the years ahead would be a slow progression to becoming one of those old coots at Rite Aid or CVS, arguing with the cashier for not accepting an expired coupon for a dollar off a twelve-ounce bottle of Lemon Scent Joy. He'd resigned himself to spending the rest of his life alone. Then thirteen months ago, on Valentine's Day night, he was sitting in one of the hole-in-the-wall *tacquerias* popping up throughout the neighborhood, swirling chips in a big bowl of guacamole while Jack counseled the owner, one of his parishioners, in the tiny kitchen. Frankie had tried not to stare at the beautiful young Mexican hunkered over a plate of rice and beans, bopping his head to the loud tunes leaking through his earphones. Frankie had quickly looked away when his gaze caught the boy's attention. When he finally summoned the courage to sneak another peek at this exotic creature's butternut skin and dark canine features, he saw the young man smiling at him, his eyes inviting Frankie to introduce himself.

His name was Mariano and his English was so rudimentary that further conversation was difficult if not nigh on impossible. The boy quickly scribbled his number on the back of a napkin and shoved it into Frankie's hand before Jack returned to the table. Mariano was intuitive, knowing not to allow a look of recognition to pass between them as Jack paid the check and said *adiós* to the owner. Frankie called three hours later and they've been together ever since. The prospect of being alone again is far bleaker than suffering an occasional nuisance like a minor bruise. The first blissful days of a new romance aren't meant to last and the past few months have been tense. Mariano's been on edge, his fuse short, his temper quick to flare, the outbursts more frequent.

Frankie understands his frustration. Mariano's frightened, his future uncertain until his situation is settled. Frankie's promised to find a way to keep him in the country legally. Mikey knows a thousand lawyers who can get Mariano the right papers, but he keeps dragging his feet about recommending one. Things will settle down and Mariano will once again be the sweet-natured boy he fell in love with when they can stop looking over their shoulders, wondering every time a stranger appears at the door if this is the dreaded day Mariano will be exiled to his mother's shack back in Puebla.

Michael hangs up the phone, his dogged persistence eliciting an unconvincing *maybe* from his brother, and turns up the volume of the car radio.

Give us twenty minutes and we'll give you the world.

It's a slow news day and Tommy Corcoran is the top story of the morning.

Corcoran had been scheduled for execution by lethal injection for his role in the hate-crime murder of Ridley resident Carmine Torino. Chief Deputy District Attorney Michael Gagliano, speaking at a press conference, expressed the prosecution's disappointment in the decision and informed reporters the Commonwealth was considering whether to request a retrial of the first-degree homicide charge.

Yesterday afternoon, at precisely 4:58, a three-judge panel of the Third Circuit Court of Appeals affirmed the district court's conditional grant of habeas corpus, vacating the first-degree murder conviction and death sentence of Tommy Corcoran, an accomplice to the torture and murder of Carmine Torino, execution of the writ to be stayed for 180 days to allow the Commonwealth to seek a new trial on the capital offense. Michael's suffered a few professional disappointments in his career; it goes with the territory. But this one hurts. The Three Stooges of the Third Circuit—Moe, Larry, and Curly—weren't satisfied with stabbing the dedicated prosecutor in the chest. They're twisting the knife, enjoying watching him squirm.

Michael flips the station to sports radio to listen to predictions about the Phillies upcoming season and postmortems on the Eagles' last one. The jokers on the morning show are riffing about the competition for the starting rotation, shifting to an argument about whether *Entourage* has jumped the shark, then segueing into a Freudian analysis of the fragile ego of Donovan McNabb. No one is talking about Tommy Corcoran or Obama and Hillary and the goddamn primary campaign. The hosts are about go live with the marble-mouthed Phillies manager in Clearwater for a spring training update when the telephone beckons. It's from his office.

"Michael, are you almost there? The kid has to be back at school by nine thirty."

He remembers he's supposed to be sitting in the dining room of the Four Seasons, doing a service for both his alma maters. Michael's been enlisted to recruit a National Merit Scholar and All-Catholic League tackle to bolster the Princeton Tigers defensive line the next four years. The kid and his father and an academic adviser from Matteo Ricci Preparatory Academy have been cooling their heels for a half hour.

"Call them back and tell them I'm running late. I'll be there in twenty minutes," he instructs his assistant Carol before hanging up. He changes stations, back to news radio for the traffic report, hoping to avoid any congestion on the expressway on his drive into the city.

He thinks of the perfect excuse as he hands his car keys to the valet. He'll say that early Mass ran late. The legendary Academy alum who'd lettered at Princeton and made Penn Law Review goes to Mass every morning during Lent! The kid will never know this paragon of virtue only crosses the threshold of the House of God one day a year. He apologizes profusely as he introduces himself to the boy and his father. The kid is nothing like Michael was at his age. He's cocky, unlikable, uninterested in anything Michael has to say. He's been offered preferred walk-on status by Notre Dame and, after five minutes, Michael's ready to hand him a first-class ticket to South Bend. It'll serve the little shit right to be ground up and tossed aside by the unsentimental Fighting Irish, his gridiron career over by his sophomore year. A decade from now when he's the bitter alcoholic manager of a car dealership, he'll hate himself for fucking up his entire life because he was too arrogant to take the advice of Michael Rocco Gagliano and accept an academic scholarship to Princeton.

Michael's anxious to end this little fiasco and get on with his day. He wishes the boy the best of luck, assuring him he'll make the Academy proud whatever decision he makes. The academic adviser is clearly embarrassed by the kid's behavior and thanks Michael, a major contributor to the alumni association, for his generosity to his high school, citing him as a model alumnus. The father, a massive, red-faced hulk of a man, seems truly humiliated. He pushes his chair from the table and, standing behind his son, places one of his enormous hands on the boy's shoulder. His *basso profundo* voice trembles with barely contained rage as he asks Mr. Gagliano—*Call me Michael, no need to be so formal*—to excuse him and his son for a minute, please. The boy seems shrunken, diminished, and the father calmer, his authority asserted, when they return.

"I want to apologize to you for being so rude, Mr. Gagliano. I know you are an important man and I really appreciate you taking an interest in me," the boy says, sounding, to Michael's ears, sincere and contrite.

His father, Officer Ivan Scalzo, is a city cop raising six kids in a Roxborough row house. He's a Father Judge alum, a massive middle guard during Michael's glory years at the Academy as an All-Catholic center and linebacker, the unanimous choice for the league's Most Valuable Player in his senior year, a sixty-minute-man hailed by local sportswriters as the prep school incarnation of Chuck Bednarik, the legendary hero of the 1960 NFL championship. Their paths would cross again years later when Michael, a young ADA in the Philadelphia District Attorney's Office, newly promoted to the Major Crimes Unit, won the conviction of the punk who crippled Ivan's partner in a random shooting during a routine investigation of a domestic disturbance. Michael suspects Officer Scalzo has just threatened a felony assault offense himself, promising to smash his kid's face against the wall of the fancy hotel bathroom if he didn't show Mr. Gagliano the respect and deference he deserved.

Michael quickly assesses that the boy actually is smart, with an obvious brain between his ears despite the fact his head looks like it should be attached to his eighteen-inch neck with a steel rod. Young Scalzo asks thoughtful questions and is eager to talk about his interest in mechanical engineering. He'd look more intelligent if he didn't buzz his hair so short, and he's rough around the edges, but he's no more awkward and lumbering than Michael had been at the age of seventeen. He nods, half listening to the kid, who suddenly seems hell-bent on impressing him. He wonders if he's doing the kid any favors, if the boy's chances for happiness wouldn't be better if he settled for a career driving a beer truck. No decisions are announced on the spot, but Michael's confident that, come September, the policeman's kid from Roxborough will be suiting up as a Princeton Tiger.

"My wife and I would like to have you over for dinner one night to show our appreciation, Mr. Gagliano," Officer Scalzo says.

"It's Michael, please," he says, handing the fellow his card. "I'd like that."

"Mrs. Gagliano, too," Officer Scalzo insists. "It would be an honor."

"Sounds great," he lies, hoping the invitation is nothing more than a polite formality, but fearing it isn't.

Yes, it sounds terrific. Three or four hours of uncomfortable tension. Kit, well bred to a fault, will praise her hostess's accomplishments in the kitchen while trying to avoid actually swallowing more than a forkful of the food on her plate. She's mastered the art of discreetly not eating. Mrs. Scalzo, solidly built, will compliment Kit's figure, self-conscious of every bite she takes in her guest's regal presence. After a few Crown Royals, Officer Scalzo will feel at ease; made wise by a lifetime of defending the streets of the city from the scum of the earth, he'll share the insights he's learned about *those people.* On the drive home, Michael and his high-born

Episcopal wife will agree that the Scalzos are the salt of the earth, up every morning at five, out of the house by six, in bed by ten. Michael will defend their unenlightened attitudes, blaming the lack of opportunities taken for granted by the privileged sons and daughters of Chester County. Kit will strongly disagree, arguing that people can rise above their circumstances, citing the shining example of her husband, son of a South Philly barber, raised in a cauldron of ignorance and prejudice, an inspiration and role model for the Scalzos' fortunate young son as he embarks on his own journey through the land of golden opportunity.

March 9, 2008

Michael is ready to concede defeat and trot back to the car, but the rusty hinges of the front door finally yield to Kit's efforts and there's no retreating now. He has no choice but to meekly follow his wife.

A yapping mongrel, the Beast from Hell, comes charging down the hallway, its unclipped toenails clattering against the hardwood floors. Half blind and completely crazed, it crashes into his ankles with a force that would break a mortal canine's neck. But the demon dog merely rolls on its back and springs to its feet, howling in defiance, its bloodshot eyes full of fury, baring every one of its broken, haphazard teeth.

"Oh my dears, what have you done to upset poor Daisy Mae?"

The voice calling from a distant room is clear and strong, as prosecutorial as Michael during a closing argument, accusing her guests sight unseen of heinous acts of animal cruelty.

"It's Katherine and Michael, Miss Peterson," Kit shouts, enunciating every word clearly since the old woman's eardrums are not nearly as well preserved as her vocal cords. "I'm so sorry we're late."

"I'd given up on you! I thought you'd abandoned me."

"Just give us a minute," Kit calls back. "I told you there'd be hell to pay," she whispers to her husband.

"You could have come without me."

"I don't ask much of you, Michael."

She's right. She doesn't, but she insists he accompany her on these biweekly pilgrimages. His fearless wife is easily intimidated by this snake of an old lady.

"I brought some things that need to go in the refrigerator, Miss P," she hollers. "I'll be in the kitchen, but Michael's going to bring you an aperitif."

He trudges down the long hallway to the sunroom, his footsteps raising a cloud of ambient dust, a glass of cheap jug sherry, thick and sweet as syrup, in hand. The panorama outside the ancient panels of thin, brittle, mud-streaked glass is magnificent—rolling, gentle hills and lively streams and thick copses of bare hardwood trees. From this privileged vantage point, the Brandywine Valley, splendid in every season, even the gray, wet days of early March, seems to exist for Miss Peterson's exclusive pleasure. Random crocuses peek through the last lingering patches of unblemished snow. A quick red flash—a fox, most likely—streaks through the boxwood hedge. He remembers his first sojourn into Chester County and this sepia-tinted Wyeth landscape of weathered barns and winter fields. His destination was Highbrook, the Morris family seat, no street address necessary, an imposing sixteen-room stone pile at the end of a long, meandering private road through property the maternal line of the woman who would one day be his wife had owned for nearly two centuries.

"Oh, Daisy Mae, you naughty girl, come here," Miss Peterson insists, reaching to gather up the dog. Michael, of course, is ignored.

"Hello, Eleanor," he greets her, managing to suppress the instinct to kneel in her royal presence.

"Oh, Michael, so good to see you," she says, entirely insincere. She shifts in her chair and allows him to offer a chaste kiss. She doesn't bother to conceal her irritation at being distracted from the sonorous proclamations of the smug, overstuffed bratwurst moderator as he introduces the combatants on *Meet the Press.*

Eleanor Peterson will be one hundred years old next month.

Her training as a ballerina is still apparent in her carriage. Grace and agility long ago deserted her joints and muscles, but she moves with the speed and determination of a much younger woman. Her arrogance and narcissism and almost sinful pride are undiminished more than six decades after her final curtain call. And her conviction in her own immortality remains unshaken even as she refuses to acknowledge the persistent signs of frailty such as memory lapses and frequent bouts of incontinence. More and more, her world is confined to this Prairie Style mausoleum, the folly of a second-rate architect and disciple of Wright.

"My dear, what *have* you been eating?" she asks as Kit enters the room.

Formalities like polite salutations aren't necessary when you share a bond as long as theirs. Honesty is valued above any reticence over causing bruised feelings. Directness is a virtue. Miss Peterson's hypercritical eye observes what the black leggings and cashmere turtleneck, the native costume of a Parisian waif, so expertly camouflage. Kit is putting on weight. A whole pound. Possibly two!

"I know, I know," his wife confesses, abashed. "I'm barely eating anything and I can't lose this extra baggage."

"Well, you're going to have to be more careful now that you're approaching the change," Miss Peterson warns.

"I've got years until that happens!" Kit protests. "My mother didn't start menopause until she was fifty-six!"

"Well, my dear, I couldn't *wait* for it to start. All that fuss and bother and bloating once a month."

The very thought of it disgusts her. She pinches her lips and frowns, not amused by the memory of bulky belts and napkins. "This sherry is absolutely delightful!" she exclaims, polishing off her drink in three swift draws.

"Michael, why don't you get Miss P another glass."

Gladly. He'd do anything for the briefest respite from the carping and barbed insults. He walks back to the kitchen, the vintage fifties appliances still in working order. Michael fishes around the deep recesses of Miss P's refrigerator, a brave and desperate act. Christ only knows what he might find in here . . . fossilized vegetables, cheese rind penicillin, the Lindbergh baby. It's not even noon, but he's earned a beer for agreeing to spend Sunday morning with

Miss P. He doesn't care if it was bottled before Prohibition. He's going to need to build a small buzz if they're going to make it through the visit without him breaking the old bitch's neck. He finds an ancient can of Miller High Life, vintage unknown, buried deep in the recesses of the antique Philco, and plops down on a chair. He pulls out his cell and dials a number with a Western Pennsylvania area code. Even enduring a few moments of his half sister Polly's monosyllabic, caustic remarks is preferable to returning to the sunroom to suffer through the interminable running commentary of an ancient, virginal narcissist.

"She's sleeping," Polly's step-granddaughter informs him. "I'll wake her up."

"No. Let her sleep. How's she doing?"

"The same," the young woman answers. "She's as mean as ever."

"Tell her to call Frankie today. It's his birthday."

"Does she have his number?"

"Repeat it to me," he insists after giving her Frankie's cell, suspecting the little brat couldn't be bothered to write it down. "Make sure she calls him."

"I will. I will," she insists, before hanging up.

He leans back and exhales, staring out the kitchen window. He wonders who's going to inherit this acreage after the old girl finally croaks. (Then, of course, he's been wondering that ever since his first visit to the Shrine of Terpsichore all those many years ago when he was naïve enough to think the reading of the will was imminent.) Miss Peterson grew up on the property, returning after her "triumph" in New York. She's lived here ever since, supplementing the monthly sums from a trust fund with private lessons for little girls with dreams of tutus and footlights and Prince Charmings in tights, including one aspiring ballerina named Katherine Morris Scott. The closest Kit ever got to a grand career on the stage were the recitals scheduled to demonstrate the progress of the aspiring prima ballerinas to their check-writing parents. None of them, Michael's future wife included, ever displayed any promise of becoming the next Dame Margot Fonteyn, but Miss Peterson's influence has been profound, her protégés distinguished by their lifelong devotion to the classical ballet, their morbid obsession with their caloric intake and the bathroom scale, and their ability to sneak up and catch their husbands red-handed, a benefit of all those years prancing about *en pointe*.

"Michael, why are you sitting in here alone getting drunk before lunch?"

"I'm hardly getting drunk on half a can of beer."

"God, she's in a foul mood today. You can't leave me alone with her in there."

"What's she complaining about now?"

"She's on a tirade about Obama. She thinks he's being fawned over because he's black. Come on, fifteen more minutes. That's all I'm asking. We have to get home and make sure everything is under control. I don't want the entire neighborhood showing up and have nothing to offer but a bag of Oreos."

They could have bought a warehouse of Oreos with the money they're paying for the spread being prepared for their guests. "Life Is Sweet," the coyly named caterer renowned for its baked goods and sugary confections, is perfectly capable of preparing a dessert buffet for forty guests without any interference from the woman paying the bill. The hypercritical subscribers of *Main Line Life* have voted its services the best in the western suburbs six years in a row. But, for once, he's grateful for his wife's conviction that, no matter the task at hand, it can only be performed correctly under her strict supervision. The usual two-hour biweekly pilgrimage to the Shrine is being cut to sixty minutes.

"Have you talked to your brother this morning?"

"He didn't pick up the phone. He was probably at Mass. I'll call again a little later."

"I left him a message yesterday reminding him about the open house tonight. I feel like we've abandoned him on his birthday. The caterer did a beautiful job with his cake. It'll be a shame if he doesn't show."

"Oh, for Christ's sake, Kit. You didn't tell him he could bring that little wetback, did you? We agreed on that one at least, didn't we?" he asks, suddenly suspicious.

"Charming, Michael. I see you really took the lessons of your diversity training to heart."

"I think I prefer the company in the other room," he says, only half joking, as he stands up, a half-drunk beer in one hand and a cream sherry refill in the other.

All Frankie wants for his birthday is twenty-four hours of serenity. At least he was spared an argument this morning. He can't fight with himself and Mariano hasn't been home for two days. These suspicious disappearances are getting to be routine. The first time Mariano stayed out all night, Frankie had panicked. He'd paced the floors until dawn, certain the boy was lying in a gutter, bloodied and broken. He'd been too relieved to be angry when Mariano walked through the door, more than twenty-four hours after having gone missing, looking like he hadn't slept. He'd claimed he'd gone to Baltimore to see his brother and missed the last train back; he couldn't call because he'd forgotten to take a charger for his phone. Now he doesn't even bother with excuses for his vanishing acts. Weeks will go by without incident, then Mariano will receive a phone call and disappear, often without even saying good-bye. If he's not back by midnight, Frankie will pop an Ambien and succumb to pharmaceutically induced sleep. Mariano's usually exhausted when he returns, but occasionally he comes back jacked, wired, flying into a rage if Frankie has the temerity to ask where he's been.

He's trying to be an indulgent husband. He'd sworn he'd never be a doormat again after Charlie Haldermann died, but a man pushing fifty can't expect fidelity if he takes up with a boy with raging hormones and the energy to fuck two or three times a day. But today is his birthday, for Christ's sake, and he shouldn't be sitting alone in his usual pew trying not to doze off during Jack's uninspiring sermon on the path to salvation. The service seems interminable. His knees are creaking and his back aches and he wants to shout hallelujah when Jack announces the Mass is ended, Go in Peace. They have sixth row, center orchestra seats at the Academy for the matinee performance of *Le Nozze di Figaro.* But Jack has two baptisms after his last Mass and they'll have to rush to make the three o'clock curtain. Frankie decides he may as well use the time to run a few errands. He has prescriptions to pick up and needs a few groceries for the week.

"Happy birthday, Mr. Gagliano!"

The pretty young Cambodian pharmacist laughs as he hands Frankie a refill of his Lipitor and Niaspan.

"Don't look so surprised. Your birth date is in our records," he says cheerfully. "Doing anything special?"

"I'm too old to celebrate birthdays," he says, trying, unsuccessfully, to sound like a grumpy curmudgeon.

"I know how old you are and you're not old!"

The kid is actually flirting with him. Frankie's astonished by the effect he still has on people. He's been told all his life how good-looking he is. Handsome. Striking. Drop dead gorgeous. But he's never quite believed it. He looks in the mirror and all he sees is an aging man with a beak of a nose that seems to grow more prominent with each passing year.

"Well, I hope you've got better plans for your birthday than hanging around here, waiting for your prescription to be filled!"

"Actually, I spent the best birthday of my life right here," he says to the confused young pharmacist, remembering a magical evening at the famous South Philadelphia nightclub that occupied this site before the series of devastating fires, accidental or otherwise, unleashed an army of arson investigators and claims adjusters.

Leaving the drugstore, he stops at the grocery to pick up a can of San Marzano tomatoes, leaving him with hours to kill. It's a soggy, ugly day. The sky's a dull steel gray, overcast with lingering clouds from last night's heavy rainstorms. The wet paper trash littering the streets—napkins and wrappers and dirty paper plates—sticks to the soles of his shoes. The venerable Ninth Street outdoor curb market of sidewalk stalls and cramped and weathered shops smells like garbage, flavored with a tangy spritz of cat piss. It's a pale shadow of its storied past when the street bustled with short-tempered vendors and obstinate housewives haggling over prices in a symphony of dialects—Calabrese, Abruzzese, Sicilian, and Neapolitan. Now it's Vietnamese hawking half-rotten vegetables and Mexican mom-and-pops stocked with industrial-size cans of refried beans. There's a half-dozen boarded-up storefronts on every block. A few upscale purveyors of artisanal cheeses and luxury-grade olive oils survive by selling their wares to the *medigan'* who descend on the neighborhood for weekend field trips, but the butchers who sold Papa's wives beautiful filets and crown roasts have fled to Jersey and the meat counters are piled high with chicken necks and cheap, fatty cuts of pork. You can still get decent antipasti and butter cookies if you know where to go. Frankie stops to admire the Easter decorations in the bakery window. The yellow and lavender straw and pastel plastic eggs are a welcome splash of color, promising springtime on a dreary late-winter day. He stops in to place his order for marzipan Paschal Lambs for the Easter baskets and decides to treat himself to a cannoli. You only have one birthday a year. The baker's wife insists he buy a half dozen. She'll make a deal, six for the price of five.

He makes a spur-of-the-moment decision and, instead of going home, turns left at his block toward the Ninth Street Merchants Alliance Leisure Timers "clubhouse." The "boys," the youngest in their mid-seventies and more than a few over eighty, will appreciate a box of cannoli, and spending an hour or two listening to a bunch of cantankerous old men bitch and moan will at least be more cheerful than sitting in his house alone. The goats have been here since early Mass; the ones who are married are hiding from their nagging wives; the widowers are hoping they'll be extended a last-minute invitation for Sunday dinner.

"Francis, what do you make of all this? We got to choose between a woman and a colored guy," Albert Costellano asks as Frankie breezes through the door.

The "clubhouse" is an old storefront stripped down to a few card tables and a couple of cast-off easy chairs. The dues are ten bucks a month, which covers the heating oil bill with enough left in the kitty for a few cans of Maxwell House and a jar of powdered nondairy creamer. Generous offspring pay the rent and the monthly cable charge for the enormous high-definition flat-screen television, a gift from Francis Rocco Gagliano to honor his late father, Luigi. It's usually tuned to a ball game, played at an ear-piercing volume, but today they're cheering the governor of the Commonwealth, who's sparring an Obama-loving senator on *Meet the Press.* The governor is disparaging the junior senator from Illinois as inexperienced, a lightweight, a cream puff who'll melt in the heat of action and burst into tears if a terrorist says boo.

"He looks like a fairy," Patsy Cipriani announces. "No offense, Francis. You know what I mean."

"Who looks like a fairy?" Pete Delvecchia asks, pushing his glasses up the bridge of his nose as he looks up from the death notices in the Sunday paper.

"That Obama. He looks like a fairy."

"He looks like a nigger to me," Sal Pinto announces, cardiomyopathy and a two-pack-a-day habit leaving him short of breath, as he blows cigarette smoke through his nose. "I don't believe he's half-white."

"I seen his mother married a Chinaman after she dumped his daddy."

"I woulda killed her if she'd been my daughter."

"It's all bullshit, this stuff about his mother, to make us think he doesn't hate white people. He hates us. They all do."

"Goddamn it, Francis, why the fuck do you buy these things?" Patsy complains, frustrated by a crisp cannoli shell that's a challenge for his poorly fitting upper plate. "Next time bring a box of donuts. Soft ones. Jelly or cream."

Sunday nights are for sprawling on the sofa, watching the NFL in the fall, HBO through the winter and spring. (Michael still misses *The Sopranos,* though it was never the same after Adriana got whacked.) But tonight he refrains from complaining about being forced to abandon his comfortable routines; he even manages to rustle up a bit of enthusiasm over spending an evening with his neighbors. As he dresses, he decides to go for the extra point and please his wife by putting on a tie without an argument. A foulard seems too formal for the occasion and it isn't the season for a casual madras. After a few moments of careful thought he chooses a cheerful rep pattern with bright stripes of yellow and lime green on a navy field.

"I can't believe I didn't have to ask you to put on a tie!" Kit stands on her tiptoes and gives him an affectionate kiss on the cheek.

An hour ago, he'd left his nine-year-old son, Danny, in the kitchen with the nanny, recounting the plot of *The Forbidden King-*

dom in exhaustive detail, complete with sound effects. He'd surprised Kit as she stood in her closet, trying to decide if a black cocktail dress was too dressy for an informal Sunday evening dinner. The familiar sight of his wife in lace bra and bikinis was oddly provocative, her prominent shoulder bones and swan-like neck arousing. She'd hesitated, her back stiffening, when he placed his hands on her waist. She'd protested lightly, saying she'd just finished blow-drying her hair and putting on her makeup; they were due at the Stapletons' in an hour. But he pulled her toward him, his erection leaving no doubt of his intentions. She'd shivered as he slipped his thumbs into the waistband of her panties and whimpered as he laid her down on the bed. Afterward, she'd made a small fuss, complaining about needing to do her face again, but he heard her singing "I Dreamed a Dream" in the bathroom so he knew he had pleased her.

"You look very handsome tonight," she says, her voice barely more than a whisper in a rare, shy moment, as she straightens the knot in his tie.

He starts to make a small joke, but desists, understanding any response other than a compliment will be a disappointment.

"You look very lovely every night," he says.

"I better get downstairs and soothe Jocelyn's ruffled feathers one last time," Kit says.

The nanny had begrudgingly accepted a two-hundred-dollar gratuity to assist the lady of the house this evening. She'd resented being asked to help pour coffee and tea. *You would think I'd asked her to wear a uniform and call the guests sir and ma'am.* Jocelyn had protested she wasn't a domestic, some Mammy or Aunt Jemima. She had driven a hard bargain, insisting on both cash under the table and a full day off, with pay, the next time her Christian Missionary Alliance tent show revival pulls into town. "Life Is Sweet" has certainly earned all the accolades heaped upon it by the readers of *Main Line Life.* The dining room table looks like a photo spread in the pages of *Food & Wine,* with whimsically folded napkins and a glorious floral centerpiece of white lilies and red tulips in a museum-quality vase. The tarts and cakes are artfully displayed on sterling serving dishes and there are banks of candles that will cast a soft glow on the charming Chinese export porcelain on loan from Dodie.

"Okay, then," Kit says, her roving eye confirming that, in fact, every detail is perfect. "Danny, we're leaving. Don't give Jocelyn grief when she says it's time for bed." She shrugs when he doesn't answer and tells Jocelyn to call on her cell if there are any problems. The nanny arches an eyebrow, skeptical, unable to imagine a crisis she's not better equipped to handle than her employer. "And please tell Scottie to be dressed and downstairs to greet our guests when they arrive."

Michael is waiting outside, strolling the parameters of home-sweet-home, inspecting for evidence of damage from last night's heavy rains. He places his palm on a black watermark on the wall, hoping it's dry, nothing more than an ancient stain that had improbably escaped his notice. But, of course, it's wet, meaning Jupiter Pluvius has found yet another leak in the seams of the roof. He'd known this house was a folly the first time he'd laid his experienced eyes on it. His childhood had been spent as forced labor in Papa's Sisyphean struggle to preserve the decaying charms of a city property constructed the same year real estate developers were building this neighborhood of Shingle Style classics on the Pennsylvania Railroad line. But Kit was insistent, impressed by the majestic front gables and soaring chimneys and charmed by the fine period details like the exposed beam ends carved into an exotic bestiary and the diamond-paned, lead-glazed windows.

Kit had never considered the expense of the upkeep of a century-old residence an impediment. She'd grown up in a House with a Name, the legacy of her mother, Dorothy Pugh Morris. They'd put a large down payment, a gift from her parents, on "Sleepy Peter's Quiet Nook," a minor architectural gem with a wraparound porch of locally quarried stone, shaded by a cluster of massive oaks older than the nation. He's invested blood, sweat, tears, and endless weekends in maintaining "the Nook," as they call it. He acts like it's a sacrifice and a burden, but he loves their home as much as his wife does, having dreamed as a boy growing up on a city block that one day he would live in a house he could walk around.

"Let's do this," she says when she finally emerges. She picks up his hand and they stroll along Walnut Avenue, headed for the first stop of the night.

In a few weeks, flowering trees and shrubs will greet the arrival of spring and the air will be fragrant with peat moss and cedar chips. The stately houses are solid stone and brick, most sheathed in shingles, all lovingly restored and maintained. The luxury imports parked in the driveways confirm the prosperity of the residents at each address. Michael hadn't balked at their thousand-dollar donation to support the community library association, the tribute tendered to participate in the neighborhood's progressive dinner, three courses served at different households with the entire group convening for coffee and dessert at the final venue of the night.

First stop is drinks and hors d'oeuvres at the Stapleton residence. He's an ophthalmologist at Penn and she's the development director at a nonprofit energy company. But their professions are merely incidental to their true vocations as "travelers," constantly departing to and arriving from exotic locations like Katmandu and Papua New Guinea, the Incan ruins and the Russian steppes. Jonathan's wrist is in a cast, broken on a kayaking expedition to New Zealand; Sydney frets it won't be healed before the archeological dig on Crete that's scheduled for May. The house is full of eclectic clutter collected on their journeys to every continent on the planet. Kit is across the room, listening to a youngish matron whose scalp is wrapped in a Hermès scarf describe the horrors of chemotherapy. She gives him a concerned look as he reaches for another helping of cocktail weenies, forever concerned about his HDL levels and triglycerides. He'd like a second bourbon and water, but exercises discretion, having put nothing solid in his stomach all day but a peanut butter sandwich after the pilgrimage to Miss P's and now a handful of hors d'oeuvres.

Anyway, it's time to move on to the next venue, the home of the president of the Anthony Wayne Film Society, for the soup-and-salad course. Madame President is an intimidating figure despite being a tiny sparrow of a woman. She dresses in flowing caftans, hiding her withered right arm and claw-like hand in the deep folds of the fabric. Five decades haven't tempered her bitterness at contracting polio just months before the announcement of the Salk vaccine. She runs her provincial film club like a sour autocrat, imposing her taste on the meek and insecure. Her house is sparsely furnished so as not to distract the eye of visitors from the walls where original movie posters are framed behind museum-quality glass and expertly displayed by professional installers and lighting designers. The classics, *The Maltese Falcon* and *L'Avventura, Jules et Jim* and *Vertigo,* hang side by side with obscure little cult films, *You'll Like My Mother,* a B-movie thriller, and *Duel of the Titans,* a Cinecittà sword-and-sandals epic. The hostess backs Michael into a corner while he's chewing a mouthful of arugula, assaulting him with what, in most circumstances, would be a benign enough question.

"What movies have you seen lately?"

Any response is likely to elicit a lecture on the crippling impact of Hollywood economics on artistic expression, tendered with a healthy dose of withering contempt for the taste of the mass audience, including one Michael Rocco Gagliano.

"Kit and I took our son to see *The Forbidden Kingdom* this weekend," he says, expecting to receive a good tongue lashing.

But Madame President heartily approves, launching into a lengthy appreciation of Asian martial arts exploitation flicks and a surprising affection for the talents of Mr. Jackie Chan. He's flattered to receive the seal of approval, especially after she moves on to excoriate the pregnant wife of an investment adviser who foolishly admits that her favorite movie is *Titanic.* Kit whispers in his ear that she'll only be staying at the next stop a few moments. Soup and salad have satisfied her appetite and she needs to get home to help Jocelyn prepare for the big rush when the traveling party convenes at the Nook for coffee and dessert.

"I'll leave with you," he offers.

"No. You stay. You don't want to hurt Pattycake's feelings, do you?"

Patricia Morehouse Rush, known as Pattycake since childhood, is the North Wayne neighbor he's most genuinely fond of. He feels a kinship with her rebel spirit, both of them having escaped the restraints of their very different upbringings. She was born in the Oak Lane Queen Anne where she resides, having returned several decades ago from the Bay Area to nurse her invalid father, one of the Pennsylvania Railroad executives ordered to move from the city to populate the communities on the suburban line. Rumor has it she's an old lesbian and her close-cropped silver hair and her habit of wearing sandals in even the dead of winter is enough evidence to confirm the Sapphic suspicions. She's the cheeriest octogenarian he's ever met, with a sunny disposition, even when raging against clitoral circumcision in sub-Saharan Africa and the creationist assault on secular humanism being waged within the local school board. There's an agreement on a moratorium on political discussions tonight, but Pattycake wears her huge Obama '08 button without comment or protest, a concession to her age and standing in the community. Her frayed, shabby house is warm and welcoming. Her Moroccan chicken tagine is legendary and the music softly playing in the background is as comfy and familiar as an old slipper—Joni singing about big yellow taxis and the ladies of the canyon, Sweet Baby James warbling about trials of fire and rain. She's introducing a young Organizing for America campaign worker she's invited to the party to browbeat her more politically diffident neighbors into voting for the charismatic young senator from Illinois.

Finally, the traveling party is herded to the Nook to gather for a speech about the importance of supporting community libraries. His house is crowded with well-meaning donors patting their tummies, insisting they're too stuffed to even look at the dessert table while loading slices of hazelnut cake onto Dodie's china. They swear to go back on their diets tomorrow, after burning off these extravagant calories with a five-mile run. Jocelyn has decided to be gracious to their guests. She's lavishing special attention on women of an age to soon be interviewing prospective nannies. Good career planning, Michael decides, as Danny soon will no longer need the services of a full-time minder.

"Where's Kit?" he asks her, not finding his wife engaged in any of the clusters of conversation around the dining room table. She's not in the living room where the chair of the board of Literary Legacy is charming her audience by praising their willingness to pledge substantial tax deductions to the coffers. She's not in the kitchen, where he surprises a junior partner from Kit's firm, married to a newly tenured professor at the Bryn Mawr College Graduate School of Social Work, in an intimate clutch with the sinewy wife of a cardiac surgeon who's hitting on the neighborhood's newest trophy bride in the next room. Kit's absence is noted by the guests who are anxious to shower praise on the marvelous baked goods. Michael makes excuses, promising to convey their compliments.

He swings through the rooms of the first floor a second time, then slips upstairs, unnoticed. Kit's behavior is completely out of character. Rudeness to guests is anathema to his well-bred wife. Something must be wrong. Danny's in his room, reading past his bedtime. Michael kisses him on the forehead and takes away his book. It's time for lights out and the adventures of the Wimpy Kid can wait until tomorrow. He hasn't seen his mother; she hasn't come in to say good night.

Scottie's bedroom door is open. His stepdaughter's sprawled on her bed, tapping her foot to the beat in her earphones, absorbed in the message she's texting into her cell phone. He bangs on the door and she looks up and pulls the buds from her ears. She's still wearing her lacrosse gear; her hair's unwashed, pulled into a tight ponytail.

"Do you know where your mother is?" he asks, irritated by her blatant defiance of Kit's wishes that she look presentable when the traveling party arrived.

"Your bedroom, I guess?" she says.

He finds Kit sitting on their bed, engaged in a one-way conversation with a voice-mail box.

". . . so, I hope you had a wonderful birthday. I miss you. I'll talk to you soon."

"He never called you back?"

"No, and it's been bothering me all night. I need to get back downstairs. Call that priest and make sure your brother was at that opera. I want to be able to sleep tonight."

"Now who's overreacting?"

"I've been married to you too long, I suppose. Dodie warned me I'd end up a big drama queen like all you Eye-talians."

"I think the word she uses is *dago*."

"I was being polite," she says, laughing, as she stands to rejoin their guests.

* * *

The performance was glorious, the cast in fine voice. Afterward, Jack announced they had reservations at the Fountain Room. Frankie insisted they go dutch, but Jack was adamant. His generosity has been almost embarrassing. Diocesan priests aren't flush with cash.

"What else do I have to spend my money on?" Jack scoffed, dismissing Frankie's protest. "You can't take it with you when you go."

He at least allows Frankie to pay the cab fare home and buy the nightcap the birthday boy insists they have at the bar of one of the Ninth Street red gravy houses. Jack was up at six to say the first of two Sunday Masses and must be exhausted, but Frankie dreads going home, not knowing what to expect. His phone has been turned off since before morning Mass. He didn't want to spoil the celebration spending the day on high alert for a call from Mariano. Jack apologizes, stifling a yawn. Frankie settles the check and walks the priest back to the rectory. They embrace at the front door and Frankie makes his way home alone.

It's seven blocks on foot from door to door, enough time for him to clear his head. He pauses to stare at the imposing building at the corner of Eighth and Carpenter, the house he's lived in his entire forty-eight years. It's the third incarnation of the building, a three-story late-nineteenth-century property first known as F. GASPARI CO., DRUGS, the name memorialized in the mosaic floor tiles that still greet customers as they cross the threshold.

Frankie's grandfather had bought the property from the widow of the prosperous apothecary. Papa had shared his father's fierce pride in the faux-Georgian details—the modillion cornices, the limestone keystones, the oriel windows sheathed in decorative cast-iron panels—that distinguished their impressive domicile from its brown-paper-wrapper neighbors. Its careful preservation was his consuming passion and he put his boys to work as soon as they were able to climb a ladder and handle a brush, forcing them to spend countless hours scraping the rust from the ornamental metal Wedgwood swags and funerary wreaths and applying fresh coats of paint to the Corinthian column that anchors the portico at the corner entrance to the barbershop. But he'd refused to upgrade the living quarters upstairs, ignoring the complaints of each of his wives, believing that only spoiled *medigan'* insisted on expensive modern conveniences like dishwashers and central air. Under Frankie's tasteful supervision, the refurbished interiors, stripped to their essence and reconceived with stark and sparse surfaces, rivals, even surpasses, the lovingly maintained exteriors.

A light in the window of the second floor means that Mariano has found his way home. Frankie unlocks the shop door, finding everything in order, neat and tidy, ready for the next appointment. The silence is encouraging as he creeps up the steps, making as little noise as possible. Mariano's sitting at the kitchen island, his bare feet hooked around the spokes of the counter stool, issuing battle commands to the miniature Japanese Bakugan action figures he'd found in the kitchen drawer dedicated to odds and ends, forgotten toys Frankie's nephew had left behind more than a year ago.

"*Hola,* Frankie. Do you want to play?" he asks, looking impossibly young, an innocent, no more dangerous than a child. The power of his sweet smile to charm is undiminished by the regrettable state of his teeth.

Frankie's body aches for sleep, but he kicks off his shoes and boils water for a cup of Cozy Comfort tea. He pours Mariano another of the sugary Mexican fruit sodas the boy adores, then sits down at the island, selecting a serpent, a dragon, and a winged predator for his army, ready to answer the call to battle.

"Te amo," Mariano says shyly, uncertain if he's been forgiven for his latest disappearance. "*Feliz cumpleaños.* Happy birthday," he says, handing Frankie a box of drugstore chocolates tied with red ribbon. The card expresses his sincere birthday wishes for a special love, signed YOUR MARIANO, in crude block letters.

"*Te amo,* too," Frankie assures him, squeezing his palm and planting a gentle kiss on his forehead.

March 11, 2008

"I don't feel like I'm forty-eight, Mikey," Frankie says, unfolding his napkin and placing it on his lap.

He could pass for ten, even fifteen, years younger than a man rapidly approaching his half-century mark. Strangers probably assume he's the younger of the two brothers. Michael's own hair, clipped close to the scalp, is thinning slightly on top and he hasn't escaped the curse of a big man, his solid weight constantly threatening to settle into pounds of fat.

"Mikey, good to see you. You never change," the waiter greets him as he approaches their table.

He's either blind or angling for a good tip. Michael's known him since the first day of first grade at Saint Catherine of Siena Elementary. Donnie's his name, Dante on the baptismal certificate.

"Hey, Donnie. You're looking good," he lies.

Donnie's looking like a pack-and-a-half of Marlboro Reds a day and a steady diet of gristle and grease on a fresh-baked hoagie roll. But Michael's always on his best behavior whenever he returns to the neighborhood, solicitous, full of compliments, remembering to ask after people's parents, sending them his best. He's under constant scrutiny. People who have known him since he was born study his body language, the inflections of his voice, searching for any telltale sign that success has gone to his head, that he thinks he's better than they are and needs to be reminded who he is and where he came from. Everything about him is suspect. His wife. His address. His car. Even his choice of apparel—his suits boxy rather than fitted, button-down collars, no cuff links or French cuffs, blunt-toed lace-ups, never loafers—is questionable in a neighborhood where success is measured by sartorial excess.

"I still hate that asshole," Michael confides in a stage whisper after thanking Donnie for reciting the menu specials twice. "I can still hear his fucking voice mocking me in the changing room at the Montrose Street pool. *Moolie Cazzo,* he called me. Now he acts like we were best friends, hoping for a big tip."

"Mikey, they didn't circumcise baby boys back in the old country. Papa probably thought some witch would steal our foreskins and use them to put a curse on the family. He believed in that kind of stuff."

"It was fucking embarrassing. Donnie told all his friends I must be half-*moulinyan* because the black guys who came down from South Street were the only other boys at the pool who were uncut. Papa should have stayed in Italy if he didn't want to live like an American."

"He was eight years old when he came over. I don't think he had any choice in the matter."

"He could have gone back and left us alone."

"Why are you getting so worked up about a waiter making fun of your uncut cock thirty-five years ago? Your wife isn't complaining, is she?"

Donnie appears and uncorks a bottle of very expensive Barolo tableside.

"That's fine, Donnie. Thank you," Michael says, turning his attention back to his brother. "She's just happy it's bigger than three inches," he says, almost gargling a glass of wine. "I don't know how that piece of shit she was married to before me gets so much action with such a tiny *cazzo.* He must be a magician when it comes to using his tongue."

"You're such a damn hypocrite, Michael. You're forgetting I changed your son's diapers."

"Things are different now. Times change."

"How so?" Frankie asks, skeptical.

"Kit and I decided it would be traumatic for Danny when he got older if his penis didn't look like his father's. Besides, she's a progressive woman and thinks the ritual is barbaric."

"So there you have it. Give Papa credit for being ahead of the times. Oh, I almost forgot. Paulina left me a birthday message Sunday, Mikey. She didn't sound well when I called her back yesterday. Maybe we shouldn't wait for her birthday to visit."

"She's been dying for five years. I think she'll make it to the end of the month."

Their childhood memories of their half sister are shrouded in a cloud of smoke from her Lucky Strikes. She returned to Philadelphia only for state occasions like funerals and christenings, and contact with her father's second family is now limited to annual birthday visits by her half brothers, infrequent telephone calls, and monthly deposits to her bank account to supplement her meager disability checks. The tenuous connection is one Michael would happily sever. He's never understood his brother's attachment to their resentful half sibling. But Frankie is sentimental and believes that blood is thicker than . . . well, if not water, than at least apathy.

"Speaking of my wife, she was really upset about Sunday night."

"I told both of you I'd get there if I could. No promises."

"Well, you scared the shit out of her when she couldn't reach you. Why the hell did you have your phone turned off? Isn't that the point of modern telecommunications? So you can be reached at any time?"

"My Way" is being piped in through the speakers. It's the lousy late-vintage Ol' Blue Eyes who's revered here. Michael wishes they would play the classic Capitol recordings or gems from the exquisite Columbia era. Donnie brings Michael a fourteen-ounce strip steak, oozing blood, and filets a Dover sole tableside for Frankie. There's a sudden buzz in the restaurant, the distinctive energy when a *presence* enters the room. The maître d' is seating the head coach of the Villanova basketball team two tables away. Men young and old approach him, wanting to wish him success in the upcoming tournament, offering unsolicited advice on how to deploy his point guard. The Gagliano brothers, the sons of a barber, appreciate his fine tailoring and impeccable grooming. Frankie admires the sharp lines of his razor cut. Michael takes advantage of the time-out in their argument over Polly to reach for the envelope in his pocket and hand Frankie a birthday card enclosing a very generous Nordstrom gift certificate.

"And I've got tickets for the Red Sox series in June. You and me and Danny. A Gagliano family outing. Men only. No women permitted. How about it?"

"Maybe Mariano would like to go, too," Frankie dares to say, knowing that the subject is going to spoil the rest of the evening.

He wants to seem appreciative, but his brother's resistance to his relationship with Mariano is frustrating. Marriage and fatherhood have mellowed Michael, who, at times, can be the true son of the father he'd hated: obstinate, hot-tempered, quick to criticize, judgmental. He's become more tolerant, though Frankie isn't so dense as to not recognize that his brother's comfort level with homosexuality is directly correlated to the level of sexual activity in Frankie's life. Charlie Haldermann's presence irritated Michael, but the arrival of Mariano clearly angers him.

"What I really want for my birthday is a little help. It's not like I'm asking you to do it yourself. I know you're not an immigration lawyer. But you said you'd help me find one, a good one."

"I never said that, Frankie. You're putting words in my mouth."

"What have you got against him, Mikey? Is it because he's Mexican? You're no different from the boys down at the Leisure Timers clubhouse, bitching and moaning about how the wetbacks are taking over."

The refugees from Puebla are the latest wave of immigrants to infiltrate South Philadelphia. Ten, fifteen years ago it was the Vietnamese and Cambodians who were struggling to save enough money for down payments on the row houses of dead Italians whose heirs had decamped to housing developments across the bridge in Jersey. The Asians, their hard work rewarded, are moving on to greener pastures, meaning suburban real estate with more convenient parking for their pho shops and nail salons. Now it's the Mexicans who gather at the corner of Ninth and Washington at sunrise, seeking offers of day work. At night, they return to crowded apartments meant for families of four, sleeping in shifts on mattresses thrown on the floor. The mom-and-pop groceries do a brisk business in phone cards and CDs of mariachi music.

They don't seem to shy away from backbreaking labor. Michael certainly admires their work ethic. Overnight, they seem to be everywhere he goes. Emptying wastebaskets and scrubbing toilets after the office closes for the night. Hauling sod and pruning azaleas at his home in lovely Wayne. Clearing tables in the front rooms of expensive restaurants. Hell, there are probably four or five of them chopping onions and scrubbing skillets back in the kitchen. He's sure they're all perfectly nice people wanting nothing more than a little piece of the American dream. They're no different from the first Gagliano to reach these shores, arriving at the Port Authority of New York with three dollars in his pocket and the drive to become a respected citizen with his own prosperous business and a legacy to pass on to his son. Michael, the child of an immigrant, has got nothing against Mexicans, but this Mariano is a different story. He's been a prosecutor long enough to recognize a stone-cold sociopath when he sees one.

"Has he ever told you how he got here?" Michael asks, trying to sound like a rational lawyer rather than a suspicious brother.

"What difference does it make how he got here? He's here. And I want him to stay."

"Look, Frankie, I'm no expert, but I think immigration would like to know if he came here legally or if he snuck across the border."

"If you don't want to help us, I can ask Jack. He's done counseling for one of the immigration advocacy groups and has a lot of contacts in the Mexican community. I'm sure he knows someone who can refer us to a good lawyer."

Frankie's rolling the dice, banking on his brother's inbred resentment of the priest. Mikey's never completely overcome the jealousy he'd felt as a motherless boy competing with the future pastor for his brother's attention and affection. Michael doesn't know Jack dislikes Mariano even more than he does and has already refused to be a party to what he thinks is a disaster in the making.

"Hey, Donnie," Michael calls. "Can you bring me a bourbon on the rocks? Is this what you really want, Frankie? Are you sure?"

"Yes. Please."

"Don't make me regret it," Michael grumbles, trying to ignore a small, nagging voice in the back of his head warning him he's making a big mistake, urging him to put an end to this folly before it's too late.

"You won't. I promise," Frankie swears, as Donnie presents him with a surprise tiramisu, complete with a single burning candle, leading the diners at the neighboring tables in a chorus of "Happy Birthday." Even the famous coach joins in, his loud, unmusical voice, used to issuing commands from the sidelines of the basketball court, drowning out the others.

MARCH 17, 2008

"I'd love it if the campaign could get his endorsement. Maybe we could peel away some of these kids who think Obama's the Second Coming of Christ."

Steven Kettleman is staring wistfully at the dog-eared copy of the *Born to Run* album cover, the Boss's autograph scrawled across his youthful face, preserved for posterity under museum-quality glass and proudly displayed on Michael's office wall. Back in high school, Michael beat his rusted-out Gremlin to death making countless road trips up the New Jersey Turnpike, blasting "Hungry Heart" and "Prove It All Night" full volume on the cassette deck. He was a true fan boy, obsessed and demented, chasing Springsteen up and down the Atlantic Seaboard, from the Spectrum to the Meadowlands to the Garden, spending every spare penny he earned bussing tables five nights a week on gas and tolls and tickets and official tour merchandise. His 3.9 average at the Academy earned him special dispensation to make school-night road trips to North Jersey and Manhattan, though his father blamed Bruce for costing him a perfect score when he got home from a Long Island Coliseum show at three in the morning the day of the SATs. (Princeton didn't hold it against a heavily recruited sixty-minute player that he only scored 1580.)

Tonight is a command performance. No excuses permitted. Perfect attendance is mandatory at the Clinton fund-raiser hosted by Steven Kettleman, the first Democrat in living memory to be elected District Attorney of Delaware County. His legal career is almost an afterthought these days. Kettleman's taken up residence on the Acela line, his life in constant transit up and down the Northeast Corridor as he travels to and from top-secret campaign strategy sessions, accessible by BlackBerry in the event a crime occurs that's salacious enough to warrant an interview on the evening news. He's certainly more fashionably attired these days, always prepared to give a sound bite to the national press on behalf of the campaign.

"Ride with me into town, Michael. We'll talk about it in the car," Kettleman says, his exasperation at Michael's insistence they discuss the Corcoran stay of execution apparent by his mirthless smile. His tiny eyes bore through the lenses of his stylish glasses. Designer frames might be rakish on the angular faces of the young models in *GQ* and *Men's Vogue,* but they look slightly ridiculous on a middle-aged lawyer from Media, Pennsylvania.

"I got roped into it," Michael complains when he calls his wife at her office. "I'm coming into town with him. It's the only goddamn time he can find to do his actual fucking job."

"Well, thank him for not allowing me to be a grass widow again tonight."

This evening will be the third fund-raising event she's attended this month despite having reached the permissible limit on individual donations to the campaign two days after the senator announced her intention to run. God knows how much she's given to PACs and the DNC and senate candidates in states she never has and never will visit. Kit is hell-bent on spending her share of the family trusts paying reparations to progressive causes for generations of misfeasance by reactionary right-wing ancestors who'd called Highbrook their home.

"Don't leave me alone tonight to justify my existence to all those bitter, middle-aged dragon ladies," he says, only half joking.

"You've got a dispensation to have more than one bourbon if you promise to be a good boy and be on your best behavior tonight.

Just come tell Mommy if any of those mean girls aren't being nice to you," she tells him with a laugh.

This is the first anniversary in nine years that Frankie hasn't driven two hours to Ephrata, Pennsylvania, to lay a memorial wreath on Charlie's grave. He remembers as if it were yesterday the afternoon the principal of Washington's Crossing High School had called and asked if he were speaking to Charlie's "friend." Charlie had been taken by ambulance to the emergency room. The kids in the Drama Club had arrived for rehearsals and found him slumped in a seat in the auditorium, a heart attack, most likely. Frankie will trek out to Lancaster County next week and lay an offering on his tombstone. Life goes on. He's sure Charlie would understand. He'd want Frankie to be happy, after all.

The grating voice of Cathy Criniti snaps him to attention. She's clearly irritated that he isn't jumping up and down and clapping his hands because she bumped into Jennifer Aniston in the feminine-hygiene-product aisle at Walgreens while she was visiting her daughter's family in Miami.

"No, I'm listening," he insists.

He tries to sound interested, but he doesn't really give a damn whether the former Mrs. Pitt is a tampon or a napkin girl. Mondays are sacred to him, his one day of freedom from the litany of woes and troubles of confiding women. But tonight's a big night for Cathy, and Frankie has never refused a loyal client just because it was his day off. Jimmy O'Connell, a widower of three years, is going to propose to her tonight at the Ancient Order of Hibernians formal dinner in observance of the Irish high holy day. Frankie's determined to help her look her best, knowing all too well how rare a chance it is to have a last, best hope at finding your one true love.

Michael wonders if the starstruck contributors to Hillary! 2008 realize their hard-earned dollars are making it possible for him and Steven Kettleman to endure rush traffic in a luxury town car provided by the campaign, their privacy ensured by a thick glass partition separating them from the disinterested driver.

"I should have taken a piss before we left the office," Kettleman complains.

A full bladder is only one of the many distractions Michael is competing against.

"Will you please turn that fucking thing off for ten minutes, Steven? Ten minutes. The least you can do is give me ten fucking minutes of your undivided attention."

Michael has made Kit swear to stand him before a firing squad if she ever finds him barking self-importantly into a Bluetooth headset. Kettleman, of course, believes it's the perfect fashion accessory, complementing his collection of John Varvatos Trim Fit suits. He holds up two fingers, silencing his Chief Deputy while he urges whoever he's speaking with to get on with it so he can move on to more urgent business.

"Sorry, Michael," the District Attorney apologizes, sounding almost sincere as he removes the offending electronic earpiece. "McAuliffe can wait. You now have my undivided attention."

Michael makes his pitch quickly, knowing Kettleman won't be able to resist taking the next incoming call.

"I don't know why you're struggling with this. It's not a difficult decision. What we need to do next is as obvious as the substantial nose on my face," Michael argues.

"I know this is killing you, Michael. You got the conviction. You got the death sentence. You did everything within a conscientious public servant's power to put that piece of shit in the morgue."

"So, you're saying you've made up your mind."

"I'm leaning toward my decision. Strongly leaning. We're talking about the capital count here. Nothing more. The rest of the convictions still stand. Second- and third-degree murder, kidnapping, aggravated assault, unlawful restraint, false imprisonment, conspiracy, possession of an instrument of crime. Heady stuff, Michael. A second-degree conviction carries a life sentence without the possibility of parole. It's not like he'll be skipping out of the penitentiary and traipsing down the Yellow Brick Road."

"Twelve of his peers found him guilty of a capital crime. I got a first-degree conviction and the death penalty at the first trial. I'll get it again."

"Stop feeling like all of this is your responsibility, Michael. You need to let go of it at some point. You didn't fuck up. It's all part of the game. It's too bad your father-in-law isn't still on that bench,"

Kettleman says wistfully. "He would have injected the fucking bastard himself despite believing the little fairy probably had it coming for offering to suck some lowlife's dick."

Michael understands why Kettleman's hesitant to roll the dice again. The Court of Appeals has concluded the artfully worded and carefully crafted jury instruction proposed by the Commonwealth and adopted by the trial court failed to adequately charge the jury of the necessity of finding beyond a reasonable doubt that the defendant charged as an accessory had the same requisite intent to kill as the actual perpetrator in order to find him guilty of a capital offense. The Commonwealth's star witness will not be available to testify at a retrial. Last Christmas Eve, Thornton's Harley was broadsided by a drunk teenager who lost control of his SUV on the icy road. Steven Kettleman is reluctant to risk the chance that, without a dead biker's damning testimony about an agitated and blood-splattered Corcoran's statements that fateful night, a second jury might find Tommy's histrionic denials of culpability believable.

"Look, you need to get your mind off this. Focus. I've been talking to the Big Dog. He said he's willing to meet you. As a favor to me. Think about what his support will mean when you run to succeed me. Name one other candidate for a fucking county office who will be endorsed by a former President of the United States."

Michael's patient suffering under the yoke of this self-promoting blowhard is about to pay off in spades. Kettleman's just accepted the governor's offer to head the Office of General Counsel of the Commonwealth of Pennsylvania. He's being advised by an established team of political operatives that a move to Harrisburg will better position him for a run in the next midterms at a House seat in a congressional district rapidly turning blue. Michael will be named as the interim DA and is being encouraged to place his name on the ballot and run for the office at the end of Kettleman's current term.

Michael Rocco Gagliano. District Attorney of the County of Delaware of the Commonwealth of Pennsylvania. Back on track for an appointment to the federal bench or election to the state supreme court. The promise of the Note Editor of the Penn Law Review and member of the Order of the Coif, his ambitions having lain fallow for too many years, is about to be fulfilled at long last.

* * *

"Christ, I loathe this place. Why does he always schedule these events here?" Kit sighs, with the exasperated resignation she reserves for those who are definitely NOCD, Not Our Class Dear.

"He worked his ass off to get his mug up on that wall," Michael says derisively. Steven Kettleman, son of a dry cleaner from the village of Forest Hills in the Borough of Queens, takes an inordinate pride at being among the elected officials and political dealmakers whose crude charcoal caricatures have been selected to grace the mural of local personalities and sports icons on the dining room walls of the Philadelphia political establishment's favorite haunt. His portrait, vaguely resembling some cursed offspring of Colonel Sanders, is front and center, between the governor and Julius Erving. Kettleman's mug is visible from every table in the room, more prominently featured than two United States senators and the last three mayors. "You think he's going to pass up any opportunity to let it be admired?"

"Bitter, party of one," she says teasingly.

"You haven't just spent an hour sitting in traffic with him, listening to his bullshit rationale for not retrying that fucking savage on a capital charge."

Even Kit is surprised by this news. Kettleman's insistence on a vigorous prosecution of one of the vicious predators charged with killing that harmless young gay man had earned him national attention. He'd received an award from GLAAD and now has a second career as the keynote speaker at the annual banquets of the Human Rights Campaign Fund and Lambda Legal. It's impossible to believe he'd alienate a possible constituency when he's about to run for the House of Representatives.

"He's worried about an acquittal on the capital charge without that Thornton kid's testimony. He says that justice will be served by letting that animal rot in jail."

"Michael, maybe he's right. I don't know. You're out for blood. You're too close to the situation. You need to put some distance between yourself and the ghost of that poor dead boy."

"Let's get the fuck out of here," he says, in no mood for sage wisdom and advice. "I've had enough Steven Kettleman for one day. I don't think I can stomach watching him swanning it up for the goddamn governor."

"Go get a drink" she says. "An hour. We'll put in an hour and leave," she promises as she heads toward the Women's Way contingent huddled at the end of the dessert buffet. These are serious women of a certain age, none younger than perimenopausal, all well groomed and expensively coiffed, with a flair for obscenely expensive scarves from exclusive London and Paris shops and pieces of large jewelry purchased at museum craft shows. Their excitement is palpable from a safe distance across the room. The campaign has been a call to arms for this army of accomplished Boadiceas, women who, despite their numerous professional accomplishments, feel they've been shunted aside and ignored, rendered invisible, marginalized, since their bodies started to sag and their faces began to show the signs of age.

Kit comes rushing back to share the news, giddy over the rumor racing through the crowd that the President of the United States of America is about to make his grand entrance.

"Bush is coming to a Democratic fund-raiser?" Michael asks, incredulous.

"President *Clinton,*" she says. "I just heard President Clinton is going to make a surprise appearance."

A lousy evening now threatens to be even worse. Michael grows depressed at the thought of anticipating the spectacle of a room full of awestruck middle-aged women reduced to bobby-soxers, swooning over a legendary cocksman you'd think they'd want gleefully castrated for the epic humiliations endured by the long-suffering wife they adore. Instead they defend his integrity, refusing to hold him accountable for his despicable betrayal. They want to wrap him in their arms and give him a big, reassuring hug. And none of them will mind if he pinches their ass. In fact, they'll be disappointed if he doesn't.

A wave of nervous energy races through the room as all heads turn toward the entrance, hoping to see the famous shock of thick white hair. Steven Kettleman is gesturing theatrically at his anxious assistant to clear a path for the wildly anticipated arrival. But the excitement peaks and quickly plummets when the governor comes bounding through the doorway and the former president is nowhere to be seen.

"Maybe he's stuck in traffic," Kit says hopefully.

"You can always have a lovely chat with the governor," Michael says, needling her.

"Oh God, look. He's coming this way."

The room seems more crowded, much more densely peopled than just a few moments ago. Everyone is gravitating toward the gubernatorial presence, a magnet that pulls mere mortals into its orbit. He can't be, won't be, ignored, sucking up all the oxygen in the room and leaving the masses gasping for air. The governor slowly plows through the sea of bobbing heads; his awkward-looking body—a thick, brawny trunk tapering to spindly legs and dancer's feet—is surprisingly agile. He grabs every extended hand and slaps every back, satisfying his carnivorous need to touch. His smile is actually a wicked grin, all exposed teeth, confrontational, daring you to resist him. He's a man of the people, the salt of the earth, an unrestrained id with no use for nuance and subtlety. He sweeps through the room, stuffing his face with smoked salmon and capers from the trays of the passing waiters and spitting tiny pieces of pink fish into the faces of the well-heeled contributors he greets by name.

"Mike, it's good to see you!" the governor shouts as he vigorously pumps Michael's arm.

The governor is the only person on earth granted a pass to get away with using the hated diminutive "Mike."

"Governor. You're looking good."

"It's great, just great, that Steve's naming you the interim. You deserve it, Mike. You can count on me to do whatever I can for you after you announce," he assures Michael as he moves along to pounce on his next victim.

It's after seven o'clock. Mariano had promised to return in an hour when he left early this afternoon to show off his brand-new Cannondale bicycle, a gift from Frankie, to his less-fortunate friends. Frankie's going to trim his thick black locks, give him a clean, sharp neckline and trim around his ears so he'll make a good impression on the lawyer Michael's arranged for them to meet tomorrow. He'd taken a cab to Macy's in Center City late this afternoon to buy Mariano a white oxford-cloth button-down and a pair of chinos, knowing Immigration and Citizenship Services isn't likely to be impressed by a black shirt of clingy rayon and high-waisted pants chosen to flatter a bubble butt. Mariano won't be pleased with the outfit Frankie's chosen for him, but, in the end, pragmatism must prevail over a commitment to fashion, at least until he has the appropriate papers.

He tries Mariano's cell, getting only voice mail, Spanish gibberish he assumes are instructions to leave a message. Finally, at long last, his own phone rings, but it's only Jack, calling to update Frankie on the events of the day. He'd spent the morning with the parish finance director, reviewing the revenues and bemoaning the low balance of the building maintenance account. The roofers were in this afternoon for an estimate on the repairs to the flashing and tomorrow an engineer is scheduled to assess the water damage to the ceiling. He had a Pre-Cana meeting with Pete Delvecchia's teenage grandson and his six-months-pregnant fiancée.

"And I just got back from Pennsylvania Hospital, where I gave Sal Pinto the last rites."

It's the fourth time in the past year the old bastard has received the sacraments.

"What's the matter with you, Frankie? You don't seem too concerned."

"I am," he lies, anxious to get off the telephone. "It's just that I'm expecting a call from my brother. I'll call you in the morning."

Michael had one too many bourbons at the fund-raiser and slept the entire drive home, to the great relief of his wife, who was able to listen to the BBC report on the uptick of sex trafficking in North Africa without the distraction of her tipsy husband bitching about the Third Circuit and Steven Kettleman and Tommy Corcoran's lucky break. But now that he's undressed and lying in bed, he's wide-awake and his mind is obsessing over the injustices of the world. It's not fair to Carmine Torino. Not fair to the young man's heartbroken parents. Not fair to the law-abiding citizens of the Commonwealth. And not fair to Michael Rocco Gagliano, who'd earned that conviction with blood, sweat, and tears only to have it stolen from him by a panel of constipated judges. These days it's easier to get away with murder than it is to get a mortgage.

"Michael, please," Kit pleads, unable to sleep lying next to her agitated husband. He apologizes, gets out of bed, pulls on his boxers, and closes the bedroom door behind him.

His wife is right. He's obsessing. He should never have accepted the assignment, but Kettleman had appealed to his vanity, citing his years in the pressure cooker of the Philly DA's Office, insisting he didn't trust any of his other deputies to handle such a high-profile case. It was too personal, too familiar. From the moment he heard of the crime, mere hours after it was committed, he couldn't think of Carmine Torino being tortured and murdered without seeing his brother's charred body lying in that bed, dying in excruciating pain, hideously punished for being different.

He considers a nightcap, but heads for the freezer instead. He wolfs down a bowl of vanilla ice cream with chocolate syrup. Still hungry, or at least still needing to eat, he carries the leaky carton to the family room and sprawls on the couch. There's a DVD in the player in the family room, *Pinocchio,* much to his surprise, a movie Danny hasn't watched for years, having moved on from Disney fairy tales to the noise and flash of video games and live-action adventure. Anything less than a nuclear blast elicits a yawn and complete disinterest, if not utter contempt. But apparently a nine-year-old who's been pulverized by *Spy Kids* still seeks out the gentle charm of Jiminy Cricket when no one is around to tease him for being a baby. Michael has loved this fucking movie for forty years. And now technology lets him skip all those cloying scenes in the workshop with the kitten and the goldfish and start the movie as Geppetto sends naïve and trusting Pinocchio off to school with nothing more than an apple and a book satchel to defend himself against the conniving and treacherous Honest John and Gideon.

"Dad."

Danny's timid voice startles him. He looks forlorn and scared in the soft blue light cast by the television screen. His eyes are puffy, ringed with dark circles. Hobgoblins and ghosts are keeping him awake again tonight.

"What's the matter, buddy? Why aren't you in bed?"

"I heard something."

"It's just the television."

"No. Upstairs. In my room."

"You want me to go up with you? Make sure there's no one there?"

"No. I want to stay down here with you."

It's going to be hell getting him out of bed in the morning. House rules are lights out by nine, but Kit's the enforcer and Michael welcomes the company tonight.

"Can I have some?" Danny asks, looking longingly at the carton of ice cream in his father's hand.

"Just don't drip it all over your mother's carpet or we're both dead meat," Michael warns him. Danny's satisfied after a few bites and they lie together on the sofa. Danny's back is against his father's chest; Michael drapes his arm over his son. Danny, content, safe from the wild things stampeding three floors above, is completely absorbed in the little wooden boy's adventures. Sleep is out of the question as Pinocchio and Lampwick disembark from the ship and step onto Pleasure Island.

"Whoa, buddy. You smell like a wet dog."

"No way."

It's obvious Danny hadn't showered before bed and his hair needs a strong dose of shampoo. Michael remembers the long-ago days when he couldn't resist pressing his nose to his son's sweet-smelling, powered skin. That little baby has grown into a stinky kid, just as his father had been at his age, always coming up with some excuse for avoiding a bath. But the poor hygiene of boys about to enter adolescence doesn't deter his dad from hugging him and kissing the crown of his head.

"Way."

"Bullshit."

"Hey, don't let your mother hear you talking like that or she'll wash out both of our mouths with soap."

"She just says that, Dad. She never does it."

"I wouldn't bet on it. I thought you said this movie was for babies."

He kicks Michael in the shin, hard. His feet are almost comically big for a boy his age. He's growing every day. His favorite jammies are already too small; soon he won't fit into them at all. His body feels both remarkably strong and impossibly fragile. He's still got a trace of a cold. His breathing is shallow and his nose is chapped from constant wiping. He shudders as Lampwick sprouts a pair of donkey ears and a tail and, finally, morphs into a shrieking jackass.

"Dad?"

"Yep?"

"How come those boys turned into donkeys?"

"You know why. They were being punished for being bad."

"Did they turn back into boys when they said they were sorry?"

"Well, it was too late. Donkeys can't talk so they couldn't say they were sorry."

"Did those boys die when they turned into donkeys?"

"It's only a fairy tale, Danny. It's not real."

Because if it were, Tommy Corcoran would morph into a jackass and be marched to the slaughterhouse to be melted down into glue.

Halfway through Leno's monologue, just as he's about to wash down an Ambien with a glass of white wine, Frankie hears the front door slam shut, then a terrible crash and a blast of angry Spanish, followed by hysterical laughter. He races down the stairs and finds Mariano sprawled on his ass. The front wheel of the Cannondale is wedged between the broken shelves of the étagère and jars and bottles are spinning across the tile. Mariano doesn't look like he's hurt. No fractured bones are protruding from his arms and legs and there aren't any bloody gashes. He doesn't even seem uncomfortable. As a matter of fact, he looks perfectly content to sit on his bum, amused by the wreckage. He slaps away Frankie's hand when he reaches down to help him up.

"Are you all right?"

It's obvious all's not well, but Frankie doesn't know what else to say. All he can do is start picking up the shampoos and conditioners and styling gels and try to salvage the salon so nothing looks out of the ordinary when Della Infermiera arrives for her cut and color at nine. He's uncomfortable and wary. This isn't his Mariano. It's some imposter with the same face and a key to his front door. The boy seems harmless enough, giggling as he tries to pull himself to his feet. Frankie's not exactly afraid of him, but he's apprehensive. Some wild energy is emanating from him and Frankie knows a frisky, playful kitten can quickly turn into a vicious and nasty cat if it's feeling threatened. And then Mariano pounces, jumping on Frankie's back and knocking him to the floor. He laughs like it's all fun and games. He says he wants kisses, big kisses, but there's nothing that feels like love in his frantic, grasping hands. This isn't desire or passion. There's no trace of alcohol on his breath; his erratic behavior can't be explained by *cerveza* or tequila. But something's unleashed this feral beast, some drug or chemical.

Frankie pushes him away, pleading with him to calm down. Mariano's inflamed by rejection, furious, his eyes wild. He's screaming in Spanish, growing more and more agitated at his inability to make himself understood. Cursing, out of control, he punches Frankie in the face, then slams his hand on the case where Frankie displays Stevie's hat, his most treasured possession. A jagged shard of shattered glass slashes his palm. Mariano is sure he's bleeding to death and grabs Frankie by the shirt, sobbing. Frankie pushes him toward the sink and forces his hand under running water. It's a nasty cut, deep and painful, but nothing serious, no arteries compromised. Still, it needs to be stitched and bandaged and he can't drive to the hospital with a hysterical boy clinging to him. He doesn't want to attract the attention of a curious cabbie. He's going to have to call Jack and tell him not to panic, everything's under control, but he needs a ride to the emergency room.

MARCH 18, 2008

He's standing on a deserted platform, waiting for the train to arrive that will deliver him and Frankie to their half sister's faraway home. Sal Pinto gave him strict orders to not move a muscle until he returns from taking a leak. The clanking motor of the escalator to the waiting room sputters and dies. He can hear Sal Pinto upstairs arguing that someone needs to open the security gate. His godson is alone down there . . . he's just a little boy.

He shoves his hand in his pocket and touches his ticket as the train approaches the station. It wheezes to a complete stop and the doors to the passenger cars open. Frankie is standing inside, urging him to hurry. "Come on! Come on, Mikey! The train is about to leave the station!" But the suitcase is too heavy to lift. He grabs the handle and tries to drag it across the platform. Papa will be angry if he leaves it behind. It's filled with change—quarters, dimes, nickels—he's sending to his daughter. He begins to cry, not understanding why Frankie won't get off the train and help. Frankie waves as he disappears behind the closing door.

He chases the train down the tracks, but the faster he runs, the farther it recedes into the smoky distance. He hears a shrill whistle behind him and feels a charging engine speeding toward him, bearing down and . . .

And then he awakes. Just as he always does at this same, exact point of his most frequent dream.

Kit's lying on her back, her arm thrown across her eyes, breathing through her open mouth. He lifts the quilt and crawls out of bed, careful not to disturb her. She rolls onto her side and faces the wall, a notorious light sleeper. He reaches for the boxers he'd dropped on the floor and retreats again to the family room. He flops onto the sofa and picks up the remote. Those saucy little marionettes—the Dutch girl, the French can-can dancer, the Russian tsarina—will distract him from the helpless feeling he always awakens to after the dream. It's after two when he finally dozes off, Pinocchio's song, *I've got no strings to hold me down,* lulling him to sleep.

A priest comes in handy in a crisis. Jack sized up the situation quickly and bundled Frankie and the boy into the backseat, warning them to not get blood on the upholstery.

"Just let me do all the talking," he insisted.

The triage nurses and crisis workers know Jack well. They've got his number on speed dial and he never complains or hesitates when the hospital calls at all hours, day and night, seeking an ordained priest to give the sacraments to a gunshot wound or vehicular manslaughter or accidental overdose. The attending physicians are polite, deferential even, when Jack balks at the suggestion Mariano be admitted for observation after they stitch and bandage the laceration. The staff is reluctant to discharge the boy until he starts coming down from whatever high he's riding, but Jack assures them Mariano is being released to capable hands. But a quick escape is impossible. The registration clerk reminds them Methodist Hospital is entitled to compensation for its services and asks if Mariano is uninsured. Jack instructs the boy to sign whatever's thrust in front of him, knowing full well the signature's not worth the paper it's written on, then hustles him out the door. Jack's speaking in Spanish so Frankie has no idea what's being said, but Mariano is nodding his head, acquiescing to all conditions and expectations being established.

"¿Comprende?"

Jack's voice is quiet, but the tone is stern, warning of the unpleasant consequences of anything less than an unconditional surrender.

"Good boy . . ." he says, opening the back door for Mariano to meekly crawl into the backseat.

"I really think you ought to let them take a look at you," Jack says, making one last futile effort to persuade Frankie to allow the ED to treat the fresh bruise on his face. "Jesus Christ, Frankie. You're going to have one hell of a black eye in the morning. And your nose is starting to swell. It could be broken. Give me one good reason to not call the feds to haul this tripped-out little shit's ass back to Mexico," he sighs, completely exasperated as he settles behind the wheel. "I need a cigarette. There's a pack in the glove compartment."

"But you promised you'd quit!"

"You hungry?" Jack asks, taking a long drag on a Marlboro Light as he turns the key in the ignition. "I'm starved."

"What about him? Shouldn't we get him home?"

"Why? You think you're going to tuck him in and he's going to fall asleep? You'll be lucky if he's ready to crash by sundown tonight."

There are plenty of available booths at the diner. A few all-night stragglers linger at the counter, staring into their coffee cups. The waitress is doing double duty as the cashier. The morning shift won't arrive for another hour when the earliest of risers, delivery truck drivers and the loading-dock workers at the food distribution center, wander in for coffee and breakfast. Jack grabs Mariano by the wrist when he tries to get up from the table.

"Don't even think about it. Sit down and wait for your food," he snaps. "What am I missing here? What is the attraction of this kid?" he asks, turning his attention to Frankie. "Can't you find someone more suitable to satisfy your needs? Go back to paying for it, if you have to. I'll absolve you at confession."

"It's not what you think," Frankie protests weakly.

The waitress sets a Western omelet in front of him. He's got no appetite. Why did he order it? But Jack rips into a heaping plate of scrambled eggs, sausage, and hash browns, and Mariano attacks a grilled cheese like he's been deprived of nutrition for a month.

"You don't know what I'm thinking," Jack challenges him.

"I know it's nothing good."

"You need to throw him out and change the locks. Today."

Mariano seems almost cheerful, chomping on his greasy sandwich, his cheeks stuffed with bread and melted American cheese.

"You don't know him. He's a nice boy. Very gentle, most of the time," Frankie says, suppressing the urge to reach across the table and caress Mariano's bandaged hand.

"Yeah, he seems like a real sweetheart," Jack says sarcastically.

Frankie feels like being defiant and declaring that Mariano is, in fact, a sweetheart, *his* sweetheart, but he knows it's wise to be conciliatory under the circumstances.

"He must be sick. A virus or something."

"Is that what they're calling methamphetamine these days? A virus?"

Mariano's English must be returning quickly, as he thinks this last remark is terribly funny. His snaggle-toothed smile still breaks Frankie's heart. It's costing a king's ransom for multiple oral surgeries and orthodontia to repair the damage a childhood cursed by poverty has done to his mouth. Jack, though, is unsympathetic and snaps at the boy, his tone harsh and commanding, the angry voice of the priest reducing Mariano to tears. The boy nods his head, chastened and humble, struggling to find the English words to express his contrition.

"I am very sorry, Frankie, to hurt you and promise to not be bad again."

"I know you are," Frankie says, forgiving him once more.

But the instinct for self-preservation is strong. He excuses himself, saying he needs to pee, and, alone in the men's room, dials the immigration lawyer's office and leaves a message with the answering service canceling the appointment Michael had scheduled for eleven this morning.

March 19, 2008

He wants to grab a *New York Post* for the flight, but there's a Tumi roller carry-on blocking the narrow path between the newspaper stacks and the rack of bagged candies and travel-size personal items.

"Pardon me, I'd like to get a paper," Michael says to the fellow flipping through a copy of *Muscle & Fitness*.

The man looks up from his magazine and stares him down.

"That way," he says, refusing to step aside, flipping his finger to wave Michael around the Twizzlers and root-beer barrels and FDA-approved three-ounce bottles of Scope.

The goddamn paper would be two steps from where Michael's standing if this asshole's precious luggage weren't in his way. His antagonist's red skullcap is pulled over his ears and the tinted lenses in his aviator frames are intended to intimidate. The thin line of scar tissue below his left eye is definitely menacing. He's not a large man or a young one, but he's a solidly built brother and his muscles are taut, coiled. He could be a former prizefighter or a military veteran injured in the line of duty. He's well dressed, wearing a cashmere turtleneck and a Burberry scarf. But the snarl is pure street.

"This isn't supposed to be an obstacle course," Michael says as he grabs the handle of the carry-on and pushes it to the side, refusing to let this motherfucker emasculate him. The man challenges him, seething. He doesn't bother to lower his voice, fully aware that the staff is consciously looking away, feigning ignorance of the confrontation.

"You shut your fucking mouth, white boy. Now get your fucking paper and get out of my fucking face."

This brightly lit, climate-controlled airport terminal, temperatures and noise levels carefully modulated, is no different from a bus depot in the shittiest part of town. Michael's enraged by the man's threats and frustrated by his complete and total impotence. What could this piece of shit do to hurt him? The bastard's been cleared by airport security. Metal detectors and X-ray cameras have confirmed there's no risk of him pulling a blade or a gun. The asshole's only weapons are his bare fists. But Michael's elevated position on the feeding chain, despite its many advantages, can be a prison, too, rendering him incapable of acting. He's restrained by the fear his life will come crashing down around him if he's caught up in an altercation, a public disturbance, charged with assault and battery. A golden opportunity to ascend to the office of the District Attorney of Delaware County will have been squandered. The gridiron warrior he once was, all muscle and grit, adrenaline and sweat, pure aggression, would have torn that prick to pieces. What happened to the fearless kid who went face-to-face with gruesome middle guards twice his size, grinding them into the mud of the field, taunting the vanquished with savage words and scorching profanities after he'd knocked them flat on their asses, his perspiration dripping in their faces?

Success has civilized him, tamed him, turned the raging beast into a docile house pet. He can only take some small satisfaction in knowing this motherfucker would get his skull smashed in if he tried this bullshit on an Italian block in South Philadelphia. Even today. In 2008. The girl at the register looks down at the counter when Michael hands her the price of the paper. The security guard stares at some vanishing point at the far side of the newsstand. Michael slinks away, defeated, his rage defusing, his fury receding, feeling nothing but the lingering sting of humiliation. All he wants is for this fucking flight to be over, to be home at the Nook, trying to get a rare eight hours of sleep. The past few days have been especially grueling. He and Kit had stayed late at the Clinton fundraiser Monday night, not getting back to Wayne until ten, and he had a restless night, up and down, before the alarm rang at five thirty.

This trip was supposed to be some sort of reward. In Steven Kettleman's mind, an opportunity to represent him at the biannual meeting of the Standards Committee of the ABA Criminal Justice Section is a rare honor, an opportunity to bask in reflected glory. Michael, of course, understands Kettleman's real purpose is to ensure a dissenting voice is present in the event one of the District Attorney's equally narcissistic rivals attempts a power play in his absence. He'd scheduled a late-afternoon flight to Boston yesterday because he'd agreed to meet his brother and the immigration attorney in the morning, only to have Frankie cancel as Michael was about to leave for the lawyer's office. Then his four thirty departure was delayed due to weather conditions at Logan and he didn't check into his hotel until after eleven. He was awakened this morning by a call from Frankie. Sal Pinto had died of congestive heart failure during the night and his widow is burying him Thursday morning before the beginning of the Easter Triduum. The viewing begins at seven this evening, and Michael, his godson, is expected to be present. The first available flight doesn't depart until three thirty.

He's stranded inside the terminal, having been forced to arrive hours in advance. Federal marshals have peered at every vial of liquid in his Ziploc bag of toiletries, making his preferred brand of toothpaste and deodorant public knowledge and forcing him to put his sweaty shoes in a basket and pad through the metal detector in his stocking feet. It's two in the afternoon, not too early for a beer while he waits for his flight to be called. The friendly bartender, a short, wiry black guy with a happy gap between his two front teeth, a dead ringer for the reigning MVP, is keeping an eye on the television broadcast of a spring training game being played under a brilliant Florida sun. Michael flips through his *Post,* scanning the headlines. *Rev's Rants Shake Voters' Obama Faith.* The preacher's inflammatory comments enrage the hysterical columnists, who accuse the candidate of being an accomplice to treason.

The man sitting next to Michael abruptly stands and walks away, leaving his copy of *USA Today* on the bar. According to the national weather map, last night's New England storms are moving south. But it's just been announced Michael's flight is boarding on time and he's being summoned to the gate. God once parted the Red Sea for Moses to deliver His Chosen People from Egypt and now He's thoughtfully holding severe weather conditions at bay until the landing gear of Michael's plane safely touches the tarmac at Philadelphia International Airport.

Frankie's arches are killing him and he's got a headache that feels like a shiv being driven between his eyes. He's going to scream if he has to explain his black eye and swollen nose to one more person. He's running on empty at this point. He'd spent the entire day Tuesday racing between the salon and the bedroom, keeping Mariano under close observation, one ear tuned for any telltale signs of escape, like footsteps on the back staircase or the slamming of the door to the house's private entrance. He'd given Mariano two Ambien in mid-afternoon and had taken one himself after a long soak in the sunken tub in the master bath at the end of his workday. He was dead to the world when his cell phone rang long after midnight. It was Jack, calling from Methodist Hospital to tell him Sal Pinto had passed, his body on its way to the Casano Funeral Home.

Frankie had intended to stay at the viewing just long enough to pay his respects—after all, Sal Pinto wasn't his godfather and he's sacrificing a half day of revenue to attend tomorrow's funeral. But it's almost eight thirty and his brother has yet to arrive. Mikey's phone is turned off, meaning he must be stranded mid-flight, and Frankie frets that heavy thunderstorms arriving from the north are causing havoc with his brother's travel plans, causing re-routing and delays. He can't leave now, abandoning the widow and her daughters. It's a disgrace, this pitiful showing, a sign of a lack of respect. Even Sal Pinto's sons-in-law have found better things to do this evening, and his sullen grandchildren look resentful at having to sacrifice *American Idol* to mourn an unloved old man.

"You sure he's gonna make it tomorrow, Frankie?" the widow asks.

"Nothing in the world could keep him away, I swear," he

promises, the bitter aftertaste of a bald-faced lie lingering on his tongue. His brother has no fond feelings for his godfather. In fact, Frankie was surprised he'd agreed to cut short his trip and fly back from Boston without needing to be begged.

"Well, you can say a few words, can't you? Just in case."

The thought of preparing a eulogy feels like a bucket of sand being dumped over his head. All he wants to do is crawl into bed and sleep until morning. He's nervous, not knowing what to expect when he gets home. He'd told Mariano he'd be back an hour and a half ago. Black thoughts, a sense of dread, a constant fear of the unpredictable, have begun to seep into his feelings for the boy.

Jack sweeps into the funeral home shortly before the end of viewing hours. The widow and her daughters have been waiting patiently for the priest to arrive to lead the rosary at the open casket.

"Where are you going, Frankie?" Jack asks as he drapes his stole around his neck.

"I'm exhausted, Jack. I need to get some sleep before tomorrow morning."

"I really think your nose may be broken. What the hell was I thinking when I let you walk out of that hospital without being looked at? I'm taking you back to the ER for an X-ray as soon as we're done here."

"I'm all right. Just drop it for now. Please."

"Did you do what I told you to do? Is he gone?"

"I was too busy today. I'm gonna do it. Right after the funeral."

"Whose fucking funeral, Frankie? Yours?" he hisses under his breath. "You can't piss around with this kid."

Mariano must be telepathic; the timing of his text message is perfect.

cum home te amo c u soon

"After Easter. I'll do it after Easter. I already made his basket."

The priest rolls his eyes, disgusted by his friend's obtuse refusal to recognize the urgency of the situation.

"You are fucking crazy," the priest whispers, careful not to be overheard spitting obscenities on this solemn occasion.

Frankie says a few more days won't make a difference. Who knows? It's the season of miracles, of transformation. Mariano seems sincere, promising to stay away from bad influences, to be a good boy and never be any trouble again. He deserves another chance before being banished to that firetrap flophouse on Snyder Avenue where Frankie had found him, sleeping in shifts on a dirty mattress he shared with other refugees from his home town, making little more than a subsistence living chopping vegetables and scouring skillets for cash under the table.

The grieving daughters approach, ready to begin the prayers.

"Are you coming, Frankie?" Jack asks.

He follows the priest into the viewing room, kneels beside the dry-eyed widow and her distracted children, and tries to concentrate on the words of the Five Sorrowful Mysteries.

March 20, 2008

Rain the day of the funeral, died happy the corpse, according to the old folk legend.

Well, that miserable old fuck Sal Pinto must have waited until his very last day on earth to experience an hour of joy because it's a goddamn monsoon out there. Michael's stranded under the awning of Mastroianni's Italian Coffee House, unwilling to ruin a perfectly good pair of Church's Consuls trying to cross the torrent of filthy water flooding Ninth Street. A strong gust of wind tosses a metal trash can into the window of the spice shop across the street and a shard of glass shatters at his feet. He's putting life and limb at risk standing out here and retreats into the safety of the coffee shop, where he's greeted by the rich, earthy smell of freshly ground beans and Ol' Blue Eyes singing "Strangers in the Night" to an empty house. It's warm and humid inside. Sweat drips from his armpits, dampening his undershirt.

"Oh my God, you almost gave me a heart attack! I didn't hear you come in!" Carla Tucci wheezes as she emerges from the dark basement, cradling a cardboard box of paper cups in her arms. "You're the last person I would have expected to find loafing in the middle of the morning, Mr. Big Shot."

"Very funny, Carla. Just get me a double."

"How about a cookie?"

"I don't want a cookie."

"Why not?"

Because I don't want an ass that could plug the Delaware Water Gap, he thinks as she turns her back, allowing him an unobstructed view of the enormous buttocks wobbling in her sweatpants.

"So to what do we owe the honor today, Mikey? They don't have Starbucks out there in that fancy place where you live?"

She has the sarcastic tongue of a pulp fiction hash house waitress without the heart of gold. She's always been a resentful bitch, even when she had a body like Pat Benatar. She'd peaked at sixteen, expelled from high school by the Sisters of Charity for getting pregnant. Life hasn't been kind to her. The handsome sociopath she married left her with three kids to support before being sent up to Graterford Prison to do a twenty-year sentence for armed robbery.

"Sal Pinto's funeral is this morning," he says. "You know what? Why don't you bring me a couple of biscotti? This doesn't look like it's letting up any time soon."

He tries not to cringe as he watches her pull the cookies from the glass jar with her bare hand. Her nails are grimy, caked with black coffee grounds.

"Why are you going to that old bastard's funeral?"

"He was my godfather."

Don Vito Corleone he wasn't. He was just a cranky old son of a bitch, a real *faccia di merda* who never had a decent word to say about anyone. A cheap motherfucker, too, who resented having to slip a lousy dollar bill into Michael's birthday card. Frankie's godfather, Dominic Ferri, a gentle and generous soul, was always good for five bucks on his godson's birthday and a twenty for Christmas. Frankie got a diamond-chip ring *and* a Norelco electric razor when he graduated from high school; that asshole Sal Pinto gave Michael his Sunoco thirty-year-service tie clip when he got his diploma from the Academy.

But Michael begrudgingly concedes the debt he owes to Sal Pinto, the father of three daughters, without a son of his own to teach how to track the trajectory of a football as it sailed across the field and to precisely calculate where it was destined to fall to earth.

Sal Pinto taught him how to block and tackle, the difference between the two- and three-point stance, the proper way to protect the ball, how to use his feet and shoulders for maximum effect. Sal Pinto took his responsibilities seriously, determined his godson would be tough, not a *finook* like his older brother. Michael's father was Sal's closest friend, but stubborn as a jackass, *testa dura*. He'd brushed off the barber's protests that ball games were the folly of the *medigan'*, and signed Michael up for Pop Warner. And it was Sal Pinto who invited the business agent for the pipefitters union, who also happened to be the brother-in-law of the athletic director at Matteo Ricci Preparatory Academy, the most elite Jesuit institution of secondary education in the city, maybe the country, to watch Michael, fleet of foot for a boy his size, tear up the field playing youth football on a team sponsored by the Ninth Street Merchants Alliance.

"The Mass starts at eleven. I'm a pallbearer."

The bell above the door announces the arrival of a pair of solemn little men bundled up in black overcoats more suitable to the depths of winter than the warmer temperatures of spring. They stamp their tiny feet and carefully shake the raindrops from their ancient homburgs. Their suits are clearly custom-made, the finest tailoring with perfect topstitching and cloth-covered buttons. They play a ritualistic game—*after you, my dear Alphonse*—and the younger (by only a few hours it would seem from their wizened faces) prevails, approaching the counter to order two cappuccinos, extra froth, and a bagel with cream cheese and grape jelly.

"You sit down and I'll bring it right over, Mr. Galante," Carla says, almost kindly.

The old fellows settle down at the table next to Michael. The elder, Mr. Angelo Casano, smiles and nods. He's a neighborhood legend; the *South Philly Review* did a front-page feature when he retired at the age of eighty-seven as the oldest practicing undertaker in the Commonwealth of Pennsylvania. He still makes himself useful, a window cat padding about the quiet corners of the family funeral parlor, always available whenever his son who now runs the business needs someone to collect the cash envelopes for the family of the deceased or to fill an empty pew at a Mass for a dearly departed who outlived his friends and acquaintances. He sits contentedly at the table, nibbling the corners of his bagel, a fleck of cream cheese in his mustache.

"You heard about Filomena Constanato?" Mr. Galante asks, making conversation.

Mr. Casano shrugs, engrossed in his bagel. After spending a lifetime in the service of death (and making a damn good living out of it), there's nothing tragic or even sad about an old woman's comfortable passing after a long, contented life.

"What are you gonna do?" Mr. Galante sighs, a rhetorical question.

"You know, I worked for her father when I was a boy," Mr. Casano recalls, his voice barely audible. "He used to sell fresh-killed chickens at Ninth and Wharton. Cut off their heads right there on the street." He laughs, daintily dabbing his whiskers with a paper napkin. "Paid me and my brother a dollar a day to pluck their feathers. Fifty cents each. That was big money back then. We thought we was rich! I could never eat chicken again after that. Turkey neither. You never forget the smell of wet feathers," he says, still wincing at the thought eight decades later. Michael smiles, amused by the delicate sensibility of a man who had spent his life draining the blood from cadavers and pumping them full of toxic embalming fluids.

"How are you, Mr. Casano?" Michael asks the old man. "Do you remember me? Michael Gagliano, Luigi and Sofia's boy."

"Of course. Of course." He smiles, trying to place Michael's vaguely familiar face.

Not so long ago the old undertaker would have immediately recalled his name. He'd taken great pride in his ability to recognize the features of the generations of South Philadelphians he'd prepared to meet their Maker in the faces of their living descendants. He stares at Michael, seeming to recall that one of Luigi's sons was a *finook,* but this young stranger is wearing a wedding band on his left hand. Frankie hates this man and refused to let him bury their father, though their grandparents and all of Papa's wives had been entrusted to his able hands. At the height of the epidemic, the Casano Funeral Home had refused to accept the body of Frankie's dear friend Michael Montello because the certificate listed AIDS-related infection as the cause of death. It seems like a cruel and a cowardly act now, depriving a heartbroken mother of the comfort of a traditional viewing, but it was the time when newspapers and magazines were full of images of hollow-eyed, emaciated men, and otherwise rational people believed a handshake or sharing an eating utensil could sentence them to an early, hideous death. Michael, unlike his brother, remembers old Mr. Casano as a kinder, more considerate man.

"So what the hell happened to your brother?" Carla asks as she gathers Michael's empty cookie plate.

"Nothing's happened as far as I know."

"His left eye is practically swollen shut and his nose is the size of a grapefruit. He said he tripped on the curb. I've never heard of anyone falling on their eye."

Mr. Galante is helping Mr. Casano into his overcoat. The rain has let up enough for the short walk to the church.

"I haven't seen him. I didn't make it to the viewing last night," Michael says.

"Well, he looked like he'd gone three rounds with Smokin' Joe Frazier when he came in for coffee this morning," she elaborates as he swallows the last of his espresso and makes his way to the door.

Frankie's waiting in the vestibule of Saint Catherine of Siena, impeccably dressed. His brother is truly their father's son, able to keep a sharp crease in his trousers in a soaking downpour, his shoes spit-shined and gleaming. He's wearing sunglasses in a dark and gloomy church.

"What time did you get in last night? The widow Pinto is frantic, thinking you weren't going to show," Frankie greets him. "Why didn't you answer my calls this morning?"

"They re-routed us through Columbus Fucking Ohio. I didn't get home until midnight. My battery was dead and I forgot to charge my phone."

Four neighborhood kids, pimply-faced vo-tech dropouts fresh out of rehab, wearing cheap suits and old black sneakers, pallbearers-for-hire, wait for their marching orders. It's an easy fifty bucks, under the table. Some old geezer is buried every day and they can pick up two hundred, two fifty, a week if they're willing to haul themselves out of bed and put on a tie. Young Casano doesn't make them sit through the Mass and they're free to grab a slice at the pizza shop across the street and shoot the shit until their services are needed.

"It stopped rainin'. Tell Mr. Casano we're going out for a smoke, okay, Frankie?" the scruffiest of the young fellows asks.

"You have your gloves?" Frankie asks the boys as he hands Michael a pair of the white pallbearer gloves required by sacred tradition.

Mr. Galante and old Mr. Casano cross the vestibule, arm in arm, and, creaking and croaking, bless themselves as they enter the nave.

"Why the hell are you wearing sunglasses? The glare from the votive candles too much for you?" Michael asks, grabbing his brother by the arm.

"I tripped on the curb crossing Christian Street. Went down on my face."

"Jesus Christ," Michael says as he snatches the glasses off his brother's face. Carla was right. Frankie looks like Quasimodo with a huge purple bruise almost sealing his eyelid to his cheek. His swollen nose is the size of a paperweight. "What the fuck did that goddamn kid do to you?"

"Nobody did this to me. I told you. I fell on the street. You want to see what I did to my knees? Here. I'll pull up my pant legs so you can survey the damage."

"Settle down, for Christ's sake. You want someone to hear you? I was just asking."

"Straighten your tie. Jack's about to start the Mass," he says. "I told Sal's daughters you'd say a few words."

"No fucking way. No one asked me to prepare a eulogy."

"Oh come on, Mikey. You're his godson. Just tell some stupid story. About him taking you to a ball game for your birthday or something."

"You say a few words."

"He was your godfather, not mine. Besides, you're a better liar."

You're damn right, Frankie, Michael thinks. *You bet your sweet ass I would have come up with a better story to explain a nasty black eye and a fucked-up nose than tripping on the sidewalk.* But Frankie's already halfway up the aisle, stopping to shake hands with Mr. Galante and, yes, even old Mr. Casano before he slides into the pew beside Sal's daughters.

Even Sal Pinto deserves better than this pitiful turnout, fifteen mourners, sixteen if you count the priest. Michael supposes he can come up with a few words for the occasion. Fuck it. Why begrudge the old son of a bitch a grand send-off? He'll spin an inspirational tale of cross-generational bonding and affection, *Tuesdays with Morrie* with a South Philadelphia twist, the first act in the eventual canonization of the deceased. Sal Pinto's daughters will dab their eyes with a tissue, grateful to learn their selfish and critical father had a kind heart and giving nature after all. Mr. Galante and Mr. Casano will lean forward in their pew, intent on hearing every word. And Frankie, well, Frankie will be rapt in his seat, beaming with pride at the easy eloquence of his little brother, foolishly assuming that the subject of bruises is officially closed, not suspecting Michael intends to buttonhole him in a quiet corner at the sorry little funeral lunch at the Speakeasy and subject him to cross-examination until he breaks down and admits it's time his little Mexican friend is moving on, if not willingly, then with the friendly assistance of a few federal agents.

The morning storms have swept through the area and a bright sun blazes overhead. The grass is wet from the drenching rain; Michael's tempted to take off his shoes and socks and walk barefoot across the cemetery lawn. The graveside service was mercifully brief, with only Sal's daughters, their children, a single resentful son-in-law, and the Gagliano brothers in attendance. The trek to the cemetery was a pitiful convoy of four cars, including the hearse, a mere shadow of the police-escorted processions of fifty vehicles Frankie and Michael remember from their youths. The prayers over, Sal committed to the earth, his youngest daughter says she's driving Father Jack back to South Philly and reminds Michael she has something of her father's she wants to give him at the funeral lunch.

"Probably his retirement cuff links from the refinery," he grumbles when he and his brother are alone.

"I bought a couple of Mass cards in your name," Frankie says.

"What do I owe you?"

"Ten minutes of your time."

"Please, Frankie," Michael pleads. "Don't ask me to do this!"

"Mikey, there's no way we're coming all the way out here and not paying our respects."

Frankie snatches a fresh floral tribute off Sal Pinto's grave.

"My godfather's gonna come back and haunt you for stealing," Michael warns him with a laugh.

"Fuck Sal Pinto," Frankie snarls, sounding almost fierce.

"Do you even remember where it is?"

"Of course. Jesus, Mikey, how long has it been since you've made a visit?"

Visit is an odd way to describe a pilgrimage to their father's grave. *Visit* implies a pleasant conversation over a cocktail or coffee and cookies, catching up on the latest news; it hardly describes staring slack-jawed at a granite tombstone, counting the minutes before you can leave without seeming disrespectful.

"I don't remember," he says, knowing perfectly well he hasn't *visited* the old man's grave since Frankie forced him to do it on the first anniversary of Papa's death.

The long walk to the Gagliano family plot is downhill, which means a trek back up the driveway to pick up the car. He complains that they aren't driving, but Frankie insists the walk will do them good.

"So, are you going to tell me who did this to your face?" he asks, taking advantage of the forced march to extort a confession. "And don't lie. Remember, I'm a prosecutor."

"I told you what happened. I tripped on a curb crossing Christian Street. Fell flat on my face," Frankie swears.

"Give me one good reason to believe you. I bet your priest buddy can tell me what happened."

"So what do you think?" Frankie asks, pointing straight ahead. "Impressive, huh?"

"Jesus Christ, Frankie!" he gasps, his mouth agape.

Impressive is one way to describe the garish monument that's been erected in the center of the Gagliano family plot. A seven-foot weeping marble angel, a strange hybrid of a Biblical messenger and a minor god of classical myth, stands vigil over the graves of Luigi

Gagliano and his many wives, brandishing a sword in one hand and a lantern in the other.

"What the fuck!" is all he can say.

"I didn't tell you because I knew you'd try to talk me out of spending the money."

"It's . . . it's . . ." he mumbles, finally giving up, a rare occasion when words fail him.

Even in death, Papa remains the center of his own little universe, the bantam rooster surrounded by his hens. His first wife, Teresa, lies to his right in the plot she shares with the ashes of the grandson she never knew, Sonny F. Shevchek, LCP, a casualty of the Gulf War. Her daughter Paulina's urn will be buried with her son and the sainted mother she'd lost when she was still a girl. Frankie and Michael's mother, Sofia, sleeps at Papa's left. Miss Eileen Costello rests at his feet, and Frannie Merlino lies next to her, interred after a protracted legal battle between Papa and her sister's children, who fought to have her buried with her first husband in the Merlino family plot. Rubbing salt into the wound, Papa had also refused their request that he return an expensive watch that had once belonged to the late Mr. Merlino. Their marriage had been miserable, but the law was on his side as she had died as Papa's wife and not as the widow of the man interred in a cemetery in Lansdale. Only Helen Constanza is missing, her daughter having cremated her body and scattered the ashes in California. There's room in the plot for at least one more Gagliano, and Michael's astonished to see Frankie's name and date of birth already sculpted into the monument, the date of death to be inscribed in the future.

"Tell me you're not planning to spend the rest of eternity under the same tombstone as that miserable motherfucker."

"You're too hard on him, Mikey. He did the best he could. He loved us, Mikey."

"That is absolute bullshit. Why are you always defending him?"

"He brought us up the only way he knew how. We turned out all right, didn't we? Better than all right. Especially you," he says calmly as he lays Sal Pinto's flowers on their mother's grave.

"Can I have a few of those, please?" Michael asks.

Frankie plucks a few gladiolas from the bouquet and offers them to his brother to place on Miss Eileen's plot.

"You know what I could go for right now, Mikey? A nasty old cheesesteak and a chocolate shake? What do you say?"

"What about the funeral lunch?" Michael asks, grateful for the reprieve.

"Fuck Sal Pinto. You've done enough good deeds for the day." Frankie laughs, breathing a sigh of relief that the subject of the cause of his bruises seems to be closed, at least for the moment.

MARCH 21, 2008, GOOD FRIDAY

"Trust me. Just this once. I know what I'm talking about. You won't regret it. I promise you."

Jack's fringe just looks awful. Frankie's been trying to persuade him to agree to a shorter cut for years now, but the damn priest is so stubborn, refusing to give up a style he's been wearing since the seminary. His wispy hair is shoulder length, carefully groomed to cover the pointy ears that make him look like a malevolent elf. Even worse, Jack insists on combing a few thin strands over his bald skull, apostasy to any self-respecting stylist.

"Just give me the usual, Frankie. Don't take off too much. Maybe we'll try something different this summer."

If only he would agree to a clean, sharp buzz cut. There's no law that says a priest shouldn't make the best of the looks God gave him. Not that there's a lot to work with. It's a sin, totally unfair, that so many beautiful people have hideous souls yet a man who would give you his last piece of bread if he were starving and the shirt off his back in a blizzard is as ugly as ten puckered assholes. Poor Jack has always been homely, a *faccia di culo.* He was saddled with the nickname Secretariat in high school after some wiseass remarked on his resemblance to the Triple Crown winner. His teeth are crooked and his skin pitted with acne scars because his parents thought dermatology and braces were an expensive vanity wasted on a son who was destined for the priesthood. Papa claimed the Centafore family had been hideous for generations. Legend had it that Jack's great-grandmother, a *puttana con coscia lorda,* a whore with dirty thighs, had given birth out of wedlock to a hideous Cyclops. She'd smothered the baby and buried it in the woods so its evil soul wouldn't defile the consecrated ground of the cemetery. The one-eyed monster had cast the *maliocch'* as its mother dispatched it to hell, and the curse of ugliness has plagued the family since that day.

"You are coming to stations of the cross this afternoon, aren't you?" Jack asks, watching Frankie like a hawk in the mirror, ever vigilant against the possibility of the scissors snipping away more than a half-inch of hair.

"If I can get out of here on time. I'm taking Mariano to the dentist after I finish you and then Mary Gianfranco is coming in for a perm at one."

"Do you want to go for fish and chips tonight? My treat."

"I promised I'd color Mariano's hair later. He wants me to take him blond."

Mariano's been begging Frankie to strip all the gorgeous color from his beautiful head of hair and transform him into a spiky lemonhead. Frankie feels Jack's neck and shoulders stiffen and senses he's about to hear a sermon about the consequences of failing to do what the priest insists needs to be done. He has no intention of tossing Mariano into the street. He'd made a mistake the other night, one he now deeply regrets. He wasn't thinking straight. His bruises were fresh and painful. There'd been too much confusion and he'd allowed Jack's melodramatic concerns about his personal safety to cause him to impulsively cancel the long-awaited appointment with the immigration lawyer his brother had begrudgingly recommended.

"But if you want to come over to the shop tonight we can order an anchovy pizza and have a glass of wine."

"Careful," Jack says, wincing. "You're taking too much off around my ears."

* * *

Arnie Strong knows the Deputy District Attorney's reputation for fairness and reasonableness. He'd thought Michael would recognize his client's not a bad kid. He's got no priors. He's not a junkie or a drunk. He's just an unlucky schmuck who drank too much at his brother's wedding, almost a prerequisite for accepting the responsibility of being chosen best man. No punishment the Commonwealth can mete out could be as cruel as having to live until the day he dies with the image of his own fiancée's crushed skull and broken neck. Arnie argues Michael will never get a conviction of vehicular homicide. The kid's inebriation didn't cause the collision. A truck driver, sober as a judge, trying to beat a red light, had crushed the passenger side of the boy's car. His client will plead guilty to a DUI and a charge of reckless endangerment to avoid a mandatory three-year minimum sentence. But Michael's intent on nailing the poor guy to the cross, no pun intended considering the significance of the day. *Let's take it up again next week,* Strong suggests, hoping that Michael will come to his senses.

"No more calls today, Carol," Michael shouts after getting off the phone, forgetting for a moment his assistant is off today, observing the Crucifixion of Our Lord by picketing Planned Parenthood to protest the tragic disregard for the sanctity of human life. Every judge in the courthouse has adjourned for the holiday weekend. It's just a little after one when he shuts down his computer and turns off the office lights, locking his door behind him.

Frankie hopes Jack is taking notice of Mariano's piety and perfect genuflections. The boy's spine is rigid as his knee touches the floor, no slouching or lazy shortcuts. His voice is loud and clear; he doesn't mumble his prayers to hide his poor pronunciation. He's dressed respectfully, in a white shirt and tie, and wearing polished black leather shoes. His attire is far more appropriate for Good Friday services than the Leisure Timers' baggy sweatpants and dirty sneakers. Jack will surely give Mariano proper credit for being one of the two males of the congregation under the age of seventy, the other being Frankie, willing to give up an hour of this beautiful spring afternoon to spend inside a gloomy church.

We adore You, O Christ, and we bless You.
Because by Your Holy Cross, You have redeemed the world.

The elderly crucifer entrusted with carrying the processional cross seems overwhelmed before he and the priest reach the second Station. It's been a good six or seven decades since the man first donned the vestments of an altar boy. It's obvious his knees are aching and he's longing to sit down in the nearest pew. The consternation is visible behind the Coke-bottle lenses of his eyeglasses. The incense is making him feel faint. He's never going to make it until the end of the service. It's a sad time we're living in, Frankie thinks, when the superannuated and feeble are forced to perform what had once been the responsibilities of children. Suspicious parents insist their sons are too burdened by other commitments to take on the added responsibility of serving at Mass. Dinosaurs will roam the earth again and the country will be handed back to the British Crown before a Catholic priest will be left alone with their boys.

We adore You, O Christ, and we bless You.
Because by Your Holy Cross, You have redeemed the world.

Mariano's stomach is rumbling, loudly. He hasn't eaten since this morning's dentist appointment, his gums too sore and swollen to chew. There's reconstructive work yet to be done before they can even think about beginning purely cosmetic treatments. Implants, crown lengthening, caps, veneers, retainers—the estimates to date are staggering. It's going to set Frankie back seven, maybe eight, grand. But this isn't the time or the place to be thinking about money. His mind is wandering when he should be paying attention to the service. There's a spirited competition among the women of the parish, each trying to outdo the others with florid displays of piety. They crank up the volume of their groans and moans lest anyone doubt the physical challenge of kneeling and rising, up and down, again and again. Joanne Portella is headed for the doors, the first to throw in the towel. The service is dragging on longer than it should and she can't go forty minutes without a cigarette.

* * *

It's insurance, pure and simple, that draws Michael back to stained glass windows and padded kneelers. He's agnostic the other three hundred sixty-four days of the calendar, or would be if he bothered to give much thought to God and religion. Yet, year after year, he returns on Good Friday to make his annual confession, indoctrinated as a schoolboy in his Easter duty to purge his soul during this most sacred season of the liturgical year. He's hedging his bets, just in case he's wrong and someday finds himself trying to cross the threshold of the pearly gates. His sins are barely worthy of being disclosed in the ancient ritual of confession. His most grievous offense is being guilty of impure thoughts about women who aren't his wife. Actually, one woman. Charlize Theron. It's something a chastened adolescent boy, too embarrassed to use more graphic descriptions for the act of masturbation, might sheepishly confess. But here he kneels, under the reproachful watch of marble saints and martyrs shrouded in the mourning black of Lent until the Easter vigil, the air he's breathing redolent of incense.

His penance is as trivial as his venial wrongdoings. Two Our Fathers, three Hail Marys, and an Act of Contrition. How easy it is to satisfy the demands of such a generous God. He's running late and Kit has given him a long list of chores for the Easter festivities so he rushes through a rote recitation of the assigned prayers and, making the sign of the cross, solemnly vows to go forth and sin no more, at least until his next fantasy date with the lovely Charlize.

Frankie should have told Jack to wear his clerical collar tonight. His Neil Diamond World Tour 2005 souvenir T-shirt and Nike cross-trainers aren't nearly as intimidating as black priestly garb. Mariano's been pouting since Frankie announced he'd invited Jack for pizza and now he's acting out. He's putting on a show for their guest, arguing with Frankie, lapsing into Spanish when he can't find the right words in English to express his displeasure with the progress on his new look. Frankie's losing his patience. Mariano is embarrassing him in front of Jack, squandering any goodwill he might have earned with his pious behavior in church, proving all of the priest's dire prognostications correct. It's a relief to finally stick

Mariano's head under the dryer for thirty minutes and hand him copies of *Vogue* and *Celebrity Hairstyles* to keep him distracted.

"I wasn't going to say anything," Jack protests, his smug smirk suggesting otherwise, when Frankie shoots him a *don't-even-think-about-it* look.

Frankie washes his hands and pours a glass of wine.

"The stitches are making him irritable. It's only a few more days until they come out."

"What time is your first appointment tomorrow morning?" Jack asks.

"Eight thirty, why?" Frankie asks, claiming to be stuffed after one slice of the cheese-and-anchovy pie, since you can't be too careful about calories at the age of forty-eight.

"I'm going to the hospice to give Father Parisi the sacraments around seven. You ought to come."

"How much longer does he have?"

"He should have been dead six months ago."

Frankie can't even imagine what would have become of the Gagliano brothers if it hadn't been for that kindly old man. His rectory was their refuge, a quiet place where Mikey spent countless hours with a glass of milk and a plate of Hydrox cookies, reading inspirational (at least in the opinion of Father Parisi) books written for much older readers and watching reruns of old black-and-white shows like *Hogan's Heroes* and *The Beverly Hillbillies.* Frankie would sit on the floor, rubbing the priest's arthritic bare feet and pouring his heart out, talking about their difficult home life, their critical father, and the flame-haired woman trying to take their mother's place.

"When Mikey and I were boys, I used to pray that Father Parisi would adopt us," Frankie says.

Jack lowers his voice to almost a whisper, ensuring the boy under the dryer, deeply engrossed in the glossy pages on his lap, can't hear his question.

"Frankie," he asks, using his confessional-box voice, soothing, inviting the sharing of shameful confidences, promising understanding and compassion. "Did Father Parisi ever touch you?"

"No! Of course not!" Frankie sputters, startled and offended. Mariano looks up from his magazine and, seeing nothing of interest, returns to his intensive study of Angelina Jolie's latest cut. Frankie's indignant at being forced to defend the honor of a harmless old man. Absolutely not, the answer is an unequivocal no. Never, not once, did Father Parisi ever put his hands where they didn't belong or show Frankie and Mikey things their innocent eyes shouldn't see or ask them to do anything a young boy shouldn't do. He's glad now he never told Jack about the Polaroids. It's obvious he wouldn't have understood.

"What would make you ask such a thing?"

"I shouldn't have said anything. He goes in and out of lucidity. Nothing can comfort him. The poor soul is terrified of dying."

The old priest had survived into his nineties, though he'd been confined to a wheelchair for nearly two decades, crippled by arthritis. He became a recluse, an odd duck in his old age, sometimes going weeks without speaking, obsessed with penance, becoming inconsolable whenever he made his confession. He's spent the last few months in the hospice unit of the Sisters of Mercy nursing facility. His wasted body barely makes an impression under the heavy bedclothes. Jack confided that the staff was shocked by the scars on his back from years of self-flagellation. On his last visit, Frankie brought a big, beautiful bouquet and box of Godiva chocolates, remembering the priest's love of bright flowers and his insatiable sweet tooth. But Father Parisi was beyond sensory indulgences. The old man's voice was barely strong enough for Frankie to hear his insistent apology for some transgression that existed only in the dying man's mind. His ancient, bloodshot eyes were wet with love and longing and shame. Frankie leaned over and kissed the priest on his parched lips, unable to absolve him of unknown sins.

Mariano doesn't hear the shrill ring tone, "Picture to Burn," of his insistent cell phone. Frankie grabs it and answers rather than letting it go into voice mail. He's made up his mind to do what he can to separate Mariano from bad influences. He doesn't recognize the harsh voice on the line, spitting a torrent of incomprehensible Spanish words, obviously angry about something.

"Excuse me?" is all Frankie can think to say.

The caller turns gracious, friendly, inquiring after Frankie's health. Frankie's flustered, completely rattled when the stranger calls him by his name, speaking in flawless English, his accent more

California than South of the Border. He casts a quick glance at Mariano, who's still leisurely flipping through the glossy pages of his magazine, unaware of the conversation occurring with the caller on his cell.

"Of course, we haven't been introduced. I'm Mariano's brother. Randy. Our little *burro,*" the gruff voice says, sounding cheerful. "He forgets our mother's birthday is today. She calls me in tears. She's afraid something has happened to him. I could wring his neck."

Frankie's confused. This man who claims to be his boyfriend's brother must be mistaken. He drove Mariano to the bank and helped him facilitate a wire transfer to Puebla of a thousand dollars, a generous tribute by Frankie to a mother-in-law he's never met for her sixtieth birthday. On February twenty-ninth. Leap Day. Mariano didn't understand Frankie's joke about his mother being fifteen years old.

"Do you want to talk to him?" Frankie asks, anxious to get off the phone.

"Just make sure he calls our mama. You will do that, won't you, Mr. Gagliano? And tell him I need to speak with him. Soon."

"Call me Frankie. Of course," he says, hanging up.

Frankie's apprehensive, suspecting secrets and deception, a pattern of lies.

"What the hell was that all about?" Jack asks. "Is something wrong?"

"No. It was nothing," he says, sounding unconvincing even to himself, certainly not fooling Jack. "Call me when you're ready to leave for the hospice in the morning. I'll wait for you outside."

March 23, 2008, Easter Sunday

"I've got a gun and I'm not afraid to use it!" the mighty warrior shouts as he races down the hallway.

Darth Vader couldn't intimidate him, but the fierce little commando isn't so tough and ornery when he finds himself nose to chin with an odd-looking creature who resembles a canary-yellow Easter Peep.

"Danny, this is my friend Mariano. Mariano, this is my favorite nephew, Danny."

"I'm your only nephew!" Danny insists, recovering a bit of his lost bravado. He's cocky and bursting with blustery self-confidence whenever he feels safe and secure, but shy and reticent among the unfamiliar and unknown. Kit and Michael have agreed to meet Mariano for dinner or brunch on a few occasions, but, being responsible parents, they believed it would be too confusing for Danny to deal with his uncle's new relationship until they were satisfied that young Mariano wasn't just some fleeting infatuation. There'd been hard feelings at Thanksgiving and Christmas. But Frankie's unwillingness to come out to the Nook and blow out the candles on his birthday cake and his obstinate refusal to accept a solo invitation for Easter had broken Kit's resolve. She'd insisted her stubborn husband concede to the inevitable. Frankie and the boy have been a couple for more than a year now and it's time to welcome the young man into the family circle. Danny's curious about this odd-looking visitor, a dead ringer for a Bakugan Battle Brawler. Clearly not a kid, but not quite a grown-up, this Mariano is something in between, like a Jonas Brother, with his tight clothes and spiked, gelled hair.

Michael's almost as dumbstruck as his son. It's worse than expected. The invitation was a mistake, no doubt about it.

"Mariano, you remember my brother, Mikey."

"Michael," he corrects him, introducing himself, reaching to shake the young Mexican's undamaged hand.

Mariano's palm feels boneless, a plush lily pad that wilts under the slightest pressure. The kid isn't masculine enough to be called handsome. Striking, that's how Michael would describe his appearance, like an oil portrait on a gallery wall that forces you to stop and admire, demanding your attention. Michael squints into the daylight, assuming his eyes are playing tricks, but, no, he's not mistaken. The young man is wearing makeup, eyeliner and mascara. His hair is the unnatural color of fool's gold and his manner is either shy or haughty, it's hard to tell. He mumbles, looking down at his feet, when forced to utter a simple greeting. He covers his mouth with his bandaged hand, self-conscious, obviously ashamed of the pitiful condition of his teeth.

"Happy Easter," Michael says, trying to sound sincere.

Michael had stood his ground as long as possible. To say the kid and his brother are a mismatched pair, a dress sock and a sweat sock, black wool and white cotton, would be an understatement. They're pieces of a different puzzle. Nothing fits. The whole fucking idea of this boy taking up residence, installing himself as the lady of the house at Eighth and Carpenter, once the home of the imperious and demanding Papa, doesn't feel right.

"Were you in a fight?" Danny asks his uncle.

"Of course not. Do I look like a fighter, Danny? I fell."

Maybe, for once, Michael ought to give his brother the benefit of the doubt. Frankie could be telling the truth when he swears the kid poses no threat to his physical well-being. It's hard to believe this Mariano could have bloodied his brother's face with one marshmallow fist.

"The baskets are still in the car. I could use a hand," Frankie says before Danny grabs him by the wrist to drag him to his bedroom to admire the pair of toxic guinea pigs he persuaded his mother to buy him for Easter.

"How bad is it?" Kit asks as her husband wanders into the kitchen.

"Bad."

"On a scale of one to ten?"

"Let's put it this way. He must have stolen his shirt from an ice dancer and his hair looks radioactive. And I'm pretty sure he's on a first-name basis with Estee Lauder."

"Jesus."

"Maybe your father won't notice."

"Michael, that boy is a guest in our home. As is my father. And he'll treat Frankie's friend with dignity and respect or he's welcome to leave."

His father-in-law, who's been sipping from a tumbler of Maker's Mark since the backyard Easter egg hunt, has become a disciple of Rush Limbaugh and *Fox News*. The Judge once had been a deeply practical man who'd taken great satisfaction in knowing his favorite child had the wits to end up with one of his Tastykakes, an olive-skinned South Philly kid with a high IQ and unlimited prospects, the Note Editor of the Penn Law Review, rather than an anemic member of the Philadelphia Club whose highest ambition was to sing a solo at the Orpheus Club Christmas concert. He'd even respected his son-in-law's decision to choose public service over the generous offer to join the storied Philadelphia white-shoe firm where the Judge had been managing partner before being appointed to the federal bench in the first term of the Reagan administration.

The old man's got nothing but time on his hands since declining cognitive functions forced him to resign his lifetime appointment on the bench. The hours of his day are consumed by his obsession with right-wing conspiracy theories like the Clinton Body Count and, more recently, Obama's indoctrination by Muslim jihadists at an Indonesian madrassa. He's taken to the Internet since the neurologist ordered the confiscation of his car keys and is the author of daily e-mail blasts soliciting funds for crackpot organizations. His latest favorite is something called American Sentries that wants to build a fifty-story impenetrable steel wall from the Pacific coastline to the shores of the Gulf of Mexico. He'll either detonate or collapse into an alcoholic stupor when he finds himself seated next to Pancho Villa at the dinner table.

"He's your father. I'll let you inform him of the house rules."

"Frankie, they are beautiful!" she gushes, looking over Michael's shoulder as Frankie and Danny enter the kitchen, laden with bounty to celebrate the Resurrection of Our Lord. "Don't move," she says abruptly.

He obeys without question. Men of all ages respond instinctually to the voice she uses to insist that Danny clean his ears and brush his teeth and that her husband tuck in his shirt and straighten the knot in his tie.

"What happened to you?" she asks.

"I tripped on the curb and went down on my face."

"You should have seen him a few days ago. His nose was the size of Bozo the Clown's. I told him he ought to sue the city," Michael says, still skeptical of Frankie's explanation of the mystery bruises.

"Why would I sue? It was my fault for not paying attention."

"Doesn't stop the good people of the city of Philadelphia from hiring some ambulance chaser with his face and phone number on the side of a bus to extort a few bucks from the treasury for their pain and suffering. One of those better be mine," Michael says, eyeing the baskets.

The Easter Bunny arrives every year bearing marzipan Paschal Lambs, solid chocolate crucifixes and bunnies, heaping mounds of jelly beans and buttercream and nougat eggs in shiny foil, all of it artfully piled on a heap of bright pastel straw in cheerful spring colors. Danny and his father rip off the cellophane wrappers, making short work of Frankie's meticulous creative efforts. Their greediness is exasperating and Kit chastises the two of them.

"My God, Michael. I don't know who is worse, you or your son. You didn't even give me a chance to get a picture!"

Scottie saunters into the kitchen, enticed from her bedroom by the promise of peanut butter eggs. Kit snaps the neck of an ill-fated bunny and pops it in her mouth.

"Take this basket away from me! This candy is going straight to my hips." She laughs, giving Frankie an affectionate hug.

"Michael, you ought to leave for Miss Peterson's now," she says. "And stop and pick up another pint of heavy cream on your way. The expiration date is next week, but I don't like the smell of this," she says, wrinkling her nose as she sniffs the lip of the carton. "Remember to give her a dressing drink before you put her in the car. Maybe she'll fall asleep before she and my father can start a political debate."

"I'll come with you, Michael," his stepdaughter says, an unexpected offer.

Her friendly smile as she buckles her seat belt is ominous. She even asks permission before changing the radio station. She's over her high school girl crush on that irritating little girl who sang that ubiquitous ode to Tim McGraw and is now an enthusiastic fan of hip-hop. Just last week she lost an epic battle with her mother over attending a concert by a rapper with the ludicrous name Ludicris.

"Did she tell you?" she asks as the disc jockey launches into his moronic patter.

"Did who tell me what?" he asks.

"Doozy."

The Italian son in Michael, Papa's boy, will never understand the casual nonchalance with which the children of his wife's tribe refer to their parents by their given names. His son may have Anglo-Saxon blood in his veins, but he will never call his mother Kit or, God forbid, Doozy, in his father's presence.

"Did she tell you about my father? He's getting divorced again."

The news is hardly surprising. Scottie's father is too arrogant and reckless to conceal his serial infidelities from his wives. Kit loathes him, wishing him dead on occasion, offended by his complete disregard for the damage he wreaks on the people in his life, first and foremost his eldest daughter.

"I'm sorry to hear that," he says.

"It's okay. I don't care," she insists, her bravado ringing false. Michael is very conscious about keeping his eyes on the road ahead, knowing she would be mortified to be seen fighting back tears. They ride in silence, listening to Top 40 radio.

Kit and Michael have sworn that Danny's childhood will be different from that of his half sister. He'll grow up secure, knowing that he's loved, the center of their universe, protected, his innocence preserved as long as possible. He's nine years old and has never even heard his parents argue. The worst thing Danny has suffered in his happy life was a broken heart when they were forced to find his beloved golden retriever a new home when he experienced a severe allergic reaction to dog hair.

"Michael?"

"Yeah?"

"Who do you think Doozy would rescue if both Danny and I were drowning?"

"She'd go down saving both of you."

"Do you think you and Doozy will get a divorce someday?"

"Scottie. There are few things in life you can be certain of. But one of them is that your mother and I will not be getting a divorce."

"That's because you're a dago," she declares, trying, without success, to get a rise out of him. "Dodie says dagos never divorce no matter how much they hate each other."

Michael is tempted to, but refrains from, revealing the sordid marital history of her grandmother and his mother-in-law's own misguided commitment to her nuptial oath.

"Good try, but I'm not taking the bait this morning, Scottie."

"Dodie says dagos spoil their kids."

"Dodie didn't know my father."

"Was he a bastard like mine?"

"In a different way."

"You're not a bastard."

"Thank you for acknowledging that."

"But you're a real jerk sometimes."

"Well, I guess I'll have to try harder to live up to your expectations."

"You're not that bad. I'd probably pick a dago if I got to choose my father," she says before turning her attention to an incoming text.

Eleanor is raring to go this afternoon. She's almost pleasant in the car, full of cheerful criticism of Michael's route between the two domiciles and his waste of expensive fossil fuel. He persuaded her to have two sherries before they embarked (not a difficult task), hoping she would doze off after he strapped her into her seat. She's wide-awake, completely absorbed in an NPR broadcast of an ancient memoirist reading a selection about a wartime Easter celebration in Provence. But he should have been less generous with the alcohol. The obstinate old cow refuses to wear the adult diapers Kit bought her and the car reeks of piss. He does a half-assed job wiping down and sanitizing the leather seat, knowing he'll need to do it all over again after driving her home after dinner.

He washes up in the utility room, his heart sinking when he hears the raucous commotion of loud voices. He tosses aside the towel and rushes into the house, preparing to throw himself into the middle of the fracas and act as a referee, separating the combatants and sending them to their corners. He'll issue a stern warning of dire consequences if the parties don't sit down, shut up, and learn how to behave like civil human beings. He's surprised to find Kit in the kitchen, preoccupied with pulling baking dishes from the oven. Her mother is tossing a salad, and Frankie is calmly slicing a Virginia ham.

"What's going on in there?" he asks, shocked by this calm in the eye of the storm.

"You forgot the whipping cream, didn't you?" Kit accuses him.

"Just add a couple of tablespoons of vanilla extract," Dodie advises. "You won't be able to taste anything else."

"How thin do you want these slices?" Frankie asks.

"Dodie, go check on Miss P and see how's she's doing," Kit insists.

It sounds like 8.5 on the Richter scale and they're blithely going about their business in the kitchen, ignoring the catastrophe in the next room. He throws up his hands and enters the lion's den, determined to keep the battle troops from pulling his house down around their heads. Three generations of Ballard-Morris-Scotts and the visitor from South of the Border are gathered around the video screen, hard at play, whooping and shouting as they run up their scores in a round of *Rock Band*. The volume is jacked to earsplitting levels. His father-in-law is pounding the drumsticks and Kit's jug-eared, thick-browed brother Henry is picking out the bass line. Danny's on lead guitar, tossing his head and wagging his tongue, and the Mexican kid is wailing at the top of his range, hitting the high notes and mumbling the words, his English too rudimentary to master the lyrics of Jefferson Airplane's "White Rabbit."

The day went better than expected, almost a complete success. Mariano was unfailingly polite and, once he was comfortable in strange and intimidating surroundings, he demonstrated the charming and considerate good nature Frankie has been insisting he possesses. He'd helped Kit and her mother clear the table and load the dishwasher, then offered to serve Dodie's coconut Easter cake, a Pugh family tradition, at dessert. Before they left, Kit promised Frankie to arrange a meeting with an immigration specialist in her Center City law firm about Mariano's dilemma. The permanent residency project is back on track and moving full-speed ahead. The whole family is on board, Michael begrudgingly so. He still intends to run a fingerprint check (he'd quietly confiscated the microphone the boy had been using—thank you, *Rock Band*), on the sly of course, nothing reportable to immigration authorities, just to make sure Mariano is on the up-and-up. But Mariano's passed an important test today and a celebration is in order. On the drive back to the city, Frankie surprises his young boyfriend by suggesting they go dancing. The shop is closed tomorrow and they can sleep late in the morning. But first there's a question he's been putting off, one that needs to be asked.

"Why don't you ever talk about your brother, Mariano?"

"You no ask, Frankie."

Frankie's relieved by his calm, nonchalant response. Surely he'd be nervous if he had something to hide.

"I have three sister. Two brother. Two sister and brother in Puebla. Sister and husband in New Jersey."

"And Randy?"

"Randy in Baltimore with his baby. You and me talk about Randy before when I go see him."

It all sounds perfectly reasonable to Frankie. He wants to know everything there is to know about Mariano's family. But it can wait until tomorrow. Or the next day. Mariano's already happily preoccupied, shimmying in his seat to a new release, undeniably catchy, by some improbably named singer called Lady Gaga, pumping up his adrenaline in anticipation of a night on the dance floor.

"Dad, my stomach hurts."

"Are we watching a video, pal?" Michael asks as Danny shuffles through the discs, looking for *Transformers,* his favorite. "How much candy did you eat?"

"Not too much."

"Go poop if your stomach hurts. You'll feel better."

It's Michael's one-size-fits-all solution for every childhood complaint.

"I don't have to poop. What are you eating?"

Danny's caught him red-handed with a big chunk of a marzipan lamb in his palm.

"Can I have some?" he asks.

"You don't like this kind of candy," Michael insists.

"Yes, I do."

"You always spit it out of your mouth."

"I won't."

Michael pinches off a big piece of the rump for his son. Soon enough there's nothing left of the sacrificial lamb but the sugary paste beneath their fingernails.

"Dad, can I ask you a question?"

He's clearly not completely absorbed in the careening Autobots wreaking earsplitting havoc on the television screen.

"Sure."

"Is Mariano a boy or a girl?"

"He's a boy, Danny. You know that."

"Why are he and Uncle Frankie friends?"

Michael thought the day was too benign to be true. He tosses a fistful of jelly beans into his mouth and slowly cogitates on how to answer the question in a way that's honest but won't overload his son with information a nine-year-old is too young too process.

"I know why, Dad. It's because Uncle Frankie is gay," Danny announces, growing impatient.

"Then why are you asking?" Michael's eager to change the subject before the inevitable twenty questions begin. "Now either watch the movie or go up to bed."

Kit enters the room with a glass of wine for herself and a tumbler of small-batch bourbon for her husband.

"I think you've earned a reward today," she says, settling on the sofa next to her husband. "Oh God, Danny. *Transformers*? Again? Run upstairs and tell your sister to stop texting for one hour and join us."

"Just so you know, she told me about the divorce in the car," Michael confides when they're alone.

"That fucking bastard. I hope he's in a car wreck tomorrow."

"Hey, hey, hey. Don't talk like that. You want the evil eye to come searching for us?" he asks, making light of superstitions in which he still half believes.

"You are so predictable, Michael, always believing a baby grand piano is about to fall from the sky and hit you on the head," she teases, giving him an affectionate kiss on the cheek.

MARCH 29, 2008

Somewhere around the two-hundred-mile mark on their annual spring trek across the great Commonwealth of Pennsylvania, the Gagliano brothers will consider the consequences of killing each other. Spending six hours trapped together in an automobile, one brother complaining he's too cold, the other that he's too hot, can strain even the closest relationship.

"You better pull off here, Frankie, unless you want me to piss in this empty coffee cup."

The rest stop ahead is the last fuel and food for the next forty miles. The elegant roadside dining rooms conceived by visionaries like Fred Harvey and Howard Johnson have gone the way of the Automat and curbside service, razed to rubble and replaced by industrial-looking food courts where a potbellied, fat-assed army traipses between fast-food counters, lured by the smell of fryer grease and charred meat. The thermostat is still cranked for the dead of winter despite the spring-like warmth outside. Mothers in sweatpants and flip-flops dispatch their broods to line up for pre-cooked burgers and buckets of greasy fried chicken. An obese trucker ambles toward the door, sucking a *venti* Frappuccino, extra whipped cream, through a straw and squeezing a handful of greasy soft pretzel in his fist.

A small corps of gray-haired service workers in blue smocks shuffles through the cluster of cranky guests, going about their duties without complaint. Their stiff gaits betray the sheet-metal tightness in their lower backs and the fiery flashes of pain in their fallen arches. They plod through their shifts, hoping for overtime because their Social Security checks don't cover the rent and groceries and the car insurance. The granny behind the Starbucks counter struggles with a paper cup sleeve; a wiry old gent drags a bag of trash behind him, leaving a trail of napkins and soda cups.

"Mikey, come here, over here," Frankie shouts, his voice carrying across the crowded room.

He's in a quandary and needs Michael's expert opinion to help him decide which stuffed animal Polly will find more adorable.

"This one?" he asks, holding up a floppy brown rodent. "Or this one?" he asks, pointing at a stuffed bear.

Michael doesn't know. Polly never seemed like the plush-toy type, but he thinks she'd prefer the generic baby-blue teddy bear with the **I♥ PA** bib.

"Why the hell would she want a stuffed rat?" he asks.

"It's Punxsutawney Phil, the most famous groundhog in the world."

Frankie rolls his eyes, smiling, clearly in cahoots with the cashier.

"You've got beautiful eyes," Frankie says as he hands her the signed credit card receipt. "I bet people told you looked like Rita Hayworth when you were young."

After all these years, Michael is still amazed by, and a little envious of, Frankie's ability to look at a sad-faced, scrawny old duck and see a beautiful swan.

"It just breaks my heart," Frankie says as they walk to the car. "Did you see her hands? Jesus Christ, I bet she hasn't been able to straighten her fingers for years. Can you even imagine how much it must hurt for her to try to count change all day long? It's just plain wrong that a woman her age needs to work that hard."

"Maybe she likes working."

Frankie spins on his heels to confront his brother, the expression on his face suspended between being flabbergasted and furious at his ignorance.

"Please tell me you don't believe that."

"Maybe she doesn't want to sit at home all day," Michael says, provoking an argument.

"Yeah. That must be it. She'd be bored to death with nothing to do but watch Whoopi and the girls go at it on *The View.* Maybe you should try standing on your feet on a concrete floor eight hours every day before you start making a speech honoring the dignity of old-fashioned, backbreaking labor."

Michael sighs, conceding the point.

"What is it you want me to do about it, Frankie? You want me to write the poor woman a personal check? How much should I make it out for? Do you want me to do it anonymously or can I at least take a deduction for it? You tired? Do you want me to drive for a while?"

"No, you drive like a maniac. It makes me nervous," Frankie says, calling a truce.

Confined to her wheelchair by a dual diagnosis of MS and emphysema, their half sister Polly's world has shrunk to the small rooms of the first floor of a musty clapboard mill house in a dying industrial town in western Pennsylvania. The town's hanging on like her, barely, on life support, sustained by pipe dreams of civic revival and rumors of the imminent arrival of eco-friendly manufacturing jobs. But there are whispers of layoffs at the last standing steel manufacturing plant, and the brewery once renowned throughout the world for its iconic green beer bottles is shuttered and scheduled for demolition. The local Polish and Croatian clubs are boarded up and a single train a day stops at the once-busy station. Kids bolt for the Sunbelt and California as soon as they graduate high school. The nursing homes are filled to capacity.

Illness and aging haven't ennobled Polly. If anything, she's more ornery than ever, barking orders at the pierced and inked Cinderella in residence, a step-granddaughter on hiatus between stints in rehab. It's a source of family pride that young Melissa has conquered her street-drug habits; her current addiction to prescription painkillers is more socially acceptable. She's out on bail, up on charges of trying to pass a forged script for Percocet at the neighborhood CVS. She's hoping for a short sentence at another treatment facility, anything to escape the purgatory of confinement to her grandmother's home. Frankie and Michael arrived an hour ago and have overstayed their welcome by fifty-five minutes. Polly's more interested in the histrionic prognostications on Fox than in her flesh and blood.

"What sounds good for dinner, Polly?" Frankie asks. "We passed a Red Lobster on the highway. An Olive Garden, too."

He's insisting they treat her to a birthday dinner at one of the local chains. Melissa's up for the prospect of a brief reprieve from these four walls, even if mealtime requires vigilant supervision to make sure Polly doesn't choke on her food.

"You go," Polly wheezes. "I'm going to finish the macaroni salad I had for lunch."

As far as Michael's concerned, they've done their duty, made the trek across the state, six hours to get here, six hours going back. But Frankie won't hear of cutting their losses and heading home. They agreed to stay twenty-four hours and they are not leaving one minute earlier, no matter what fresh hell they are forced to endure.

"Turn that up, Melissa," Polly demands. "Look at him," she practically spits, disgusted by the smiling young black man shaking hands on the screen.

"He's coming to Latrobe today, Mimi," the younger woman says, enthusiastic over the prospect of the campaign trail rolling through her hometown.

"Why? There aren't any niggers here to vote for him."

The epithet rolls off her tongue casually, without passion or venom, no more remarkable than if she were describing someone as tall or short, blonde or brunette.

"Mimi, please," the girl pleads, eager to distance herself from the old woman's unapologetic racism. After all, Melissa's not like the small-minded people who live in this town and has a biracial daughter she gave up for adoption to prove it.

Polly is squirming in her wheelchair, obviously in pain. The MS has progressed rapidly in the past few years, the relapses occurring more and more frequently, exacerbated by the gradual corrosion of her lungs. She's nothing but a stick figure, all elbows and ribs, her pink sweatsuit a literal bag of bones. Her stocking feet are warped and twisted and her face resembles a dried apple. But her blue eyes still blaze with the fury that's sustained her for a lifetime.

"Well, I think Hillary's going to be a fantastic president!" Frankie says.

"She wants to kill our babies," Polly hisses, spoiling for a fight.

"Do you think I should vote for Hillary?" Melissa asks Frankie. "I just don't know."

"Not if you're going to live in this house," her step-grandmother pronounces.

"You can't tell me who to vote for," she insists, teeming with resentment.

It's academic, this argument. Michael suspects Melissa isn't even a registered voter. Besides, the topic under fire hardly matters. If it's not politics, they'll find something else to bicker about, sparring to pass the time.

"I suppose *you're* going to vote for *him,*" Polly says, her voice confrontational, accusing Michael of a multitude of sins, among them stupidity, naïveté, and blind loyalty to the liberalism that threatens to bring down the country.

"I don't know who I'm voting for," he admits.

Frankie and Melissa have lost interest in any further political discourse and turned their attention to the stuffed groundhog.

"I don't know why I even give a damn." Polly sighs. "I'll be dead before it's all said and done."

"You think he's going to win?" Michael asks.

"It's their turn now. There's too many of them to stop it. I'm just glad I won't be here to see it."

Polly calls for Melissa, coughing and wheezing, her oxygen levels depleted by the effort required to raise her voice above a gruff monotone.

"I'm ready."

"Already, Mimi? It's still early."

"I'm tired. I want to go to bed."

Melissa sighs, resigned to the fact her rare opportunity to indulge in an all-you-can-eat-shrimp-and-lobster buffet has slipped away. She shuffles off to the kitchen and returns with a pack of cigarettes and a lighter. Frankie and Michael are speechless as she shakes a Benson & Hedges 100 from the pack and fires up, swallowing a chestful of smoke and exhaling through her nostrils. She walks over to the wheelchair, drops to her knee, and holds the burning cigarette up to her step-grandmother's lips. Polly leans forward, twisting her entire body in the chair, pumping every bit of energy in her frail body into a Herculean effort to draw enough breath to suck the precious smoke into her brittle lungs. Her tongue makes a dry clucking sound against the roof of her mouth as she pauses between each labored puff.

"Shouldn't you turn that thing off?" Frankie asks, the flammable oxygen tank nearby obviously making him nervous.

"It's okay," Melissa assures him. "Are you done, Mimi?"

The old woman shakes her head no and opens her mouth, anxious for another jolt of nicotine.

"Two a day. That's all I let her have. And she won't rat me out to the agency nurse for taking some of her Oxys. That's our deal. Right, Mimi?"

Michael looks down at his feet, uncomfortable witnessing the final indignity of a dying woman being forced to agree to a Faustian bargain to indulge in the one small pleasure left in her miserable life.

"Okay, Mimi. Done," Melissa says, stabbing out the butt in an ashtray. "Time for bed. Say good night. Your brothers will be back to say good-bye in the morning," she promises, anxious to put their sister down for the night and indulge in whatever substances she's stashed away.

"I'm not doing anything about it," Michael insists. "And neither are you."

Frankie's up in arms, arguing that they need to report Polly's dire circumstances to the county Department of Aging. They'll have a caseworker at the house by Monday morning to investigate; they might even send someone out tonight if they can persuade them it's an emergency.

"It's elder abuse, pure and simple. She's our sister. We need to rescue her. It's our duty."

"So you think those caseworkers are going to let her smoke?"

"She shouldn't be smoking anyway."

"Why not? You afraid it's going to kill her?"

"That kid could be high as a kite on whatever drugs she's stealing. She's going to get too close to that tank with that cigarette and blow the place up."

There's a commotion growing toward the front of the bar, some whooping and hollering and a smattering of applause.

"I don't think one lousy cigarette is going to cause an explosion."

"We need to do something, Mikey!" he pleads.

"Why? She looked okay to me, all things considered. Did you see any bruises? Any bedsores? Was she lying in filth? Her clothes were clean. She was eating her fucking macaroni salad and bitching at the television screen. You call that being abused? If she wants to trade a few of her pain pills for cigarettes, what business is it of ours?"

The patrons seem to have lost interest in the NCAA tournament game on the widescreen televisions mounted above the bar, Davidson versus Wisconsin, score tied at thirty-six apiece. They've turned their attention to the racket on the far side of the room.

"Where's that girl? This shit is undrinkable," Frankie complains.

"I told you not to order red wine in a sports bar," Michael reminds him. "I wouldn't use that crap for salad dressing."

They've still got time to kill before the seven o'clock feature at the mall multiplex. Polly's early bedtime has freed up their evening and there are plenty of hours to fill before an early turn-in at the budget chain hotel where Frankie booked a room. Sharky's Café looked like a good place to grab a bacon cheeseburger before the movie, and Frankie says the chicken Caesar salad is better than he expected, though he's positive he'd told the waitress to bring the dressing on the side.

"What the fuck is going on up there?" Michael asks, perplexed by the arrival of news cameras and spotlights.

A burly, wide-shouldered tackle in a black suit has positioned himself in front of their table. He's speaking into his security headset, summoning two large bodyguards, who quietly hustle a drunk kid out of the room.

"Oh my God! I don't believe it!" Frankie gasps.

"What?" Michael asks, mumbling through a mouthful of cheeseburger.

"It's him!"

Standing across the bar, daintily sipping a draft beer from the lip of his glass, leaning forward to listen intently to the flannel-shirted local who's giving him an earful, is the man who would be President of the United States of America. He nods thoughtfully, though the bar is so loud it's hard to imagine he can actually hear the opinionated citizen's words, then tosses back his head and rewards the fellow with his blazing, irresistible smile.

"He is so thin!" Frankie gushes.

"He is so fucking young," Michael says, trying to seem blasé, though Obama is so compelling it's impossible to take his eyes off him.

Their Democratic senator is chaperoning the candidate, an exotic stranger from parts unknown and untrustworthy. They stop to introduce themselves to a table of young soldiers wearing camouflage and heavy boots. The kids stare at one another, clearly embarrassed, too uncomfortable for small talk. Obama's persistent, unflappable; he points at a television screen and makes a graceful little dunking motion with his arm. The soldiers relax, laughing, and stand to shake his hand as he thanks them for their service and sacrifice and wishes them Godspeed.

"I hope he isn't coming over here unless he wants to hear why I'm voting for Hillary," Frankie says, pumped full of bravado.

"Yeah, right," Michael says, mocking him. "I fucking dare you."

A pair of chubby girls, one with a very prominent Hillary button, plead with the candidate to pose for a picture. He smiles for their tiny camera phone, an arm chastely draped over each of their shoulders. The bar is in good cheer. Michael doubts a single person here intends to cast their ballot for him, but, for the moment, they're basking in the reflected glow of his star power, thrilled to have the man of the hour, a constant presence on their television screens, among them.

"Oh, no! I don't believe it! Here he comes!" Frankie gasps, twitching nervously.

"Hey, guys," the senator from Illinois says as he approaches their table. "Enjoying the game?"

Michael stands and introduces himself, pausing to let his brother follow suit.

"And this is my brother, Frankie," he finally says. "He usually isn't at a loss for words."

"Nice to meet you, Frankie," the senator says, offering his hand. "What do you do here in Latrobe?"

"We're from Philly," Frankie corrects him when he finally finds his voice.

Obama shakes his head thoughtfully, squinting as if he's trying to formulate the perfect question to solicit their advice on an important issue.

"So, who do you guys have in the Final Four in your brackets?"

"I'm going with UNC to take it all. Frankie isn't much of a fan. But I know he's got something he's dying to say to you."

He sees murder in his brother's pupils.

"Shoot," the senator says.

"I just wanted to tell you that's a really beautiful tie," Frankie stammers.

"Thanks. I'll tell Michelle. She picked it out." He smiles, waving good-bye as he's gently nudged to the next table.

"You are a complete asshole," Frankie hisses, tossing back his glass of swill in a single gulp.

"What's the matter, Mr. Tough Guy?" Michael laughs. "God, I thought you were going to ask him for a hug."

"Well, I'm not voting for him," he insists, demanding the immediate attention of the server to bring him an Absolut and tonic to calm his nerves.

"Oh, I bet you will."

"Never," he insists. "Not in a million years."

MARCH 30, 2008

The motel was the best Latrobe had to offer. The mattresses were lumpy and the rugs and curtains reeked of mildew and industrial shampoo. Frankie was dozing when he was awakened by the telephone long after midnight. Mariano was in the mood to talk, chatting up a blue streak, barely pausing to catch his breath. But it was strictly a one-sided conversation, conducted entirely in Spanish despite Frankie's pleas that Mariano speak English, slowly, so he could be understood. Something, or someone, distracted Mariano and he'd wandered off. Frankie waited ten minutes for him to return, then hung up.

He should have insisted they bring him along. Mariano would have been perfectly content in the backseat of the car watching videos on Frankie's laptop and listening to his iPod and there's a decent selection of in-room movies that would have kept him occupied while Frankie and Michael visited with their sister. But his presence would have only further irritated his brother, who was already grumbling about making the dreaded trip. He slept fitfully after the call, having foolishly left his Ambien home, not thinking he would need it. He dressed before dawn, showered and shaved, made a run to Dunkin' Donuts, and roused Michael from a deep sleep when he returned.

"No donuts until you're dressed and packed," Frankie announces. "If you hurry, we can be on the Turnpike by eleven."

Suddenly, Michael is full of energy, raring to go. They were supposed to spend the entire day with their sister before driving back to Philly in the late afternoon. Michael suspects this unexpected good fortune has something to do with Frankie's phone ringing in the middle of the night and Frankie barricading himself in the bathroom to answer. He's in and out of the shower and ready to check out in twenty minutes.

"You better stop at that Dunkin' Donuts again," Michael says as they drive away from the motel parking lot. "I wouldn't mind another cup of coffee."

"How many of those donuts have you eaten?"

"Three," Michael admits sheepishly. "Maybe four. Who called you in the middle of the night?"

"It was Jack. Father Parisi's probably not going to make it through the night," he lies, a convenient alibi for their early departure.

"Jesus, is he still alive? How old is he? A hundred?"

"I told you he's in hospice. Do you ever listen to anything I say? I feel like I'm talking to a brick wall. I'm going straight to the hospice when we get home. Do you want to come?"

Frankie knows it's bad luck, tempting fate, to lie about death, especially the passing of a priest, but it's better than Michael knowing Mariano was high as a kite, alone (hopefully) in the house where they grew up.

"I haven't seen the man in thirty years. Why would I show up at his deathbed? You're the one who's made him a saint of the church. You know what I remember best about the guy? I've been in a lot of locker rooms in my life and I don't think I've ever seen a cock on a white man as big as the piece of equipment that fucking old priest was packing. He was even bigger than Papa. What a waste!" Michael laughs.

Frankie is speechless, his brother's casual observation a punch in the gut.

"What the fuck are you talking about, Mikey? I never saw Father Parisi naked and neither did you!"

"Don't bitch at me about this. I get enough lectures about the evils of refined sugar from Kit," Michael pleads as he helps himself to yet another donut. "I never get to eat these fucking things at home. Don't you remember showering with him, Frankie?" he asks as he licks the last of the sticky glaze from his gooey fingers. "Are there any napkins?"

"Never. I never showered with him. Never. Ever. Father Parisi was the most modest man I ever knew!"

Frankie remembers Jack saying the old man is terrified of dying, fearing an eternity in the burning flames of hell. He can't grasp the idea of that gentle priest exposing himself to his little brother, refuses to believe it's possible. He's surprised to hear himself calling his brother a liar.

"Don't get yourself all twisted over nothing, Frankie," Michael says, amused by his brother's indignant defense of the old man. "It's not like I'm accusing him of being a child molester, for Christ's sake. Remember when he took us swimming at Neshaminy State Park? There was one of those big open showers in the dressing room. There were at least twenty guys with their kids in there at the time. He caught me staring at him and promised me I'd be as big as he was when I grew up. Fucking priest was a liar!" Michael laughed.

Frankie remembers now being too shy to undress in a room full of naked men and riding back to the city in cold, wet trunks, sitting on a towel to protect the upholstery of Father's new Plymouth sedan.

"Jesus, Frankie. I can't believe how you overreacted. That old man was a little weird with his Polaroids and shit, but he wasn't a pervert."

Polly is almost pleasant, pleased with the offering of donuts, her mouth and cheeks dusted with powdered sugar. She's even turned down the volume of the television so that *Fox News Sunday* is barely audible. She has something to discuss with her brothers, with Michael especially as the lawyer in the family, something too important to be entrusted to her stepfamily. Michael can recite her instructions word for word, the same directives she repeats year after year. She slowly and solemnly reminds him where to find her last will and testament and to use the proceeds of a small life insurance policy she maintains to pay for the disposal of her remains.

She insists he write down the name and number of the local mortician (just as she had the last time he'd seen her), and solicits his solemn assurance as her executor that he will ensure a direct cremation, no viewing or service. Finally, he agrees, again, to personally transport her ashes back east to be interred in the family plot. Frankie shows her photographs of the new headstone for her approval. She's pleased to see her name etched in marble below her mother's and next to her son's.

"And you," she asks, pointing a half-chewed donut at Michael. "Where are you going to be?"

"I'm being cremated, too, and my wife's gonna sleep with my ashes under her pillow," Michael jokes. It's a sore subject with Frankie that his brother's urn will be buried with the family of his wife in the ancient columbarium of St. Peter's Episcopal.

"What about my dad? You just gonna leave him here alone?" a deep voice inquires, startling Frankie and Michael, neither of whom had heard Carl, Polly's morbidly obese stepson, silently enter the room on his padded feet.

"You can be buried with him if you're so worried about him being lonely," she snorts. "He can rot in hell, for all I care."

Her relatively benign mood is short-lived. The mere presence of her stepson irritates her. Michael had hoped to escape back home without seeing the giant ne'er-do-well, but Carl wouldn't miss an opportunity to hit up his prosperous kin for enough cash to tide him over until his next worker's comp payment is deposited in his account. He disgusts Michael, always has, though now for different reasons from when he was the malevolent tormentor of his gentle older brother. Carl stands six-five. His large frame and broad Slavic shoulders can support a lot of weight, but he's clearly pushing north of three-fifty on the scales these days. He wheezes as he shuffles toward the donut box on the kitchen table. His fingers are gnarled and swollen; the nails are broken stubs, covered with a thick fungus. He pokes the donuts, searching for one filled with yellow custard.

"How are you, Carl? How's your back?" Frankie asks, forever polite and solicitous.

"I got good days and bad, Frankie," he responds with a shrug. "I been seeing a pain guy down in Pittsburgh."

Michael suspects the health-care professional he's consulting works out of the backseat of a beat-up Camaro in a Wal-Mart parking lot, dispensing pharmaceuticals in Ziploc bags.

"You look like you've lost some weight since last year," Frankie says.

"Yeah, ten, fifteen pounds. Still got a ways to go," Carl says, patting the flabby pouch drooping over the elastic waistband of his sweatpants.

"Then keep your filthy hands off my donuts," his stepmother curses. "Where is that daughter of yours? Go see if she's passed out somewhere."

"I'm right here, Mimi," Melissa announces. She's obviously just crawled out of bed, her hair unbrushed, her stale breath noticeable even from a distance. "Who stuck their fingers in these donuts?"

"Ask your father," her step-grandmother sneers.

She looks at her dad and giggles. Michael, the prosecutor, doesn't miss a trick. He sees the meaningful look between father and daughter as Carl subtly taps his finger on the zippered pocket of his nylon jacket. How sweet of him to supplement the dosage his kid can extort from her grandmother. For a small price, of course, probably ten bucks a pill. Carl and Melissa excuse themselves, seeking privacy to conduct the transaction.

"I should have been nicer to your mother," Polly mutters. "I'm going to apologize to her as soon as I get to heaven. Right after I see my Sonny." She's been patiently awaiting her reunion with her only son since he came back from the Gulf War in a body bag. "She used to tell me how pretty I was, how she wished her eyes were as blue as mine. I still have the sterling comb and brush set she gave me for my sixteenth birthday. They're in a bag in my dresser drawer. You should have them, Frankie. Take them home with you. They'll just sell them for drug money after I'm dead," she says, spitting contempt.

"Your mother was too good for Papa. Mine was, too," she says, taking a sip from a cup of cold coffee and clearing her throat. "He slapped me so hard he knocked me to the floor when I told him I was pregnant with Sonny. Even marrying that drunken hunkie was better than living with Papa. I don't think he ever said a nice word to me, not one. Maybe he did, but I just don't remember."

The thought of Papa makes Polly irritable. She turns up the volume of the television and devotes her attention to the histrionic ranting about the liberal agenda. Frankie goes to the bedroom to retrieve his bequest. Michael sees a pack of Benson & Hedges and a Bic on the counter and steals a cigarette, slipping out the back door to sneak a smoke. He'd taken up the habit to cope with the pressures of law school and had smoked until Kit, then his fiancée, forced him to give it up. Sometimes he still yields to temptation. Three or four low-tar-and-nicotines a year aren't going to kill him.

He stands under an awning, protected from the light drizzle. The first drag sears his throat and sets him off on a coughing jag, but, after a few puffs, he's sucking the smoke into his lungs as if he never quit. The fucking yard looks dystopian, post-apocalyptic. The metal garbage cans are overflowing with empty wine bottles and beer cans. A trash bag on the porch has been torn open by vermin—raccoons or stray cats—and the lawn is pockmarked with sinkholes. A rusty propane grill is upended in the mud.

How the fuck do people live like this? he wonders, flicking his cigarette butt in the wet grass. Not just people, *these* people, tied to him by blood and marriage? It's a goddamn joke. This fucking squalor mocks all his accomplishments and achievements, linking him to a lineage that feels like the history of a complete stranger. He looks at his watch and sees it's nearly eleven. It's time to say their good-byes and put this weekend in the rearview mirror. He goes inside, catching Frankie red-handed in an act of misplaced charity. Frankie's wallet is open and he's counting out twenties—one, two, three, four, five—into Carl's open palm.

A man's home is his castle, impregnable, a fortress surrounded by a moat teeming with flesh-eating sharks and crocodiles and secured by a raised drawbridge and iron portcullises to fortify the gate. The dreaded annual visit (most likely, the last) is over and Michael's safely ensconced in his National Register of Historic Places–designated neighborhood. He's lying on his leather sofa, digesting takeout pad thai, watching highlights from the early rounds of the Big Dance while sipping an IPA from a local craft brewery. His son is fast asleep upstairs; his stepdaughter is in her room, sharing confidences with her electronic social network. His wife is reading P. D. James in bed, nursing a mug of herbal tea. He can finally relax now that the barbarians are on the far side of the ancient mountain range, out of sight and out of mind.

He's going to insist there be no further contact with Polly's stepfamily once her ashes are tucked away in the family plot. The chasm between their worlds is unbridgeable. Their lives are case studies in self-destruction, their lack of ambition incomprehensible. Frankie will put up an argument, insisting that, like it or not, they are family, even if they aren't blood relatives. He's naïve and gullible, easily manipulated, a sucker for their plots and schemes. But right now there's a more immediate problem than the Shevchek tribe three hundred miles away. He's confirmed Mariano doesn't have a criminal record, at least under the name by which Michael knows him. There aren't any prints on file. He's certainly not enthusiastic about fighting to keep the kid in the country legally, but he isn't objecting, either, conceding to his wife and brother's united front. But it doesn't feel right. His gut instinct, rarely wrong, is telling him it's only a matter of time until that fucking little Mexican disappears with the clothes on his back, the cash in Frankie's wallet, and Papa's ridiculously expensive timepiece that had formerly belonged to Frannie Merlino's late husband. And that's the happiest of the many bad endings he can imagine for their toxic relationship.

After the ominous phone call from Mariano in the wee hours of the morning, Frankie wouldn't have been surprised to arrive home and find the doors wide open, the windows busted out, the entire contents looted and destroyed. He's relieved to discover the shop in perfect condition, not a comb or scissor out of place, and a strange blonde calmly sitting in a stylist chair, holding a drowsy toddler in her lap. He's startled, not knowing what to say, when she rises to greet him.

"You must be Frankie. I am so glad you made it home before we had to leave. We really wanted to meet you."

She's a rough-looking woman, with a ravaged complexion and brittle hair.

"Cameron, say hello to Uncle Frankie. Be a good boy and shake his hand."

Cameron isn't interested in making a new acquaintance, much to the embarrassment of the woman Frankie assumes is his mother.

"He's really tired. He's been up since seven this morning and missed his nap."

"Would he like some juice? There's apple cranberry in the refrigerator," Frankie asks, before ascertaining the identity of these strangers who seem quite at home in his shop. His instinct for hospitality trumps curiosity.

"Thanks, but he's already had plenty. Mariano was sweet enough to find him something to eat and drink."

Frankie is finally about to ask how this woman and child ended up in his salon when Mariano and an older, taller man—busily engaged in an animated conversation—enter through the shop door.

"*Hola,* Frankie!" Mariano shouts as he embraces his confused boyfriend with an affectionate hug. "This is my brother, Randy. From Baltimore. And his baby."

Frankie's finding it hard to see the family resemblance except in the broadest sense, in the way that a rhinoceros and a hippopotamus are both enormous mammals that live in the jungle. Randy is a scary guy, his skin thick as hide and pebbled with scar tissue. His lazy left eye drifts from object to object, never settling, finding nothing worthy of engaging its interest. His bloodlines are pre-Columbian; his bulk is solid muscle, his body a blunt object built for power.

"My father brought our mother and me to Los Angeles when I was three," he explains when Frankie compliments his command of the English language.

Frankie's curious, of course, but is too polite to ask prying questions. And, he's afraid of probing areas that might be sensitive, not meant to be shared beyond the intimate circle of blood relatives. But Randy generously offers more details of the Garza family history.

"After he was killed, our mother returned to Puebla and married his younger brother, who is Mariano's father."

Despite his thuggish appearance, Randy's manners are impeccable, almost florid. He's got an old-world sense of dignity and propriety as he extravagantly praises Frankie's generosity, expressing his gratitude for rescuing their little *burro* from a Snyder Avenue flophouse.

"Have you eaten?" Frankie asks. "We can walk over to Ninth Street and have a late dinner. My treat."

"No, no," Randy insists. "We must be going. It's late and we should be on our way."

"Well, I hope to see you both again soon. Come for the weekend. You are always welcome to stay with us."

"That's very kind of you. I have business here in Philly and hope to see you often."

"What do you do?" Frankie asks.

"Distribution. Mostly soda from Mexico and candy."

Frankie notices Mariano is distracted by a new telephone. Randy says something in Spanish, growling in a harsh voice, sounding intimidating.

"Excuse me. That is very rude, speaking our language in your home," he apologizes. "You'll help him with his English, I hope. We don't want our little *burro* to sound like a wetback forever."

April 5, 2008

"Roll over, please."

The spa attendant grabs Frankie's arm and twists it behind his back, exposing a wide patch of dry skin to attack with his loofah sponge. Something stronger than a gentle touch is needed to scrub away the damage caused by four months' exposure to the winter air.

"Turn on back, please."

Frankie's treating himself and Mariano to this small indulgence tonight. It's almost sinful, lying splayed across a table, buck naked, not moving a muscle to lift an arm or a leg while his chapped and flaking skin is restored to a pink, healthy glow. He feels like a decadent Roman senator, Laurence Olivier in *Spartacus.* Closing his eyes, he imagines the young Tony Curtis, not a buck-toothed, ancient, half-naked Korean midget with garlic breath, is giving him a soothing bath. The attendant dumps a bucket of warm water over his supine body.

"On stomach, please."

The man's probing fingers find all the pressure points in Frankie's muscles. The little gnome's hands are surprisingly strong. His thumbs work their magic, releasing the tension in his neck and shoulders. Frankie marvels at how the man finds the energy to do ten, twelve, body scrubs a day.

"Is good?"

"Very."

He melts on the table as the Korean picks up his loofah and goes to town on his back and buttocks.

"Too hard?"

"No. It feels great."

Actually, it feels like a thousand tiny pinpricks and he winces as the attendant rinses his raw skin with the spray hose.

"Turn on back, please."

He feels completely unselfconscious, lying here, his big floppy pecker fully exposed. He admires these Asians and their lack of modesty about their bodies. Men of every age and size, tall and short ones, bony scarecrows and roly-polies with sagging bellies, are going about their ablutions. Wrinkled, dimpled, creased, some surprisingly hairy, many of them shockingly smooth, they squat on overturned buckets, scrubbing, shaving, rinsing, and brushing their teeth with single-minded determination. Mariano had seemed embarrassed by all the naked flesh and was reluctant to remove the towel he'd wrapped tightly around his waist. He'd covered his crotch with his hand in the steam room and tucked his penis between his crossed legs in the soaking pool, shyly averting his eyes from the parade of phalluses on display. Not that there's much to stare at—they're Asians, after all—except for an impressively hung Russian, a heavily tattooed cement block of a man, who struck up a conversation with Frankie in the hot tub after Mariano was called for his appointment with the shiatsu therapist. He seemed like a friendly enough guy. His foot kept brushing against Frankie's shin and his gap-tooth smile suggested the wildly inappropriate thoughts of an overactive Slavic libido.

"Sit up, please."

The Korean wraps his arms around Frankie's chest and squeezes tightly, cracking his back, then gives his shoulder blades a spirited thumping for the grand finale.

"All done," he announces.

Frankie slowly lowers himself from the table and steadies himself on his feet before wandering off in search of creams and lotions to soothe his raging skin. He uses Crème de la Mer at home, but the economy moisturizers provided by the thrifty Koreans will have to do in a pinch. The lotion feels slick and oily on his face and arms; he slaps it on his chest and legs, but he needs Mariano's hands to smear it across his back. As usual, he's nowhere to be found when Frankie needs him. The attendant is padding around the locker room in his bare feet, collecting wet towels and emptying trash cans. Frankie has time for a shave while he waits for Mariano and retreats to the steam room to soften his prickly whiskers. A blast of steam sears his face as he opens the frosted glass door, surprising the Russian, who flashes a wicked grin, not knowing or not caring it's Frankie's boyfriend whose spit-slicked ass he's enthusiastically fucking with his enormous cock.

"Tight. Very nice," the Russian says as he graciously withdraws and steps aside, inviting Frankie to take his turn.

April 6, 2008

Every day's a holiday in the Gayborhood, but this Sunday afternoon is even more festive than usual. The sunshine is glorious, no clouds in the sky, proving that God surely can't hate fags, despite the insistence of the militant fundamentalist protesters marching behind police barriers with their Bible-quoting picket signs. The burly cops, working-class Irish and African Americans, eye the God-fearing marchers suspiciously, finding them even more freakish than the elaborately coiffed drag queens and leather-clad muscle bears celebrating the diversity of pride with a beery and boisterous street fair. Miss Bonnie Faye Crawford, a travesty of femininity in a size twenty-two sequined gown, takes the outdoor stage at Twelfth and Locust to introduce an eager pack of buff, shirtless bartenders who are gyrating and lip-synching to a fabulous new single called "Just Dance" by Mariano's latest favorite diva. The crowd is squealing like teenage girls at the height of Beatlemania. Frankie didn't know it was possible to scream *ohmygod!* at the top of your lungs for three minutes running without taking a breath.

"Well, Francis, are you going to introduce me to your young friend?"

If Frankie had seen him approaching he would have grabbed Mariano by the arm and disappeared into the crowd. Seamus Ferguson is the nastiest bitch Frankie's ever had the misfortune of encountering. A red-faced old drunk, his fat cheeks mottled by a lifetime of imbibing, he's never really forgiven Frankie for being unable to conceal the appalled expression on his face when Seamus made a drunken advance at Frankie shortly after Charlie's death.

"And what might your name be?" the old queen asks Mariano.

Frankie's seen this act of Mariano's too many times now. It's lost whatever charm it once had: the feigned shyness, the fluttering eyelashes, the exaggerated look of deference as if Frankie were his lord and master and he's the subject who needs permission to speak.

"His name is Mariano," Frankie says briskly, not trying to hide his irritation.

"Cat got your tongue?" Seamus asks, hoping the lascivious twinkle in his eye might appear seductive. But Mariano's already lost interest in the old ogre. His gaze is fixated on the glistening torsos of the dancers on the stage.

"Looks like you're going to have to keep this one on a short leash, Francis. Unless you two have one of those modern relationships, anything goes."

"I suppose," Frankie says.

He hadn't expected a *modern* relationship when he asked Mariano to share his home. He'd never believed Mariano, a very young man with a strong libido, would be faithful. He's older and wiser than when he'd met Charlie Haldermann and had expected a lifetime of unwavering monogamy. But Frankie is old-school and had expected discretion. Outside sexual activities were to be conducted in secret, never admitted or openly discussed. He doesn't remember ever agreeing to an open relationship with Mariano, but he's adapted quickly, even enthusiastically at times. You won't hear him complaining when Mariano invites one of his pretty little friends to join them for a romp in their king-size bed.

"Well, more power to you. I don't know where you get the energy. I can't stay awake for the late news anymore."

A gaggle of Mexican boys rushes up to embrace Mariano. They're painfully effeminate, their eyelids streaked with eyeliner and lashes caked with mascara. They surround Mariano, deferential, as if he's the alpha male or, more appropriately, the queen bee. They admire his tight Diesel jeans and polished Cole Haans, charged to Frankie's

American Express, and listen with rapt attention when he speaks. Frankie doesn't know Spanish, but Mariano's patronizing, grandiose tone of voice needs no translation. Mariano opens his mouth, showing them where he'll be fitted for a bridge. They nod appreciatively, impressed by his ability to exploit the endless opportunities in the promised land. His friends plead with him insistently, tugging him by the wrist, trying to drag him away.

"They are going to dance, Frankie. I want to go to the club," he says petulantly, already having made up his mind to join them. Frankie gives his blessing, wishing that Seamus didn't seem to be so thoroughly enjoying witnessing him being abandoned at the kid's first opportunity to flee.

"What say we old farts go for a quick drink?" Seamus asks, but Frankie's already turned his back and is walking away. He sees a group of friends from the Charlie era, librarians and real estate agents who are counting down the years until early retirement, making monthly payments on mortgages on second homes in Rehoboth Beach, where they intend to live out their dotage, collecting pensions and Social Security. He hopes to escape his old posse without notice, but it's too late to turn his back and disappear. His friends have sighted him and are shouting for him to join them.

They share a haunted past, these men of a certain age. The ghosts of the victims of the virus will always walk among them. Survivors of the horrors of the eighties, they cling to their interrupted youths with stubborn pride, still wearing the clownish bright pastel polos and the designer jeans of the decade that defines them, though with wider waistbands and larger collars.

"You know, bitch, I shouldn't even speak to you. Don't you bother to return phone calls these days?" his friend John, a proud alumnus of the Naval Academy, pouts in mock indignation. A barrel-chested six-foot-seven with a chin that should be immortalized in bronze or marble, he's an impressive specimen of masculinity, even in his late fifties.

Frankie's been drifting from his friends for years, spending more time with Jack, feeling awkward in the midst of their insistent couplehoods. He's been actively avoiding them since meeting Mariano, knowing they would scorn the boy and talk about Frankie as an object of pity and ridicule, just another of those deluded old queens blindsided by the splendors of youthful beauty.

"Where have you been keeping yourself? I was going to drop by the shop the next time I'm in your neighborhood to make sure you're still alive," John asks.

"Well, you look good. But you always look good," John's animal-loving partner, Timmy, assures him. "Sophie, behave yourself or Mama's going to have to take you home!" he snaps, chastising the mongrel tugging on his leash, another rescue dog he's adopted to pamper with his nurturing personality.

"We're having an early dinner and you're coming with us," they insist, but before Frankie can accept, a wave of excitement rushes through the crowd. *Oh God, it's her! She looks fabulous! Get up closer, I want to meet her!* Frankie strains his neck to see which remarkable diva is passing through their midst, wondering if this mysterious new goddess whose name Frankie keeps forgetting, Lady Goo Goo or something ("It's *Gaga,* Frankie. GA-GA!"), is making an appearance.

"Chelsea! Chelsea! Over here!" Timmy shouts, waving his frightened dog in the air, trying to get the former First Daughter's attention.

The big gorilla of a governor is guiding her through her adoring public and leads her over for a nice little photo op with the puppy. John and Timmy swear an oath of allegiance to her mother; they can't wait to see Hillary's gown for the inaugural ball. Chelsea asks the breed of their pet while tickling it under its chin. The camera doesn't do the girl justice, Frankie decides; she's much prettier in person. He hears his phone ringing and sees that Mariano's calling, mostly likely needing to replenish the cash reserves Frankie had given him this morning. He hesitates, then hits ignore, and goes off to join his friends for a raucous and boozy meal.

April 7, 2008

At first, Frankie thinks it's 1978 again and he's dancing shirtless, his smooth chest glistening with sweat, spinning, spinning, Donna chanting she feels good, she feels good, she feels good . . .

But the heavy stomping up and down the staircase, the shrieks of laughter and pulsing bass lines, are an ugly reality, not a pleasant dream. It's four in the morning, only a few hours until daylight. Yesterday's revelries are still at fever pitch, having moved from some after-hours dance club to his living room downstairs. The Ambien has left Frankie woozy and he's unsteady on his feet as he reaches for his bathrobe. He makes the descent slowly, carefully placing one foot after another on the steps.

Every light in the house is burning brightly. Mariano's being a gracious host, offering vodka and tequila to his guests. The windows are wide open and a breeze ripples the sheers, but a thick layer of smoke lingers in the room. Cigarette butts smolder in makeshift ashtrays and two boys on the sofa pass a small glass pipe between them, inhaling and holding the smoke in their chests. Dance music from Frankie's youth, a track from *I Remember Yesterday,* is pounding through the speakers, not at earsplitting volume but loud enough to be heard by anyone who might be passing on the street below at this ungodly hour of the morning. The boys on the leather couch giggle and tussle, swapping spit as they work their hands into each other's pants. *Get a fucking room,* a sallow, pock-marked blond snickers as he sucks on the pipe. Frankie knows him from the neighborhood; he waits tables at one of the spaghetti houses that cater to tourists seeking "authentic" South Philly cuisine.

"*Hola,* Frankie. You want some vodka?" Mariano asks.

"I don't want any vodka," Frankie balks, asking Mariano if he knows what time it is.

"Is Monday. No work for you today," Mariano reminds him disdainfully. "You go up to sleep now," he says, dismissing Frankie as he takes the pipe from the blond.

"What is that? Who told you you could bring that into my house?"

"It's chill, man. Don't worry," the waiter assures him.

Enraged, Frankie snatches the pipe from Mariano's hand and runs to the window, throwing it into the street. The waiter raises his hand as if he's going to strike, but the usually passive Frankie picks up a heavy piece of crystal, brandishing it as a weapon.

"Get the fuck out of my house. Tell them to leave, Mariano. All of them."

The boys on the sofa zipper their pants and, still giggling, scamper toward the back staircase. The waiter hisses at Frankie, calling him a motherfucker, and tells Mariano *adiós*.

"Where are you going?" Frankie shouts as Mariano rushes to follow his friends.

"I hate you, Frankie," the boy spits. "I hope you die."

Frankie takes a deep breath, the crisis over. He gathers the smoldering ashes and flushes them down the toilet, then pours himself a vodka that he swallows in one long draft. He slowly climbs the stairs, wanting only to crawl back into bed, not caring that the extra Ambien he's going to take will put him down until late in the afternoon.

Marshall Culpepper's mind is obviously elsewhere. Kit and Michael are barely seated before he announces he's been rehearsing his performance of "nappy lord fauntleroy," the signature work that won him the Langston Hughes Medal for Poets of Color Under Thirty. He reminds them he'll be reading at an Obama rally on the Swarthmore campus tomorrow, just in case they've missed the many press releases. He doesn't feel the need to pretend he isn't bored to distraction reading adolescent analyses of *Slaughterhouse-Five* by the young scholars of the Charlotte Ingersoll School, the rigorous preparatory academy that has shaped the minds of generations of Morris-Pugh-Scott women. Come September, he'll be three thousand miles away from such dreary obligations, living in Palo Alto, a Stanford Wallace Stegner fellow in poetry with no responsibilities but chasing his muse.

Marshall's narrowed the list to three candidates for the cash award to a graduating senior funded by the modest endowment established by Kit to honor the career of Miss Eleanor Peterson. Forever self-aware of the impression he makes, he tosses his golden dreadlocks as he reviews the accomplishments supporting each of their cases for being selected as the class's most distinguished student musician. *The New Yorker* Talk of the Town correspondent who covered the Hughes Medal ceremony couldn't come up with anything more original than *café au lait* to describe his skin pigment. He's fairer than cinnamon, as pale as cashews, the perfect shade for a blue-eyed Hip-Hop Poet whose father is a direct descendant of the founder of a long-extinct shipbuilding company and whose mother, a former beauty queen and Bond girl of the Roger Moore era, is heir to the African-American beauty products empire started by her great-grandmother, a kitchen domestic from Durham, North Carolina.

Michael despises this Tupac in J. Press at first sight. All these years later, despite his many accomplishments, the boy from South Philly is still self-conscious around the privileged elite of the storied clans who summer in Bar Harbor, winter on St. Simons and Sea Islands, and gather each December at the Assembly Ball. Kit says he's being ridiculous, unfair even, but he knows they condescend to him, subtly of course. It's part of their heritage, in their blood. A young male cousin of Kit's, a junior at Bowdoin in dire need of a haircut, who spent his undergraduate summers touring the youth hostels of Europe, had once expressed shock that Michael had never seen the Tuscan countryside from atop the campanile of the Duomo. Her drunken brother Henry had attempted solidarity by confiding he'd once gotten a great blow job from a South Philly girl during an Eagles game behind a fire door at Veterans Stadium. His future mother-in-law was unnerved the first time she saw the tarnished Saint Rocco holy medal he's worn on a chain around his neck since the morning of his First Communion. To this day, they can still make Michael feel like a Tastykake—a Butterscotch Krimpet or a Peanut Butter Kandy Kake—in a box of patisserie pastries.

"They all seem deserving," Kit frets, unable to choose.

None of the young women selected as a finalist is going to find herself on the wish list of the Curtis Institute of Music. One's a pianist, one's a cellist, and the third has a sweet, if slight, soprano.

"What do you think, Michael?" she asks.

"They all look fine to me," he mumbles.

"Marshall, can we have a moment? I'd like to speak to my husband alone," Kit asks politely.

"I have to take this," he says, implying that his conveniently ringing cell phone is an urgent call and the Dean of Stanford is dying to speak with him. More likely, the video store is calling to remind him his new release rentals are a week overdue.

"You offered to come along this afternoon. Can you please stop sulking over not getting your pound of flesh from that pathetic young man and try to muster up some enthusiasm?"

Michael had been scheduled to make his opening statement this afternoon. But just as they were about to pick a jury, Arnie Strong had made a last-ditch pitch to persuade the zealous prosecutor he'd never convict his client of vehicular manslaughter. Michael finally conceded to the obvious and made a reasonable offer. The kid will do ninety days and be eligible for release after thirty, pay the maximum fine, and have his license suspended for a year. But it doesn't seem like justice to Michael. The young man has a promising future. He'll marry and have children and with any luck enjoy a long, happy, and prosperous life, while the ill-fated and long-forgotten college sweetheart he was supposed to marry rots in her grave.

"I like this one," Kit says, pointing to the photograph of the cellist.

"She looks fine to me," Michael agrees.

"You're not going to read the recommendations?" she asks.

He rubs his tired eyes with a clenched fist, squinting at the small print. She hands him her readers, a thoughtful gesture.

Marshall Culpepper gently knocks on the door, good breeding apparently well engrained, and asks if his guests need more time.

"No, we're ready," Kit announces, inviting him to return. "Libby Guilfoyle is awfully impressive. She's the perfect young woman to honor Miss Peterson's legacy."

"Excellent choice. She's a delightful young woman. She's quite the scholar, our Libby." Marshall Culpepper does an impressive impersonation of an Oxford don. "Nearly perfect board scores. A gift for the Romance languages. A talented writer. And, of course, a skilled cellist."

He finishes with a flourish, a final dramatic toss of his dread-locks.

"Well, that's that and I'm sure you want to get back to preparing for tomorrow," Kit says, smiling too broadly as she kicks Michael under the table. She knows that look on his face, the one where he's entertaining fantasies of grabbing the man by his braids and bouncing his head off the wall, and quickly hustles her husband out the door.

April 9, 2008

Randy Salazar, age 37, of the thirteen hundred block of Snyder Avenue.

Frankie holds this morning's edition of the *Daily News* close to his face, seeking absolute confirmation in the blurry Pointillism of the newsprint. There's no mistaking the flat, broken nose and the black nostrils wide enough to inhale a passing warm front. Randy Salazar, the suspect who was booked and printed, whose mug shot is prominently featured on page three, is the same man introduced to him by Mariano as his brother Randy Garza from Baltimore, with a girlfriend named Christine and a son named Cameron. He's one of six desperados, four Mexicans, a scurvy white guy Frankie doesn't recognize, and a hollow-eyed Richie Capuano, whose father owns a vegetable stall in the Ninth Street Market, who were apprehended in a raid of a crystal methamphetamine laboratory operating in an abandoned warehouse on Washington Avenue. The newspaper account says Salazar is being held without bail, awaiting extradition. He's wanted for distribution in California and Nevada and for murder and trafficking in Arizona, where, according to law enforcement agents, he'd ordered the gangland-style execution of the leader of a rival drug ring.

Frankie races through the story, searching for Mariano's name in the article, and is relieved to find he's never mentioned. He assures himself he's overreacting. Mariano's no drug dealer; the boy he knows would never be involved in violent crime. This Randy Salazar or Randy Garza, whatever his name is, may not even be his brother. There's no family resemblance between Mariano and that odd-toed ungulate. They don't sound alike. They don't share any physical mannerisms. But what reason would Mariano have to lie to Frankie? Why would he claim this man is his flesh and blood if he isn't? Jesus, he thinks, suddenly worried that a criminal has been using, or God forbid paying, Mariano to hide money or drugs in his house, implicating Frankie in felonies with long sentences in the federal penitentiary.

A sense of dread weighs upon him. There's some connection, genetic or otherwise, between the boy he invited to live in his home and the tabloid headlines. He hasn't heard from Mariano, not a call or a text, since he'd run off with his druggie friends. He wonders if he's coming back at all. Maybe he's slipped into that black hole where illegals disappear to stay one step ahead of the law. Maybe he's already taken a new name, in a different city, waiting until things cool off before emerging to find work in yet another kitchen where he's paid in cash at the end of the night, no questions asked. Maybe he'll reappear, with a posse of Scarfaces, needing a sanctuary where they can hide, holding Frankie hostage in his own home. Or he could simply show up, as always, tail between his legs, full of affection and endearments, swearing his undying love and promising to never hurt Frankie again. It won't work, not this time, Frankie swears. He longs to return to his old life, the peace and contentment of solitude. It's easier, and cheaper, to purchase affection at an hourly rate from a reputable agency.

The shop bell is ringing. Jesus Christ, it's 9:07; his assistant, Connie, has called out sick again and Dottie Griffo is waiting for him to unlock the front door for his first appointment. The kitchen is a mess, at least by Frankie's high standards of domestic maintenance. There's an uneaten slice of toast on his plate, an open jar of peach preserves, and an unwashed coffeepot. An empty carton of Chinese takeout is beginning to stink. He's used to everything being in perfect order, spic-and-span, before he begins his long workday: bed made, bathroom wiped down, the dishwasher loaded, and the garbage bagged and tied and placed in the trash cans outdoors. The current state of his housekeeping is adding to his anxiety.

"I'm coming, I'm coming," he mutters as he bounds down the stairs to unlock the door.

"Where's Mariano?" Dottie asks, clearly disappointed when she's greeted by the proprietor.

The battle-axes have rendered judgment and, by unanimous consent, have deemed Mariano to be adorable, delightful, charming, and sweet, with beautiful eyes and lovely pouting lips, as docile and friendly as a housebroken cocker spaniel.

"Mariano went to Baltimore. His brother lives there," Frankie says impulsively, knowing Mariano could prove him to be a twisted liar by sauntering through the front door in the next sixty seconds.

"When's he coming back?" she asks as she settles her bulky frame into the stylist's chair.

"Soon," he says, begging God to keep Mariano away until Dottie with her freshly lacquered classic waitress upsweep is taking her first lunch orders at the sandwich shop in the Market.

He's carefully snipping Joan Forte's thinning hair when he hears the back door slam shut and Mariano's footsteps on the creaking staircase. She's his last scheduled appointment of the afternoon, but he welcomes a walk-in at six, delaying the inevitable confrontation upstairs. He finally locks the door to the shop at seven, still needing more time to summon his courage to announce he's ending their relationship and that Mariano needs to find somewhere to live. Fresh air and a little exercise will bolster his courage.

The notorious warehouse in the morning paper is an anonymous slab of whitewashed brick on the commercial strip. The asphalt of the neglected parking lot is crumbling and vehicular access to the loading docks is restricted by a rusted chain-link fence. The only evidence of its recent infamy is the yellow crime scene tape across the padlocked entrance. A patrol car slows as it approaches from Broad Street. Frankie turns and starts to walk away, not wanting to draw attention for showing an unnatural interest in the scene of the crime. A loud voice calls his name, causing him to freeze in his tracks.

"Yo, Frankie! How's it going?"

Paul Ottaviano steps out of the patrol car, stretching his limbs and adjusting the waist of his pants.

"You hear about this shit, Frankie?" Paul asks, nodding at the site of the illicit meth lab.

"I read about it in the paper."

"Fucking unbelievable, huh? Right here, a few blocks from where we grew up."

Frankie refrains from commenting that nothing is unbelievable in a neighborhood with a long history of the bodies of mob rivals being found in the trunks of abandoned cars with bullets in their skulls.

"Yeah, kind of makes you wonder," he says.

"Keep reading the papers, Frankie boy," Paul shares. "A lot more of these fucking greaseballs are going down before this is all over."

Frankie's heart races as he rushes home. He runs up the stairs, calling the boy's name, but no one answers. He's alone in the house, the only evidence Mariano has come and gone an empty juice bottle he'd left behind on the kitchen counter.

APRIL 11, 2008

The bright morning sunlight is cruel to her. The other night Frankie had thought Christine marginally attractive despite her bad skin and overly processed hair. He'd appreciated her good bone structure and recognized how she might once have been considered pretty. But he barely recognizes the hyper and agitated creature who had appeared unannounced as he was opening the shop. Her T-shirt is vintage boardwalk, VIRGINIA IS FOR LOVERS, and flip-flops are a poor choice of footwear for a woman in desperate need of a pedicure. The little boy, Cameron, is tugging at her elbow, demanding attention. His clothes are rumpled and dirty and Frankie suspects he never saw a bed last night, sleeping, if at all, in the backseat of a car. His mother grabs his wrist and twists his arm, threatening physical retribution if he doesn't shut up and stand still. Frankie offers the boy a juice or a Coke, but Christine declines, saying they're in a rush and he'll need to use the bathroom if he drinks anything.

"I haven't seen or spoken to Mariano since he took off in the middle of the night," he repeats.

"Not once?"

"No."

He's not lying. Hearing footsteps on the back staircase doesn't count. He never actually *saw* Mariano during his brief pit stop at the house and certainly didn't talk to him.

"Have you tried calling him?"

"No. Well, maybe once or twice, but I finally gave up," Frankie lies. "He won't pick up if he's still angry."

"Are his things still here?" she asks, clearly suspicious.

"His clothes are upstairs."

"And he hasn't called you?"

"No."

It's urgent they find him, she insists. Randy has already left for Puebla and he's made arrangements for several of his friends to slip Mariano out of the country for their mother's deathbed vigil. Frankie expresses his deepest sympathies, asking if there is anything he can do to help. It's obvious she believes he's buying her bullshit about a dying mama. She clearly thinks he's in total ignorance, knowing nothing about the bust of the meth lab and the subsequent arrests.

"Just have him call me the minute you see him. And don't let him out of your sight until I come to get him," she says, preparing to leave, the visit no longer than ten minutes. "Give me your number," she insists, almost as an afterthought. "I'll call your phone so you can save mine."

He knows he has to suppress even the slightest hesitation. Reluctance would raise suspicion and give her reason to suspect he knows more than he's letting on. He slowly repeats the digits, a sick feeling in his gut. He's seen enough *CSI* to know a single record on a subpoenaed phone log is enough to drag him into a major narcotics investigation.

"Now give Uncle Frankie a kiss, Cameron," she insists and Frankie bends at the waist, offering his cheek to sticky lips that have been pacified with several Tootsie Pops. What fucking chance in the world does that poor kid have? he wonders as he watches them disappear down Carpenter Street.

"You look like you've just seen a ghost. Who was that?"

Connie's breathless, a half hour late for work as usual.

"Who?" he asks, acting as if he has no idea what she's talking about.

"Her," she says, pointing at Christine, who's strapping Cameron into his car seat in a Silverado parked across the street. "I saw that little boy give you a kiss when they left."

"Oh, that's just Mariano's little nephew. From Baltimore. His mother is married to Mariano's brother. Or they live together. Or something. I didn't ask."

"You really don't look good, Frankie. You must be coming down with something. Probably that bug that's going around."

It's her idea to cancel the day's appointments and reschedule, pleading a sudden onset of flu. He's probably contagious and shouldn't risk exposing his clients to the virus. She'll make all the calls, she assures him, as she dispatches him to bed.

He locks the master bedroom door and closes the blinds, not knowing where to start. He can't decide which room Mariano would choose to hide any contraband. He suddenly realizes he has no idea what he's searching for. *The Daily News* called it crystal meth; he recalls Jack using the word *crank*. Are they the same thing? What does it look like? Is it a pill? A powder? Something grainy like sugar or fine like baking soda? No, that's cocaine. It's not a liquid, is it? Is it bright and shiny like actual crystal? Should he be looking for needles and syringes? Mikey would know, but he can't call and ask. He could search the Internet, find a description, and, if he's lucky, a picture. But how would he explain a word search for *methamphetamine* if his laptop is confiscated? He'll know it when he sees it. It'll be obvious, something out of place, intentionally concealed, hidden in a sock, rolled in a handkerchief. He starts in the dresser drawer in the master bedroom where Mariano stores his clothes, then rummages through the pockets of the boy's shirts and jackets and trousers hanging in the closet. Nothing. He searches his own drawers and closets, then under the bed, moving on to the linen closet, the bathroom vanity and medicine cabinet, and the blanket chest. Nothing. Either Mariano is very clever or Frankie is wildly paranoid. His heart is pounding, his brain pulsing in his skull. He needs to take a deep breath and slow down.

The room looks like a riot zone, upended, clothes and papers tossed to the floor. He picks up Mariano's shirts and pants and folds them, then gathers his shoes and underwear, and carefully packs the boy's belongings in a huge roll-on, a five-hundred-dollar investment he'd bought for a long-ago fortieth-birthday-celebration cruise and never used again. He checks the time. It's not quite eleven o'clock and he's exhausted. His body aches for a deep, dreamless sleep, something that feels like death, and he swallows an Ambien and throws himself on the bed. Twenty minutes later he's lying on his back, still staring at the ceiling, and reaches for another sleeping pill.

"Wake up! Are you taking something? Wake up!"

"What are you doing here?" Frankie asks, trying to shake off the effects of the pharmaceuticals he'd taken and appear reasonably coherent to the worried priest.

"When you don't answer the fucking telephone for four hours I start to get worried. I guess I'm overreacting," Jack says sarcastically.

"I was sleeping."

"It's seven thirty at night. How long have you been out?"

"I don't know," Frankie says honestly.

"What are you taking?"

"Nothing. I'm not taking anything!" he says indignantly. "Connie says I have that flu that's going around. I'm trying to sleep it off."

"What the hell happened here? Looks like someone's planning a trip," he says, gesturing toward the packed suitcase and the scattered clothes from emptied drawers. "Where's your little friend?"

"I don't know. I told him to move out."

He dreads the coming inquisition, but, surprisingly, the priest decides this isn't the time for an interrogation.

"Get up. I'm calling out for Chinese. You have to eat something. But first, you're getting in the shower."

The cold water revives Frankie a bit. He pulls on a pair of jeans and a clean polo and ties his shoes, looking longingly at his unmade bed as he trudges toward the steps. The priest is busy in the kitchen, spooning food from paper cartons onto dinner plates.

"Only soda for you tonight," Jack says as he pours himself a beer. "I want to know what the hell you took to make you sleep the entire day."

"Nothing. I told you. I have the flu."

Frankie's stomach clenches tight as a fist at the sight of a greasy pile of fried rice and pork bits. He nudges little shreds of scrambled egg yolk with the tines of his fork, forcing himself to swallow a mouthful before he pushes his plate away.

"You have to eat something," Jack insists again, deftly clacking his chopsticks in a nest of Shanghai noodles.

"I'm not very hungry," Frankie says, opening a can of ginger ale.

He stares at the man sitting across the table as if he's a complete stranger, not a friend since his first day at school. He doesn't want his advice; he resents the intrusion. No one asked for his help. Jack's jealous, as he always is when someone else is the focus of Frankie's attention. He hates Mariano for taking Frankie away from him. He wants Frankie to be as lonely and unhappy as he is. He needs someone to share his miserable existence, eating noodles from soggy cartons and watching *The* fucking *Golden Girls,* then falling asleep reading a book.

"Maybe I should stay here with you tonight. So you won't be alone when he comes back."

"I'm okay. It's all right," Frankie responds, trying to discourage a sleepover. Jack acts like he's concerned for his safety, but Frankie knows the real reason he wants to stay is to ensure his resolve doesn't weaken, that a coy smile and Mariano's promises to be a good boy won't persuade him to change his mind.

He doesn't want to listen to Dorothy and Sophia trade wisecracks tonight. He wants to be left alone. Jack's unwelcome presence is irritating. He hates the sound of the methodical grinding of the priest's jaw as he chews. The lank fringe of hair tucked behind Jack's ears angers him. They've seen this episode a half-dozen times. It's the beginning of another Lifetime channel marathon and Jack seems to be settling in for the long haul. At ten o'clock, Frankie announces he needs to go to bed. Saturday's his busiest day.

"I wish you'd let me stay here with you tonight."

"No. I'm fine," Frankie insists, anxious to pour a glass of wine, go upstairs, and pop a pill. He'll set his alarm early, six, enough time to restore order in the bedroom before a long day of work.

APRIL 12, 2008 (THREE O'CLOCK IN THE MORNING)

Frankie, Frankie . . .

The stairs are impossibly steep, the walls unbearably close, but Frankie is compelled to keep climbing. His legs are dead weight, his chest tight, every muscle constricted, his lungs starved for nourishing oxygen. Papa is summoning him, demanding his presence. His father's voice grows less patient each time he repeats his errant son's name. Frankie tries to answer, hoping to appease him with promises of his imminent arrival, but he's out of breath, unable to speak. The stench grows stronger the higher he climbs; the atmosphere is sulfurous, corrosive, bringing tears to his eyes. At the top of the stairs is an unlocked door; it opens into a large room flooded with dusty sunlight, airless, the only furnishing a hospital bed in a distant corner. The buzzing drone of circling flies, mechanical, relentless, is ringing in his ears. Papa stands waiting, his arm wrapped tightly around his younger son's shoulder to keep him from running away. Michael's once crisp white shirt is smeared with melted chocolate. The red imprint of Papa's palm is still visible on his cheek.

A woman wearing an emerald-green dress with a plunging neckline lies on the mattress. Her orange wig is combed and lacquered, the ruby-red lipstick perfectly applied. Are you happy now? Papa gloats. Isn't this what you wanted? What you prayed for? A plump rat pokes its snout in his stepmother's eye socket. It bares its teeth, hissing at Frankie, slapping the corpse's cheek with its long tail as it scurries off the bed. Papa pushes his terrified younger son into Frankie's arms. Tell him to kiss her good-bye, Papa insists, growing impatient. Frankie can see the thread Casano used to sew together her lips. Something, a nest of maggots most likely, is squirming just below the surface of her skin. Be a man, you filthy little finocchio, *and make him kiss her good-bye.*

He opens his eyes, adrift in the twilight where the ghosts that dwell in the deep recesses of memory emerge in unsettling dreams. He vaguely recalls taking another Ambien after Jack finally left, then a second when drowsiness refused to come, then remembers nothing more until Papa's voice demanded he climb the stairs. The image of Miss Eileen is fading now, water swirling down the drain.

"Frankie, Frankie . . ."

The shrill tones and heavy accent sound nothing like Papa's commanding voice. It's Mariano, home at last; the poor kid is tired, sure to be hungry. There's cheese in the refrigerator, eggs and milk, sausage. A loaf in the bread box. Enough for Frankie to make the boy a simple meal. But he stumbles as he tries to stand and throws out an arm to steady himself against the wall. The bedside alarm clock says it's 3:12 and he's still fully dressed, wearing shoes and socks. Mariano is climbing the stairs, calling his name. Dizzy, unsteady on his feet, Frankie slumps back on the bed, gazing at the packed suitcase in the middle of the room. He panics, not wanting Mariano to discover he's being banished from his home. He doesn't have the stamina for the fighting and tears, the accusations and threats. He drops to his hands and knees, grunting. The oversize luggage won't fit beneath the bed. Mariano snatches the suitcase from his hands and dumps its contents, all of the boy's earthly possessions, over Frankie's head.

It's impossible to read the boy's expression, to determine whether his crooked smile is benign or evil. Mariano lifts his leg and gently places his right foot on Frankie's throat. Frankie braces himself for a swift, crippling kick, but the boy has a change of heart and removes his foot and lifts him onto the bed. Mariano sings a familiar song, "Rhiannon," as he unbuttons Frankie's shirt and removes his shoes.

Frankie looks up at him helplessly, grateful for a simple act of kindness, not expecting the hard slap that bloodies his lip, followed by a backhand that sends him sprawling across the mattress.

"I stay here with you now, Frankie," Mariano says and Frankie feels the sharp tip of a blade, either scissors or a knife, pressed against the soft flesh under his chin. "I go nowhere."

Frankie closes his eyes, tasting the blood in his mouth. He hears water running in the bathroom. The pills are dragging him down again. He's slipping away, drifting off.

Charlie Haldermann steps forward and emerges from the gloaming. Impatient as always, he turns his back on Frankie, who follows him down a long, narrow corridor. Huffing and puffing, gasping for air, Charlie insists they're going to join a gym tomorrow, both of them. Frankie suddenly stops, finding himself standing alone in a church. Charlie is nowhere to be seen, gone, vanishing without a trace, though the room has no doors or windows through which he could have made his escape. A young woman sits in a rocking chair, cradling a blanketed bundle on her lap. She's singing quietly, her weary voice barely more than a whisper. He takes a cautious step forward, charmed by her lovely song, and she looks at him and smiles. He recognizes her familiar face, the Madonna of the Pilgrims, and falls to his knees, asking for her blessing. She speaks softly, asking if he wants to hold the baby. Don't be afraid, he won't hurt you, you've been waiting for him, praying for this day to come. His name is Mariano, she tells him, placing a scaly, hairless, brown-eyed Cyclops with a coiled, spiny tail, slick with blood, in his arms.

He rolls on his back, emerging from a trance, eyes wide-open again, staring at the ceiling. He hears the gentle splashing of water and a voice, neither masculine nor feminine, singing in Spanish. A ring tone, Taylor Swift's "Our Song," announces an incoming call on the cell phone in the pocket of the jeans Mariano tossed on the bedroom floor as he undressed. Frankie rolls off the bed and retrieves it. It's one of those cheap disposable phone card cells they sell in all the bodegas, not the expensive iPhone Mariano had pleaded that Frankie buy him. He presses his thumb on the answer button, but doesn't speak. A woman—is it Christine?—repeats

Mariano's name, once, twice, three times, finally exploding in a rage when he doesn't respond. He turns off the phone and shoves it back in the boy's pocket.

He tastes blood on his tongue, feels it dripping down his throat. His left eye is beginning to swell shut and his nose, still not completely healed from the last beating, is throbbing. Who was that shrieking woman, what urgent message was she attempting to convey? What if the paper is wrong and bail has been made, or, worse, that Randy Salazar or Randy Garza, whatever his name is, has escaped custody and is making his way to Eighth and Carpenter, knowing a conspiring hand will unlock the door, allowing him to enter and take Frankie prisoner, a hostage in his own home? He picks himself up off the floor, emboldened by the blood he's swallowed, and walks to the bathroom. Mariano, soaking in the Jacuzzi, vamping and posing like a pop star luxuriating in her bath, is too distracted to notice him enter. He doesn't see Frankie lift the heavy ceramic lid from the toilet tank, never knows what hit him as Frankie smacks him on the head, fracturing his skull. The blow isn't fatal, but the boy knows he's defeated, barely struggling as Frankie holds his head under water until the last bubbles of his dying breath break on the surface.

April 12, 2008 (late afternoon until evening)

"How old is she, Frankie?"

"I'm not sure. Fifty? Fifty-one?"

"Don't be silly. She was a star in the seventies. I can't believe you don't know how old she is."

Angela Marcaccio is incredulous that Frankie doesn't know the exact year, month, day, and hour of Stevie Nicks's birth. Connie hovers close by, monitoring the tone of the conversation. Ever vigilant, she listens for lapses in Frankie's concentration, ready to jump into the fray and ride to the rescue.

"I bet she's at least sixty," Angela insists. "Google her on your BlackBerry."

"You heard what the weather's gonna be like the rest of the weekend?" Connie asks, trying to distract the chattering woman so Frankie can finish her highlights.

"You got plans, Connie?" Angela asks.

"I'm goin' down Ventnor tomorrow for my nephew's baby's christening. He had a little girl."

"Which nephew?"

"My sister's boy. Vincent. He's a dealer at Bally's."

"I only go to the Borgata," Angela sneers. "What are they calling her?"

"Mara. Mara Christine Luongo. Her mother's Irish."

"Did you look it up, Frankie?" Angela asks, clearly bored by Connie's family tree. "I'm sure Stevie Nicks is at least sixty years old."

In the span of two minutes, he's lost track of the conversation. His thoughts are in the room at the top of the stairs, on the highest floor, behind closed doors. He's climbed the steps five times today, each time expecting to discover his mind has been playing tricks on him, that he'll open the bathroom door and find an empty bathtub, dry as a bone, everything in order, nothing out of place. He feels like he's inhabiting someone else's body. Muscle memory is guiding the scissors and combs.

"If I were you, I'd sue that cab driver. He probably don't even have insurance. When was the last time you got into a taxi and the driver spoke English?" Angela complains.

Connie's wits are quicker than he gives her credit for. That was the story she gave when his first customer this morning commented on his fresh bruises. They've stuck by it all day: He'd been riding in a cab and smashed his face into the plastic protection screen when the driver slammed the brakes after running a red light.

"Don't worry, Frankie. Your pretty face won't have any scars," Angela comments. "Speaking of pretty faces, where's my little Mariano today?"

Connie tenses and Frankie's at a loss for words.

"He's going back to Mexico," Connie finally volunteers, the answer she's repeated throughout the day.

"When will he be back?"

"We don't know. His mother is very sick."

"Good Lord, I wouldn't want to get sick in Mexico. We crossed the border to Nogales when we visited my sister in Phoenix. It was the filthiest place I've ever seen. You couldn't pay me to go back there," Angela opines. "I'll keep her in my prayers," she says, subject closed, her curiosity satisfied.

Frankie appreciates that Connie's been a loyal soldier, a saint today. He doesn't know what he would have done without her. He swears he will never, ever, criticize her again. He appreciates her discretion. She may not be terribly bright, but she's awfully cunning. She knows there's more to Mariano's sudden disappearance than

Frankie's admitting, but she's refrained from asking for details. Twice today, he's almost taken her into his confidence before suppressing the powerful urge to confess that Mariano's lying dead in his bathtub. Not even Connie would believe he doesn't know or can't remember how the boy got there.

The first thing he's going to do after closing up the shop is flush the rest of the Ambien down the drain. How many did he take? He's counted and recounted the pills in the bottle and the numbers always come up the same. A thirty-day prescription, refilled five days ago, only sixteen tablets remaining. He's certain he swallowed one last night; he knows he took a second. He remembers fretting, anxious for sleep to come, trying to relax with a glass of wine, refilling his glass, unable to wind down, resisting the temptation to take a third pill . . .

. . . And then recalling nothing until he woke up lying on his bed, drool on the pillowcase, his eyes as dry as cornflakes. Connie was calling him, shaking him by the ankle, insisting it was time to wake up. Nine o'clock had come and gone and he hadn't appeared. Reluctant to invade his privacy, but worried when he didn't answer his cell phone, she'd climbed the stairs to his private sanctuary, up to the top floor, finding clothes scattered across the bedroom floor, and Frankie, asleep, breathing heavily.

"Where the fuck is Taco Bell?" she'd asked, confronting him as he stirred on the bed, struggling to come back to life. Connie, unlike his clients, had proven immune to Mariano's charms. She'd grabbed Frankie's chin and leered into his face, angered by the blood and the bruises.

"I don't know," he'd answered truthfully.

"Well, it looks like he's planning to take a little trip," she'd said, eyeing the empty suitcase lying by the bed.

Frankie had sat up on the bed and dropped his aching head into his hands.

"His mother's dying. He's going back to Mexico," he says, remembering the unpleasant and unexpected visit from Christine.

"I'm calling the locksmith to change the locks. Today. You can leave his suitcase on the street for all I care."

He'd looked up from the bed, conceding, acquiescing in her decision.

"Just don't say anything to Jack. Please!" he'd pleaded.

"You go jump in the shower. Patty Corella is downstairs for her appointment. I'll put her off until you're dressed. Hurry up, now. Don't you lie back down when I go downstairs."

He'd touched his swollen face as she turned and left, wondering if he'd fallen on the stairs. Everything would be better after a hot shower and a strong espresso with a teaspoon of sugar to kick-start his engine. He'd stood and stretched, resisting the strong urge to curl up and go back to sleep, and walked to the bathroom and opened the closed door, his tenuous equilibrium shattered by the shock of discovering Mariano lying in the cold water of the Jacuzzi and finding the toilet tank top on the floor.

Kit and Michael had placed bets on whether Kettleman would actually show. She'd predicted that some pressing obligation or imagined crisis at Clinton headquarters would require him to board the next Washington-bound Acela to hold the hands of a distraught campaign adjutant. Michael had assured her not even a summons from the lady herself would be enough to keep him from being in attendance when the legendary director of three of the top-ten-grossing movies in Hollywood history is feted as this year's honored recipient of the Abraham and Selma Grossman Foundation Humanitarian of the Year award. Abraham and Selma's son and his well-born wife are the most influential Democratic fundraisers in the Commonwealth, and Kettleman has decided to make a midterm run in 2010 for a House seat against the dyspeptic seven-term Republican incumbent. The congressional district, once a solid red, has been turning purple the past few cycles, and is projected to be a dependable blue two years hence. The support of the Grossmans is essential and Kettleman's contribution to the Foundation was exceedingly generous.

"You better get used to it. It's part of the territory," Kit cautions her husband, who seems unusually skittish as they enter the thousand-dollar-ticket event.

He doesn't like crowds except at a Springsteen stadium show and the thought of glad-handing makes him nauseous. But Kettleman has ignited the embers of Michael's ambition. He's suggested his deputy approach the Grossmans, but Michael scoffs at the idea they would devote precious time and assets to a county race for District Attorney. Besides, he's having his doubts. He knows he's no damn politician. He can be brusque to the point of seeming arrogant and he doesn't suffer fools gladly—character traits that aren't appreciated on the campaign trail. Kit brushes aside his protests that he's charisma-challenged and resembles a haunted vampire in photographs. Women are attracted to his looks and his deep voice, sensing the gentleness beneath the gruff, aggressive exterior. Men want to be his friend, a member of his crew. And, of course, juries love him.

"I think you're afraid of losing."

Her insight, as always, is right on the mark.

"You'll look damn sexy in the campaign mailers," she assures him as she straightens his collar.

"We have plenty of time to think about it," he insists. "It's not like we have to make a decision tomorrow."

Kettleman is seething at being banished to a table in the Siberian quadrant of the Academy of Music Ballroom. Whoever assumed he'd appreciate being seated with his deputy and their respective spouses didn't know much about Steven Kettleman. He wolfs down his petite filet in three bites, anxious to free himself from present company. Even Kit, who he usually fawns over, receives the cold shoulder when he's surrounded by so many potential contributors to his latest ambition. Kettleman's young wife, clearly humiliated by his indifferent treatment, is near tears and Kit comes to her rescue, requesting her assistance in the ladies' room for an unexpected wardrobe malfunction.

"At last, I've got you all to myself. I came over to see if you needed help cutting your meat."

Amy Grossman's flirting is harmless, hardly sexual, certainly not in Michael's eyes. He doesn't encourage it, knowing it bothers his wife, who suspects many of the middle-aged woman in the room, single or otherwise, would like to take a run at her husband. Amy Grossman is still a great beauty in her forties, with magnificent sculpted cheekbones and azure eyes, her bearing as patrician as his wife's. A Morganthau by birth, a direct descendant of the Ambassador to the Ottoman Empire, she's recognized as royalty in the most exclusive addresses of the Upper East Side. She and Kit have been careful adversaries since Penn Law, respecting each other's ability and genealogy. Kit will make snide remarks about the exquisite craftsmanship of the surgical corrections to the minor imperfections of Amy's face, just as Michael is certain Amy has commented to her husband that it's tragic that a woman with such fine, fair skin as Kit's would so carelessly expose it to the sun. There are rumors aplenty about an "arrangement" between the Grossmans. Kit has taken to calling Amy a cougar, which Michael says she ought to find very reassuring because he's far too old to be desirable prey for a middle-aged female on the prowl for virile young men.

"God, I despise that man," Amy Grossman says, commenting on Kettleman's unctuous style of working the room. "I have to admit he's no slouch. It's the smart move to join the governor's staff. He'll have a much larger profile in Harrisburg when he runs for Congress than he ever could in Media. Your boss certainly thinks big. He's already scheduled a breakfast meeting with my husband to gauge our interest in supporting his congressional ambitions. I'm a little hurt you haven't come to us now that you're considering a political career yourself."

"Amy, we're talking about the DA's Office, not the presidency. I'd hardly call that a political career. And we haven't decided yet if I'm going to run."

"Of course you're going to run. And campaigns are expensive. Even local ones. You'll burn through your cash before you know it. But I'm going to be strong-arming every deep pocket on my donors' lists to make sure you're well financed. Good God, look at him. Preening like a smug little baronet," she sneers, gesturing toward Kettleman, who's holding the exhausted but gracious Humanitarian of the Year hostage. "If he can be a congressman we can get you elected senator."

"That's ridiculous."

She stares him down, daring him to challenge her.

"One thing I can assure you, Michael, is that I never joke about politics. My husband and I don't back losers. Look at yourself. The barber's kid from the hardscrabble neighborhood. Football star. What did they call you at Princeton? The Godfather, wasn't it? Phi Beta Kappa. Penn Law Review. Pugnacious prosecutor. Man of the people. Defender of our sacred way of life. With your raw material and those solid-citizen good looks, the District Attorney's Office is just the beginning."

"I think you're overstating the appeal of my biography."

"Do you? The world loves the story of a self-made man. They see you and believe they're still living in the land of opportunity where every little boy can be President. You're going to need a few lessons on working the room." She laughs. "It will help that you'll already be the incumbent by the time of the special election. You've got the face of an honest man. Better yet, a *good-looking* honest man. Perfect for television. But we'll need to put you on a diet."

"I'm in decent shape!" he protests, straightening his spine and sucking in his once trim but now softening gut.

"The camera puts on ten pounds."

"You sound like you're going to run my campaign."

"No, I'm going to *hire* someone to run your campaign. A professional. I've already approached him. He's balking at taking on a candidate for a local office, but he'll listen to reason. My husband and I can be a very persuasive."

He hopes Kit is out of eyesight as she fusses with his tie.

"There's just something about you that brings out the maternal instincts. I should have grabbed you for myself in law school. You'll always be my knight in shining armor, Michael. Those two animals would have killed me after they'd finished having their fun. Now come on. There are quite a few people here I want to introduce you to."

April 13, 2008

Michael has been assigned a place of honor at the table of senior-class athletes and their beaming fathers. Young Scalzo is the reigning alpha male of the season, the recipient of the Father Theodore Sullivan Award for outstanding scholar athlete, a worthy successor to Michael, Class of '83, and every other alumnus of Matteo Ricci Preparatory Academy who once held the distinction of being honored as the year's most accomplished graduate. Various cliques huddle together, stratified by age and the status assigned to them in the rigid hierarchy of an all-boys prep school. Michael fondly remembers the deference he was awarded during his final years at the Academy. He's always known his own son won't follow in his footsteps. Maybe some dramatic change will occur in the years before Danny is old enough to enter the freshman class. But Michael expects his son will continue to prefer the company of awkward comic book geeks and video game enthusiasts, boys who will pass through high school anonymously, waiting to distinguish themselves at some later stage of life. The best he can hope is that Danny doesn't begin to take an unnatural interest in drama club or chorus, forcing his broken-hearted father to affirm his liberal politics by loudly proclaiming his support for the choices his son makes.

Faces he hasn't seen for years seek him out to offer congratulations. Michael's astonished that Kettleman's move to Harrisburg and his own accession to acting District Attorney of Delaware County is a matter of public knowledge, since the formal announcement won't be made until after the presidential primary. But the alumni of the Academy, both his own contemporaries and the succeeding generations who've been schooled in his legend, are well connected in the city and state governments. Their effusive enthusiasm over his accepting an interim position has the unintended effect of making him feel his life so far has disappointed their expectations. It's a foregone conclusion in their minds that he'll run for the office in the next election.

"You remember to mention us in your victory speech," the Dean of Students says, prompting Michael to remind him they shouldn't be getting ahead of themselves.

"Whatever you need just let me know. All you have to do is ask," the president-elect of the Philadelphia Bar Association promises.

A Madison Avenue advertising executive with a national profile wants to kick around a few ideas for a campaign slogan. Gratis, of course.

The prizewinning journalist with a twice-weekly editorial column in the *Inquirer* is ready to go with an early endorsement as soon as Michael makes the formal announcement.

"I never understood why you retreated to the wilderness," a two-term city councilman comments. "Never made any sense. I should have known you were thinking three steps ahead. It looks like it's all paying off in spades."

Michael just smiles, allowing the councilman, rumored to be the target of an ongoing grand jury investigation, to assume his life's been scripted to a clever master plan. The truth is he'd decamped to the suburbs and a House with a Name after growing restless and frustrated with the endless vicious politicking and backstabbing among the would-be heirs to the throne of the District Attorney, a woman who clings to her office like a barnacle, promising that each successive campaign for election is her last, only to announce her intention to run yet again as the current term is coming to its end.

He'd seized an opportunity when she'd agreed to loan him to Kettleman to serve as a special prosecutor to avoid any question of a conflict of interest in the trial of a Delaware county commissioner on charges of bribery and influence peddling. He hadn't needed much persuasion to accept Kettleman's offer to be his Chief Deputy after winning the conviction. Kit was enthusiastic, grateful to be released from the bonds of the Philadelphia residency requirement and free to pursue her dream of finding a home like Sleepy Peter's Quiet Nook. The work has been challenging and it's deeply gratifying when justice is served. He's convicted the spurned lover who'd murdered a popular high school guidance counselor, a sexual pervert who panicked and strangled a seven-year-old girl who resisted his attempts to molest her, and the gang leader who disposed of the bodies of his enemies with chain saws and gasoline. And, of course, his ultimate achievement was securing the death penalty for one of the killers of Carmine Torino. His experience in Philadelphia had soured him on the political maneuvers necessary to advance his career as a prosecutor, and he's become complacent, too comfortable as an adjutant. Kettleman's decision to decamp for Harrisburg has awakened the competitive beast that's been in hibernation too many years.

The tinkle of flatware on water glasses summons the last malingerers to their tables. Men and their sons persevere through the blessing—heads bowed, hands clasped, stomachs rumbling—then grab their plates and storm the buffet table. Michael runs through his remarks one final time, tweaking here, tinkering there, while alumni and the current student body stuff their faces with scrambled eggs and breakfast meats. There's a short list of minor recognitions before the main event on the printed program, the presentation of the Father Theodore Sullivan Award to the member of the class who best embodies the character and piety of Father Ted, that tough Irish street kid from the Philadelphia river wards, a champion middleweight pugilist who'd dedicated his fists to the service of Saint Ignatius Loyola.

Michael suspects Father Ted would have approved of the man he has become, believed him a worthy recipient of his eponymous award. He would have admired Michael's commitment to public service, earning less than newly minted law school graduates at the major law firms. He would have applauded Michael's refusal to cash in on his years of experience in the criminal justice system by representing drug lords and insider traders. He would have encouraged Michael to stay the course while watching his peers on the Law Review rocket past him on their career trajectories, compiling biographies that will earn them an obituary in the *New York Times* or, at least, the *Philadelphia Inquirer.*

Fuck Father Ted and modest ambitions. Of course he's going to run in the next election. The Hamlet act is getting a little shopworn. His wife, who has always sworn she wouldn't care if he chucked it all to pull espressos at Starbucks, can't conceal her excitement (and, likely, relief) her husband is seeking his destiny after a long hiatus from the fast track. He and Kit will accept the Grossmans' invitation to dinner after the primary to discuss the platform of his campaign. The days of needing to defer to Kettleman are about to end. His first decision after being sworn in as the interim will be to announce the Commonwealth has reconsidered its earlier decision to not request a new trial and will seek a capital conviction and the death penalty for Tommy Corcoran. Michael Rocco Gagliano receives a loud and enthusiastic round of applause as he approaches the mike, ready to shed the cloak of anonymity and fulfill the world's expectations for the former Father Theodore Sullivan Award recipient, All-Catholic and All-Ivy, Penn Law Review Note Editor and Order of the Coif.

Frankie's locked himself in the bathroom and is sitting on the toilet, trying to think. He remembers an episode of *Law & Order* about a murderer who'd confessed to a priest, seeking absolution. Dick Van Dyke was in it, but he can't recall if he played the priest or the killer. No, it wasn't *Law & Order,* it was *Columbo* and Dick Van Dyke was a murderer who *pretended* to be a priest, but he couldn't fool a detective as clever as Peter Falk. Why is he thinking about old television shows when he needs to concentrate on the problem in the Jacuzzi? He knows a priest can't turn him in if he confesses. That's all that matters.

Jack will be here in a few hours. They have tickets for the touring production of *Phantom of the Opera* and the curtain is at three. Jack will be suspicious, start asking questions, if Frankie cancels at the last minute. He'd considered asking the priest to hear his confession when he arrives before realizing Jack will never let him get away with this. His penance won't be two Our Fathers and three Hail Marys or even a rosary every day for a year. The price he'll be asked to pay for God's forgiveness will be a phone call to the police. A priest can absolve Frankie of his *sin,* that's the job he's paid to do, but he can't acquit him of his crime. All Jack can do is send him to his executioner without a blemish on his immortal soul.

Frankie jumps off the commode and kneels beside the Jacuzzi. Mariano's body is half submerged in the water. He can't leave him here, where someone is bound to discover him. The bloating is ominous, proof that nature had begun to take its natural course of rot and decay. Frankie wants to pour a drink to bolster his courage, but he needs a clear head. He drains the cloudy water, cringing at the sight of Mariano lying in the empty tub. The boy's face is unrecognizable, mottled with a blue-and-purple mask of livor mortis. Frankie grabs the body under the armpits and drags it from the Jacuzzi. He winces and chokes, sickened by the eerie sensation of Mariano's skin sloughing off his torso. He looks away from the gash in Mariano's skull and concentrates on dragging the surprisingly heavy body to the top of the staircase.

The occasion demands that Michael deliver a short speech extolling the virtues of an Academy education before bestowing the award he'd won a lifetime ago on the young football hero who will follow his path to Princeton. He scribbles a crude cross on a napkin that he places on the podium to remind himself he's expected to bless himself at the end of his remarks. He leans into the microphone and pauses, his gaze sweeping across the room, a bit of theater to grab their attention. He begins softly, repeating the *sacramentum* every boy pledges when he joins the exclusive ranks of Academy scholars.

"Each man for the other and every man for Christ."

He speaks nostalgically of his own years at the Academy and how the lessons he learned within these walls have shaped his life. He artfully balances humor and solemnity. He inspires without lecturing. He praises the accomplishments and character of young Mr.

Scalzo and reminds him of his solemn obligation to honor the school by example, living his life according to the values he has been taught.

"The road ahead won't always be smooth and easy. Difficult decisions will need to be made. But the sacred oath you swore when you entered this school as a boy four years ago and now leave as a man will help you find the strength and the faith to overcome any challenge you will encounter.

"Each man for the other and every man for Christ."

Michael brings the room to its feet. His inspirational words have renewed the commitment of all within the sound of his voice to honor the Academy mission. One or two of them might even attempt a good deed or two before forgetting the stirring passion he feels at the moment. Michael calls the man of the hour and his father to the podium for the awarding of the trophy. According to time-honored tradition, he gives the bronzed image of a boxer standing on a stack of books to the young man's father, who will then place it in the hands of his son. Michael can't help but be touched by the unembarrassed tears of the grizzled cop as he embraces his boy. Officer Scalzo unexpectedly turns and wraps his thick arms around Michael, crushing him against his massive barrel chest.

"Your old man must have been as proud as I am when you were my Joey's age," he says when he's finally able to speak.

"It was a day he remembered the rest of his life," Michael assures him, ending the story there, not wanting to spoil the cop's perfect afternoon.

He'd never had any intention of inviting Papa to the ceremony. But Matteo Ricci custom demanded the presence of the father of the honoree at the ceremony, and Sal Pinto, without telling Michael, confided in Frannie Merlino that Luigi's son was going to receive the coveted award. When Michael descended the staircase the morning of the breakfast, Papa was waiting in the barbershop, dressed in his finest navy-blue suit and a starched white shirt, *la bella figura,* as dignified as one would expect of the father of such an exceptional young man. Frankie, who'd double-parked the car, blocking the traffic on Eighth Street, stood in the doorway, unsure of the next move.

"Your father is very hurt and disappointed," Frannie Merlino announced haughtily. "But he's willing to forgive you so you can both enjoy this special day."

"Forgive me for what?" Michael snapped, intending the cutting edge of his voice.

"How can you be so cruel and disrespectful? This is how you show respect to the man who raised you?" she challenged, refusing to back down.

"You want to see the man who raised me? Look over there," he spit, pointing at Frankie. "So shut your fucking mouth and stay out of it, you fucking cunt."

Papa wasn't a tall man and his arms were too short to deliver a stinging slap to his son's face. The blow landed harmlessly on his chest. It wasn't pain or even humiliation that enraged Michael, but the arrogance of a scrawny old man who believed he still had the power to make his youngest boy cower and yield. He grabbed his father by the collar and, lifting him off his feet, slammed him against the wall.

"Michael," Frankie said, his voice calm and steady. "Michael, put him down. I left the car in the middle of the street and we're going to be late."

Frankie placed the trophy in his brother's hands at the ceremony, just as Michael had wanted. Afterward, they went directly to the Giorgini household and Frankie huddled with Barbie's father, the men speaking in low tones. He returned an hour later with a suitcase of Michael's clothes, promising he and Jack Centafore would move the rest of his things later in the week. The Giorginis had offered a refuge, a place at their table and the bed of their son who had married and moved to a home of his own. Frankie sensed Michael was anxious and he lingered, sitting on the stoop beside his younger brother. There was a full moon and the street was awash with the dusty light of streetlamps. Michael finally stood and turned his back, facing the Giorginis' door, not wanting Frankie to see the fear and uncertainty in his eyes. He would be a man soon and had never spent more than a handful of nights in his short life alone, without his brother sleeping in a bed an arm's length away.

"I'm sorry, Frankie."

"I love you, Mikey."

"I love you too, Boo," he said quietly, words he hadn't spoken since he was a little boy, afraid of monsters in the dark, and disappeared into the house.

Frankie brokered a tentative peace between his father and brother. Michael finally crossed the threshold of Papa's door on Christmas Day. They never spoke of his behavior the morning of the award ceremony. He returned occasionally, always at Frankie's insistence. But he never slept again under the roof of the house at Eighth and Carpenter until his father was dead and in the ground.

Book Three

sepoltura in mare

April 15–22, 2008

APRIL 15, 2008

"He was in here. This is where I found him."

"What happened to him?"

Michael stares into the dry Jacuzzi. The idea of his gentle, harmless brother killing someone is preposterous. The poor kid must have overdosed. Or passed out in the tub and drowned. Or lost his footing on the slippery surface, falling on his head. But the ceramic lid doesn't have magic powers and didn't jump from the tank to the floor by itself. He suspects the coroner will find a fracture in the victim's skull and bathwater in Mariano's lungs.

"Why is there an open suitcase on the floor?" Michael asks.

"I was going to throw him out."

"And he beat the crap out of you when you told him, right? You need to tell me now. Don't give me some bullshit about tripping on the curb or your cab running a red light."

"I don't know."

"You expect me to believe you have no idea why there's a dead kid stashed in the freezer in the basement?"

Frustrated and frightened, he grabs Frankie's shoulders and shakes him, setting in motion a spinning pinwheel of seemingly random information. Randy Garza and Randy Salazar. Washington Avenue. Methamphetamine. A bleached blonde with a young son. Baltimore. Disposable cell phones and suspicious calls. He'd taken a sleeping pill. More than one. He doesn't know how many. Then he remembers finding Mariano in the bathwater in the morning. He didn't know what to do with him, so he dragged the body to the basement.

"Why didn't you call 911 when you found him? Why did you think you had to hide him?"

Michael pleads with his brother to come clean. Frankie's only hope of getting out of this mess is to tell the truth. A lie is a labyrinth and a liar is inevitably trapped in the maze.

"I don't remember. I don't know why I didn't call. I must have been scared and didn't know what to do."

Frankie's affect is disturbing. His calmness is eerie. His diffident, fatalistic attitude is out of character. Someone else, some strange spirit, has possessed him. Michael considers and quickly dismisses any thoughts of his brother taking his own life. Frankie's a devout Catholic despite the Vatican's disapproval of his sexual conduct. Jesus Christ may tolerate the occasional blow job, but suicide isn't a sin to which even the most indulgent of gods would turn a blind eye.

"It's okay, Frankie. I'll figure something out," Michael says, trying to reassure him. "Don't worry. I'll take care of it."

A call to 911 now will bring the circus rolling into town. The responding officer will arrive and secure the scene of the crime. Homicide detectives and a young ADA will be summoned. Photographers and investigators will descend like flies on a carcass. In the midst of pandemonium Michael and his brother will be asked to give statements that neither is prepared to make before securing the best representation money can buy.

It will be hours until Michael can make the call to Walter Rudenstein, the legendary prosecutor and Michael's one-time mentor who had switched allegiance a decade ago and now uses his prodigious gifts in the service of the enemies of society. He'd been in the headlines last month for getting life in prison for the white serial killer the NAACP wanted guillotined for cannibalizing a half-dozen little black boys. This will be a walk in the park by comparison. Walter Rudenstein will make the arrangements for Frankie to turn himself in. Michael will be by his side, of course. Rudenstein will ask for and get reasonable bail. Frankie's not a violent man and has no criminal history. He's no danger to society. He acted in self-defense. The condition of his face proves he was the real victim. And it hadn't been the first time Frankie had been beaten. Only a few weeks earlier he'd had to hide his cuts and bruises behind sunglasses. The only fly in the ointment is Frankie's bad decision to deep-freeze the evidence.

Frankie's phone is ringing.

"Who the fuck is calling at this hour?

"It's Jack."

"Answer it."

The conversation, no longer than a few minutes, feels interminable to Michael.

"I will," Frankie assures the priest as he hangs up the phone.

"You will what?"

"Be ready to leave by five thirty."

Michael is speechless. He'd thought his brother had grasped the seriousness of his situation and, instead, he's running off for a day of fun and games.

"Father Parisi is being buried today in Scranton. You should come, too, Mikey."

For the first time in his life he's grateful that fucking horse-faced priest is lurking in the background. Frankie can't be left alone and his presence would be a constant distraction while Michael makes the arrangements with Walter Rudenstein.

"You can't say a word about this to anyone, not even him."

"Do you think I'm crazy?"

No, but you're trusting and impulsive. Michael pulls the ace from his sleeve, the only thing that will ensure Frankie's silence.

"I could lose my license for not calling the police and letting you go to Scranton. I might even face charges. Do you understand?"

"Don't worry, Mikey. No one will ever know you were here," he promises. "Do you think I should call Connie now and wake her up to tell her to reschedule today's appointments or just leave a note for her to find when she comes to work?"

Michael questions the wisdom of allowing her free rein to wander through the house.

"She won't go down into the basement, Mikey. She's terrified of mice."

"You don't seem yourself this morning, Mr. Gagliano. Are you feeling under the weather?"

The judge is truly concerned. The Chief Deputy's attention to detail is known throughout the courthouse. A suppression hearing like this morning's is approached with no less gravity and passion than a jury trial. It's completely out of character for Michael to appear in the courtroom unprepared. He fumbles through the case file. His ability to think quickly and speak extemporaneously has deserted him.

"I didn't sleep last night, Your Honor. A family situation."

He'd boarded up the back door to the building. Then he sat in his parked car, waiting until he saw Frankie leave the house and drive away in the priest's Ford Explorer. The sun had risen by the time he finally got home.

"Nothing serious, I hope."

"No, nothing like that."

"Would you like a continuance?"

"That would be greatly appreciated, Your Honor."

"Jesus Christ, Michael. You look like shit," the lead defense attorney informs him after the judge has left the bench.

"I'm really sorry about this."

"I'm going to mark this day in my calendar! Michael Gagliano is actually human!" she says with a laugh as she turns her attention to the messages on her cell phone.

He should have asked one of the junior attorneys to cover today. The short walk between the courthouse and the DA's office feels like a death march. He expects there will be a message waiting for him on his desk. Rudenstein or his assistant will have returned the call Michael had made before leaving for court. His brother's life will never be the same after they speak. He'll never be a truly free man again. No matter the outcome of the negotiations and pleas in the months to come, he'll wear the yoke of notoriety around his neck until the day he dies. *Isn't he the one who killed that young man? Yes, isn't it hard to believe someone with such a sweet face would be capable of doing such a thing?* It seems like a lifetime since he scarfed down a couple of slices on the street last night. It's past one and he makes a sharp left on the sidewalk, walking away from the office, seeking the comfort of food before he destroys his brother's life.

The Bishop's words are generic. It's his one-size-fits-all eulogy. In all fairness, he hadn't known the deceased, had never even met him. Father Parisi spent his entire clerical career in the much larger archdiocese to the south. But his last instructions were clear. He wanted his funeral Mass in the city where he'd been born and to be buried in the soil of his native Scranton.

It's a High Mass, of course, and a Latin one at that. The chants and prayers are mysterious, a secret language between men who have dedicated their lives to the work of God. No ambient noise disturbs or disrupts the solemnity of the occasion. No coughing, no wailing of babies, no banging of kneelers echoing off the walls of the cathedral. Frankie is seated among a clutch of laypeople here to pay their last respects. No one from Saint Catherine of Siena has traveled a hundred twenty-five miles north to say farewell. He'd always thought Father Parisi was beloved by his congregation, only to learn from Jack after the priest was transferred to another parish that he was considered an odd duck, someone who made his parishioners uncomfortable. They were polite, respectful of his standing in the community, but would breathe a sigh of relief when he excused himself after making the briefest of appearances at their wedding receptions and funeral luncheons. Only Frankie had held any affection for him.

It takes more than a single celebrant, even one who's a bishop, to bury a priest. The altar is crowded with ordained men in billowing white cassocks. The organist and choir begin the communion hymn, and Frankie joins the line to receive the Body of Christ. Only after receiving the sacrament, kneeling in his pew, his head bowed, does he realize what he has done. He remembers Father Parisi's voice, instructing him that it is a grievous sin to take Holy

Communion while unconfessed, unforgiven sins still blacken the soul. He remembers the vivid tale of the wafer turning to blood in the mouth of the cynical nonbeliever who had flaunted God's law.

The Mass is ending and the processional to the waiting hearse begins. A long column of prelates, hands folded in prayer, accompany the flag-draped casket (Father Parisi was a chaplain in the Second World War) down the aisle of the cathedral. Their voices—tenors, baritones, basses—blend effortlessly, all in perfect pitch, as they sing the closing hymn. Frankie, who's been dry-eyed throughout the service, feels tears welling in his eyes. He's not crying for the deceased, who had lived a long and useful life, but for the boy he once was, the reverent young man who posed with his little brother in a pressed shirt and tie for the kind and generous priest, solemn and dignified as they stared into the lens of his camera.

There's a long, detailed message from Walter Rudenstein's office when Michael returns to his desk. Mr. Rudenstein is at his St. John's residence until Thursday morning. His secretary assures the Chief Deputy that Mr. Rudenstein will contact him when he returns. Michael is tempted to call back and remind her satellite service reaches the Caribbean, but pressing would make him sound desperate. The little Mexican's going nowhere in the next forty-eight hours. No suspicious odors will be drifting up from the basement. He and Frankie had collected the rotting meat and stashed it in sidewalk trash cans blocks away from the barbershop under the cover of night. But the delay means Michael's going to have to retain Rudenstein to represent both him and his brother so that the timeline between finding the body and the report to the authorities is protected from disclosure by the attorney-client privilege.

His phone is ringing. Frankie is checking in. Michael had told him to call when the service was over and they were on their way home.

"Mikey. Jack wants to drive to New York since we're so close. He's going to try to get standing-room tickets for *Jersey Boys* and stay overnight. I called Connie and asked her to reschedule tomorrow's appointments, too."

Michael rubs his bloodshot eyes. Everything is spinning out of his control. A trial is out of the question. Not even Walter Rudenstein could win an acquittal on charges against his brother for the death of his young house pet. What jury of his peers will ever sympathize with a man who runs off for an evening of show tunes while a human Popsicle is lying in his freezer chest?

"Breathe. Just breathe."

Jack's doing his best to calm and reassure him, but Frankie's claustrophobia resists his best efforts to achieve tranquility through measured intakes of oxygen. Traffic has come to a complete stop. Pungent exhaust fumes seep through the closed windows. They've been sitting ten minutes at most, but Frankie feels like he's been captive in the Lincoln Tunnel for days. The filthy walls seem to be shrinking and the dim lighting feels threatening. Frankie's heart is racing and his knuckles are white from gripping the dashboard.

"Maybe this will help," Jack suggests, slipping Mozart's *Six Quartets Dedicated to Haydn* into the disc player.

But the music only agitates Frankie. The screeching violin strings are hardly soothing.

"Just breathe. Take deep breaths. You can do it. I think I see some movement ahead. It won't be much longer."

His words are no comfort to Frankie. If he can't find the courage to do what he needs to do, he'll be confined to a space not much larger, and far less comfortable, than the interior of Jack's Ford Explorer. He dreads the thought of spending the rest of his life pacing ten steps between the wall and the bars of a cell. He would never survive it. He reaches into his pocket to touch the iPod Mariano had given him and takes comfort in knowing the last thing he'll hear in this life is Stevie's voice singing about the mysteries of Rhiannon.

April 16, 2008

Michael is sitting at his desk, staring at the ungrammatical affidavit presented by the officer seeking a search warrant in a high-profile narcotics distribution investigation. Nearly a decade after Kettleman's first election, Delaware County law enforcement still resents his decision to impose the option under the Criminal Code allowing the DA's Office the discretion to approve every application for a warrant before it can be presented to the court. The consensus among the cops was all you could do was cross your fingers and hope you didn't pull that bastard Gagliano, who was known to cross-examine you as vigorously as he would a defendant on the stand before he would even consider signing the fucking thing. The officer is loaded for bear, expecting even more rigorous scrutiny than the Deputy's usual vigilance. It's not often, after all, the Commonwealth wants to raid the neat and tidy little bungalow of an eighty-nine-year-old woman. But if three months of observation and the detailed recording of the suspicious comings-and-goings of a steady stream of jittery and paranoid-seeming young visitors to a churchgoing lady's home sweet home isn't probable cause to search the premises for evidence of a prescription narcotics operation, he doesn't know what is. The cop is shocked when the Chief Deputy approves his affidavit without asking a single question.

Michael rises from his desk and shuts and locks the door. At this very moment, some fresh-faced, eager young member of the Philadelphia police force could be standing in front of a judge, asking for a signature to enter and search the premises at Eighth and Carpenter. An hour later investigators will be dusting for fingerprints and the photographer will digitally preserve a series of images of the frozen body in the freezer chest. The prosecutor will enter the photographs into evidence. Michael's witnessed the scene a hundred times: the pinched faces of the jurors, flinching as the grisly pictures of the victim are passed through the jury box, the abject disgust when they look up to stare at the accused sitting at the defense table.

He unlocks the bottom drawer of his desk and retrieves a worn manila envelope. He's been tempted several times since the Corcoran reversal to look at its contents, but resisted, afraid his anger, already bubbling on low heat, would ignite. He arranges them in a morbid solitaire pattern so he can see the images all at once. The face, battered beyond recognition. The glazed, unseeing eye, staring at the lens of the camera. The charred skin from the clumsy attempt to burn the body. The filthy duct tape sealing his mouth. And, most hideous of all, the shredded ribbons of skin and muscles that once were his throat, the naked bones of his neck and the severed vertebrae exposed. The defense had tried to exclude them as inflammatory. Michael argued that a jury of Tommy Corcoran's peers deserved to see the monsters' handiwork. One of the jurors had to be excused to regain her composure after viewing the evidence.

A light tap on his door snaps him to attention.

"Michael, it's almost three o'clock. You need to leave soon if you're going to be there on time."

The opening statements in the mock trial are scheduled to begin precisely at five. Michael takes his work as an instructor in Penn's trial-advocacy program seriously. His team—the earnest daughter of a Pittsburgh machinist, a boisterous Cuban-American princess from Miami, and a wisecracking Orthodox kid from Brooklyn—is expecting a last-minute pep talk to boost their confidence. They've rehearsed their opening statements and closing arguments. They've mastered the art of direct examination and sharpened their skills at cross. His presence will be an unnecessary crutch. He doesn't need to be there at all. But the dean wouldn't look kindly on an adjunct clinical professor who blew off the grand finale to his semester's efforts. And it might help him to forget, for a few hours at least, that it's Frankie's last night as an unmarked man, who, come tomorrow when Rudenstein returns to town, will be betrayed by an ungrateful Judas Iscariot who once had been a motherless boy he'd loved and protected.

"Come on, Mary Wilson. How about some backup vocals?" Jack insists, taking the lead on the refrain to "Close to You." Jack's finally given up trying to get him to admit he hadn't acquired this fresh set of bruises in a traffic accident and can't cajole Frankie into joining in a sing-along to the Carpenters' *Ultimate Collection*.

The New York getaway hadn't lifted Frankie's dour mood. Jack knew he was lying when he said he'd enjoyed *Jersey Boys.* He'd had to be prodded to join the curtain call standing ovation. He'd stayed in bed this morning until checkout. Even a shopping expedition to the menswear department at Saks failed to brighten Frankie's spirits.

A road sign informs all southbound travelers the Joyce Kilmer Service Plaza is two miles ahead.

"We need to stop here," Frankie says, clutching his gut. "I think I'm going to be sick."

"Please. You're coming," Kelly, the machinist's daughter, pleads. "We couldn't have done it without you."

Frankie hasn't given him a set of keys for the new locks and the thought of waiting at the bar at the Speakeasy until the priest delivers his brother into his custody isn't terribly appealing.

"Just one," he concedes. "I'll meet you guys there."

The young South Floridian is shepherding everyone out of the law school building. Michael admires her brisk efficiency. The Orthodox kid is on his cell, giving a blow-by-blow account of the victory.

"I'm coming to find you if you're not there in ten minutes," Kelly warns him as she runs off to join her classmates.

He calls Kit and leaves a message, telling her not to wait up. He expects the celebration will go on until last call. He'll probably drink too much and will stay at his brother's. He says he'd stopped by home on his way to the city to pick up a clean shirt and underwear and his toiletry kit (which he had) and will go directly to work (which he won't). He has an idea, he says, trying to make it sound spontaneous. Why doesn't she send Danny to Dodie's tomorrow after Little League? He's been so busy and preoccupied the past few days and she deserves a date night. *Good night. I love you,* he says, hanging up. He feels sleazy and dishonest for using the promise of a romantic evening as a setup to finally disclose his brother has been arraigned and bail set and they are all about to be implicated by association in a tabloid scandal that will drag their son's family name through the mud.

Fuck it all, he thinks. How did he let himself get involved in this mess? If only he hadn't answered the call from the township police. If only he had insisted Frankie spend the night in Wayne instead of driving him back to the city. If only Frankie had never changed the locks. If only he'd never kicked in the door. If only, if only . . .

The phone in his pocket begins vibrating as he opens the front door of the appointed meeting place. It's a text from Jack Centafore sent from Frankie's phone.

Please call me.

Calling from inside the bar is out of the question. He's already fought his way in. He'll have one drink then fight his way out. The crowd is at least twice the maximum occupancy posted by the Philadelphia Fire Department. Young men and women in varying states of intoxication are packed into the narrow bar. Most of them have been drinking since happy hour. Frat boys, nerds, and a few stray hipsters are three deep at the bar, vying for the bartender's attention. It's Wednesday night. Hump Day. Even students whose greatest stress is getting out of bed in the morning feel the need to celebrate passing the halfway mark of the workweek. He sees Kelly standing with her group at the back of the room. She's waving to get his attention.

"I was just about to send a search party after you," she shouts in his ear.

She hands him a glass and offers a toast. It's cheap liquor and burns going down.

"Another!" the Latina princess shouts as they raise their glasses again.

"One more!" the kid in the yarmulke insists.

Sweat is dripping from Michael's forehead. The alcohol and the crush of human bodies are taking their toll. He chugs a bottle of Yuengling that's thrust into his hand, then a second, trying to wash the taste of cheap whiskey from his mouth. The Orthodox boy snakes his way through the crowd with yet another round, using his elbows to clear a path to Michael. He's full of questions about the life of a prosecutor, few of which Michael can hear in the deafening noise. Kelly manages to wedge herself between two hockey fans screaming at the hapless goalie on the television screen and comes to his rescue.

"You look miserable," she laughs.

He starts to respond, only to find his tongue has grown surprisingly thick. It's been years since he's done shots and tonight he's tossed back three, chasing them with beer, all on an empty stomach. He needs to make his way to the door. Fresh air will revive him. The phone in his pocket is vibrating again. His blood alcohol level is soaring. There's no way he can get behind the wheel of his car.

"I have to go," he says.

Someone bumps Kelly from behind, pushing her against his chest. Her body feels soft, squishy, padded with flesh. She's a bit drunk herself and sloshes beer on his shirt. Her hip is pressing against his inner thigh. It feels intentional. The Boss is on the jukebox, singing "Glory Days."

"I need to make a call," he says, thankful for the excuse to escape the heat of her body.

"Michael?"

"Jack?"

He expects the priest can hear he's not completely sober.

"Thanks for calling me back."

"Where's my brother? Is he home? You didn't leave him alone, did you?"

"He's upstairs. I gave him a Xanax and put him to bed."

Michael panics at the possibility of the priest wandering down to the basement. He's not a shampoo girl and won't be deterred by the odds of encountering a mouse.

"I brought him back to the rectory. It was easier than taking him home. He'll sleep through the night."

There's a lingering chill in the April night air. Still, Michael shouldn't be shivering on the sidewalk with all the alcohol in his bloodstream.

"He got very agitated and wanted me to drop him at the Trenton train station. He said he was transferring at Thirtieth Street and you were picking him up in Wayne. Something about leaving his car out there. He wasn't making much sense. He told me to forget it, just take him home, when I said I would drive him out to your place. Something's off, Michael. None of this feels right."

The priest clears his throat. He hesitates, knowing he's about to cross a boundary.

"I have to ask you something, Michael. I know you don't want to talk about it."

There's an awkward moment of silence.

"Please be honest with me, Michael. Please. Did that old man ever do anything to him? You know, anything inappropriate. Sexual? Your brother shuts me down whenever I bring up the subject. So, please. Tell me if you know. I can't think of any other reason why Parisi's death is affecting him like this. He barely seems himself."

Jack says he's all too familiar with the tragic pattern. Of course Frankie is dissembling. Death has robbed him of any chance to bring closure to a lifetime of guilt and shame. Michael agrees that the wounds of abuse never completely heal. He asks for Jack's solemn oath before confirming the priest's long-held suspicions about the deceased.

"You can never let Frankie know I told you. He'd never forgive me. This is between you and me."

"Never. Don't worry, Michael. Never. I swear."

Michael feels a sharp pang of regret about smearing the reputation of an old man who'd been nothing but kind to him and was guilty of nothing except photographing two young boys with a Polaroid Land Camera. He remembers eating chocolate cake at the rectory on Saturday nights and the grown-up books Father Parisi had given him to read. The priest was strange, but oddness isn't a crime.

"Give me an hour. I'll stop at the rectory and pick him up."

"He can stay here tonight, Michael. It isn't a problem."

But Michael is adamant about taking his brother home. Jack knows not to argue. There's just one thing he wants to say.

"Thank you for trusting me, Michael. I really mean it."

Michael wanders into the latest hot spot in University City, seeking food to soak up the alcohol sloshing in his belly. He tells the hostess he'll sit at the bar and asks the bartender for a menu, but nothing looks appealing. In fact, his stomach clamps down, rejecting the very thought of eating. He should start sobering up, but instead orders a bourbon on the rocks, an inconspicuous middle-aged man in a roomful of privileged undergraduates armed with platinum American Express cards provided by their generous parents. He still can't order in a restaurant without looking first at the prices. These spoiled brats blithely run up the bill, then haggle with one another over the amount of the miserly tip.

He crushes an ice cube between his molars, a habit that's cost him thousands in crown repairs. He shrugs off the bartender who's complaining about the Phillies' abysmal April record.

"Michael?"

His stepdaughter seems shocked to find him in such an unlikely place.

"Man, are you shit-faced," she laughs.

"Don't tell your mother," he mumbles, sounding sober and clear-headed only to himself.

"Only if *you* don't tell her. She thinks I'm spending the night at my father's. You remember Meaghan?" she asks, introducing her companion. "We played lacrosse together for three seasons. She graduated last year and was recruited by Penn."

He vaguely remembers the girl as a fierce competitor on the playing field. Kit doesn't like her, thinks she's a bad influence on Scottie. His wife will never admit she's bothered by her daughter's friendship with an obvious lesbian. She's tried broaching the subject with Scottie, hoping to allay her own suspicions about her daughter's sexual orientation, but their relationship has deteriorated to raised voices, tears, and slammed doors.

"Aren't you going to answer that?" she asks, pointing at his ringing phone.

It's Kit, returning his earlier call. She says she didn't expect him to pick up, just wanted to leave a message. There's an emergency hearing in the Southern District of New York in the morning. They may have to postpone their date night. Is he near a television? Hillary is wiping up the floor with her adversary.

"Michael, are you there?"

Scottie grabs the phone from her stepfather's hand.

"Doozy, it's me. You better come get him. He can't drive. He's really, really drunk. He's acting weird. I don't know what to do."

Danny's asleep; it's a school night and Kit doesn't want to wake him. She can't leave him alone in the house. She tells her daughter to call a cab.

"I'll be at the door when you get here. Tell the driver you're going to pay double the fare. Don't let him out of your sight. Not even to go to the bathroom. Get him home safe and sound and you have a free pass. I won't even ask what you've been doing tonight."

April 17, 2008 (morning through late afternoon)

He's standing on a deserted platform, waiting for the train to arrive that will deliver him and Frankie to their half sister's faraway home. Sal Pinto gave him strict orders to not move a muscle until he returns from taking a leak. The clanking motor of the escalator to the waiting room sputters and dies. He can hear Sal Pinto upstairs arguing that someone needs to open the security gate. His godson is alone down there . . . he's just a little boy.

He shoves his hand in his pocket and touches his ticket as the train approaches the station. It wheezes to a complete stop and the doors to the passenger cars open. Frankie is standing inside, urging him to hurry. "Come on! Come on, Mikey! The train is about to leave the station!" But the suitcase is too heavy to lift. He grabs the handle and tries to drag it across the platform. Papa will be angry if he leaves it behind. It's filled with change—quarters, dimes, nickels—he's sending to his daughter. He begins to cry, not understanding why Frankie won't get off the train and help. Frankie waves as he disappears behind the closing door.

He chases the train down the tracks, but the faster he runs, the farther it recedes into the smoky distance. He hears a shrill whistle behind him and feels a charging engine speeding toward him, bearing down and . . .

* * *

Then, as always, he's wide-awake. His indulgent wife had force-fed him three aspirin and two bottles of spring water before tucking him into bed and, miracle of miracles, Michael is dry-mouthed and foggy-headed but doesn't have a smashing hangover that would have lingered the entire day. He panics, thinking his brother is alone, with no one watching his every move, then remembers making a drunken, barely coherent call to Jack Centafore in the cab, asking him to keep Frankie overnight and to not let him leave until Michael came to collect him in the morning. Kit's gone—he vaguely recalls something about her needing to take the 6:05 Acela to New York—so he'll have to take the train into the city to pick up his car and collect his brother from the rectory.

Michael's assistant is already at her desk, sipping her first cup of coffee, and answers on the second ring. Something has come up, he says. Thankfully, it's a rare day he doesn't have court appearances scheduled. He doubts he'll make it in today. Reach him on his cell in the event of an emergency. And give Walter Rudenstein his personal number when he calls. Jocelyn's returned from taking Danny to school and offers to drive him to the station. He thanks her and says he can use a brisk walk to clear his head.

It's a beautiful day. He reaches in his pocket and turns off his phone, needing an hour without interruptions to collect his thoughts and prepare for what is going to be the worst day of his life. The weather forecast was right on the nose, the perfect spring day with a few passing clouds. The kid at the coffee shop, too young and pimply to have earned the distinction of being called a barista, manages to pull a decent café Americano. The train is due to arrive shortly. He drops several quarters in the honor box for a copy of the morning paper and settles on a bench on the platform. He flips through the front pages, his eyes glazing over the editorial debates about Obama and bitterness and religion and guns. One article gets his attention. Springsteen will be endorsing Obama later in the day.

It's difficult to concentrate while an agitated, nasty-tempered lapdog is barking farther down the platform. *Please, lady,* he thinks, *keep that damn thing far away from me.* He's going to report her to the conductor if she tries to board the quiet car at the front of the train. A Haverford Prep boy flops onto Michael's bench. The kid's a classic model, straight from central casting: wrinkled khakis, an unpressed oxford shirt with the tail untucked and collar unbuttoned, his rep tie loosely knotted, a band of duct tape wrapped around his fashionably well-seasoned Sperry Top-Siders. The boy squirms and shuffles his long legs, searching for a crumpled pack of Marlboros in his pocket. Trained to be polite to his elders, he offers Michael a cigarette. God knows he's tempted, but good sense prevails and he thanks the kid and declines. The boy fumbles with the matches and swallows a chestful of smoke, barely suppressing a cough. He's a novice, obviously, needing a bit more practice before the Brad Pitt attitude seems natural.

"I think that stupid dog is losing it," the young man says.

The frantic animal's mistress leans forward, admonishing the little fucker, wagging her finger like a mother disciplining a naughty child. Across the tracks, the westbound train from Center City is approaching the north platform. The crazy mutt is spinning in circles, chasing its tail, clearly distressed by the shrill pitch of the air brakes. The woman drops her backpack and squats to pick up the dog, but can't control it, letting it slip through her hands. It jumps off the platform and runs onto the tracks, racing toward the arriving train. The woman is hysterical, shrieking at the barking dog as she pushes aside a young girl who tries to stop her from making a mad dash across the rails. The little devil hears her voice and turns, wagging its tail, thinking his mommy wants to play. Too quick and clever to be caught, it bolts back toward the south platform and into the path of the eastbound 9:14 as it pulls into the station.

Head down, never hesitating, the woman tries to outrun a thousand tons of irreversible momentum, seeing nothing but her little dog as it disappears beneath the moving train. Everyone is on their feet, trying to warn her, shouting *No! No! No! God, no!* Some are already sobbing as the inevitable unfolds in slow motion. Her body makes an oddly soft thumping sound as she's struck and thrown under the metal wheels. The steel flange is a perfect meat slicer, scattering pieces of flesh along the tracks. The schoolboy howls in horror, his face distorted in anguish; he drops to his haunches and vomits between his knees as the train comes to a stop in the station.

"There's a woman!" Michael shouts at the conductor disembarking the train. "There's a woman under the front car!" he insists, his voice surprisingly calm. Her headless torso is lying on the track bed. A leg, severed at the hip as cleanly as a country ham, is on the far side of the rail. The bright white Keds on her foot looks new, unscuffed; her sock is hot pink, something a child might wear.

The passengers descending onto the platform are confused and frightened, not understanding why they're being greeted by tears and sobbing. Michael hears a plaintive cry, almost human, beneath the train. The dog, a small black Chihuahua, is shaking, frightened, not knowing what to do.

"Come here, boy," Michael calls and it jumps onto the platform and runs toward the large black backpack abandoned by its mistress. The young girl who tried to stop the foolish woman from running on to the tracks is standing guard over the bag, holding a leash. Her face is streaked with tears, her eyes red, and snot dribbles from her nose. She's fighting to compose herself, overwhelmed by the unwanted responsibility of being the last person to speak with the victim before her tragic end. She throws her arms around Michael when he gently touches her shoulder, an act of solidarity. The other eyewitnesses, frightened and suffering from shock, scatter before the arrival of the police.

"I didn't know her," she confesses without Michael's asking. "We just started talking. About the dog. She let it off the leash. I should have tried to stop her," she says, breaking down.

The animal is eerily quiet, content, snuggling against the canvas backpack. Its green vest identifies it as a medical assistance animal, a service dog. What kind of physical assistance could a small Chihuahua give a grown woman? None, of course. She was a petty scofflaw, scamming the exception for legitimate service animals to flaunt the prohibition against companion pets traveling on public transportation. Michael picks up a worn composition book the dead woman had left on the platform. Its pages are filled with wild scribbles and doodles, the ramblings of a disordered mind.

The tragedy ghouls, those morbid vultures who appear at crime and accident scenes at the first scent of blood, are arriving, alerted by the call for response on the township police scanner. Michael is asked to give a statement. The young officer asks if there are any questions before he's released. One, Michael, the veteran of hundreds of crime scenes, says. Why was there no blood? The cop confirms the prosecutor's theory that the scorching heat of the metal wheels cauterized the wounds.

The officials throw a tarp over the train car, shielding the gruesome spectacle from curious eyes. A patrolman is restricting the area with crime scene tape. Michael feels awkward just walking away. He feels a strange attachment to the woman whose death he'd witnessed. A bond of intimacy exists between them. He should wait until the body is removed, piece by piece, an act of respect. But he's starting to feel conspicuous standing here, unneeded, his civic obligation fulfilled. He blesses himself, pure reflex, muscle memory, and wades through the throng of gawkers gathered at the perimeter of the station. He ignores their questions and walks away.

He wishes he had one of the boy's cigarettes now. The bright sun is burning off the last lingering traces of the slight morning chill. The brilliant yellow forsythia are in full flower and the magnolias are just beginning to blossom. He crosses the street, against the light; a truck driver, forced to swerve into the opposite lane to avoid hitting him, leans out his window and calls him a stupid fucker.

"What you doin' home, Mr. G?" Jocelyn asks in her West Indian lilt when he walks through the front door.

"The trains aren't running, Jocelyn. I'll have to drive into town. I need the keys to the Pathfinder."

The adrenaline rush from the accident is fading quickly. His briefcase feels like it's packed with bricks. He's exhausted, his legs too heavy to lift. The staircase is as forbidding as the Matterhorn. He wants to collapse on the nearest sofa but someone is vacuuming in the front room. There's a mop and bucket in the foyer. The cleaning lady smiles shyly, acknowledging his presence without speaking. She doesn't know his name, can't call him anything but *señor.* They're at equal disadvantage. She could be Consuela or Carmen or Maria, from Guatemala or Nicaragua or Peru. He doesn't know if she's the same woman who scrubbed the kitchen floor on Tuesday or the one who will wash his socks and fold his towels next week.

Somehow he finds the energy to climb the stairs to the bedroom. He needs to call the priest to let him know he's running late and to expect him in an hour. But first he needs a few minutes, five or ten, to rest. He locks the bedroom door, kicks off his shoes, but doesn't bother to undress. He's too tired to pull back the sheets. (Kit is incapable of leaving an unmade bed, even when it's scheduled to be stripped before noon.) The reel keeps playing after he closes his eyes. One second, she was a manic dervish, alive, charged by surges of fear and anxiety, surrounded by a nimbus of crackling energy that propelled her onto the tracks and into the face of a moving train. Then, at a speed faster than can be measured by time, she was nothing but a butchered carcass, perfectly still, lifeless. He finally collapses into something more profound than sleep, a black hole, no, a tunnel, and he's running from the train that's bearing down on him.

Connie is already setting up for the first client when Frankie arrives shortly before nine.

"When did you get back? How was the show? God, I'd love to see *Jersey Boys.* Have I ever told you Frankie Valli is my mother's second cousin twice removed?"

Only once a week for nine years, he wants to say.

He feels liberated, not having Jack or his brother watching his every move. He and the priest had argued this morning. Of course he was going directly to the shop. Why would he wait for Michael? He has a business to run, he'd insisted. He'd snapped at Jack when the priest insisted on walking him home.

"Did anyone complain when you called to cancel?"

"One or two. Just the usual impossible-to-please bitches. I told them you didn't pick the day for the funeral. Of course, I didn't mention you were also taking a mental health day in New York. Not that you don't deserve it."

"Thank God," he says, looking at the schedule. "All wash-and-sets this morning."

"Oh, there was one strange thing yesterday," Connie remembers as Frankie chooses the rollers he'll need. "I'd finished going through the appointment book and was about to make the last call when that woman started banging on the front door."

"Who?" he asks, feeling his heartbeat accelerate.

"I saw you talking with her the other morning. The woman with the kid. She was acting like she was high on something. Her hair was dirty and she wasn't wearing makeup. Blond. Not a natural. Not a professional job, either. Strictly Lady Clairol. She kept trying the door, but I told her we were closed for a funeral. She got really pissed off when I wouldn't unlock it."

His heart is racing now.

"What did she want?"

"How do you know this skank, Frankie? She wanted to know if I'd seen Mariano."

"What did you tell her?"

"I told her he left. She wanted to come in. Said the little boy needed to use the bathroom."

"Did you let them in?"

"Are you crazy? I knew I'd never get them out of here."

"Did she ask where he'd gone?"

"I didn't like the tone of her voice. I said I'd driven him to the bus station myself, but he wouldn't say where he was going."

Connie's proud of her resourcefulness. She asks Frankie if he's okay because he looks like he's been shot by a stun gun.

"Fine. I'm fine," he says, trying to look cheerful as he unlocks the door to let Monica Delfina into the shop.

"Mr. G, Mr. G. Missus wants you to call her."

He's awakened by the nanny's insistent rapping on the bedroom door. He opens his eyes and stares at the ceiling. He hasn't moved since falling on the mattress. He's sweating and his clothes are damp and sticky. He rolls on his side and stares at the face of the alarm clock.

One forty-three.

"I'm up!" he shouts, swallowing the sludge that gathered in his throat as he slept.

He rolls off the bed and reaches for the phone in the pocket of his pants. Eighteen voice messages and thirty-two texts have been received since he turned off his phone at the train station. Kit answers on the first ring. Her voice sounds concerned.

"Michael, what's going on? My calls went straight to voice mail.

What's the matter? Jocelyn says you've been asleep all day. Are you still hungover?" she asks.

"No. I'm not hungover."

"Your office tracked me down in New York. They said you called out and they haven't been able to reach you since early this morning."

"Uh-huh."

"You sound strange. Are you going to tell me what's wrong?" she asks, growing more distressed.

"I saw a woman get hit by the train this morning."

"Oh my God," she gasps. "Is she okay?"

"What do you think?" he asks, regretting his brittle, sarcastic tone. He hears the clacking keyboard on her end of the call. She's accessing the Action News Web site, seeking the facts.

"Good Lord," she utters, obviously having found a link to the breaking headlines. "It says the dog survived."

"Yes."

"Where is it?"

"I don't know. How would I know? They took it, I suppose."

"Poor little thing must be traumatized."

"It seemed all right."

"And what about you? How are you?"

"I'm okay."

"I can be on the next train home."

"Don't. Please. I mean, I'm okay. I really am," he swears.

His sense of time is distorted. He tries shaking off the fog of confusion.

"What day is this?" he asks.

"It's Thursday, Michael. I think I should come back."

"No. No. I'm fine. I just need a moment."

"Are you sure? The negotiations aren't going as well as I'd hoped. I'm going to be late. Tell Danny I wish I could be at his game tonight. You're going to have to cheer loud enough for both of us," she says before hanging up.

He skips through his messages, searching for one from Walter Rudenstein. The first is an unfamiliar voice, heavily accented. The caller identifies himself as an attending physician at Presbyterian

Hospital in Pittsburgh and asks Mr. Gagliano to return his call. Jack Centafore has made several phone calls; Frankie insisted on going home and refused to cancel his daily schedule. His heartbeat accelerates at the thought of Frankie being unsupervised and on his own. Calm down, breathe, he tells himself. Jack Centafore said he'd walked him back to the shop and the shampoo girl can keep an eye on him until Michael arrives. He'll call her as soon as he gets through his messages, deleting any from his wife or his office until he reaches the one he's been awaiting.

Michael, it's Walter Rudenstein. I understand you need to talk to me. It's ten fifteen. Ask my assistant, Susan, to put you through when you call back.

It's nearly two now. His carefully-thought-out plan for the day has been shot to hell. He'd wanted to allow Frankie several hours to absorb the enormity of the profound changes about to occur in his life before calling Walter Rudenstein. By now they should be sitting in the lawyer's office while Walter speaks to the Dowager Empress (Walter Rudenstein, of course, has direct access to the District Attorney herself) making arrangements for Frankie to surrender himself and securing her agreement to instruct her adjutants to not oppose his request for a nominal bail at his preliminary arraignment on charges of manslaughter. He realizes how jumpy he is when he's startled by the ring tone of the phone he's holding in his hand. Frankie's number flashes on the screen.

"Michael?"

The voice is vaguely familiar, but he can't associate it with a name or a face.

"Michael, it's Connie. Frankie's assistant."

He tenses, sensing something's amiss if the shampoo girl is calling on his brother's phone.

"Michael, just let him know his phone is here when you pick him up. He's going to panic if he thinks he lost it."

"He isn't there?" he asks, sounding as nonchalant as possible under the circumstances.

"No, he left. He said his car is out there and you were taking him to pick it up."

Michael had forgotten the impounded car. Monday night feels like a lifetime ago.

"He was rushing to meet you and must have forgotten his phone," Connie says. "I told him to call the station first to ask if the trains were running on schedule after that accident this morning. It's all that Jackie Fontana could talk about when she was in the chair. She saw it on the local news. They said the woman was chasing a dog. I think it happened out near you. Michael? Are you there?"

"Yes," he says, unable to process this unexpected news and needing to force himself to speak. "Tell me again. What did he say he was going to do?"

"He said he was taking a train to meet you and you were going to take him to pick up his car."

He has a vivid flashback to the grisly aftermath of the tragedy he'd witnessed on the station platform. But the dead flesh he sees scattered along the tracks aren't pieces of a woman, a stranger. The butchered body is his brother's.

"When did he leave?"

"I don't know. Fifteen minutes ago maybe."

"Which station was he leaving from?"

"He didn't say. Thirtieth Street, I guess. He borrowed twenty dollars for cab fare and a train ticket."

He shouts for Jocelyn as he jams his feet into a pair of Nikes beside the bed. He strips off the damp dress shirt he's slept in and shoves his wallet and badge into his wrinkled suit pants. He doesn't waste precious minutes changing his T-shirt.

"Jocelyn!" he screams with a pitched urgency in his voice. The nanny looks hesitant, even a bit frightened, as she appears in the doorway.

"Where are the keys to the Pathfinder?"

"On the counter," she says, following him down the staircase, arguing she needs the car to pick up Danny at school. He slams the door, cutting her off, and peels out of the driveway. He tears through the meandering back roads to the entrance of the expressway, praying there are no bottlenecks created by roadwork or an accident. The steering wheel is slick with sweat and his cotton undershirt is sticking to his skin. Angry drivers blast their horns as he weaves between lanes, cutting them off. There's a metallic screech as he sideswipes the concrete median and he nearly loses control of the vehicle, coming close to capsizing to avoid rear-ending a cement truck. He ignores the traffic light at the top of the exit ramp and jumps the sidewalk, parking at the station door. Startled commuters scatter, probably fearing a terrorist attack. A pair of transit cops pursue him on foot and he spins on his heel and flashes his badge without breaking stride. He races through the majestic marble waiting room and bounds up the stairs that lead to the commuter platform at the far end of the station.

A lone woman is arguing with someone on her cell phone. Michael paces the entire length of the platform, though it's obvious Frankie has already boarded a train that has left the station. If, in fact, he's on a train at all. No matter. He's gone. Michael's let him slip through his fingers. A pair of Philadelphia cops, one of whom remembers Michael from his days with the city DA, are conferring with the Amtrak police at the station entrance. They're all members of the fraternity of law enforcement and ask if there is any way they can be of assistance. He thanks them for the generous offer and drives away.

Frankie finds the last unoccupied seat on the airport express train in a car overrun with boisterous high school girls headed to a soccer tournament in North Carolina. The conductor has raised the white flag, abandoning any effort to collect tickets and impose some modicum of order. The ride is one long Chinese fire drill with everyone competing to prove she can shout the loudest. A roll of Mentos is making its way through the car and Frankie politely declines the offer of a mint. Headphones are passed from girl to girl, prompting squeals and outbursts.

He'd had to abandon the original plan to drive to the freight yard near the cargo terminals since his car is still in the possession of the suburban police. He's improvising, traveling on the same form of transportation he'll use to end his life. He'll ride to the airport, the end of the line, then walk the length of the platform where he'll wait for the next incoming train to approach. A sudden stop sends one of the soccer players tumbling into his lap. She giggles, prompting an outburst of laughter from her teammates.

"Sorry," she halfheartedly apologizes as she struggles to stand, but the car is rolling again and the rocking makes it difficult for her to steady herself.

One of the taller girls grabs her wrist and pulls her to her feet, calling her a doofus.

"Are you all right, sir?" the Samaritan asks. "She didn't hurt you, did she?"

"Thanks. I'm fine. No damage."

The tall girl's gaze makes him uncomfortable, as if she can read his mind and knows his intentions.

"Are you sure?" she asks again, seeming genuinely concerned.

"Yes. I'm fine."

She asks where he's from and where he's traveling to.

"Florida," he says, naming the first place that comes to mind.

"My uncle lives in Florida. Fort Lauderdale. He and his boyfriend have a condo on the beach. They're old guys, too," she says matter-of-factly.

Cheerful mayhem erupts as the train arrives at the airport station. The girls good-naturedly jostle one another, racing to be the first to grab her travel duffel from the overhead luggage rack. Frankie sits patiently until he's alone in the car. The platform is deserted as he exits the door. The earbuds of his iPod are a snug fit and he cranks up the volume of Stevie's greatest hits. He places his wallet with his ID where it will be easily found and faces the rail tracks, transported by "Landslide" as he waits.

The evening rush begins in mid-afternoon and the expressway will be log-jammed by now. Michael decides to drive home through the city. The ramshackle row houses and crumbling bodegas begin to give way to tidy neighborhoods of well-kept bungalows with manicured lawns and finally to wide residential streets canopied by ancient trees that camouflage the large and stately stone houses set back far from the road.

He's deflated, resigned to accepting he's powerless to change the course of fate. All he can do is sit in his comfortable home and wait. He pours a glass of bourbon and collapses on the nearest sofa. In hindsight, he realizes he'd missed all the obvious signs.

Monday night, driving Frankie back to Philadelphia.

Just take me to the nearest train station, Mikey. It's late and I can get back home on my own.

Yesterday, on the New Jersey Turnpike, the call from the priest.

He got very agitated and wanted me to drop him at the Trenton train station. He said he was transferring at Thirtieth Street and you were picking him up in Wayne.

This morning, being awakened by his most terrifying nightmare. Papa believed dreams were prophecies not to be ignored.

His phone is ringing. Walter Rudenstein is calling again and, getting no answer, leaves another message.

"Michael, I'll be leaving my office shortly. Reach me on my cell phone if you still need to speak to me."

The walls of the house are closing in on him. The bourbon doesn't relax him. He's pacing between rooms, trying to assure himself his fears are foolish. He'd jumped to conclusions and is making assumptions with no basis in fact. He's overreacting. Imagining catastrophes. Thinking like his father. Papa was a superstitious old peasant. You can't read the future in dreams. It will be a long haul until this journey is over and he can't allow himself to go crazy at every little bump in the road. It's post-traumatic stress, this obsession with trains and death. It's poisoning his judgment, scrambling his logic, affecting his ability to think clearly. The shampoo girl said Frankie was leaving for Wayne. He's coming to retrieve his car. He may be at the station now and Michael isn't there to greet him.

He snatches the cut flowers Kit has delivered twice weekly to fill the enormous Ballard family heirloom vase to contribute to the tributes that strangers will have left on the platform to commemorate this morning's tragedy. He'd been cynical as a younger man, mocking the impromptu memorials for accident and crime victims until he'd found himself quietly crying as he stood before the stuffed animals and bouquets, the poems and balloons, left in remembrance of Carmine Torino.

The tarp has been removed and the crime scene tape taken down. Frankie's train must be late and he has yet to arrive. A young woman is tapping on the keyboard of her laptop. An older gent approaches Michael and asks if he has a schedule. No one has bothered to lay even a single flower on the sacred ground where a woman was violently killed just a few hours ago. Michael carefully places his bouquet of Gerbera daisies and snapdragons between the rails. They look sad and pathetic, unworthy, and he reaches for the medal he wears on a chain around his neck. Saint Rocco has had no religious significance to Michael since he was a boy, but the image is a talisman. He tosses it onto the tracks, a more meaningful offering than blossoms.

He shouldn't feel this exhausted after having slept the day away. But the thought of the short walk home overwhelms him and he slumps onto the same bench where he'd sat this morning. His body feels heavy, as if he's wearing an iron yoke and his sneakers are cement shoes. He drops his head into his hands and squeezes his temples in a futile attempt to quiet the throbbing pain behind his eyes. He stares at his feet as a train approaches from the city. His brief moment of sanguine confidence that Frankie is still alive has passed and he's broken and defeated, unable to stand between his brother and his destiny.

It's magical thinking believing Frankie will be among the tired commuters getting off at the Wayne station. Somewhere along the miles of tracks leading into and out of the city, his body lies mangled beyond recognition, more pieces along the tracks. This morning's tragedy has repeated itself, two similar fatalities in a single day, the newscasters will report in amazement. He regrets his impulsive gesture. Saint Rocco is their family's household saint, an offering for Frankie, not some nameless stranger. But the medal is a tiny thing, too tarnished to catch the light of the sun. He falls to his knees and sweeps his palm along the pebbles between the rails, determined to find it by touch if not by sight. He's absorbed in his treasure hunt and doesn't hear the inbound train approaching the station or the frantic voice shouting his name. Someone grabs him by the shoulders, tearing the cloth of his undershirt, and pulls him back from the tracks.

"What the fuck are you doing, Mikey? What the fuck? Jesus. What the fuck are you doing?"

Michael attempts a response, but his voice is weak and quivering, unable to utter a coherent sentence. He's reduced to stammering, blubbering, fighting the powerful urge to sob. Self-conscious about attracting unwanted attention, he breathes deeply and slowly composes himself, using the back of his hand to wipe the snot dripping from his nose.

"I'm sorry, Boo," he apologizes. "I saw a woman run in front of the train this morning. She went under the wheels and was cut into pieces. It's got me . . . it's got me . . ." Michael says haltingly. "I thought you might . . . I thought you had . . . tried the same thing. She got into my head. I'm sorry. You must think I'm crazy. I know you'd never do anything like that to me."

"You don't have to worry, Mikey," Frankie assures him. "I'm too much of a coward."

April 17, 2008 (evening into night)

He'd stood there as the train approached the airport station, not moving until the car stopped and the doors opened, then stepped inside and took a seat. The conductor collected the fare, Philadelphia International Airport to Wayne, where he would surrender himself to Michael and place his fate in his brother's hands. He'd lied when he said he was a coward. It wasn't fear of dying that had stopped him from stepping onto the tracks. It was something Connie said when Jackie Fontana was running at the mouth about that woman who was struck by a train chasing a dog this morning.

Say a prayer for that poor woman's family. They'll never be the same. It's hard enough when someone you love passes. Do you remember Marsha Carbone who lived at Twelfth and Wharton? Her son was killed in an explosion at the refinery. They had to identify him by his dental records. I don't know what I would do if something like that happened to one of my boys.

A coward *would* have stood in the path of a moving train. It's the bravest thing he's ever done, choosing prison and confinement to spare Michael from spending the rest of his life thinking of him as bloody pulp on a slab to be packed in a box to be buried in the earth. How could he ever face their mother in heaven and explain how he could have been so selfishly cruel?

* * *

"Dad!"

Danny comes rushing from the kitchen, excited by the unlikely surprise of hearing his father and uncle come through the door. It seems to Michael he's grown a half foot since yesterday. The resemblance between them grows stronger as Danny begins to lose the features of a boy and develop into a young man: the soft brown eyes shadowed by dark circles, the strong jaw and peaked Roman nose, the cleft in their square chins, the black hair shorn close to the scalp, their natural bearing somber and dignified. Danny's happy to see his dad, but he's a bit conflicted. Any variation on the settled routine is ominous. He looks anxious, seeking reassurance.

"Are you sick?"

"No, buddy."

"How come you're home so early?"

"Your mother is stuck in New York and I'm taking you to Little League."

"Why is Uncle Frankie here?"

"He left his car near here and he came to get it back."

"Where?"

"It doesn't matter, Danny. Don't ask so many questions," he says, growing impatient and irritated about needing to answer to a nine-year-old boy. "Go tell Jocelyn I'll pay for a cab if she's too fu—if she's too lazy to walk her fat ass to the train station."

Danny returns a few minutes later with his glove and his North Wayne Falcons jersey, emblazoned with the logo of Ace Hardware, the team's generous sponsor. It will be almost dark before the game is over and Danny is fed and put to bed. The call to Walter Rudenstein should have been made hours ago. More time is being wasted when every minute counts.

"Hey, aren't you coming?" Danny asks his uncle.

"Of course he's coming. Get in the backseat, Frankie. How many times do I have to tell you to buckle your goddamn seat belt, Danny?"

His tone is harsh. His son stares in amazement. His father has never sworn at him before today.

The radio's tuned to News Radio 1060 and he quickly changes the station, not wanting Danny to hear an account of this morning's accident. Adult alternative public radio is playing an Emmylou Harris track, a soothing lullaby by a Nashville madonna.

"A lady got hit by a train this morning," Danny announces as they drive past the station.

Michael's startled by his son's casual observation. He looks in the rearview mirror to see his brother's reaction. Nothing. Frankie is staring out the window, adrift in another world.

"She was chasing a dog," he adds.

"Where did you hear about it?"

"Jocelyn told me when we were coming home from school."

He bites his tongue to keep his temper under control. He's going to fire the lazy bitch for overstepping her authority. She's nothing but a car service anyway. Danny hardly needs a nanny. The team has already taken to the field for batting practice when they arrive.

"Let's go," Michael snaps, irritated by his son's stalling tactics. "Goddamn it. Stop acting like a fucking spoiled little brat. Pick up your glove and get out of the car."

Michael knows Little League is a burdensome chore for him. His son is acutely aware of his lack of skill, having inherited none of his father's athleticism. His ambivalence and clumsiness infuriate his coach, who plays him as the fourth outfielder so he can do the least harm. Balls the other boys would catch fall from the sky and land at his feet. Michael's told him time and again he doesn't have to play if he doesn't want to, but Danny soldiers on bravely, not wanting to be marked as an outcast, a pariah. It's painful to watch him flailing at the plate, a study in frustration.

"Dad . . ."

"Shut up and do what I tell you!" Michael shouts, his tone sharper and more menacing than intended.

Even Frankie is stirred by his outburst. Danny's clearly frightened by this stranger who raises his voice and swears and refuses to let him speak. There's an unspoken threat of physical punishment, of being roughly pulled from the car and slapped. He grabs his glove and slinks away, dragging himself to the field, his shoulders sagging as if being sent off to certain doom. He finally spins on his heels and stares at his father from a safe distance. Michael is unsettled by the fear and apprehension in the boy's eyes.

"Hey! Hey! Come back!" Michael calls after him. "Come on. Come back."

Danny stalls, not knowing if he can trust this man who only resembles his dad.

"Come on. You don't have to play tonight. We can just go home."

Danny's hesitant and approaches his father warily.

"Why are you mad at me, Dad?"

"No. No. No. I'm not mad at you. I'm just having a bad day. A really bad day. You hungry, buddy?"

"I guess so," Danny says tentatively, testing the waters.

"Don't tell your mother about this," Michael warns as they pull into the parking lot of McDonald's.

Danny's appetite has outgrown Happy Meals, though he looks longingly at the excited little boy at the next table playing with his cheap plastic toy giveaway. He orders Chicken McNuggets and fries and a strawberry shake. The father he knows has returned and life is back to normal.

"You have to eat something, Frankie," Michael insists when his brother refuses even a cup of coffee.

Frankie hasn't said ten words since Michael gently explained how this was going to go down. *I need you to trust me. Walter Rudenstein is the best in the city.* Michael said he doesn't see the prosecution going for a murder charge. No jury will doubt the words of a priest when Jack takes the stand to testify to Frankie's bruised and battered face and the prior history of violent beatings by a volatile young man. Throw in Frankie's diminished capacity from excessive doses of sleeping pills and it's voluntary manslaughter at most. *It's serious shit, Frankie. I won't lie to you. But it isn't murder and the prosecutor will agree to reasonable bail at the preliminary arraignment.* Frankie has no record. He lacks any propensity for violence; he's a danger to no one. And he has a brother who's well respected by the entire Philadelphia office, even by the DA herself. The bad idea of stashing the body in a freezer chest complicates things, but that's why Michael will be paying Walter Rudenstein his considerable fee. It's possible he won't have to do any time. Frankie's only reaction had been to ask when they could retrieve his car. *Is that all you have to say?* Michael asked. *You think you're in this alone? This is going to affect me, too. You know that, don't you?*

Kettleman is going to distance himself from anyone associated with a dead boy found in a freezer and he's certainly not going to anoint someone knee-deep in the muck of a tabloid scandal as his successor. The Grossmans will offer their sympathy as they move on to more promising, untainted candidates. His political career is over before it ever started. As for the impact on his wife and son, why state the obvious?

Danny's tugging at his uncle's shirtsleeve. He's grown frustrated with Frankie's out-of-character lack of interest in debating who would emerge victorious—Spider-Man or Superman—in a battle to the death.

"Danny's talking to you, Frankie. Aren't you going to answer the question?"

"What's that?" Frankie asks, as if being aroused from a deep sleep.

"Never mind," Michael says, exhausted by the effort of playing the charade that all is well in the world, that it's just another day. "You finished, Danny? Tomorrow's a school day."

Danny's patter during the drive home is a welcome distraction. His father insists he go straight up to his room and change into his pajamas when they get home.

"Lights out, buddy," he announces when he goes to say good night and finds Danny propped against his pillow with his frayed copy of the *Diary of a Wimpy Kid* in his hand. "Your mother is going to be really pissed if she comes home and finds you awake."

"Ten more minutes."

"No more minutes."

"Can I have a glass of water?"

"Are you thirsty?"

"Yes."

He gurgles the contents, hands back the empty glass, and asks for another.

"No more water. You're just stalling for time."

Michael listens to his prayers. Tonight he asks God to bless the lady who got hit by the train and to take good care of her dog. His father kisses him good night and turns off the bed lamp. On impulse, Michael picks up his son—he's getting to be a heavy little bugger—and hugs him. He'd recognized that voice earlier this evening, cruel, impatient, threatening. It was Papa speaking and it shocked him to realize he was capable of striking his child. He asks if Danny knows how much he loves him.

"I'm sorry for upsetting you tonight, Danny. It won't happen again. I promise."

The boy looks him in the eye, his expression as grave as a church elder's.

"It's okay, Dad. You're allowed to be mean sometimes," he solemnly pronounces, the son comforting the father, assuring him all is well.

Michael leaves him safe in his bed to dream of X-Men and Bakugan Brawlers, beyond the reach of the dangerous and unpredictable world for a few hours. He closes the bedroom door and walks downstairs to call the lawyer. It's late, but it won't be the first time Walter Rudenstein gets a phone call from a desperate client at ten o'clock. Frankie's sitting where he left him, watching the local news. The anchor is using his fake somber voice as he announces the most urgent matters of the day.

A little dog's excitement led to tragedy on the Main Line this morning. Eyewitnesses say the victim had bent down to pick up the animal after it wandered onto the tracks.

What eyewitnesses? The woman was running, goddamn it, head down, chasing the dog as it disappeared under the train. Michael was there. Never took his eyes off her.

The victim's identity is being withheld until next of kin can be notified.

Michael's phone starts vibrating as the anchor moves on to another tragedy, a four-alarm fire in North Philadelphia. It must be Kit, calling in with a status report and her estimated time of arrival. But the area code of the incoming call is 412 and he remembers he never responded to the earlier message from western Pennsylvania.

"Am I speaking to Mr. Gagliano? Mr. Michael Gagliano?"

The man's English is fluent, his diction is formal, and his accent is decidedly Indian or Pakistani. He identifies himself as Dr. Patel, an attending physician in the Coronary Intensive Care Unit, and is calling about Mrs. Shevchek, Mr. Gagliano's sister. He apologizes for the late hour, but Mr. Gagliano never responded to his call. The doctor explains Mrs. Shevchek had been transported by ambulance and presented in respiratory distress. She was still alert and oriented and had consented to allow them to drain the fluid that had gathered around her heart. But now she's gone into an acute episode of COPD and he's calling Michael as her medical power of attorney, needing his consent to intubate her.

Goddamn it, Michael thinks. He would never have agreed to assume this unwanted responsibility if Frankie hadn't pleaded with him. Polly spent her dying years fearing the motives of her impaired stepson and his children. Her stepdaughter Laurie had died of uterine cancer and Polly and Marybeth have been long estranged after a bitter dispute over money, leaving her no one to trust but her half brothers by the father she hated. Michael, being the lawyer, was the obvious choice. His first instinct is to refuse to allow them to do the procedure. He recalls the instructions in her advance declaration, locked in a safe upstairs, and her decision to forgo any extraordinary measures to extend her life.

"It would give us the opportunity to see if she responds to antibiotics. If there is no improvement, we would agree that the appropriate course would be to remove the breathing tube."

The doctor recommends a family meeting between the legally authorized power of attorney and Mrs. Shevchek's next of kin. As soon as possible. The son has been argumentative, unwilling to accept he's been excluded from any decision about his mother's treatment and care. *Stepson,* Michael clarifies, without legal standing to challenge the decisions of her blood kin and the appointed power of attorney. The physician says the hospital social worker, expert at building consensus and trained in grief counseling, will facilitate. When can they expect Mr. Gagliano's arrival?

"I don't need consensus. Her instructions are clear. No tubes," he says decisively. "Let her go peacefully."

"Was that the lawyer? Is it time?" Frankie asks when Michael finishes his call, his voice surprisingly strong and even.

He can't read the strange expression on Michael's face.

"That was Presbyterian Hospital in Pittsburgh. Polly's dying. They wanted to put her on life support to give her a chance to rally. I told them to let her die."

April 18, 2008

The phone call to Walter Rudenstein was postponed once again by a lengthy debate between Michael and the suddenly engaged Frankie about his decision as the power of attorney. It wasn't his brother's plea for mercy and kindness that had caused Michael to call back the attending physician and consent to the procedure. He'd come to realize Polly's bleak prognosis was a gift, an opportunity to improvise an elaborate ruse about needing to drive across the Appalachians and rush to her bedside, a reasonable explanation for the sudden absence of a reliable husband and father and his uncharacteristic behavior of neglecting his office and duties as a dedicated public servant. He hates lying to his wife but she has to be kept in the dark, unaware of her husband's plots and scheming, until Frankie is arraigned and he can he come clean without implicating her in a possible charge of harboring a criminal. Then he'll take Polly off life support after she's outlived her usefulness, no pun intended.

He'd slept fitfully, checking on Frankie periodically to ensure he hadn't disappeared while the household was sleeping. In the morning, Kit, exhausted from her sixteen-hour-day in Manhattan, had promptly announced she was postponing Miss Peterson's birthday party scheduled for Sunday. He'd said he appreciated the gesture but that it would be ridiculous for his wife to drop everything to travel across the state for what could be a lengthy vigil for a comatose woman being kept alive by a ventilator. He'd reminded her she'd been planning Miss P's centennial for over a year and the spiteful old bitch will have her revenge if the party is postponed. He knew Kit was relieved, having been decidedly uncomfortable on the rare occasions she'd encountered Polly and her brood. Addicts in the Ballard-Morris-Scott clan are far better bred.

She'd packed Michael enough casual clothes for several days. She didn't question the necessity of taking a dark suit and white dress shirt, not knowing Polly's instructions and assuming there would be a small service before the body was sent to the crematorium. She drove her husband and his brother into town. He couldn't remember where he'd left his car and they circled the law school several times before finding it. He owes the city over two hundred dollars for parking violations. Kit defused his fury, telling him to put it in perspective, then kissed him good-bye, making him promise to reconsider her offer if she can be any help out there.

He'd sent Frankie to dress for court as soon as they arrived at the house, telling him to pack whatever he'll need for the foreseeable future since he won't be returning any time soon. By noon, Eighth and Carpenter will be a designated crime scene. Law enforcement personnel will descend like locusts as soon as Walter Rudenstein arranges for Frankie to turn himself in. Five days ago Michael could never have imagined himself in this situation. He wishes he had a magic wand to turn back the clock, the world restored to its natural order.

Michael's watch says seven forty-five. He's going to call the lawyer precisely at eight. He's untying his shoes, preparing to change into appropriate attire to appear with his brother before a judge, when he hears banging on the door to the shop downstairs. Whoever wants inside so badly isn't likely to let a sheet of plate glass stand in their way. There's already one broken door in the building. He doesn't need the aggravation of boarding up a second. It's a woman. No one he recognizes from the neighborhood. She's high as a kite, filthy, wearing a souvenir T-shirt that looks like it's never been laundered.

"Can I help you?" he shouts through the glass.

"I'm looking for Frankie," she says, fumbling a cigarette, dropping it on the sidewalk and falling to her knees to retrieve it. "Mariano's mother is dying and wants to see her baby."

"Frankie isn't here," he lies. "What is it I can do for you?"

Maybe his brother's wild tales of meth labs and drug busts and nefarious characters with mysterious connections to Mariano weren't the delusions of a man on the verge of cracking up.

She starts pounding on the door again, clearly infuriated by his cold stare and refusal to answer. He has no choice but to open the door before her clenched fist cracks the glass. She's quick, but not fast enough to slip through his grasp. Her arm feels brittle, as if it could break under the pressure of his grip. He blocks her from entering, pushes her out onto the street, and confronts her on the sidewalk.

"Who the fuck are you?" she shouts, trying to wrest free from his hold.

"Who the fuck are *you?*"

"Where's Frankie?"

"He's not here. He's gone."

"That fucking faggot lied to me. He knows where Mariano is. The bitch admitted she drove him to the bus station."

His heartbeat accelerates, but his demeanor is glacial.

"I don't know what you're talking about. I don't know any Mariano. I think you better leave."

"The bitch drove him to the station. She wouldn't tell me where he was going."

"What bitch?"

"The one who works here."

"Look, I told you there's no one here named Mariano. I think you ought to leave."

"Let me go inside and talk to Frankie. Please."

She tries an abrupt change in demeanor, hoping it will be more effective. Her smile is malicious. She's a poor judge of her ability to charm and seduce.

"Look, just let me talk to him. Just for a minute."

"I told you. Frankie isn't here."

"You're not doing him any favors lying to me. He's crazy if he thinks Randy can't get to him. He'll send his boys to find his little brother. Frankie will be lucky if all they do is break his legs if he won't tell him where the little bastard has gone."

"What the fuck are you talking about? Who the fuck is Randy?"

She says time is running out, dropping any pretense that Mariano's needed at the bedside of a dying mother in Puebla.

"Randy. His guys on the street told me to find Mariano. He shouldn't be afraid. He doesn't need to hide. It wasn't his fault. Randy's not going to hurt him. He loves his little brother. He just wants to send him back to Mexico where he'll be safe. Let me talk to Frankie. He knows me. We're friends. Really."

"Safe from what?" he asks, an unreceptive audience for her little performance.

His refusal to be swayed enrages her. She tries shaking him off and attempts to kick him, losing her balance as she aims for his groin, sending a filthy flip-flop sailing into the street. She reaches for his face with her free hand, her nails seeking his eyes. He grabs a handful of her hair and slams her against the wall of the building. He yanks her head back when she spits in his face, intending to crack her skull against the bricks, but the sound of a crying child stops him. A little boy, sobbing and terrified, runs to the woman and clings to her leg. Michael leans forward and speaks quietly, his message for her ears only, careful not to further frighten the pitiful child.

"Come around here again and I'll kill you myself. Do you understand me? I will kill you myself."

He realizes he's drenched with sweat after locking the door behind him. The first thing he does is reach for the bag Kit had packed for him. His instincts as a prosecutor are deeply ingrained. He had been half way out the door this morning when he claimed to suddenly remember he'd left Polly's power of attorney upstairs. Just knowing a loaded handgun is tucked among his carefully folded clothes—legally issued, the object of Kit's scorn and fear, kept locked in a safe in their bedroom—comforts him.

"Take off that suit. What time does that shampoo girl get here? You be down there to meet her."

"I thought you said—"

"Never mind what I said."

Michael seems impatient, agitated, even afraid. He'd just sent Frankie to change and to pack. Now he's insisting he act like it's a normal day, nothing out of the ordinary.

"Just go do it. Now. Do you hear me?"

Connie is standing at the bottom of the staircase, shouting for Frankie, announcing her arrival.

"Tell her you'll be down in a minute."

"I'll be down in a minute," he hollers.

"I'm going to go out the back door. Don't mention that I've been here. Don't say anything to her. I'm trusting you."

"You said the longer we waited, the worse it will be."

"I know what I said. Don't ask questions. Just do as I say."

Vinnie's Place, a block away, sells American Spirit cigarettes, an all-natural carcinogen for suckers willing to pay premium prices to delude themselves into believing they are polluting their lungs with a healthier alternative. Michael quietly seethes while Vinnie's widow, the battle-scarred matron working the lottery ticket machine, ignores him.

"You going to see Hill-ree? Hill-ree's gonna give a speech down the street," she asks the flustered woman who's trying to concentrate on the figures scratched on the back of a Rite Aid receipt.

"What numbers did I give you?" the customer mumbles, clenching an extra-slim menthol between her teeth as she fumbles for her reading glasses.

"Twenty-three. Seven. Sixteen. Seven. Thirty-six."

"Yeah, that's right," she sighs, relieved. "Where?"

"Down the street. In front of the cheese shop."

"When?"

"Now. The cameraman was just in for sodas and coffee. He told me she's on her way. Eight bucks," she demands as she finally hands Michael his top-shelf smokes. It's extortion; the off-label brands sell for only four twenty-five.

"I'm gonna go down and see her. Maybe I'll get her autograph," her friend announces as she stashes her lottery tickets in her pocketbook and stubs out her cigarette in the overflowing ashtray on the counter, next to the Saran-wrapped slices of banana bread and day-old bagels.

"You make sure you vote next week. We can't let the nigger get in," Vinnie's widow advises as she hands the woman her lottery tickets.

"Shove these fucking things up your ass, you fucking fat cunt," Michael spits, disgusted by her casual, smug arrogance, throwing the cigarettes back in her face.

She reaches under the counter for her weapon of choice—a pipe, a baseball bat, maybe a gun—but he's out the door before she can threaten life or limb. She steps into the street and shouts after him.

"I know who you are, asshole. I remember you. Mr. My-Shit-Don't-Stink. Stay the fuck out of my store!"

His nerves are on edge; he almost jumps through his skin at the sound of the shrill ring tone of the phone in his pocket. Walter Rudenstein is nothing if not persistent. Michael can't avoid speaking to him and answers on the sixth ring, the last before it's programmed to roll into voice mail. He forces himself to sound cheerful, as if it were a pleasant but unexpected surprise to hear from Walter on this beautiful Friday morning.

"Michael, I'm flying to Chicago early this afternoon to speak at a symposium at Northwestern. I know you were eager to reach me."

He was. Is he still? Does he really want to divulge to Walter Rudenstein a body is on ice in his brother's freezer chest? There's nothing Walter Rudenstein can do to help Frankie now. There's nowhere that the man responsible for Mariano's disappearance will ever be safe from an animal seeking revenge. Retribution won't be quick and it won't be painless. Frankie says this Randy is in custody, that the papers say he'll never be released, but his network is a beast with a thousand heads intent on blood revenge. Michael's spent his life prosecuting criminals and he knows the woman, hopped up as she was, spoke the truth. The monster's nose is on the trail of the dead boy and it will eventually lead to the door of the house at Eighth and Carpenter. It will toy with Frankie, sadistic bastard that it is, threatening unspeakable things, maybe hold a knife to his throat or a gun to his head trying to extort a confession. But if Frankie can keep his wits about him, stick to the story, it might believe he's telling the truth. It could never imagine a *maricón* would have the balls to deceive it. It will move on, quickly forget the silly old fag who pampered the brat and showered him with gifts before he went on the lam, his tiny role in the drama ended unless . . .

. . . Unless it's splashed on the front page of the daily paper, the leading story on the local news, that the brother of the Chief Deputy District Attorney of Delaware County has been released on bail and is awaiting trial on charges of voluntary manslaughter for cracking the skull of a young man identified as Mariano Garza with a toilet lid and drowning him in the bathtub. Walter Rudenstein may very well succeed in winning Frankie an acquittal on a manslaughter charge, but nothing and no one can ever protect his brother from the fury of violent criminals intent on literally extracting their pound of flesh and settling the score.

"No. No. It wasn't anything important. It can wait until you get back."

Michael knows by the silence on the line that the shrewd old counselor-at-law suspects something is amiss.

"Actually, Walter, my brother and I are on our way to Pittsburgh. Our sister isn't expected to live for more than a few days."

"I'm very sorry to hear that, Michael. My condolences to your family. Call me when you're back and we can meet for lunch. Better yet, dinner. Are you still fond of aged bourbon, Michael?"

"I'd like that, Walter. We should catch up."

The man Walter Rudenstein knows isn't the one who has just made a rash, impulsive decision to risk branding himself a criminal without any thought to his wife and son. The Michael Rocco Gagliano who Walter Rudenstein mentored is an unimpeachable career public servant who's dedicated his professional life to pursuing justice for the victims of violent crimes. That Michael Rocco Gagliano would never stigmatize his family as the spouse and offspring of a felon who is certain to be convicted as an accessory after the fact if he's caught.

If he's caught.

How hard would it be to make Frankie vanish without a trace? Where can he send him? How will he get there? There's still time for him to disappear. No one is examining passports for a suspect wanted for questioning in the wrongful death of a young man buried in an ancient freezer in the basement of the building at Eighth and Carpenter. Frankie could be on a plane to Madrid or Prague or Timbuktu this evening. But what will he do when the cash in his pocket is spent and he has no credit cards or access to the cash in his accounts? How long will he survive? A week? A month? A year? He'll be on his own, unable to ever contact Michael again. Michael will never know his brother's fate, a mystery that will deny him any peace of mind until the end of his days. And what assurance does he have that the beast seeking vengeance will retreat, defeated, if somehow Frankie is able to elude its grasp? Will it follow the blood trail to a House with a Name in the Friendly Village of Wayne, where Kit and Danny reside, unaware of the threat to their peaceful existence lurking beyond their locked doors?

He slips into the Donut Connection, where a huddle of Mexican day workers are stuffing their cheeks with microwave egg sandwiches and super-size glazed coffee rolls. The radio is crackling behind the counter, announcing the time and weather. Michael's fishing in his pocket for change for two chocolate frosteds as the DJ on WMGK, the Magic of the Seventies, announces a Bee Gees tripleshot without commercial interruption, three hits from the classic *Saturday Night Fever* sound track, a record Frankie had played over and over until the needle wore down the vinyl grooves. The donuts are stale, but he eats them anyway, tasting nothing.

The Mexicans are giggling at some private joke. The youngest is a boy, no older than the kid in the freezer. He's got a chocolate-milk mustache on his upper lip and there's yellow yolk on his chin. He looks too fresh and well pressed to be soliciting eight hours of hard labor hauling sod and trimming hedges. His sneakers are blinding white and the crease in his jeans is sharp. His *Sopranos* T-shirt looks brand new, Gandolfini's face uncracked by the heat of the dryer. Tony Fucking Soprano wouldn't have broken a sweat over Michael's problem. He knew what to do when he had to take care of Big Pussy. Take him out to sea, put a bullet in his head, weight him down, and toss him overboard to sink to the bottom of the ocean. The seed of an idea begins to take root. It's brilliant, inspired, classic, straight out of *The Godfather* and Luca Brasi sleeping with the fishes. The Mexicans cast suspicious stares at the crazy gringo who is laughing to himself and slapping his palm on the counter, not knowing what they've done to deserve his generous offer of two boxes of donuts.

The plan is perfect. An undocumented illegal with no medical records or available genetic samples never officially existed. The dead boy will be laid to rest in a watery grave. It's too risky to dump him locally. The Delaware River and its estuaries are out of the question. Even Jersey is too close. Best to drive a few hours, south, to Virginia, the Eastern Shore where Frannie Merlino had had a trailer she'd been left by her first husband, a sportfisherman. Even if the body is found, they'll never trace it back to Philly.

"He's never been to the doctor, has he?"

"I took him to the ER once. For stitches."

"No X-rays, right?"

"No. Only by the dentist."

Dental records.

The forensic pathologist's Rosetta Stone.

Granted, he doubts that the Virginia State Police will ever think to issue a search warrant for office files of Vincent Calabro, DDS, "Dr. Smiles" of 738 Wallace Street, but there's always a risk. The greatest criminal minds have been tripped up by making the tiniest mistake.

"Fuck," he spits, disheartened by this unexpected glitch in his foolproof plan.

"What's the matter?"

"The X-rays. The goddamn dentist has the X-rays," he patiently explains to his dense older brother.

"The X-rays are in a drawer upstairs. Pamela Canarsi's brother is an oral surgeon in Jersey. He said he'll charge my insurance for Mariano's implants. I got his records from Dr. Smiles last week."

"That's insurance fraud! You could go to prison for that!" Michael warns, shocked and angered by his brother's casual admission of his willing participation in a criminal conspiracy. "Go get them. Right now. Go."

Michael sets a match to the flammable strip and tosses it into the kitchen sink, watching it turn to ash.

"They'll never connect a decomposed body found in a Virginia swamp to a missing kid in Philadelphia. The farther away he is, if they ever find him, the safer we'll be. Tonight's not good. It's already too late. It might take longer than we expected. People will ask questions if you don't open on time on your busiest day of the week. We'll leave tomorrow night, be back early Sunday. No one will even know we've been away. Everything has to seem as normal as possible. Nothing can seem strange or unusual."

"Why? Why are you doing this?" Frankie asks.

Michael's too distracted to answer. He wants to be alone, to be able to go over the plan in his mind, again and again, obsess over every detail. Where to buy the chains and cinder blocks. How to get the body from the back door opening to the alley behind the house to the car without drawing attention. How to hide the kid so that any curious eyes standing at the windows of the neighboring houses would never recognize the tidy package they're loading into the trunk as a human body.

"Why are you doing this?" Frankie calmly asks again.

Why *is* he doing this? He's spinning the roulette wheel, rolling the dice, dealing his hand. One small fuckup, one careless move, and he loses. They both lose. But it's not as if he has a choice. Free will has nothing to do with it.

"You know why I'm doing it."

"This isn't what she meant. This isn't what she would have wanted."

"Then I'm doing it because I want to. Just like you would do it for me. I won't ever let anyone hurt you. Never. So go upstairs and throw all his clothes into trash bags. Don't leave anything, not even a sock."

The priest arrives at the appointed hour, promptly as always, tonight's entrée in hand. This week it's stuffed shells in red gravy, forty minutes at 350 degrees, lovingly prepared by one of the women of the parish, all of whom worry that Father is wasting away to skin and bones. He's brought a bottle of Gavi and Jewish apple cake, Frankie's favorite, made from scratch by another member of his flock.

"What the fuck is he doing here?" Michael whispers in his brother's ear as Jack busies himself in the kitchen.

Frankie reminds him of his own words.

Business as usual. Nothing out of the ordinary. Don't raise any suspicion.

Michael hadn't known about his brother and his friend's Friday night tradition.

"He eats here every week. What did you want me to tell him?"

If Michael were to paint a portrait of a pedophile, it would look exactly like Jack Centafore—eyes set too close together, wispy strands of hair, and a pockmarked, sallow complexion. He really ought to cut the poor guy some slack. It's unkind to say he looks like a predator. What does a child molester look like anyway? He's prosecuted some who could pass as innocent choirboys and others who seemed as jolly as Santa Claus. It isn't the priest's fault he was born ugly. It's not a crime. It doesn't make him a bad person. But Michael doesn't like him, never has. The sound of his voice grates; his condescending words infuriate.

"Don't you have anything green in the house?" the priest shouts, rooting in the crisper drawer of the refrigerator. "I hope neither of you is dying for a salad. It's going to be a Spartan feast tonight," Jack says, uncorking the Gavi and pouring three generous glasses.

He seems oblivious to the tension in the room, unaware of the laundry list of forbidden topics of conversation this evening. Michael insisted Frankie isn't to mention the situation in Pittsburgh. Jack would question why they were sitting in Philadelphia, casually drinking wine, when their place is at their dying sister's bedside. And Mariano, of course. Jack knows he's gone and the locks have been changed. Frankie isn't to say anything more and let Michael handle it if the priest brings up the subject. The official reason for Michael's unexpected overnight visit is a seven a.m. appointment at the dealership. Frankie knows nothing about cars and Michael doesn't want to see him fleeced. Michael's uncomfortable using multiple alibis. One story for his family and his office who think he and his brother are attending a bedside vigil three hundred miles west. Another for the priest and the shampoo girl and a fully booked schedule of customers who believe there's nothing out of the ordinary. It worries him. Simplicity is the key to escaping detection.

"I thought your car was inspected last month, Frankie?" Jack asks as they take their places at the table.

"It's not an inspection," Michael corrects him. "It needs a realignment and I want to get an estimate on bodywork to clean up all those little dinks on the chassis. I keep telling him to take a monthly lease on a garage space instead of insisting on parking on the fucking street."

"I would have thought you'd be uptown tonight, Michael. Rumor has it your boy is making an appearance at the Obama rally in Independence Park."

"Danny? At a rally?" Michael asks, befuddled by the remark.

Jack throws back his head for a good, long, braying mule laugh.

"Bruce. The Boss. Springsteen. He's endorsed Obama."

It feels like it was another lifetime that he was sitting on a bench, reading about Bruce's announcement while waiting for the train. Jack opens a second bottle of wine, a red this time. Michael is grateful to cede the floor to him. The priest is a Democrat, despite the party's insistence life doesn't begin at conception, and thinks Hillary would make a fine president. But he's suffering from Clinton fatigue and he has to admit the idea of electing the first black president is exciting.

"It's the first time I could be voting for a president younger than myself. I'm starting to feel old. Who are you voting for, Michael?"

"Whoever my wife tells me to vote for. The price of domestic tranquility."

The evening passes uneventfully. Jack attributes Frankie's quietness to his grieving for the old priest.

"I'm worried," he confides in Michael when Frankie excuses himself to visit the bathroom. "Maybe he should talk to someone. Maybe he should be on medication."

Michael rises to clear the dessert plates, thinking the priest will take his leave. But instead Jack brings a bottle of Frangelico to the table, yet another Friday night tradition Michael's learning about for the first time. He proposes a toast and finally announces it's time he should be in bed. When Michael returns upstairs after letting him out, Frankie is sitting on the sofa, the remote in his hand. Michael asks to watch the last few innings of a game being played in central time. Michael doesn't make it through the top of the eighth and when he awakes hours later a man is doing a sales pitch for a miracle appliance. His head is in his sleeping brother's lap and he closes his eyes and dozes off again, too exhausted to dream.

April 19, 2008

Marianne Scavetti says she'll understand if Frankie says no. She'd done all she could do to talk her daughter out of such an expensive folly, but Amber had insisted that she would allow no one but Tocci of Tocci & Guiliano's, a perennial Best of Philly winner and the stylist of choice for all the female local newscasters, to cut her hair for the biggest day of her life. That snooty bastard had charged two hundred fifty dollars to spend less than five minutes with the poor girl before turning the scissors over to one of his many assistants, who may as well have chopped her hair with lawn clippers. She left the shop sobbing and hysterical and now her mother is begging Frankie to do damage control. *Please, Frankie. Puh . . . leeze. Her father will pick you up and take you back.* He's known Marianne since elementary school and this is the first time he's heard her cry. Michael encourages him to say yes. *Go, go. We can't leave until dark. It will calm you down if you have something to do with your hands.*

"What time is the wedding?"

"Seven."

"I'll have Connie cancel my last appointment. Have him pick me up at four."

All brides are beautiful, but Amber Scavetti needs a bit of magic and a lot of heavy labor. He assures her a bride wearing a size-fourteen gown can still be stunning. Her mother had objected to her choice of a wedding dress, worried too much unsightly back fat would be exposed. Frankie insists the strapless gown is an inspired choice that will show off her daughter's flawless milky skin, her best feature. He suggests they try a classic ballet chignon, solving the problem of the naturally frizzy texture of her hair and leaving nothing to distract the eye from the sensuous line of her long neck and shoulders. Marianne is skeptical, offering other suggestions for the best way to tame her daughter's unruly mane.

"Just shut up, Ma. One more word and I'm locking you out of the room," the girl threatens. "Frankie knows what he's doing."

It feels good, having a task at hand, a challenge, something to take his mind off the gruesome chore that awaits. The only thing that matters at this moment is that, in a few hours, Amber will be walking down the aisle, basking in the murmurs of approval, a storybook bride, Odette from *Swan Lake,* far lovelier than anyone could have expected.

Frankie's car is still in the custody of the Upper Merion Township police, so Michael will need to put his BMW sedan into service as an improvised hearse to transport the body to its final resting place. It's probably for the best as no one is going to issue a warrant to search a vehicle registered to the Chief Deputy District Attorney of Delaware County. He's outside Home Depot loading cinder blocks and chain link into the trunk when Kit calls to see how he and Frankie are holding up and to offer her support. He assures her nothing has changed.

"That pig stepson is acting out. He thinks I'm the devil who escaped from the bowels of hell. I've got it under control. You've got enough to worry about with Eleanor's big day."

"Miss P's going to miss you tomorrow."

"Please. She hates my guts."

"Do you think that matters? All she'll remember is you weren't there to pay proper homage."

For the first time in his life there's nothing he'd rather be doing than spending time with Eleanor Peterson. Kit says she has a thousand little details to look after before the party. He wishes her luck and drives to his next stop, Target, to buy vinyl shower curtains and an expandable wardrobe bag. He tears the cash receipts for his afternoon purchases into tiny pieces that he tosses to the wind.

Come nightfall, Michael plans to pull his car onto Carpenter Street and carefully back down the side alley that leads to the rear entrance to the house. It will be a tight fit and he'll be lucky to escape with a few minor scratches. He'd had the foresight to line the trunk with one of the shower curtains before leaving the Target parking lot. They'll quickly load the body and head for the interstate. They should arrive in Virginia in four hours, with hours of darkness ahead to carry out their scheme.

Neither Frankie nor Michael has an appetite and they ought to avoid spending the next few hours getting jacked on caffeine. Frankie says he wants to attend the five o'clock vigil Mass, and Michael, shocking himself, agrees to accompany him. It can't hurt to light a candle; Jesus must sometimes listen to the prayers of apostates. The days are growing longer and the weather is pleasant for the short walk to the church. Familiar faces from Michael's past greet the Gagliano brothers by name from their lawn chairs on the sidewalk. Only the most stubborn and contrary of the old guard remain rooted in the row houses where they've spent their lives. They insist they'll have to be carried out feet first, ignoring the notices from the city of overdue property taxes and the pleas of their grown sons and daughters to follow them to Jersey and Delaware County.

Michael tries engaging his brother, commenting on the changing neighborhood, criticizing the greed of real estate developers and the surplus of flashy half-million-dollar town houses being built in this suddenly fashionable zip code. A century after prosperous immigrants used their new fortunes to build ornate Georgian grande dames like the building at Eighth and Carpenter, South Philadelphia—or at least its northernmost borders—is on the rise again, buoyed by the exorbitant mortgages of a new generation lured by the promise of ten-year real estate tax abatements and a city residence with a two-car garage.

"Didn't you ever want to live somewhere else, Frankie?" Michael asks. It's intended to be a rhetorical question and an answer isn't expected.

Frankie stops dead in his tracks, seemingly spellbound by the idea.

"Could I really do that, Mikey?" he asks, no less awestruck than if his brother had suggested he pack up his belongings and take up residence on the moon.

The Mass feels endless. The young priest recently assigned by the archdiocese as Jack's assistant pastor is a less-than-dynamic speaker and Frankie's mind is elsewhere during his meandering sermon. His attempts at contrition feel hollow and forced. The truth is he doesn't feel sorry or ashamed. In fact, he doesn't feel anything but bewildered and terrified by the thought of being caught. A little boy two pews ahead is making a fuss, resisting his mother's attempts to restrain him. Poor Cameron is no older than this kid. What's going to happen to him? What chance does he have to grow up, live a decent life? Mariano had once been an innocent child, too, corrupted by the very people entrusted to protect him. It's not Frankie's fault that the boy ended up as an ice block about to be sunk to the floor of a tide pool. The die had been cast long before that fateful Valentine's Day when their paths crossed in a storefront *tacqueria*. It was always meant to be this way. Mariano was never destined to live beyond the first blush of youth. Some people are just born unlucky.

"Frankie, *muchas gracias* for the *cerveza!*"

It had completely slipped Frankie's mind that he'd generously donated three fifty-dollar bills to ensure there were enough kegs on tap to keep the Carpenter Street block party, Saturday, April nineteenth, rain or shine, from running dry. Christmas lights are strung between Eighth and Seventh Streets and speakers blare every possible style of party music, Jay-Z to G. Love to the Dead, from the open windows of the row houses. The karaoke machine is ready and waiting for the first performer to get lubricated enough to take the stage. Burgers and Italian sausages are sputtering on charcoal grills. A posse of young dads, rushing the season in cargo shorts and flip-flops, insist that Frankie and Michael join the neighborhood camaraderie and hoist plastic cups of PBR.

The residents of the 700 block are settling in for a long night. It will be midnight before a few patrol officers come around to amiably enforce the city noise ordinances. Even then a few of the revelers will malinger on their front stoops until two in the morning, the party not officially over until the last keg is dry. Michael and Frankie will be fortunate to be able to load the trunk before the approach of dawn.

The first performer is introduced by the evening's amateur karaoke jockey. Michael cringes at the off-key rendition of "Don't Stop Believing." The song's unfortunate association with Tony Soprano's final moments makes him skittish, reminding him of the rapidly dwindling window of opportunity to dump the body tonight. Doing it in broad daylight is not an option.

An urban pioneer wearing a Boston Red Sox cap offers Michael another cup of beer and makes a pitch for him to join the neighborhood civic association. He doesn't remember seeing Michael around before. Did he buy one of the old row houses, with small rooms the realtors describe as "cozy," or did he splurge on the gabled and spacious new construction? The man and his wife opted for the older housing stock—well, it's all they can afford on their salaries as bench researchers at one of the local medical schools—and now the rumors are flying that the assessment board is considering raising their real estate tax rates. The buyers getting the tax abatements are the ones who least need them. No offense, buddy, he grouses to Michael, assuming he's one of the more prosperous recent arrivals contributing to the steady rise in median household income in the Ninth Street Market neighborhood. He only wishes he and his wife had the scratch to qualify for a six-hundred-thousand-dollar mortgage themselves.

Michael feigns interest in the conversation as he gazes at all the happy faces enjoying cold libations on a beautiful spring night. He doesn't know any of them, though he definitely recognizes all of the types. They could be his neighbors in the Friendly Village of Wayne, mostly young achievers, a few empty nesters, professionals, educated and definitely of a liberal-minded bent. And here they are, living cheek-to-jowl with the likes of Vinnie's widow. Maybe coexisting is a more apt description of the demographics. Michael knows which will be the winning side. The feisty old stalwarts with names ending in vowels will die off or finally be squeezed out by the rising property values, exiled to retirement villages or tiny apartments close to their children's homes.

"How do you know Frankie?" the man asks. "We love him. He's real South Philly. Authentic. A real fucking character."

"He's my brother," Michael says acidly, walking away from his flustered interrogator.

Finally, he sees a familiar face, though it's hardly a welcome sight. Jack Centafore and Frankie are engrossed in deep conversation.

"I didn't expect to see you here tonight," Jack comments as Michael approaches.

"Kit and Danny are in New York, so I'm going to rewire the lighting in the salon tomorrow."

"Let me know if you need any help."

Michael's relieved to hear the priest has only been soliciting a generous donation from Frankie to support the annual Procession of Saints.

"What say you come down and join your brother at the procession this year, Michael? Bring your boy. It will be fun. Pass on some of the old traditions."

"My kid's Episcopalian and wouldn't know Saint Rocco from Luke Skywalker."

"See what I mean? All the more reason to bring him."

"We'll see," he says.

"I saw in the *Inquirer* that the court threw out the death sentence for one of the killers of that poor Carmine Torino. You know the Church is opposed to the death penalty, but I feel for his heartbroken parents. I'm praying they'll find peace someday and accept that everything happens for a reason. That it's all part of God's plan."

Michael refrains from asking the priest to spare him the sanctimonious platitudes. God has nothing to do with it. Men make their own plans. Just like he's taken matters into his own hands, not relying on divine providence to rescue his brother from this fucking mess.

April 20, 2008

This fucking interminable block party is more than a minor inconvenience, forcing Michael to deviate from his blueprint. He waits for the last drunken straggler to lock their front door and until every window facing Carpenter Street is dark, then brings the car around to load the body before sunrise. Frankie never flinches, doesn't hesitate, as they lift Mariano from the freezer chest. They wrap him in one of the shower curtains, securing him with rope, and zip him into the wardrobe bag. Frankie slips, nearly losing his balance as they carry Mariano's body up the basement steps and through the back door to the open trunk. It makes for a snug fit when Michael tosses in the two trash bags of Mariano's clothes, but the lid closes without effort.

Michael sends Frankie to bed, saying they'll sleep a few hours and leave for Virginia by mid-afternoon. He can't leave the car in the alley all day and street parking is out of the question. The forecast is calling for a warm spring day so he drives six blocks to a self-park garage and carefully backs into a dark corner space that the bright light and thawing heat of the midday sun will never reach. He's nervous and edgy walking back to the house. A few hours of sleep, however unsettled, will help to calm him down. He lights a new cigarette from the ash of his last. The streets are deserted, yet he feels he's being watched, curious eyes tracking his every turn. The calls of awakening birds sound like threats in the ominous silence. A car approaches from behind. He tenses as it slows, expecting to be jumped by a posse of desperados searching for a missing boy. He stops and turns to confront them and the car races down the street, running stop signs and red lights, making a speedy getaway.

The phone call wakes him at ten forty-five, two and a half hours after he was able to fall asleep.

"Mr. Gagliano, I think it's really important that you be here. The son contacted an undertaker to collect the remains when your sister passes. He's insisting his mother wanted a viewing and a traditional burial in her husband's plot."

"Stepson," he repeats. "He's only a stepson."

The social worker sounds young and inexperienced, incapable of confronting the overbearing and demanding Shevchek clan.

"Please. You really need to be here. Dr. Patel wants to know when you'll be arriving."

"There's nothing her son can do while she's still alive. I'll be there tomorrow. Sometime tomorrow."

"We'd thought you were arriving yesterday. Now you're saying it will be another day."

She sounds pitiful, lost.

"Look," he says, resenting the need to explain his absence. "My son fell off his skateboard. Complex fracture. He needed surgery. Are you saying you expect me to leave the bedside of my little boy to sit with a woman in a coma?"

"Oh God. I'm so sorry," she gasps. "Is he going to be all right?"

"Yes. Thank you. But I won't be able to leave until tomorrow."

"I understand. Please know I'll keep your son in my prayers."

Jesus Christ. Can he sink any lower? He's superstitious. He wears a Saint Rocco medal—wore a Saint Rocco medal—around his neck, hidden beneath his Brooks Brothers High Wasp attire. He won't allow a cat in his house. Why is he taunting the fates, inviting the evil eye to punish him for telling desperate lies about his innocent little boy?

He won't be able to go back to sleep. He may as well put the next four hours to good use. He begins a list of items they'll need once they return home. Rags. Rubber gloves. Goggles would be wise to protect their eyes from splashing. A case of bleach. No, two cases of bleach. Industrial strength. Mops and buckets. The entire house doesn't need to be scrubbed free of DNA evidence. The body only traveled from the master bath to the basement, then back up the steps and out the back door. The hardwood staircases will be the biggest challenge.

He stares at the scribbled list he's holding in his hand and sees an exhibit in the case against him for accomplice after the fact. He rips it into tiny pieces that he flushes down the closest toilet. His ears prick and his heart sinks, hearing voices below. That fucking priest must be downstairs, come to offer a helping hand with Michael's phony wiring project. Shouldn't he be saying Mass or something? He's gum on your shoes, a bad penny, the guest who refuses to leave.

But it isn't Jack Centafore he finds deep in conversation with his brother in the salon.

"Excuse me," he says politely as he interrupts whatever business they're conducting.

Michael, the experienced prosecutor, instinctually knows they're not police investigators or immigration officials. The stranger standing closest to Frankie introduces himself as Cesar; his friend is called Guillermo. They're well dressed, wearing pointy boots and studded belts and those metal wrist bracelets that are indigenous to the American Southwest. Guillermo, the older of the two, wears an amulet, a coral disk on a leather string around his neck.

They claim to be cousins of Mariano. Mariano's brother Randy has sent them for the little *burro.* Every moment now is precious. Confidentially, they can't just put the boy on a plane back to Mexico. Problems with his papers. They're going to take a long road trip and cross the border in Arizona. Randy is already back home. Their mother, her chest full of cancer, lingers, waiting to say goodbye to her baby, her favorite, before dying. Their story is heartfelt and sounds almost true. At least they don't seem to suspect Frankie has made the connection and knows Mariano's supposed brother Randy Garza also goes by the alias Randy Salazar, whose name and face have been in the papers.

"I told them Mariano hasn't come home for nearly a week. I'm worried something has happened to him," Frankie says, surprising his brother with his smooth delivery of a blatant lie.

Michael offers their guests water, coffee, something to drink, which they graciously decline.

"What else did Frankie tell you?" Michael asks.

He's certain firearms are concealed under the flaps of their sport coats. He wishes his own handgun weren't in a travel bag upstairs. But, touching his pocket, he realizes he's carrying a far more intimidating weapon than any gun. He sees the subtle changes in their faces, the barely detectable hint of tension in their shoulders, when he shows them his badge. They're poised, alert, cats eyeing their prey just before they strike. They've walked into the unexpected. Michael quickly shoves it back in his pocket, denying them the opportunity to discover he's just a lawyer, not a police officer. Everyone is apprehensive, uncertain of what the next few moments will bring.

"Look, guys," Michael says amiably, defusing the room. "Frankie doesn't want Mariano to get into trouble. Me? Well, it's hard for a cop to sit back and do nothing."

The two men are clearly confused.

"But Frankie's my big brother and I don't want to do anything to upset him. I had the credit cards cut off as soon as he discovered his wallet was missing. The kid charged a couple hundred bucks at Macy's. Nothing to get too upset about. And Frankie won't miss the thousand dollars in cash Mariano walked away with. It's something personal he took that's killing me. The watch he stole was worth fifteen thousand bucks. Insurance will cover the replacement cost, but they won't process the claim if Frankie doesn't file a police report. That watch belonged to our father. We miss him every day and it was all we had left of him. I'll be honest with you. I didn't like your friend Randy's brother. But he made Frankie happy and I don't want to have him hauled in and charged with theft. And I wouldn't do it if he hadn't stolen that watch."

The man wearing the amulet speaks with the voice of authority.

"Officer, it is very important to Randy that his brother be able to return as a legal someday. You are aware he cannot have a record. I know that Randy will make you whole. I will bring you the money myself tomorrow."

"No. No," Michael insists, appearing to be a paragon of generosity. "That isn't fair. Randy didn't steal the watch and we can't take his money. We can keep this between ourselves if you give me your solemn promise. All I ask is that you return the watch to us when you find the boy."

"Officer, you are a very kind man," Guillermo says, obviously relieved that a showdown at the O.K. Corral won't be necessary to keep the *norteamericanos* from filing a police report. "You have my word. I swear on the souls of my children."

Good fortune blesses the Gagliano brothers by placing a Goodwill clothing donation box in the parking lot of the travel plaza at the South Wilmington exit off Interstate 95. Michael had chosen a route to avoid any toll lanes, and they'd planned on tossing Mariano's clothes in the dumpster of a Delaware Wal-Mart or Kroger and had hoped that no over-vigilant store manager ever questioned how two bags of used clothes ended up in his trash. Instead they'll be scattered to the winds, impossible to trace. The boy's garish, gender-bending sequined T-shirts and blouses will brighten the summer wardrobes of the wives and daughters of the migrant farmworkers of the lower counties of the state. His boxy black shoes and designer sneakers will be a perfect fit for the size-seven feet of their sons. And some lucky bastard is going to become the proud new owner of Frannie Merlino's first husband's valuable watch.

"Frankie!" he shouts, looking up just in time to see his feckless brother about to swipe his debit card at the gas pump. "Cash only, I told you. No fucking records. What the fuck is wrong with you?"

Frankie looks abashed.

"Sorry, Mikey. I forgot."

"I'm going to go pay inside. Take those two trash bags of his clothes and throw them in the Goodwill box. Make sure no one can see inside the trunk. And try not to look so goddamn guilty about making a donation to charity."

Michael's self-conscious about the sweat on his forehead, but the cashier never looks up from his register as he rings up thirty dollars for gas and two packs of Marlboro Lights. The car already reeks of tobacco. He's going to need to take it to be detailed; Kit has a beagle's nose for any scent of vice.

"You're bleeding, buddy," the bruiser in a leather jacket waiting to pay for a liter of Mountain Dew tells him and, sure enough, there's a bright red blood smear on one of the bills in his hand. He inspects his thumb, uncertain where or when he got the gash at the tip. He doesn't remember cutting himself, didn't feel any pain. How long has he been leaving a DNA trail behind him?

"Look at this shit!" he panics, sticking his bloody thumb in Frankie's face as he crawls behind the wheel of the car. "We are truly fucked."

"Did you get any Band-Aids in there? You don't want that getting infected."

"Jesus, I'm dripping evidence across two states and you're worried I'm going to lose my hand to a staph infection."

"What are you getting so worked up about? I haven't seen you in a state like this since you were a kid. It's *your* blood, Mikey, and I may not be some fancy criminal lawyer but I don't think it's a crime to cut your finger in your own car."

Since when did Frankie become so maddeningly sane?

Michael taps his foot on the brake when the speedometer inches above the posted speed limit. Tractor trailers are doing eighty miles an hour in the passing lane, but he exercises self-control, wary of speed traps and the curious eyes of the state patrol. He rolls his head and cracks his neck. He needs to harness his adrenaline, to extinguish the flash fire blazing through his bloodstream. It's a rush he recalls from his playing days, this sensation of electrical charges igniting his senses, the elation of knowing he's in control, confident in his ability to channel the waves of pure energy pulsing in every cell of his body. He nearly jumps through his skin when his cell phone unexpectedly starts ringing.

"Keep quiet," he warns his brother as he takes a call from home.

"How is she?" Kit asks.

"The same."

She quickly moves on to the real purpose of her call. She's in the ED herself, waiting for Miss P to be discharged. The party ended in disaster when the old ballerina, after tippling four glasses of sherry, broke a bone in her foot attempting to demonstrate the proper way to execute a *jeté battu.*

"Good God, you're in a generous mood!" she exclaims when he doesn't object to her decision to hire—and pay for—twenty-four-hour, seven-day-a-week home care services until the nasty bitch is ambulatory.

"I doubt the lucky caretaker will thank us for our generosity after two hours on the job."

"I'm staying with her myself tonight. Dodie's keeping Danny. I promised you'd call to say good night."

His son is happy to hear Michael's voice. He doesn't remember the woman they call his aunt Polly so his father's sudden rush to leave town is a mystery to him. Before hanging up, he elicits his dad's solemn promise to bring him back a present and asks him to reaffirm his solemn oath they'll be in the audience for the midnight opening of *The Dark Knight* this summer. Michael feels a chill run down his spine. Only a cold-blooded sociopath could tell his son that he loves him and to not give Dodie any grief over bedtime while speeding down the interstate with a frozen body thawing in the trunk. He tries clearing his head by playing "Rosalita" at full volume through the powerful speakers.

"Jesus, Mikey, are you trying to go deaf?" Frankie shouts as he turns down the music. "How many times in your life are you going to listen to that same song?"

"As many times as you're going to listen to fucking 'Rhiannon,' " he answers as he lights another cigarette and blows the smoke out the open window.

A light rain, more a mist than a downpour, greets them at the Virginia border. It looks like the type of precipitation that's sure to linger though dawn. It's just wet enough to jeopardize their chances of finishing this macabre chore before daybreak. Michael had been counting on a starry night with clear visibility to execute the game plan.

"We're close, aren't we?" Frankie asks.

He'd wanted to program the destination on the GPS, but Michael was adamant, insisting there's always the chance the device could be confiscated pursuant to a search warrant. He won't even let Frankie buy a gas station map. He assures his brother his recall of the area is clear and accurate, surprising him with his admission that he'd returned to the Virginia island last summer, with Danny, for the famous wild pony swim across the channel when the annual pilgrimage to the twelve-room Scott family "cottage" in Maine was canceled due to a rescheduled creditor's hearing in bankruptcy court for Kit's largest client.

"I love this smell," Frankie says as they near the causeway, rolling down the window to inhale the pungent breezes, laced with sulfur from the brackish waters of the inlets and coves of the Chincoteague Bay. "Papa really hated it here, remember?" The Virginia coast had brought back unpleasant memories of the malarial swamps of their father's Calabrian childhood.

Between the mainland and the coastline is a vast and monotonous prairie of marsh grasses that will be Mariano's sepulcher. The clouds overhead recede suddenly, like thick velvet stage curtains parting to reveal the opening act of a play. The bright lights of the constellations in the clearing sky illuminate the weathered shacks of the truck farmers and oystermen who live on these tiny barrier islands. Rows of exposed cement burial vaults in the churchyard of a small Pentecostal church bear witness to the folly of interment below sea level. A fire-breathing Jesus, staring from a billboard in the shallow waters at the shoreline, eyes blazing with vengeance, promises sinners the tortures of hell.

"Up there, the last island before the bridge into town, that's where we're going to do it," Michael says, pointing ahead.

"Mikey!"

A white-tailed doe in mid-flight, tense as a coiled spring, leaps into the bright beams of the headlights. Michael loses control of the car, avoiding a head-on collision but clipping the animal as the sedan sails into a tailspin, stalling out on the road. The wounded deer limps away, dragging its broken leg in the sandy soil.

"We can't just leave it like this, Mikey," Frankie pleads as they get out of the car to inspect the damage.

"What do you want me to do? Take it to the vet?" he snaps, flustered and impatient with his brother's sentimentality.

"Can't we put it out of its misery?"

Michael reaches for the canvas bag on the floor behind the front seat to retrieve the revolver. The animal is exhausted by its futile attempt at escape, staggering from the loss of blood and the effort of dragging its weight. It turns its majestic head and Michael sees the suffering and fear in its pleading eyes. He takes aim and kills it with a clean hit to the skull, confident that the sound of gunfire, a single shot, won't draw attention in a rural area where every truck has a rifle rack and the roadside stands all sell discount ammunition.

He and Frankie avoid facing each other. They haven't cried for the dead boy but killing a maimed animal brings them to tears. The damage to the fender is cosmetic, thankfully, and they drive another half mile before Michael swerves onto a dirt road, breathing a sigh of relief that the rain hasn't made it impassable. It's a bumpy ride and the car bounces in the deep ruts cut by the brutal tire treads of pickup trucks and all-terrain vehicles.

"Do you know where we're going?" Frankie asks timidly.

"Danny and I went crabbing down here last summer. We can get to the marsh through this field. We can't just park the car on the causeway."

"Jesus Christ, Mikey. I remember this place," Frankie says, recognizing the ruins of an abandoned drive-in theater. "We saw *Star Wars* here."

The cinder-block screen and rusted speaker poles, awash with milky moonlight, are as imposing and dignified as the broken columns and fractured temple walls of the ancient forum of Rome. The parking lot has been overrun by pine saplings and scrub brush, forcing them to finish their journey on foot. Michael parks behind the concession stand. The corrugated roof collapsed long ago and the boards that once sealed the doorway have rotted away. The eyes of nocturnal creatures foraging inside the walls glow in the headlights.

"The screen was too small. Han Solo's head was in the trees," Frankie recalls.

"You ready to do this, Frankie?" Michael asks, uninterested in reminiscing, as he turns off the engine and kills the headlights.

He looks down at Frankie's feet, then his own, remembering an important detail he'd overlooked, forgotten in the haste to get out of Philadelphia. The only shoes they have are the ones they are wearing, sneakers with distinctive treads that will have to be dumped along some deserted stretch of Maryland State Highway 13, making it impossible to trace Michael and Frankie to any footprints that might be discovered in the muddy marsh banks. He opens the trunk, lifts the wardrobe bag, and grabs the shower curtain he'd used to line the trunk, telling Frankie to follow with the cement blocks and the chain and to stay close behind. Frankie's breathing is labored before they're halfway across the old parking lot and Michael realizes he hasn't taken into account the stress and strain of lugging heavy chunks of concrete on his brother's lipid-soaked cardiovascular system. Michael realizes he should have carried Mariano into the marsh, then come back for the blocks. Please God, don't let him have a heart attack out here in the middle of nowhere, he prays, knowing even he's not smart enough to make up a plausible explanation for his brother dying in a Virginia salt marsh in the middle of the night.

"How you doing back there?" he calls over his shoulder, his voice hearty with false cheer.

"Good," Frankie pants. "How much farther?"

Michael forges ahead, splashing through shallow waters. He can feel the muck underfoot, a sign they're near their destination. Ahead, beyond the green colonies of new spring cordgrass, the receding tide reveals the surface of a wide mudflat glistening under a clear sky of low-lying stars. The dead-of-night stillness is shattered by the rifle-shot crackling of an army of fiddler crabs as they retreat from the surprise invasion of human footsteps.

"Almost there," he promises, his arms aching from his clumsy hold on the body. He wants to drop it, relieve the strain on his lower back, but he plows ahead, wading into pools of briny water. "We'll do it here. X marks the spot," Michael announces as he unzips the wardrobe bag.

They struggle to wrap the long, heavy chain around Mariano, weighing him down at the waist and looping it twice around his neck before securing his wrists to one of the concrete blocks and tying his ankles to the other. Michael drops him in a cluster of swamp grass and they watch him sink as he's slowly swallowed by the soft mud. The entire plain will be flooded come high tide.

"How do we know he'll stay there?" Frankie asks.

"He will. And between the gases and the fish, there won't be much left of him soon."

"Shouldn't we say something?" Frankie asks, reluctant to just walk away.

"Like what?"

"I don't know. A prayer or something?"

"You should have asked your priest buddy to help you if you wanted to have a funeral Mass."

But his brother is right. The occasion calls for a formal ceremony and cathartic ritual, so Michael pulls his dick out of his fly and takes a long, steaming piss on Mariano's watery grave.

"Satisfied?" Michael asks as he shakes the last dribble from the tip of his penis. "Let's get the hell out of here."

April 21, 2008

The moon still shines brightly, but the stars are starting to recede as night fades with the arrival of dawn. The wise decision would be to drive without stopping until they're twenty miles deep into the mainland, but their throats are parched and their limbs ache, their bodies craving sleep. The local convenience store, open twenty-four hours, sells Cokes and day-old Krispy Kremes and a fresh pot of Maxwell House is on the burner. The cashier has been dozing, her head on the counter; she's too groggy to ask why their jeans are soaking wet and filthy and their sneakers caked with mud. She's anxious to bag their purchases and send them on their way so she can grab a few more minutes of sleep. The coffee is weak and flavorless, but Michael drinks it anyway, needing a caffeine jolt for the long drive home. The menacing billboard Jesus is less intimidating in the brightening sky, only a cartoon demon sprung from the childish imagination of an amateur artist. Frankie yawns as they pass the churchyard, staring dreamily out the window. Soon they're several miles deep into the mainland, where grain silos and soybean fields dominate the coastal flatlands and the stench of manure, not salt, infuses the air. No police sirens are shrieking and no flashing domes are visible in the rearview mirror.

"Throw your shoes out the window, Frankie. Now, while there aren't any cars on the road."

"Jesus, is that your feet or mine?" Michael coughs, gagging on the sweaty funk.

Frankie curls up in his seat to sleep, trying not to think about the future he'll awake to. Michael will go home to his wife and his son, leaving him alone in that house. He doesn't want to ever go back there, knowing a sense of dread will crush him every time the doorbell rings, forever fearing Christine or the two messengers carrying concealed weapons or even Randy, released on bail, will return looking for their little *burro.* The story that Mariano simply disappeared one night taking Frankie's wallet and Papa's watch will grow less credible as more time passes without anyone hearing from the boy, not even a phone call or a text. He wishes he could board up the windows and padlock the doors and walk away, never to return. If only Mikey could keep driving, to Los Angeles or Phoenix, someplace far away where Frankie can live in a house where no one has ever died and no restless spirits roam the rooms in the night. He drifts into a shallow sleep, dreaming of a home of his very own, without a history, a brand-new high-rise condo with floor-to-ceiling windows and no steep staircases or dark basements.

"Frankie, are you awake?" Michael whispers to his gently snoring brother, getting no response. Traces of blue and pink are beginning to seep into the first gray light of dawn. In twenty miles the office towers of Wilmington will appear on the horizon, just as the sun is rising on a brand-new day. He retraces every footstep from the moment they tossed the body into the trunk. Human tissue will deliquesce quickly underwater and even the denser skeletal remains will eventually crumble. The wardrobe bag will rot in the marsh and salt water has already washed away any incriminating fingerprints on the indestructible vinyl curtains. Their shoes have been disposed of. The imprint of the tire treads in the soft muddy ground will disappear with the next rainfall and, even if they don't, there isn't the remotest possibility anyone will attempt to trace them to a vehicle registered in Pennsylvania.

One possible but unlikely problem will keep him awake at night. The markings of the bullet lodged in the skull of the dead doe can be matched to the rifling of the barrel of a handgun registered to Michael Rocco Gagliano. He feels a sickness in his bowels as he berates himself for taking pity on Bambi and putting her out of her misery. He realizes he's overreacting. Who would do forensics on an obvious mercy killing of a mortally wounded animal? No one will ever waste the state's precious resources on a fucking dead deer. Unless, of course, some bright and curious investigator has a hunch, connecting a slab of roadkill to an unidentified body discovered in the salt marshes. But it would take a Rube Goldberg contraption of coincidental evidence to link Michael and his brother to a decomposed corpse found in a swamp three states away if it's ever discovered, which it won't be. He's made sure of that. He's startled by his cell phone, knowing a call at this hour of the morning can only be bad news.

"Mr. Gagliano?"

"Yes?"

"I'm sorry to have to inform you that your sister arrested ninety minutes ago."

Arrested? For what? Who would issue a warrant for a comatose woman barely able to breathe?

"Cardiac arrest secondary to end-stage emphysema."

He realizes the extent of his exhaustion and its effect on his ability to think reasonably.

"I assume you won't be requesting an autopsy?"

"Of course not. You can release her to the funeral director. The arrangements for direct cremation have already been made."

"Mr. Gagliano?"

"Yes?"

"There's a problem. The son is insisting on taking custody of the body. He says he'll own the hospital if his mother isn't given a decent viewing and burial."

There's silence on the line as Michael lights a cigarette and inhales a chestful of smoke.

"I'm going to hang up now. Give him this number. Tell him to call me back. Now."

Frankie stirs in his seat as the cell rings again.

"Don't say anything, Carl. Not a single word. I'll do all the talking. The name of the District Attorney of Westmoreland County is

Jim O'Hare. I have his personal number in my contacts. We've been friendly since the Chief Justice asked us to serve on the criminal rules committee. The courthouse opens in three hours. I will provide the District Attorney probable cause for a judge to issue a search warrant for your house and your vehicle. I will agree to personally testify that I saw you sell prescription narcotics to your own daughter. That's a mandatory prison sentence. You won't thrive in prison, Carl. You'll be dead by the end of the year. Now give the phone to the doctor."

"Hello? Mr. Gagliano?"

"You can release the body for cremation as soon as the death certificate is completed. There won't be any more trouble from her stepson."

April 22, 2008

A twenty-four-hour Acme had a large selection of flip-flops and no one had seemed fazed by the sight of two middle-aged men shopping in their stocking feet. They'd rented a room in a Red Roof Inn just across the Pennsylvania border and slept well into Monday evening. They'd showered, ate, and bought the supplies they needed at Wal-Mart and the Home Depot. Michael insisted on postponing the trek across the state to collect Polly's ashes until after they've completed the final chore. They'd waited until after midnight to back the car into the alley when any curious neighbors who might question why they're carrying buckets and mops and cases of bleach into the house are fast asleep. The basement and master bathroom are both windowless rooms and the staircase is in the interior of the house so curious eyes passing on the street won't wonder why lights are blazing brightly in the wee hours of the morning. Michael will start in the cellar, working his way up the steps, while Frankie scrubs his way down from the Jacuzzi.

Michael has the tougher job, dirt floors being porous and notoriously difficult to clean. He wipes down the freezer chest. Next week he'll have it hauled away, along with all the other shit that's accumulated in the cellar over the years, and bring in a contractor to lay a concrete floor. After an hour, his knees are aching and his back is stiff. He'd quickly become impatient with the clumsy and awkward rubber gloves and his hands are raw and chafed. The powerful chemicals have ruined the finish on the wooden steps, but Frankie's unconcerned about the damage. He's wanted to have them stripped and stained anyway. There are only a few hours until daylight as Michael and Frankie drive to the wetlands out near the airport. There's no traffic on the access road to the cargo terminal at this hour and there are no drivers to witness them quickly dispose of cleaning buckets and mops, rags and gloves, empty bleach bottles and used sponges, in the tidal pool.

"Are you hungry?" Michael asks as they pass the all-night diner on Passyunk Avenue.

"I just want to get a few hours sleep," Frankie says. "I'll meet Connie when she comes in this morning. We'll reschedule the appointments for later this week."

There's a parking space a block from the salon, a minor miracle.

"I need this shit today like I need a hole in the head," he grumbles when he sees the number of the incoming call as he locks the shop door behind him.

Steven Kettleman's priorities always take precedence over a minor inconvenience like an emergency in his Chief Deputy's family.

"You sound wide-awake for six thirty in the morning," the District Attorney comments.

"Not really."

"By the way, how is your sister?"

"She died last night. Peacefully."

"My condolences. Are you still in the wilderness across the Alleghenies?"

Michael says he has a few estate details to handle (emptying the trash, changing the locks on the doors to Polly's house) before returning home.

"Sorry to inconvenience you, but I need you to take care of something. You can do it from out there in God's country by phone conference. I'll have the office organize it. Can you get to a landline? These fucking cell phones are too fucking unreliable."

"I'm sure I can find one."

"Call in at two. The fucking press is looking for a comment for the evening news and I'm meeting the governor when he arrives from Harrisburg. I'm writing the introduction he's making at the victory celebration tonight. It's gonna be a landslide for our girl, Michael. Hillary's gonna crush that arrogant asshole. Besides, I think it's more appropriate for you to be the one to comment on Tommy Fucking Corcoran. The Grossmans are pressing me to raise your profile."

Michael's heart leaps into his throat. There can be only one reason the media is seeking a reaction from the Office of the District Attorney. Tommy Corcoran must be dead. Michael hopes it was deservedly gruesome and painful. A garroting or stabbing or his skull bashed in by an inmate swinging a dumbbell in the weight room. Maybe there is justice in the world.

"Just stay on message, Michael. Don't let your emotions run away with you. The vultures reached out to the little fucker through his sister. It's more money than that family of low-rent scum could ever expect to see in a lifetime. Do they really expect we're going to let them keep it?"

Tommy Corcoran has entered into an agreement to sell the rights to his life story to a production company with an exclusive deal with HBO. *Access Hollywood* is reporting a young teenage star from the Disney Channel is attached to the project. They'll cast an actor with shady, suspicious looks to play Michael, one who's been typecast as a ruthless climber who would never let the truth stand in the way of his ambition. Someday his son will flip the channels and stumble upon this fairy tale and wonder if the father he thought he had known, his hero, had been this villain, hell-bent on leading an innocent lamb to slaughter.

"Every goddamn penny of that blood money is going into the pockets of Carmine Torino's parents, Michael. Get that message out loud and clear. Every last penny."

Michael has an even better story to feed the public's voracious appetite for sensational tales of blood and death, if only he could sell it. It would be worth millions, set his family up for life. Hollywood would be after it like sharks in a tank. Fuck HBO. The material is too good to waste on anything less than a feature film with an A-list star. Too bad Pacino's an old man now. It's a role that would be as iconic as Michael Corleone and Serpico. Oscar bait. Michael Rocco Gagliano, an ambitious prosecutor sworn in as District Attorney after covering up a fatal felony by dumping a dead body in a tidal marsh. Imagine the fadeout before the final credits: the leading man, an accessory to a violent, bloody crime, hand on the Bible, swearing an oath to see that justice is served and that those who have broken society's laws are justly punished.

It's a true story of loyalty and obligation, the movie based upon actual events. Only the ending would be pure fiction. Michael may be many things, but a hypocrite is not one of them. His integrity is intact, despite the blood on his hands. He will never again put a man behind bars, branding him as a criminal for life, then retreat to his comfy, cozy life at the Nook knowing he is guilty of the same or worse. The press conference will be his final official act before resigning as Kettleman's deputy and successor.

The press will have to settle for audio only. All three of the local Philly newscasts offer to send camera crews from their network Pittsburgh affiliates. Michael declines, requesting respect for the privacy of his family at this difficult time. Frankie's number on his private line is blocked, so there's no caller ID to reveal the Chief Deputy is sitting in his brother's kitchen less than a mile away. The phone conference is mercifully brief. They only need a sound bite to balance the pathos of the teary-eyed sister and the producer's solemn announcement that Tommy Corcoran is an American tragedy, a cautionary tale of a young man society had thrown away. Michael is surprised by his own complacency over this unexpected turn of events. After all, Corcoran will still rot in jail, Carmine's parents will be able to buy a vacation condo in Ocean City, and the teen idol will get his chance to show his chops as a serious actor, praised by the critics for his sympathetic portrayal of a misunderstood victim of the criminal justice system.

The house at Eighth and Carpenter feels claustrophobic, airless. He needs to get out, escape this self-imposed prison, stretch his legs in preparation for the long drive. He's just going to go around the block. He'll be back before Frankie's finished showering and dressing for the long trip. It's a perfect spring day, unseasonably warm. Two kids race by on bicycles, brushing his elbows. One of them turns his head, not apologizing, shouting Obama's name. A white retiree in plaid Bermuda shorts is sitting on a lawn chair on the sidewalk, sunning his bare, hairless legs. He curses the little bastards, asking the saints to knock them off their bikes and break their necks.

"What's going on?" Michael asks.

"They want to see the guy they think's gonna be *their* president," he sneers, assuming Michael shares his low opinion of the candidate from Illinois. "I just heard on KYW he's down the street. That Obama. Signing autographs at Pat's. They're coming out like flies to shake his fucking hand."

Of course. The obligatory photo op for every politician trolling for votes in the City of Brotherly Love, captured for posterity chewing on a torpedo roll stuffed with thin slices of fried beef and waxy processed cheese food.

"He'll probably start crying when he finds out they don't serve watermelon," the old man cackles, a nasty twinkle in his eye.

More kids flash by on their bicycles, hooting and hollering, excited by their proximity to History. A young canvasser from Organizing for America is running along the sidewalk. Rail thin, with Buddy Holly glasses and a battered thrift-shop Harris Tweed cap, this dedicated hipster, forever detached and jaded, has abandoned any pretense to cool.

"Damn, man. Better step on it if you want to see O."

All roads lead to Pat's. The crowd grows denser, more excited, as Michael approaches the King of Steaks. People are bouncing on the balls of their feet, trying to see over the shoulders of the gawkers in front of them. Television and newspaper beat reporters are recording the occasion for the evening newscasts and the morning headlines. Michael is careful to stay out of camera range. Any blowhards in the crowd are too intimidated by the menacing Secret Service and uniformed police guard to heckle the candidate with epithets. Michael pushes through a thicket of high school boys waving their phones to capture a blurry shot of the back of the candidate's nappy-haired head for posterity.

Obama's got a good two-fisted grip on his cheesesteak as he listens intently to his dinner companions, a father and daughter too startled to refuse his request to join them. His missus is nibbling french fries, a casual and approachable woman who isn't intimidated by the local gastronomy.

"That's one big girl," a geezer in an IBEW Local 98 baseball cap and a filthy Flyers jersey, Broad Street Bullies vintage, remarks as he admires the strong, imposing physique of the senator's wife. "I bet she could kick his ass."

"Hey, Obama! Hey, motherfucker!" the bicycle truants shout, trying to get his attention by popping wheelies at the fringe of the crowd. They speed away, screaming obscenities, as Philly's Finest come charging after them.

The Obamas seem to have healthy appetites, both of them. They don't seem to mind being stared at like animals at the zoo; after all, they didn't come wandering to Ninth and Passyunk in search of privacy and fine cuisine. The senator leans across the table and flashes his signature smile, all dazzling white enamel, and asks his new friends if he has cheesesteak in his teeth. The candidate and his wife are hustled back to their caravan, exasperating their handlers when they stop to shake every hand and sign every autograph. The door of their SUV closes behind them, leaving the hoi polloi staring at their table. A woman grabs a french fry bag left behind, a few sticky potatoes at the bottom left uneaten, and stashes it in her purse.

"This is gonna be worth a fortune someday," she announces to her friend, triumphantly clutching her newfound treasure under her arm.

A pair of vans circles the traffic island, bullhorns exhorting the electorate with a pre-recorded message.

TODAY IS ELECTION DAY. VOTE FOR JOHN DOUGHERTY FOR STATE SENATE.

In a few hours the polls will close, the votes counted, the winner of the primary announced. Michael's been existing on the periphery of time over the past week, consumed by his brother's dilemma, only vaguely aware of the noise of the campaign in the background. This must be how an astronaut feels when he returns from the uncharted regions of space and discovers the world has gone about its business in his absence, barely missing him, leaving him feeling even more inconsequential than when he was navigating the immeasurable distance between the stars.

He's dawdled too long. Jack Centafore is standing a block away. Michael is too tired for a lengthy explanation why he's strolling the streets of the old neighborhood on a weekday afternoon. He turns and walks back to the house quickly, escaping while the priest is still too distracted by the Obamas' surprise pit stop to recognize his best friend's younger brother on the fringes of the crowd. He reaches for his phone and calls Kit with the sad, but expected, news that Polly has died. He'll be home on Thursday. He misses and loves her. He has something important to tell her, but it can wait until he speaks to Steven Kettleman.

Frankie brought a light jacket, anticipating the cooler weather in the higher altitudes of the western side of the state. They bought toothbrushes and toothpaste and mouthwash at the travel plaza. Michael tried to reason with Frankie, arguing it was a waste of money to pay the outrageous price being charged for a small can of spray deodorant. They'll sleep a few hours when they arrive in Latrobe, collect Polly's ashes from the funeral director, change the locks of her house, and drive home.

They're approaching the Hershey exit of the turnpike and the reception from the Philadelphia all-news station is fading to static as the announcer reads the shocking headline at the top of the hour. *The body found beneath the interstate overpass has been identified as Christine Palmer, a native of Ridley in Delaware County, who authorities had been seeking to question in the Washington Avenue methamphetamine investigation.* Frankie leans toward the dashboard, attempting to make sense of the string of barely audible broken phrases and isolated words of the rapidly vanishing broadcast.

"What about Cameron? Is he all right?" he asks, sounding as if he expects the radio speaker to answer.

"Is that the little boy? Is that his name? When this pack is finished, I'm done," Michael promises as he fires up another cigarette. "I don't know how the fuck I'm going to get the smell out of this car."

"Jesus Christ, how fast do you think that bastard's going?" Frankie asks, gripping the dashboard as the car sways in the backdraft of a tractor trailer doing at least thirty miles over the construction-zone speed limit.

"Too fast," Michael bitches as he swerves to avoid sideswiping a barrier of orange warning cones. At least it's a clear night, no misty rain. Maybe they'll be lucky and the mountain peaks won't be cloaked in fog.

"What do you think they did to Cameron? You know, those men who came looking for Mariano."

"He's fine. I swear. They're not interested in hurting a little boy. Not even an animal would execute a little kid. He's better off this way. Probably got taken in by his grandparents. Maybe Child Protective Services has him. Anything is better for him than the life he had before."

"I should try to find him."

Frankie's stunned by his brother's quick reflexes as Michael grabs his wrist and squeezes tightly, refusing to release him until he elicits a solemn promise.

"Don't even think about it. Don't even try. Do you hear me? Do you? I put it all on the line for you. Don't be stupid and do anything that might lead anyone back to that fucking freezer in the basement. You want to worry about a kid? Worry about your nephew. Worry that he doesn't end up with a father who's locked up in a fucking prison."

"Sorry. Sorry. Sorry. I wasn't thinking. I never meant for you to get mixed up in this, Mikey. I never wanted you to find out what I did until after I was gone," Frankie says sadly.

"You motherfucker! I knew it! I knew it! I was right!" Michael howls, pummeling his brother's shoulder with the fist of one hand, the car threatening to run off the shoulder of the road. "You lied to me, Boo! You looked me in the eye and lied to me! I knew you were going to do it! I just knew it!"

"But I didn't."

"Tell me you will never do that to me. Tell me. I want to hear you say it!"

He hates turning mawkish and, after the promise is made, the subject is dropped and will never be raised again. A loud dose of the Boss comes in handy at awkward moments and the familiar lyrics of "Glory Days" inspire him to make a confession.

"You want to know the truth, Frankie? I never wanted to play football. I only did it to piss Papa off. I wanted to be a musician. I used to fantasize about playing in Bruce's band."

"But you have a tin ear."

"I know," he laughs. "But sometimes I regret that I never even tried. What do you regret most in your life? What do you wish you'd done differently?"

"At this point? Nothing. Nothing at all."

"There's nothing you would have done differently."

"At one time, I thought there was. Do you remember Patrick Ryan?"

"No. I don't think so."

"I was only seventeen. He asked me to run away to San Francisco with him. I thought it was because he loved me as much as I loved him. But he only wanted me to come because he was afraid to go alone. He would have dumped me within a month. Papa would never have allowed me to come home and I would have ended up living on the street. Charlie and I went there years later. I thought it was the most beautiful place on earth. The steep hills and the sound of the trolley bells. I imagined myself living in a house with a hanging garden and a balcony overlooking the bay. I could sit up there at the top of the world, with the perfect view of the Golden Gate Bridge, drinking my coffee and reading a book. But it was only a fantasy. Do you know where I'd be if I'd run away with Patrick? *Morto.* Patrick died in 1983. They cremated him even though his mother was a strict Catholic because they didn't want her to see his body, wasted to the bones, covered with purple lesions."

Michael's never heard this tale before. He'd never thought of his brother wanting any life beyond the corner of Eighth and Carpenter, never knew he'd shared his own wild dreams and hopes of someday escaping that house.

"Why didn't you go with him? Why did you stay?"

Frankie looks at him as if the answer is too obvious to state.

"You, Mikey. I would never have left you with Papa. I made a promise. I would never have left you alone."

Afterward

Ciascuno sa come si chiude la porta di casa sua.

October 31, 2008

The sun has cracked open the sky and the morning is awash with bright, brilliant light. The day's as vivid and friendly as a kid's pop-up book; even the brick and stone surfaces of the houses seem alive. The forecast is calling for a beautiful October afternoon, highs in the seventies, low humidity, absolutely no chance of rain, perfect weather for a parade of champions. It's Halloween and the entire city will be in costume when the team steps off on Broad Street at the stroke of noon. The Phillies Nation, two million strong, men and women, parents and kids, rabid fans and bandwagon climbers who haven't been to a ball game in decades, will be wearing red pinstripes today. The Gagliano men will be sporting their new MLB-authorized player jerseys, Utley for the son, Lidge for his father.

"Don't let go of Daddy's hand. You have to promise me," Kit begs. "Don't take your eyes off him," she warns her husband.

"Do you have to pee, Danny?" Michael asks. "It's going to be a long ride."

Kit insists he make a last trip to the bathroom and sends her son running up the staircase.

"Make yourself useful, Michael. Put these out front while you're waiting," she insists, handing him two Obama lawn signs, as if the four already posted at the edge of their property weren't sufficient declaration of the political affiliation of the owners. What the hell is everyone going to talk about come next Wednesday? Only a few weeks ago the campaign seemed endless, eternal, and now suddenly, it's reeling to a swift, breathless conclusion. The real estate agent keeps begging her to remove the placards, not wanting to alienate potential buyers, but Kit is adamant, saying it would break her heart if Sleepy Peter's Quiet Nook, the house where they raised their son, the only home he's ever known, fell into the hands of partisan Republicans.

Michael's far less sentimental than his wife. He'd sell to Dick Cheney if he made the best offer. The house is a money pit, its maintenance a Sisyphean task. Patch a leak and two more appear. Plaster the ceiling in one room and a crack appears in another. But he's grown used to living in a world that's landscaped rather than paved. He loves this financial black hole, the fulfillment of his boyhood dream of one day living in a house he could walk around. And he'll miss his leisurely weekend afternoons running errands to the Norman Rockwell hardware store and shoe repair shop and spending Sundays in autumn drinking pints of craft beer at the local taproom, moaning about the number of turnovers by the hapless Eagles with his fellow husbands and fathers of the Friendly Village of Wayne. It's hard to leave, but he's always known he was a tourist here, that his stay was temporary and someday he would need to return home. The move is his punishment for an undiscovered crime and his unpardoned sin, and he will serve his sentence under his father's roof, without hope of parole.

"Ready, champ?" Michael asks as he and his son step outside into this beautiful morning.

"Why are we taking the train, Dad? Why can't we drive?"

"They're expecting millions of people today, Danny. We don't want to spend the entire parade sitting in traffic, do we?"

His cell phone vibrates in his pocket. It's his brother, calling to reconnoiter.

"We're walking to the station," he answers, dispensing with the formality of saying hello.

"I heard on the radio they're adding extra trains to handle the overflow."

"We'll get there. Don't worry."

"Well, hurry up. I'm so excited I can't stand still."

He'd bought Frankie a Cole Hamels jersey to wear to the parade today. His brother couldn't tell a change-up from a sinker, but he knows a great head of hair when he sees one.

Maybe news radio is onto something. Maybe he shouldn't be so blasé about getting into town. Half the population of Wayne is marching along the sidewalks, making their way to the station. The platform is already packed with folks waiting for the arrival of the eastbound Paoli local. More than a few of them look like they're sipping something stronger than French roast from their thermoses.

"Come on, here it comes!" Danny shouts, dragging his father through the crowd. The little commuter train is approaching, chugging along the rails, nearly out of breath as it wheezes toward the station, just as it had that morning a lifetime ago when a frantic woman chased a dog across the tracks. The cars are standing room only, but no one complains about spending the next thirty minutes with a complete stranger breathing down his collar. The train begins gathering speed then lurches to a halt, more bodies wedged into the narrow aisle at each stop, until it plunges underground after exiting the commuter platform at Thirtieth Street Station. The grinding wheels and screaming air brakes echo off the walls of the tunnel, delivering them to their destination below the heart of the city.

Danny squeezes his father's hand as they shuffle up the staircase to the concourse, following the flow as it meanders past the donut shops and coffee kiosks, the newsstands and salad bars. The station is decorated for a party, draped with red and white streamers and World Championship pennants. The already iconic hallelujah photo of the closer on his knees after the final pitch, his arms thrust toward the sky, is in every window. The improbable, the unlikely, the impossible, the incredible, the amazing, the astonishing, has been achieved.

Phinally! the headlines scream.

The crowd grows denser as they push toward the subway entrance. He squeezes Danny's wrist until his knuckles are white, determined not to lose him. Danny doesn't resist or complain, meaning he's intimidated by the crush of bodies surrounding them, friendly and unthreatening as they seem. No one is shoving or trying to muscle their way ahead. But all it would take is one piercing scream to ignite panic in the station and start a stampede toward the exits. The momentum sweeps them forward, past the turnstiles, and into a subway car.

"Stay close to me, buddy," he warns his frightened son.

Danny shakes his head, clearly rattled by the ripple effect of the jostling of a group of rowdy boys trying to squeeze through the closing doors. A pair of transit cops push the kids back onto the platform and the subway car leaves the station and barrels down the tracks. This crowd's a rough sort; these kids weren't fortunate enough to be born into families with budgets for orthodontia and SAT prep courses. The boys have crooked teeth and buzz cuts; the girls wear too much makeup and have long lacquered fingernails painted with elaborate designs.

"You have the most beautiful eyelashes," a pretty young teenager, weathered beyond her tender years, tells Danny, making him blush. He buries his face in his father's back, giggling.

"He's shy," Michael says.

"You tell him to call me in a couple of years. He's gonna be a heartbreaker," she says as she tries to retrieve an insistent phone from the pocket of her jeans.

The train rolls into the Snyder station and they fight through the crowd on the platform trying to board the car. Michael wraps his arm over Danny's shoulders and leads him toward the exit where, suddenly, the sea of bodies parts and they climb the stairs and step out into the glorious sunshine of the perfect morning. The police are cordoning off Broad Street though the parade won't start for hours. Gray-haired mom-moms and pop-pops have parked their ample butts in lawn chairs on the sidewalk. They'd laid claim to front-row seats before daylight and pass the time gossiping and drinking coffee and sodas. Hawkers are doing a brisk business in soft pretzels and cheap commemorative T-shirts, ten-buck knock-offs of officially sanctioned gear, guaranteed to shrink three sizes in the first wash. Kids are blowing on those cheap plastic parade horns. One of them jumps in front of Danny, demanding a high-five.

"We better step it up, Danny. Your uncle is calling again," Michael says, reaching for his phone.

"Where are you, Mikey? I got us a booth," Frankie says.

"We'll be there in a few minutes."

"We already ordered. What do you and Danny want for breakfast?"

"Relax. We've got plenty of time."

"This place is packed."

"We're right outside the door," Michael says as he stops to greet a couple of cops smoking cigarettes on the diner's wheelchair ramp.

"Paulie, this is my boy, Danny. Danny, this is Officer Ottaviano. Officer Ottaviano and your uncle went to high school together. His big brother, Bobby, is a fireman."

"Used to be a fireman. The lucky SOB's retired and lives down the shore."

The kid's eyes are wide as saucers. The cuffs and billy club are awesome. He's clearly impressed that his old man's on a first-name basis with a flesh-and-blood policeman in full riot-gear paraphernalia.

"So you're an Utley fan, Danny?"

"Yes, sir."

"Chase is my main man, too," Officer Ottaviano says as he blows a thick stream of smoke through his nostrils.

"Looking forward to today, Paulie?" Michael asks.

"Looking forward to all the overtime we're getting this week. Man, if Obama wins, they'll be dancing in the streets and I'm gonna really clean up."

"See you, Paulie. Be safe. Give my best to your brother," Michael says, hustling Danny inside before he asks who *they* are and why they'll be dancing in the streets.

"Dad, can I ask you a question?"

Too late.

"Why was that policeman smoking?"

Danny, who's been raised in a world where adults go to extreme lengths to conceal their abominable tobacco habits from impressionable children, was probably more awestruck by the sight of

Paul Ottaviano casually sucking on a Newport than by the service revolver in the holster on his hip. Michael knows it's his responsibility to launch into a lecture of the dangers of smoking. That's what a good upper-middle-class parent from the leafy Main Line suburbs is expected to do. But he passes on the opportunity to reinforce a life lesson this morning. There are worse crimes than taking a drag on an occasional cigarette. Goddamn, the man who may be President has been known to fire up a menthol now and then. Michael likes the fact that the guy is fucking human.

"I guess he likes to smoke, Danny," he says, unable to work up the enthusiasm for a sermon about the life-threatening evils of tobacco.

"But it's bad for you! That's what you and Mama always say," he spouts, challenging his father with the American Lung Association party line.

"Well, Officer Ottaviano has a really hard job," he tries to explain.

"Don't you have a really hard job?"

"Sometimes," he laughs, scuffing him on the head. "Hey, buddy, there's Uncle Frankie," he says, pointing at a booth in the back of the diner.

It's funny, seeing his brother in his Hamels jersey, his hair pushed back under a baseball cap, one more middle-aged guy dressed in age-inappropriate attire, stoking up on caffeine and carbohydrates for the big day ahead. Michael bends down and touches his face, needing physical confirmation of the stubble on his chin.

"I don't believe it. Francis Rocco Gagliano didn't shave this morning. You remember Father Jack, don't you, Danny?"

"I think so. Where's your jersey?"

"I don't have one," the priest says, smiling.

"How come?"

"Don't know. Didn't buy one."

"Don't you like the Phillies?"

"I love the Phillies."

"Don't you have any money?"

"Apologize to Father Jack," Michael says, though truth be told, it's hard to be indignant over his son mocking the priest. "Enough questions, Danny. What do you want for breakfast?"

"Pancakes."

Michael orders two short stacks of blueberry pancakes and a side of bacon to share. The grown-ups pass the meal with idle chatter, their conversation interrupted by parishioners approaching the booth to pay their respects to the padre. *How's your breakfast, Father? How 'bout them Phillies, Father? I bet you wuz prayin' for a victory! See you Sunday, Father.* Jack has a pleasant word for everyone, calling them each by name. *Beautiful morning, isn't it? Couldn't ask for a more perfect day. You get enough to eat? See you at the parade.*

Michael almost feels sorry for the pathetic priest. It's going to be hard on him once Frankie's gone, leaving him all alone. *You two are just like J. Edgar Hoover and Clyde Tolson*, he'd once teased his brother. Frankie had made it clear he didn't find the joke funny, obviously uncomfortable with the idea of a carnal relationship with a man of the cloth. Michael watches his brother making stumbling attempts to speak Spanish with the pretty young busboy, expecting it's only a matter of time before he becomes infatuated with another demanding and deceitful gold digger looking for a human ATM machine.

Today Frankie isn't worrying about calories and cholesterol. He mops up a pool of syrup with the last bite of French toast and scarfs down a greasy slab of scrapple. His brother and Jack tease him about this uncharacteristic lack of self-discipline and gargantuan appetite.

"I'll take an extra Lipitor tonight," he says.

Damn, he thinks, that's another thing he's going to have to take care of, something else to put on his list. He'll need a cardiologist in Fort Lauderdale to refill his Niaspan and statins after his prescriptions expire. No wonder people stay put in one place rather than deal with the aggravation of uprooting their lives and making a new start in another part of the country. A few short months ago he would never have considered leaving this neighborhood and settling thousands of miles from his brother. Sometimes he wakes in the middle of the night, certain he's making a terrible mistake.

Still, with each step he takes, he grows more confident. Every day that passes he's more eager to begin the next chapter of his life in the Silver Daddy capital of the eastern United States. He's already gotten his Florida license to practice cosmetology in the Sunshine State, and the manager of the Neiman Marcus in the Galleria was so impressed by his experience and poise (and, yes, his looks) he offered him a stylist position during his interview. His bid on a two-bedroom condo in Wilton Manors was accepted before he flew back to Philly, and he's ordered a leather sofa and a dining table to be delivered after the closing. He's eaten his first conch and met a handsome Cuban, a dead ringer for the young Desi Arnaz, Jr., who claims to like older men. He's learned his lesson after Mariano and had only agreed to a first date after calling the law firm where the young man claimed to work to confirm his employment as a paralegal.

It's going to be hard leaving Mikey, seeing him at most once or twice a year, but they agree it's for the best. Michael won't admit it, but Frankie knows his brother suspects it's only a matter of time before his guileless older sibling slips up and makes some careless remark, raising suspicions about the fate of the pretty young boy who'd vanished without warning one day, never to return. Jack, though, is still arguing that there is plenty of time for Frankie to change his mind, that he can flip the Florida condo or even keep it as a second home, somewhere to escape in the dead of winter. But the die has been cast. The lead feature of the current edition of the *South Philly Review* is a long piece about the closing of Gagliano Cuts and Color, Family Owned Since 1928. Connie and a few of his special clients will raise a glass in a champagne toast at the close of business tomorrow before locking the door of the shop at Eighth and Carpenter the very last time.

The contractor arrives Monday morning to begin gutting the salon, stripping the walls to the studs and ripping up the floor. Frankie will be gone by Thanksgiving, maybe sooner, depending on how quickly he can put his affairs in order. It's funny how easy it is to wind up an entire lifetime in just a few weeks, so little to keep him here. His accountant and lawyer can tend to all the details; his financial adviser assures him he has plenty to live on for the rest of his life, even before clearing another half million after selling the building. He's half tempted to simply shutter the shop after the farewell toast and drive to Florida Sunday morning. He could take up residence in the Hilton until he closes on the condo, a safe and comfortable distance from the regrets that plague him and the memories that haunt him, leaving behind a cold trail that curious strangers won't be able to follow. God may forgive him one day for what he has done, but somewhere in this world someone is missing Mariano, searching high and low for clues to answer their questions.

The young Mexican girl was in again yesterday, as always without an appointment. She'd unnerved him the first time she'd entered the shop, on a quiet afternoon in May, shy and hesitant, asking Frankie in heavily accented English if he would cut her hair. She was polite and quiet as she sat in the chair, making no suggestions, trusting his skill, her eyes carefully following his moves in the mirror. The resemblance was subtle but undeniable. She and Mariano shared the same dark brown eyes, almond-shaped, the color of cocoa, the same sharply angled cheekbones, the identical plush and sensual lips. Michael tried to reassure him, saying he had an overactive imagination and watched too much tabloid television, when Frankie confided his suspicions that the girl is Mariano's flesh and blood, a sister or cousin, determined to solve the mystery of the disappearance of the family's little *burro.* Once Frankie saw her sitting with a man who resembled Randy as he walked by the window of one of the seedy *cerveza* joints below Washington Avenue. He's tried talking to her as he cuts her hair, asking questions about her family back home and here in the city, but she simply smiles and shrugs her shoulders sheepishly, gesturing that her English is too poor to carry on a conversation. It's chilling, the way her eyes scrutinize the reflection of his face in the mirror, peering into the dark corners of his conscience, trying to expose the guilty secret he will carry to the grave.

"Having a good time, buddy?" Michael asks.

Danny's shoveling pancake into his mouth, eating like a racehorse with no one lecturing him to chew with his mouth shut and to keep his elbows off the table.

"Yes," he says, blueberry chunks wedged in the spaces between his teeth.

Frankie and Jack are regaling him with tales of the 1980 parade, a day when dogs ran wild in the street, kids swung from the low-hanging branches of the trees, confetti and streamers poured from the highest windows of the tallest buildings, fireworks exploded in broad daylight, cannons roared, and Superman and Spider-Man both streaked across the sky.

"It wasn't really like that, Danny," Michael protests, throwing a bucket of water on their nostalgia-flamed memories, not wanting him to be disappointed in the parade when chariots of fire and superheroes don't descend from the heavens.

The diner is starting to empty as folks finish their eggs and coffee and leave to stake out a good spot to watch the parade.

"Do you have to go to the bathroom before we go, Danny?"

He shakes his head no, insisting he's fine. If worse comes to worst, Michael will take him behind a building and let him piss on a wall. Hell, he'll probably love that. Michael had taught him how to pee like a big boy by standing him on the back porch and telling him to the aim for the boxwood shrubs.

The city's growing livelier as they head back to the parade route. More and more people have made their way out to the streets. There's still time to kill before the festivities begin, but Frankie and Jack have no interest in wandering the neighborhood. They're going to plant themselves right here, thank you, and wait for the motorcade to come to them. Of course, it doesn't hurt that Louise Pelusi has reserved a pair of folding chairs outside her formal-wear rental shop and is promising to crack open a bottle of Cold Duck to toast the Phillies as they pass by her storefront.

"We're going to take a little walk," Michael announces. "Danny wants to check out the neighborhood, right, buddy?"

"You better be back by the time of the parade!" Frankie warns.

Michael knows South Philly must be intimidating to a kid raised in one of the priciest zip codes in the county. The auto body shops and nail salons. The holes-in-a-wall selling cigarettes and lottery tickets. The storefront counters where you order cheesesteaks and pizza by the slice. There's a funeral home on every corner and at least two Chinese take-outs on each block. Mexican boys whiz by on their rusty used bikes, nearly clipping pedestrians on the sidewalks, racing the clock so they won't be docked for being late at their kitchen jobs. Grizzled survivors of addiction wars malinger on the street corners, drinking coffee from paper cups and filling the hours of the day with idle gossip and strong opinions. Teenage mothers push strollers down the block, threatening their babies with physical violence if they don't stop wailing. The streets smell like fryer grease and exhaust fumes. But by spring, summer at the latest, Danny will have adjusted to his new surroundings and urban life will be second nature to him. Times have changed since Frankie and Michael ran wild on these streets, unsupervised, in those bygone days when parents never worried about abductions or seductions or assaults. Still, Michael will insist his boy be given some independence. It's ridiculous to assume that stalkers and predators are lurking around every corner of the neighborhood, despite Kit's fears.

It's been a rough year on his wife, but they seem to have weathered the first real strain in their relationship after ten years of marriage. Kit had been taken aback by his abrupt resignation from Kettleman's office just as he was about to assume the position he'd coveted for years. She was furious he would make such a radical decision without first telling, let alone consulting, her. He'd said he'd lost the fire in his belly to put men behind bars and he's no politician. Glad-handing and insincerity are anathema to him. She'd asked him to consider applying his talent to civil litigation, defending pharmaceutical companies and enforcing restrictive covenants. But criminal law is his lifeblood. Walter Rudenstein, the Dark Knight of the Defense Bar, hadn't hesitated before offering Michael a partnership. In fact, he said he was greatly relieved that his protégé had been pursuing him for a job. He'd foolishly thought Michael had been trying to reach him because he was in trouble. Why would the winner of the Father Theodore Sullivan Award, All-Ivy, Order of the Coif, the straightest of arrows, ever need the services of a defense lawyer?

But it was Michael's insistence they sell the Nook and move to his boyhood home that had completely unsettled her. He'd argued he owed it to his brother. Papa had bequeathed the house to his three children. Frankie and Michael had paid cash to their half sister for her share of the appraised value when the property was transferred at the settlement of their father's estate. He had always insisted Frankie would get the full proceeds when the building was sold, in recognition of his significant investment in renovating the interiors and in recompense for his gentle caring for their demented parent. But housing prices had taken a sudden steep drop as a result of the latest financial crisis and Frankie was selling when the market was soft, at least for a century-old, mixed-use property at the fringes of gentrification. Michael was adamant his brother maximize his profit, which he insisted could only be accomplished if Kit and he purchased the property.

She said he wasn't thinking rationally. He was acting impulsively. No one, least of all his brother, expected him to uproot his family. Why couldn't he admit it made no sense? It was unfair to her and their son. Why couldn't they just buy the house and put it on the market? They could afford to take the loss, if necessary. There was no reason they needed to actually live there. She was worried about him. The past few months she'd felt as if she had been living with a stranger. She wanted to help, if only he would let her. She'd never seen the full force of his volcanic temper until she suggested he agree to "see someone."

He wanted to confide in her that he no longer dreams of chasing trains, but of crouching in the cold, dark basement as an angry Papa descends the staircase swinging the barber's strop, following a glowing blue trail of Luminol, searching for Frankie, who Michael has hidden in the freezer. Michael could never feel safe with strangers living in the house at Eighth and Carpenter. Some traces of organic evidence will always remain. Skin and hair, sources of blood cells and genetic samples, can stubbornly resist a chemical reaction with bleach. But confessing to his wife would compromise her integrity and jeopardize her own freedom by making her a party to his crimes. Better to let her believe he's crazy.

Improbably, it was her mother who persuaded Kit the Nook was only a stone-and-mortar building, albeit one with perfectly preserved period details. Houses were meant to be bought and sold, but a home was worth any price to preserve. Had Kit learned nothing from her first marriage? Dodie would have abandoned Highbrook without regret, selling her birthright to the first bidder, to share her life with an honorable man who unconditionally loved her, one born without the philandering gene. Conceding the wisdom of her mother's advice and resigned to accepting her husband's decision, Kit took to the challenge of being a bohemian urban pioneer. And in a few years Danny will be enrolling at the Academy, its campus in the heart of the city. He's excited by the promise of having a floor all to himself, Papa's barbershop and Frankie's salon converted into a bedroom and refitted into his private retreat. Michael agreed to restore the top floor to the original plan to placate the last dissenting voice. His stepdaughter, a college freshman who's rarely at home, was devastated to learn they were moving to a house without a room she could call her own. He cheated a bit, shrinking the dimensions of her bedroom to half the square footage he and Frankie had once shared, but she'll still have the afternoon sun from the window on Carpenter Street. Kit's mildly disappointed the renovations will necessitate ripping out the oversize Jacuzzi and replacing it with a conventional tub. She's hinting they ought to make love in it once before the plumbers haul it away, a house christening Michael will go to great lengths to ensure never happens.

"Jump on my back and hang on to my neck," Michael says. Danny's a bit heavier each time he piggybacks and Michael's knees aren't getting any stronger. But he's still only sixty-five pounds and off they go, taking long strides back toward the parade route.

The crowd has gotten rowdier over the past hour. A cheer rises when it's announced the Phillies have stepped off uptown. They're in countdown mode; it's only a matter of time until the cavalcade arrives to bask in the love and adoration of the city. College and high school boys strip to the waist to paint the red Phillies logo on their torsos. Kids peer into car windows, smearing whiteface on their skin and drawing baseball seams across their cheeks with black eyeliner. A young man strolls by, acknowledging the applause for his hat—a majestic construction-paper model of the championship trophy, spray-painted a glittering gold. A few people are chugging forty-fives, but most everyone is sober, stoked to a fever pitch on nothing but excitement. They're standing on mail and newspaper boxes and shinnying up lampposts and street signs. And, yes, Frankie's memories are accurate; they're hanging from the branches of trees.

They can hear the swell of cheers uptown and, in the distance, see the headlights and beacons of the patrol cars leading the approaching caravan. The cops are in a good mood as they quickly throw up the restraint lines, trying not to dampen the enthusiasm of the fans pressing into the street, trying to get a first look as the convoy appears in the distance.

"Dad, I can't see!" Danny shouts, fighting the tears of disappointment welling in his eyes.

His uncle and the priest hoist him even higher, up onto Michael's shoulders, giving him a catbird-seat view of the gelled spikes and balding crowns of the crowd and an unobstructed view of the parade as it creeps along the boulevard.

"Dad, get closer," Danny pleads as they step off the curb and into the street, propelled by the crush of bodies at their backs as the faithful press forward, needing to be closer to their heroes. The cops grow tense as the flatbed trucks carrying the team approach. Their smiles are less genial; their eyes scan the crowd, anticipating catastrophe, and their ears are pricked to pick up any ominous threats in the deafening noise. But the chubby-cheeked little officer directly in front of them, no taller than the minimum height requirement for the force, is less of a killjoy than her fretting colleagues, letting Michael and Danny inch ever farther from the safety of the sidewalk.

Women of all ages act like frenzied girls. They squeal and blow kisses, pledging eternal fealty. The crowd is chanting, howling, and yelping, happily making noise. Old men make the sign of the cross, unembarrassed by the tears streaming down their cheeks. The players look more like awestruck Little Leaguers than jaded millionaire athletes; they seem mesmerized, maybe even a bit intimidated, by the furious passion of the millions who've gathered on the streets to pay tribute. Danny starts bouncing up and down on his father's shoulders. Michael can hear him shouting at the spitfire centerfielder who's tossing cheap red Mardi Gras beads to his rapturous fans.

"Step back. Please step back, people. Please," the mini-cop finally warns, fighting a losing battle. The crowd has advanced too far to retreat now, just when they are so close. "Let's go, folks. Step back on the curb."

She's not even pretending to be friendly now, but the beast, once unleashed, refuses to be tamed. Michael lurches toward the rolling truck, fighting to keep his balance and to not lose his footing in the surging mob.

"Dad! Dad!"

He reaches up to grab Danny's wrists, to steady him on his shoulders, but the boy lunges forward, nearly breaking his father's neck and dropping him to his knees. Michael lifts his head just in time to see the newly anointed World Champion laughing as he gives his son a thumbs-up, clearly impressed by Danny's clean snatch of a string of beads he'd dispatched from the truck.

And then, in a flash, it's over and the frenzy passes like a wave, rambling down the boulevard. The parade disappears as quickly as it had arrived. Everyone is suddenly quiet, not quite certain about what to do next. The younger kids decide to follow the celebration and chase after the last truck. The older folks fold their chairs and linger, trying to decide where to go for lunch.

"This way, guys! Over here! Smile, Danny! Say cheese!"

Frankie's going crazy with his camera.

"One more, Mikey. Come on. Look happy! Good God, you look like you're about to break into tears."

The celebration has ended, and Michael is overcome by a crushing sadness. He knows this is the last time he and his brother will share a milestone in their lives. He's dreading the day he will put Frankie on an airplane with a one-way ticket to his sub-tropical paradise. Princeton, New Jersey, little more than an hour's drive, is the farthest they've ever been apart. He'd expected it would be Frankie who would be suffering pangs of anxiety, since Michael has a wife and a son and Frankie has only Michael. He's proud of his older brother's courage to strike out on his own, but he's also hurt that Frankie seems to be counting the days until his flight is announced, as if he were a prisoner who knows he's about to walk through the door of his cage. Frankie will be fine in the coming days and weeks. It's Michael who is unsettled by the rapidly approaching separation.

"Are you crying, Dad?" Danny asks, bewildered and bit frightened.

"It's just the dust blowing in my eyes, buddy. Come on, the party's over."

"This is great! Take a look!" Frankie boasts, proudly offering the camera screen for their approval.

Ah, the wonders of digital technology. There's no need to finish the roll, send the film off to the lab, wait a week to confirm you've captured the perfect Kodak moment. It's a terrific picture, a classic shot of father and son. Danny's waving his magic beads above his head. His face is wild with excitement. The game is over and he's the winner of the grand prize! His mouth is wide open; you can count all of his teeth. He's shouting something at the camera, a message for the world. Michael assumes this will be the moment Danny cherishes decades from now whenever he thinks about his dad. In the years ahead events of this day will recede into a foggy and vague recollection. But he'll always have this picture and, after Michael is dead and gone, he'll marvel at the image of the man his father had once been and he'll remember there was a time he believed his dad was the strongest, bravest, and smartest man in the world.

Michael would be puzzled if he knew that, years from now, Danny will keep a different photograph, copied and enlarged from a fading Polaroid, in a frame on his bedside table. Father and son will remain close after the boy reaches manhood, and Danny will be devastated when Michael dies unexpectedly at the age of sixty-seven from a massive coronary, three days after laying his brother to rest in the family plot. Kit will divide his ashes, keeping half to be mingled with her own, the rest to be buried in an urn at the foot of Frankie's grave. Danny will find the photo, one of dozens, in a worn manila envelope while going through his uncle's papers. The harsh lighting shrouds the serious young boys in mystery. He will never know who took these strange pictures or what they mean. Only his father and uncle could answer his questions and they are both gone. Every image is the same. Frankie and Michael stand side by side, handsome boys in crisp white dress shirts and dark ties, solemnly staring at the lens. Danny will choose a portrait where his father has nearly caught up to his uncle's height, on the verge of outgrowing him, the balance between them about to shift. But at that moment, frozen in time, the younger brother still tightly grips the older's hand, afraid of losing him, as if Frankie could step outside the frame, leaving Michael behind and on his own.

GRATITUDE

Casey Fuetsch, Rachel Klayman, Steven Salpeter, Monique Vescia, Paula Reedy, Karen Auerbach, Tova Diker, Annsley Rosner, Della Capozzi Payne and Danny Payne, Brian Corbett, Sharon Sorokin James, Lori Biondi, Diane Brown, Elliott Stein, Charles Honart, John Szubski, Daryl Levine and Carl Pelizoto (DL Salon), Mariel Freeman and Matt Derago and the staff of Shot Tower Coffee, Oliver Gallini, Peter Guido Valentino, Louis Pizzitola, Michael Burke, Burke & Payne (Philadelphia Barber Co., LLC), Larry and Jessie Mele, Shannon and Franco Sciotto, Rocco Sciotto, Terry Dougherty, Herta Ginsburgs, Janet Fries, Frank Chernak, Jean Kozicki.

The late Jerre Mangione, teacher and mentor, first encouraged me to write about our shared heritage.

Mitchell Waters conjured up Billy Wilder to come to my rescue.

Sarah Russo's enthusiasm is infectious and her energy and savvy never cease to amaze me.

Glenn Gale has the uncanny ability to visualize my ideas.

Above all, my peerless editor, John Scognamiglio, embraced the idea of this novel from the outset and encouraged me to follow my instincts. Without his unwavering support and generosity, this book would never have seen the light of day.

My parents believed that marriage is for life. They taught me well. So finally, to my *marito*, Nick Ifft.

Please turn the page
for a very special Q&A
with Tom Mendicino!

How did you come up with the idea for *The Boys from Eighth and Carpenter*?

The Boys from Eighth and Carpenter was inspired by my experience doing neighborhood canvassing during the 2008 presidential primary election. The campaign touched a raw nerve and exposed the usually dormant racial and class tensions in this rapidly gentrifying section of the city. I wanted to explore that dynamic in the context of a single family, and the completed novel focuses on the domestic narrative and the relationship between the Gagliano brothers.

You grew up in Philadelphia and still live there today. Is the neighborhood in the novel based on the one where you once lived?

Setting the record straight, I grew up in a housing development in a working-class community near Pittsburgh. (The Gagliano brothers travel to a nearby town to visit their half sister Polly in the novel.) I currently live in the neighborhood that is the primary location of the book. The Ninth Street (or Italian) Market area is struggling to maintain its traditional ethnic identity as newer waves of immigrants arrive and Lego-land construction proliferates. But the community continues to maintain its unique character and, for better and worse, change comes slowly, enough so that my mother, in her typically blunt and outspoken way, once remarked, "Well, you didn't get far, did you?" Papa's cronies and wives are all based on members of my extended family, and the dialogue is their words as I remember them. Fortunately, unlike Frankie and Michael's abusive tormentor, my father was a very gentle man who never once raised his hand to me.

Are there any aspects of your personality in Frankie and Michael?

People wrongly assume my first novel is semi-autobiographical. In fact, the adult Michael is the closest character to myself I've written, with the possible exception of Charlie Beresford in the *KC, At Bat* trilogy.

Which brother was your favorite character?
That is an impossible question to answer as I can't see one existing without the other. I love them both, and each drives me crazy.

How did the writing of this book compare to your first novel, *Probation*? Was it easier or harder?
Probation was far more difficult because you lose the freedom of the omniscient voice when writing a first-person narrative. It was perfect for that novel, which is really a confessional, but I doubt I will use it again.

How do you feel about the way Italians are portrayed in films and TV? Do you think there are stereotypes? When people hear "Italian" they instantly think of *The Godfather* or *The Sopranos*. Does that bother you?
Hell, no, it doesn't bother me. My father was born in 1921 and had vivid memories of cross-burnings by the Klan who believed "the dagos" were stealing all the good railroad jobs. His generation of children of immigrants couldn't assimilate quickly enough to distance themselves from the stigma of being "a wop" and "a guinea." My father and his brothers began pronouncing Mendi-CHEE-no as Mendi-SEE-no to appease the *medigan'*. My great-uncle by marriage actually changed his family name from Camparoni to Rose.

Flash-forward four-plus decades and my old man is handing me his copy of *The Godfather,* proclaiming "this is a great book" and insisting we make the long trek into Pittsburgh to see the movie at the Warner Theater the opening weekend. The crime sagas of Puzo and Coppola, Scorcese and David Chase mythologize the Italian-American immigrant experience on an epic scale, and today Michael Corleone and Tony Soprano are as much cultural icons as the cowboys of the "Old West" were in the early to mid-twentieth century. It's gratifying that John Wayne has been deposed by James Gandolfini.

Who are some of your favorite Italian-American authors?
I have to acknowledge my first mentor, the late Jerre Mangione. And I would like to take the opportunity for a shout-out to the great, sadly neglected John Fante, whose reputation needs to be re-

stored. *Ask the Dust* should be mentioned in any conversation about the Great American Novel, and *Wait Until Spring, Bandini* and *1933 Was a Bad Year* are books I deeply love.

What does being Italian mean to you?

Just to clarify, I'm not Italian. I'm Italian-American. My mother was of a different ethnicity, and, but for the Roman Catholic Church, I might be writing about kilts and haggis and be a practicing Presbyterian. Being Italian-American to me means plaster saints in the bedroom, *baccala,* Sinatra and Dino, Sunday dinners at one in the afternoon, a simmering pot of sauce so thick you could stand a spoon in it, superstitions and talismans and an irrational suspicion of cats, Mass cards, the old man cross-examining suspects in the theft of the last sheet of his *gabagool,* three-to-fives and seven-to-nines, my mother's gnocchi, the Easter vigil, a grandmother who made Livia Soprano look like the Blessed Madonna, *rigot,* Catholic school uniforms, the Christmas manger, and an unbreakable bond with your maddening family, no matter how hard you might try.

What's next for Tom Mendicino? Have you started working on a new novel and, if you have, can you tell us anything about it?

Travelin' Man and *Lonesome Town,* the second and third novellas in the trilogy continuing the story that began in *KC, At Bat* about the improbable relationship between an aspiring professional ball player and his Ivy-bound school mate, are being published simultaneously with *The Boys from Eighth and Carpenter.* At least once a week I announce I've given up writing and intend to spend my time watching an endless loop of *Spartacus, Blood and Sand* reruns. But before I make good on the threat, I've completed a first draft of a novel following the members of an extended Italian-American family through a single summer weekend and lately have been intrigued by the idea of a man with a troubled past assuming another identity to attempt a fresh start in a distant city.

A READING GROUP GUIDE

THE BOYS FROM EIGHTH AND CARPENTER

TOM MENDICINO

ABOUT THIS GUIDE

The suggested questions are included to enhance your group's reading of Tom Mendicino's *The Boys from Eighth and Carpenter.*

DISCUSSION QUESTIONS

1. Why does Papa have such contempt for the *medigan'*? Why does he behave so abusively toward his children, particularly Frankie, his eldest son? Can his treatment of his sons and daughter be reconciled with his supposed piety?

2. At various points in the novel Frankie comments on the similarities between Michael and their father. How is Michael like Papa and how is he different?

3. How different would Frankie's and Michael's lives have been if their mother hadn't died? Would there have still been such a strong fraternal bond? How did the arrival of Miss Eileen impact their lives? Would Frankie have eventually grown to accept Miss Eileen and return her love?

4. What is your impression of Father Parisi and why does he become so attached to the boys? What was the reason for the Polaroids and what do you think he did with the photographs?

5. Michael is clearly unsettled by his gradual awareness of his brother's homosexuality. How did Frankie being gay affect their relationship in late adolescence and, subsequently, as adults?

6. Michael is obviously a highly intelligent and driven man. What motivates him to succeed?

7. Why would Frankie become Papa's caretaker after suffering years of abuse at his hands? Why does Michael hate his father so intensely?

8. Is Frankie merely unlucky in love, or does he seek out destructive relationships? When does he realize Mariano's in-

terest in him is mercenary, as was his relationship with Charlie Haldermann? Why is he unwilling to cut the boy loose?

9. How much of what Frankie knows of Mariano's background is true? Do you believe Randy is actually his brother? What is Mariano's role, if any, in the methamphetamine operation?

10. Why can Michael never be completely comfortable with his wife's patrician family? Is he making incorrect assumptions and misjudging their intentions, or do they intentionally or unintentionally condescend to him?

11. Does a deathbed promise to a mother he doesn't remember fully explain Michael's decision to protect his brother? What other reasons would he have to willingly jeopardize the security of his wife and son by becoming an accessory after the fact?

12. Is Michael's refusal to allow the house at Eighth and Carpenter to be sold outside the family rational?

13. Kit has spent her life in quiet rebellion against her parents and their values. What are her insecurities and how would they explain her pursuit of Michael? Is it simply Michael's commitment to fidelity that persuades her to agree to walk away from their home and suburban life?

14. Which brother will more easily adjust to their separation? How do you see their relationship changing after Frankie's move to Florida?